Also by Shelagh Meagher

Non-Fiction:
The Spirit of the Garden (with photography by John de Visser)

Stoddart Press 1995

PEARLS IN THE ASHES

SHELAGH MEAGHER

Torriver Press

This edition published 2012

LIBRARY AND ARCHIVES CANADA CATALOGUING IN PUBLICATION
Meagher, Shelagh, 1954–
Pearls in the Ashes / Shelagh Meagher.
ISBN # 978-0-9880374-0-3

Cover and book design: Frank Tino

WITH THANKS

To my Mongolian guide and researcher, Bulgan-Erdene Hurelchuluun,
for showing me the best of her country,
and to Karen Connelly for teaching me how to make this a better book.
Above all to my family Glen, Nichola and Rachel,
for saying yes to my desire to travel to Mongolia in the first place,
where this story made itself known to me.

CHAPTER ONE

A FROG IN THE WELL DOES NOT KNOW HOW BIG THE SEA IS; A FROG IN THE SEA DOES NOT KNOW HOW SMALL THE WELL IS.

"It was the ninth day of the Yellow Dragon month," my father said, "when your mother told me you were ready to be born. 1923. The night had just begun, and the wind was roaring and battering our ger with the last of winter, just like it is now."

I snuggled deeper into the warmth of his arms as the thick, felt sides of our home shuddered with a fresh gust.

"But this didn't worry her. Wind is nothing to a Mongolian. According to the calendar, the next morning was a good date for births and journeys. Your mother said you were clever to start that night so you would arrive on the best possible date.

"When you came into the world you howled louder than the storm, but she held you tight to her breast and it calmed you." My father hugged me in demonstration. He always did at this point in the story. "She said we should call you Dash, so your name would bring luck."

Dash means good fortune in Mongolian. My father nodded, confirming the wisdom of the choice. That was part of the story, too, making sure I understood the power of my name. I waited quietly while he gathered himself for the ending. It was my bed time. The candle-lamp hung from a roof-pole on the other side of the ger, casting a yellow glow into the shadows.

"When the bleeding started, she said the only thing she was sorry about was how she wouldn't be able to watch her only child grow into a fine young man. She kept holding you, and calling you her handsome, clever son, until she slipped away." He lay there for a moment in silence, his breathing slow and deep. Then he kissed me and got out of the bed, pulling the covers in tight around me as I nestled into the warm imprint left by his body. "Now go to sleep and dream about your mother who treasured you."

My father told me this story often so I would know I was a boy who'd had a loving mother, if only for an instant, capturing that fleeting family moment for me almost as securely as if it had been my own real memory. I shut my eyes and let the beautiful, soft-voiced mother of my imagination sing me to sleep.

Our life as herders centred around coaxing the sheep and horses of our feudal lord to survive in a land that could barely sustain them. We worked, our master fed us, and our king the Living Buddha gave us hope for a better life next time around. But our king died when I was only a year old and the Mongolian People's Party, sponsored by Russia's Stalin, seized power themselves instead of allowing the designation of a new royal incarnation.

A few years later they came to our herding camp and took away my uncle to serve in their army. My aunt, with a baby in her arms and a toddler clinging wide-eyed to her skirts, wailed and pleaded with the officials not to take him. My father made a quiet attempt to convince them that we couldn't manage without the extra hands. We never saw my uncle again. Not long after that, the Party executed our feudal lord for resisting their appropriation of his wealth. We continued to look after the herds, but now we were collectivised and under the direction of the Party. Their zealous production goals became impossible to meet.

In my ninth year I noticed that my father rarely spoke about the strength of my name anymore. It had become ridiculous to pretend I was bringing any kind of luck. I even had to prod him to recount the story of my birth now, whereas before he'd done so easily and often.

When the Iron Frost winter arrived, killing millions of animals and leaving us all starving, my father decided we needed the help of a greater power.

We packed up our nomad's ger and its few furnishings, my aunt and my cousins did the same, and we all moved closer to the nearest Buddhist monastery. Although the Party had been doing its best to repress and even eradicate religion in Mongolia, our small local group appeared to be carrying on without much interference.

"That means it's especially favoured by the Buddha," my father told me with the same certainty he'd once had for my name.

He traded on his reputation as a dependable, tireless worker to get himself hired as one of their herders. Then he arranged for me to be accepted as a novice.

We'd barely settled into our new surroundings when he made the announcement. "The abbot says you must present yourself tomorrow, and they will take you in," he said. There had been no discussion as to what I wanted. Food was scarce, and they had it. To be accepted was a privilege.

So it was that the following morning I stood hovering outside the door of the ger that had been my home for ten years, about to take my first step away from the only life I knew. It had been a miserable life in many ways, but a comfortingly familiar one. My cousins stood nearby staring at me with wonder. My aunt, as close to a mother as I'd had, alternately hugged me and busied herself with the dried curd that hung from a rope tied around my scrawny waist, adjusting and readjusting it between flustered embraces. The hard, pale rectangles clinked against one another like a shaman's belt of bones.

My father came out of our ger carrying a sheep's stomach filled with buttery *orum*, and hefted it into my arms.

"This, and the curds, are for you to give to the Abbot when you arrive," he said, straightening the front of my *del* where the closure never lay quite flat. "They are from his own sheep, to show how well we tend them."

"Yes, *Ahv*." He was giving away two weeks' worth of his own nourishment, the only pay he got as a herder besides the occasional brick of tea.

"You're a strong boy, you'll be able to carry them."

The monastery was an hour's journey over a set of low, rocky hills. It was traditional to walk there by yourself as a kind of pilgrimage, a symbol of your willingness to walk away from your secular life.

My cousins mumbled their goodbyes, my aunt gave me a final kiss on my cheek, and my father hugged me, orum and all, and spoke over the top of my head. "In the summer, when we are nearby like this, you can come home one day every month and tell me all the things you're learning," he said. "Maybe you'll even teach me to read."

In the winter, when they changed pastures, he'd be much further away and we wouldn't see each other for months. I felt my lower lip start to wobble and bit it hard.

Unwrapping his arms from me, he stepped back. "And I'll come to the monastery on ceremonial days and watch you blow the conch shell or sound the *tingsha* bell," he said. "And I will feel very proud."

Then my father did an extraordinary thing. He brought his hands to his chest, palms together, and bowed ever so slightly towards me, as though I were already superior just for being about to take my first step along the Path. Flustered, I bowed in return, my hands awkward around the bulk of the sheep's stomach.

"Go now," he said, and I did. I didn't look back. I concentrated on putting one foot in front of the other. Puffs of dust rose up and drifted away on the wind with every step. Very quickly my arms began to ache from carrying the heavy orum. I tried to soothe myself by chanting the one mantra everyone knew: *om mani padme hum*, which is said to evoke all the compassion and knowledge of the Buddha.

Although I did my best to focus only on the mantra, the way I supposed a good monk would, my head kept filling with the image of my father watching me go. I saw how small and stooped he had become from his efforts to keep us fed. I saw him standing perfectly still, his eyes on my receding form.

Tears trickled down my cheeks and were grabbed by the wind, disappearing into its dry, unsentimental fist before they could even hit the ground. The mantra became a mumble as I trudged on through that harsh land on the northern edge of the Gobi, its summer plains as colourless as a worn rag.

The hills finally put an end to my crying; the difficulty of climbing the meandering and uneven path accomplished what my attempts at chanting had not. In the lee of the rocks it was hot, the air pungent with artemisia and dust. Flies tormented me, finding in the tear-salt on my face and the curd around my waist a welcome change from their usual diet of sheep dung. With my arms full it was difficult to swat them.

I reached the top of hills and saw the monastery below me. Khovor Khan was just a stone and mud wall surrounding a white, squat *stupa* monument, a small stucco building used as a temple and dharma hall, and a collection of gers. To me, however, its very permanence inspired awe. The monks living there didn't move several times a year looking for fresh pasture the way we did, but stayed in one place through every season. I would live that way now. I wondered how I would like it; every time I had complained about the chore of packing up our things and moving, my father had told me that if a Mongolian stayed in one place too long he felt smothered, as though he'd used up all the fresh air around him and needed a new supply. Did monks get used to breathing the same air all the time?

The golden sun and crescent moon at the crown of the stupa shimmered in the sunshine, gleaming bright against the dullness of the surrounding land. Putting down the orum for a moment, I used my sleeve to wipe the tear stains from my face, then straightened my del. My father had promised them a strong, disciplined boy. I picked my offering back up and scrambled down towards the monastery and the strange new life it offered, finding fresh energy in myself now that I could see my destination.

When I arrived outside the closed wooden gate, however, I was suddenly hesitant. I had visited the monastery rarely, at *Tsam* and other special days when the doors were open to us all. Now I heard the faint sound of monks chanting in the temple, barely perceptible as a low drone on my side of the thick gate, and I felt like a trespasser. My hand came up and back down again twice before I worked up the courage to yank the bell-pull. The resonant clanging sounded disrespectfully loud. It was a minute or so before a peephole slid open and a single, dark eye peered out.

"I am Dash," I said. "The new novice."

The peephole slid shut again and I heard bolts being drawn, then the gate swung inward and a crimson-robed monk stood in the opening. He was tall, and lean in every feature, with a narrow nose, thin lips, and long-fingered hands. He put his palms together in greeting and smiled. His teeth were very uneven, but his face was friendly.

"I am Mongo," he said, "chief administrator. Welcome."

I did my best to bow properly in return, then I was inside and the bolts were being set again behind me. On public visiting days the monastery had been noisy and bustling with people. Today it was eerily still, silent except for the continued chanting and the occasional ping of the hand bell. Mongo's presence was my only reassurance that people actually lived there, not just spirits.

In the ger that served as an administrative office and storage space, he took my offerings of orum and curd, carefully noting them in a large ledger. His hand was so sure it made the flowing script look like art.

"Possessions?" he asked.

"My clothes."

Mongo looked me up and down. "Del?" I nodded. He wrote it down.

We went through every item I was wearing: one dark grey del, one orange sash, under tunic and underpants, one pair of wool socks, boots, two felt strips for lining the boots. Each thing was entered in his ledger.

"You may keep all these things. We will provide you with novice robes, but the extra clothing will be useful in cold weather. Do you have anything else?"

My hand hovered over a small, hard object inside the folds of my del. "I've heard," I began, then stopped, unsure. "Do monks have to give up all their things when they enter the *sangha*?"

Mongo smiled. "I'm sure that whatever treasure a boy like you has, it will not interest the Abbot to take it from you."

I showed him the precious object: a small brass Buddha, no bigger than my thumb. "My father gave me this, to help me pray. It belonged to his father, too."

"Then clearly you must keep it. If it is to help you pray." It was noted in the ledger.

After that Mongo sat me down on a low stool and fetched a bowl of water from a barrel he kept inside the ger. I held my breath as he took a straight razor and began deftly slicing off my hair a finger's width from my head. Then I sat even more still as the cool blade slipped back and forth against my scalp, conscious that it was even sharper than the knives we used to slaughter sheep. He was so expert, however, that he hardly nicked me at all. I touched my head all over when he was finished, exploring the strangely smooth skin my hair had been hiding all those years.

"It feels odd," I said.

"It won't for long. Soon you won't even remember what it felt like to have hair."

He gave me a fresh bowl of water, an amazing luxury, in which to wash myself before putting on my new clothes. There were clean socks, new underthings of saffron yellow, and robes of thin red cotton that Mongo showed me how to drape and wrap. I tucked my tiny Buddha into the waist sash.

"These are novice robes," Mongo explained. "Ordained monks wear darker crimson robes like mine."

I didn't care what colour mine were. They were crisp and clean, and felt wonderful against my skin. They smelled of the incense with which they had been stored. My old clothes smelled of boiled mutton and smoke. Mongo put them aside to be washed.

The chanting that had floated dimly through the felt sides of the ger during my transformation had stopped. Now there was excited chattering just outside the door.

"Prayer is over," observed Mongo. "We can present you to the Abbot."

The door to the ger suddenly opened, replaced by a square of bright sunlight through which ducked another young monk in robes the colour of mine. He acknowledged Mongo with a casual flip of his hand, while looking at me.

"How is our new novice?" he asked, adjusting my outer robe as though I were his to care for. He was several years older than I, big and strong-looking.

"I see your prayers for good manners have remained unanswered," said Mongo, his bony chin stuck out indignantly.

The boy just smiled at me. "What's your name?" he asked.

"Dash."

"Dash! And are you lucky?"

"No."

"That's too bad. My name is Bayan."

His name meant wealthy. I wasn't sure if he meant for me to comment, so I kept quiet.

"We must go to the Abbot now," said Mongo, taking me by the elbow and steering me around Bayan to the door.

"We'll talk more later," called Bayan as I left.

Back in the brightness of the outside, I almost didn't notice another novice in the shadow of a ger a few strides away. He was wispy as a reed and inspected me with the sideways glance of someone who's pretending not to. The moment I looked at him he turned away, as timid as Bayan was bold.

The other monks were dispersing from the dharma hall. Most of them were older, the age of my father or more. Unlike my father, however, or any of the other weary herders I knew, the monks had an air of contentment about them as they smiled and nodded at me in welcome. Mongo and I wound our way around the dharma hall and along an avenue formed by rows of small gers on either side, at the end of which stood an enclosure made of upright wooden planks. The gate was surmounted by a painted archway carved with colourful, snarling guardian animals, like the doorway to a temple. Inside the enclosure was a large ger with a fresh canvas cover that gleamed clean and white against its dusty surroundings. Mongo called out our presence—knocking on a ger door brings bad luck— and entered with me in tow.

The ger where Mongo had helped me dress looked much like the one I'd grown up in, sparsely furnished and with walls that showed the accordion network of supporting wood trellis and the thick, grey felt that insulated the room from the outdoors. The Abbot's ger, by contrast, was palatial. His walls were draped with deep blue Chinese velvet trimmed with red. The floor was polished wood. He had a shrine with a Buddha inside it as big as a real man. The Abbot himself sat on a big chair with arms, not on one of the little stools normally found in gers. Behind him hung a curtain, of the same Chinese velvet as the walls, which I presumed to be hiding his private quarters. There was an odd sweetness in the air.

The Abbot was dressed in a robe of deep yellow silk spun through with gold to make it glow in the soft light of dozens of butter lamps. I had seen him before on ceremony days, but never up this close. He was as large and round as a pregnant mare. Although I knew I should be in reverence of him, my first thought was to marvel that someone could become fat when there was so little food.

Mongo presented me and I bowed, trying to look like someone who deserved to be there. "The boy has come with offerings of orum and curd from the monastery's sheep," he said. "I have noted them in the log."

The Abbot nodded. Would he even taste them himself as my father had hoped, or would they end up, anonymous, in the kitchen ger? I longed to tell him how my father's knowledge of the best pastures, even in a poor year, made the orum especially good. But it felt impertinent to speak without being asked. He rose from his chair and came towards me, laying his hot, damp palm on my newly exposed scalp by way of greeting.

"What a handsome boy you are," he said. This came as a surprise not only because I expected something holier as his first words to me, but because I had little sense of what I looked like. Our family owned one small mirror, which was special because it had belonged to my mother and was therefore kept safely wrapped up in the bottom of a drawer. I'd only had cause to look in it twice; once when my first adult tooth started coming in, and once when I'd had measles.

"Your father wishes you to follow the Path," the Abbot said. He had a strange voice, nasal and high.

"Yes, your Holiness." I kept my eyes trained on the floor as I answered him.

"Do you wish it also?"

"Yes."

"And to have enough to eat every day."

That, to my mind, needed no answer.

"The government of the People's Party has determined that monasteries are no longer to accept novices, did you not know? They don't want us shaping young minds they would rather shape to their own beliefs."

I looked up in confusion. Had my father been mistaken? Had he given away the food for nothing? The Abbot smiled slightly.

"Are you certain you wouldn't rather be a Young Pioneer?"

I had seen a few members of the Party's youth corps at the *soum* capital the last time we journeyed there. They wore army shirts and red scarves, and handed out pamphlets about the Party to people who didn't know how to read.

"I know little about them, your Holiness. But I would fear bad karma from wearing a blood-red thing around my neck."

"And so you should. Fortunately, we at Khovor Khan have been quietly continuing on with our work, which is timeless, despite the wishes of the Party, which is —like all things human—as impermanent as a dark cloud." He took his hand from my head, the residue of his sweat creating a cool spot. "Has your father taught you any of the Buddhist precepts?"

"Yes, your Holiness. I know the Ten Black Sins and the Ten White Charities, the Four Noble Truths and the Eightfold Path."

"Those are very few things compared with all you'll have to know to become a monk. They are one hair of a yak, while a monk's knowledge is as much as the whole animal," he said. "Maybe even a whole herd of yaks. Do you understand?"

"Yes."

"Can you read?"

"No."

"Add and subtract?"

"A little." I began to fear the Abbot would reject me for being too ignorant.

"The prayers, the scriptures, they're all in Tibetan. Do understand any Tibetan at all?"

I shook my head, mute now with the growing certainty that I would be turned away. As I stared at the floor, my face grew hot. The robes, the washing, the shaving of my head, they had all been a terrible mistake; the Abbot could see right away that I wasn't someone worthy of teaching. What had my father been thinking? I clutched a fold of my wonderful new robe in my fingers and foresaw the awful moment when I would have to take it off again and put my old clothes back on. Then I thought about the worse moment when I reappeared at our family ger and had to explain that I wasn't wanted at the monastery after all. The loss of the food my father had given would have been for nothing.

"Your father made me a very beautiful set of playing cards as an offering when he came to ask if I would take you in," the Abbot said then.

I had seen the cards, each one hand painted with intricate, interwoven swirls and circles that had taken my father months to complete. The Abbot probably wanted to keep them even though he was sending me back home. "He has a fine hand at decoration," he continued.

I nodded. Everyone said so; it was not bragging to agree.

"Has he passed on his talent to you?"

"I don't know," I said, not knowing the best way to answer.

"Perhaps he has. I will therefore allow you to study Buddhist art along with the other demanding studies we require of you here."

I couldn't believe my ears. "I am accepted?"

"Yes, of course, I already told your father that."

I thought I might faint with the relief. "Thank you, your Holiness."

"You will attend classes every afternoon with the other novices. We are a small monastery, but we do not lack for scholars in the dharma and sciences."

This was an amazing idea, that I should be going to school. My education until then had been strictly utilitarian. I knew how to make a good fire, how to take a ger apart and erect it again in the space of a morning, how to keep horses, sheep and camels healthy, how to butcher a sheep so not a drop of blood was wasted. But I knew nothing of school studies or religious art.

"For your spiritual guidance a dharma master will be assigned to you," the Abbot continued. "I have given this great thought, as your father says you're prone to bad fortune. Your master will be Tilik."

He nodded to Mongo, who produced a white silk prayer scarf and a book of scripture from the folds of his robes. The book was a long rectangle bound in wood covers. I extended my arms and the scarf was laid over them, then the Abbot touched the scriptures to my head as he intoned what I took to be a blessing in Tibetan.

I was a novice. Mongo folded the scarf back up and tucked it away again along with the scripture book.

"Dash, we welcome you to Khovar Khan," said the Abbot. "You may go now."

As soon as the Abbot's gate clunked shut behind us, Mongo began talking very fast, his eyebrows working up and down with excitement. "Tilik is a very powerful master. The best. He holds the *geshe* degree. Whatever the reason for your bad fortune, with Tilik as your master you will surely be able to change it. Just having the Abbot choose him for you is a sign in itself."

I certainly wanted to believe it. It hadn't been my idea to join the monastery, but having done so to please my father I was already starting to see the wisdom of his choice. A thread of optimism slipped into my heart and the feeling was so wonderful I tried not to let doubt chase it away.

We went to the kitchen ger, where the other monks were already sitting or squatting with their bowls in the dusty open area outside. Mongo gave me the bowl that would hold my meals for years to come. It was plain china, once the color of the divine blue sky but now cracked and faded, with a tiny chip at the rim.

Mongo told me to sit with the other novices, Bayan and the timid boy. Bayan introduced us.

"This is Koke," he said to me. "He's been at the monastery since he was two."

Koke smiled but didn't meet my eyes.

"You must have learned a lot," I said.

"Don't tell him that," said Bayan. "You'll swell his head."

Koke frowned but said nothing in his own defense. The monk who was serving lunch came around with salty milk tea in a large kettle, filling our bowls to the brim. I downed mine without taking a breath. "How long have you been here, Bayan?" I asked.

"A few years. Did you meet the Abbot?"

"Yes."

"What did you think of him?"

I didn't think I was in a position to have an opinion about the most elevated member of our monastery. "He seemed important."

Bayan laughed. "He'd like to hear that. Do you know what name he uses for himself? Suren. *Majestic.*"

"Mongo said we didn't use avowed names in this monastery."

"It's not an avowed name. He just gave it to himself." He lowered his voice and leaned in close to me. "He'd rather be a king than a monk."

"Our old king was both, until he died."

"And maybe Suren would like things to be that way again. But he'd never get near to a royal palace. He only dreams of having such power." Bayan straightened up again. "But you're too young to understand politics. Who did he assign as your spiritual master?"

"Tilik." I said it with a bit of pride, after what Mongo had told me.

Koke spoke for the first time, in a soft voice I could barely hear. "You're lucky."

"No, he's not," Bayan corrected him. "He told me so himself." He jerked his head in the direction of the older, ordained monks. "Do you know which one he is?" he asked me.

"No."

"He's the one looking at his bowl in silence, sitting closest to the ger door. Probably contemplating its emptiness, which would be just like him. He's sour and unfriendly, and a stickler about rules. I wouldn't consider myself lucky to have him as my master."

Even seated, Tilik looked taller than the others. Perhaps it was due to the straightness of his back. As I looked at him he raised his head and looked right back at me, as though he'd known my gaze was on him. He had an angular face and a thin mustache like in paintings of Chinggis Khan, and although he was at least ten strides from me I felt the force of his eyes so strongly that I had to look away, my heart thumping the way it did when my father caught me nabbing yak's milk directly from the teat when I thought no-one was watching.

"They say his grandmother was a great shaman," whispered Koke. "He hasn't had a novice for over ten years."

"Then he should be happy to have someone make his morning tea again," said Bayan.

My father had explained to me that novices live in the gers of their masters and make themselves useful by keeping the fire going in the stove, cleaning and tidying, gathering dung for fuel, and hauling water for making tea. This work was nothing new to me, but I did wonder what kind of master Tilik would be. I'd heard rumours from laypeople that some lamas hit their novices for the smallest reasons, treating them like slaves.

"Who is your master?" I asked Bayan.

"The Buddha himself."

"What he means," Koke began, but he was interrupted by a cuff to the head from Bayan.

"I can say what I mean perfectly well," he said, but he didn't. "Koke's master beats him," he offered instead. "See the scars on his head?"

Although I knew I shouldn't stare, I couldn't help myself. The stories of abuse were true! I wanted to know all about it. But Koke seemed to be curling in on himself, his head hunched so far over his bowl he looked as though he were trying to crawl inside it. I made do with a quick glance.

The server monk came by then, with a gruel of milk and rice, and put a ladleful into the bowls that had held tea a moment before.

"Give him a bit more," Bayan told him as he served me. "Can't you see he's been starving?"

The monk scowled, but added a tiny bit more and gave us each a hunk of bread to go with it. It was good gruel, with more rice than I'd been used to at home. I gulped it down quickly, polishing my bowl with the bread before Bayan was even halfway through his. I noticed that he broke his bread in pieces before dipping it, rather than using his teeth to bite off chunks as he went along.

He glanced over at my empty bowl. "You really have been starving, haven't you?"

"The lord of our lands, the Dalai Van, was executed," I told him. "And things went badly after that."

"They certainly did," said Bayan. "That was my father."

I was so shocked I couldn't speak. Bayan was an aristocrat, although technically we didn't have those any more. I couldn't believe I was eating lunch beside him.

"My father knew he was in danger," Bayan said, "so he put me here, for protection. Although as the middle son I would probably have ended up here in any case."

"But the other monks," I said. "Do they know?"

He looked at me as though I were the most ignorant person he'd ever met. "Of course they know. The Abbot thought it was an excellent thing to have the local lord's son enter his puny monastery. He received a hundred sheep and fifty horses for the courtesy of taking me in." Bayan snorted. "Not that it did him much good. Now my father can no longer wield power for him, and the government confiscated the animals last year as taxes."

"I'm sorry."

"For the loss of the animals, or my father? Never mind. The good monks here will teach you soon enough: we and our pitiful belongings are all impermanent. To mourn the loss of either is short-sighted."

Suddenly, he smiled at me as though none of these things had been discussed.

"Do you want the last of my bread?" he asked, tossing it to me the way we used to toss offal to the family dog when we slaughtered a sheep. I snatched the offering out of the air, trying to ignore how Koke's eyes followed it steadily, from Bayan's elegant hand to my own calloused one, and up to my waiting, hungry mouth.

Later in the afternoon we had group meditation. I'd been in the dharma hall on special days as a lay person, sitting at the edge of the room. Now I entered as a novice, to sit in the centre with the others. The hall at Khovor Khan was the size of a comfortable ger, which made me feel at home. In the intimate space the altar's huge, golden statue of the bodhisattva Avalokitesvara—the Light, the All Seeing, the Compassionate One—was an overwhelming presence. He had hair coloured blue like the Mongolian sky, and an expression that was not quite smiling but looked as though he might reach out one of his many large hands and pat you kindly on the head if you prayed well enough.

The room was heavy with the smell of dust, rancid butter lamps, and freshly lit incense, murky tendrils of which wound over us. That strange mix of smells was particular to the hall, part of the mysterious rites that were going to be revealed to me. We filed to our places in silence. Even the sounds of birds and the wind stayed outside, along with our chatter, so by the time we sat and the door was closed, only the occasional whisper of a robe was heard.

Koke sounded the tingsha. Its single, sweet ping purified the air. Then the monks' voices began, the sound rising slowly like a crane taking flight, until it filled the room with a rhythmic hum. I didn't yet know the words of the prayers, let alone understand their meaning, but they sounded hopeful to me. I closed my eyes to better let them in, so that their power might one day make me wise enough to see the Path and steadfast enough to follow it.

CHAPTER TWO

WIND ENTERS THROUGH GAPS; WISDOM ENTERS THROUGH INSTRUCTION.

Tilik was frugal with praise and affection as well as with heat, food and the luxury of sleep. I was accustomed to hard work, but it took a while before I was able to wake before he did to prepare the fire. When my chores were done I had to meditate and pray, rarely getting to play sheep bones or stick toss as I would have done at home. Tilik demanded of me the same devotion to prayer and study that he demanded of himself.

Still, he never beat me, and one thing he was never frugal with was teaching, whether I rewarded him as a pupil or not. Academically I was successful enough, quick to read and write in both Mongolian and Tibetan, and good at memorizing the many texts. Artistically I was starting to show some of the talent the Abbot hoped of me, excelling in the creation of sand mandalas. On top of that I was getting good at recognizing different herbs and knowing how to extract their medicinal value, which was Tilik's special interest.

My spiritual progress, however—the part of my training that concerned Tilik the most—was far less impressive. I took pleasure in the rituals but failed to find enlightenment in them, mouthed the words but felt no effects. Personal meditation was my weakest subject.

Tilik kept telling me that meditation sessions by myself, twice daily at least, were critical to my progress towards enlightenment. I had to start by developing the ability to focus on a single object until I reached a place of calm in my mind, then I was supposed to use that place to deeply contemplate some aspect of enlightenment. Advanced Tantric practitioners are so adept they can go there and visualize themselves as the deities they want to emulate. By slipping into the character of the being they aspire to be, they gain part of that deity's wisdom with each experience.

My own efforts fell rather short of the ideal.

"What did you achieve in your meditations today?" Tilik asked me as we gathered thyme and wormwood on the hillside one morning. It was summer again; we rose before the sun, meditated by ourselves for an hour, had breakfast and prayed with the group, then roamed the parched land around the monastery searching for herbs and discussing dharma.

It was tempting to lie. I wanted to tell him that I had entered an empty place where I had managed to focus, without interference, on something—anything—relevant to enlightenment. But, apart from the amount of bad karma there was in a lie like that, I was convinced by then that Tilik had the power to discern the truth inside me. Every time I claimed to have washed carefully behind my ears when I hadn't, for instance, he ordered me to fetch back down the rag I'd just hung up to dry. It was uncanny.

"This morning's meditations started out well," I said, looking for thyme as I spoke. "I chose the flame as my object, so it could light my way to the Path."

"That's good."

"And I got as far as seeing no other thing and hearing nothing but the breath of the flame." Out of the corner of my eye I saw he was nodding his head.

"Then I began to lose it," I confessed.

Tilik heaved a great, resigned sigh. "What happened this time?"

I spoke to a sprig of thyme in my right hand, twisting it in my fingers until its scent started to rise. "As I watched the light emanating from the flame, which of course is supposed to be yellow, it became different colours. The colours were very beautiful and I couldn't stop them from changing. They gave me an idea for a new pattern that would be very good for a mandala, and then I noticed my rumbling stomach and felt hungry. After that I couldn't get the image of the flame back at all."

"Stop mutilating the thyme," he ordered. "What did you think about for the rest of the hour?"

"Many things." I didn't want to say exactly what, but Tilik was silent so I knew he was waiting for more. "The mandala pattern. Sweetened milky rice. Hot biscuits. What the weather would be like today. The horse I used to ride and what it was like to gallop at dusk with the sunset making the whole sky pink and violet." Just talking about it made that lovely image float back into my thoughts.

"Self, self, self!" Tilik shouted, so suddenly that the thyme fell out of my hand and I almost dropped my whole basket. Tilik prided himself on being master of his anger, but he was not above using his voice to scare me into attention. "Why do you concern yourself so much with your physical self, what it sees, and feels, and tastes? It is all illusory. Recall the Hevajra Tantra: *Great knowledge abides in the body, free of all constructs. It is the pervader of all things but though abiding in the body it is not born of the body.* 'Not born of the body.' How do you expect to touch this great knowledge if you think only of its container? You must apply your mind. It is all mind; no body."

"But my mind is inside my body and can't stop listening to it."

"If you concentrate fully, your mind can transcend those interruptions, as I've explained many times. You can control these other thoughts that fly in. You close the door. Your mind becomes a quiet ger, the door shut, the air within it still. Then you create in your empty ger the images necessary for accessing the great knowledge of the bodhisattvas. You don't fill the space with pretty colours. You will never get anywhere that way."

Tilik sat down on a rock. I lowered myself beside him, haunches resting on heels, and waited until he had thought enough to speak again. I had learned not to hurry him when he was thinking. Flies started taking a greater interest in me now that I was still. They stayed away from Tilik, however. One might weave towards him, but as soon as it got close it scooted off again, as though something told it not to even consider bothering him. This allowed Tilik to remain completely still, his hawk's eyes rarely blinking, his large hands resting serenely on his knees.

"Meditation is not meant to be an entertainment for your mind. It is a discipline. It is meant to abate selfishness and egotism, not indulge them. To be successful you must first renounce your attachment to the things you perceive around you. The Buddha exists in a different world than the one you cling to."

"But I have renounced all worldly goods." I'd had none to renounce, really. In that sense, I thought, hadn't I already been in a blessed position for years?

"Renunciation isn't just about physical things. It's the ability to give up your mental attachments to illusory desires. To daydreams of physical pleasures. They are impermanent things."

It was hard for me to imagine giving up daydreams.

"When you're making a mandala," Tilik said, "what do you think of?"

Sand mandalas were finicky creations of complex patterns rendered a few coloured grains at a time. First we drew the design on a large platform, then we laid it down like a table and applied the sand through thin tubes, tapping gently so just the right amount dropped into its allotted space. It wasn't possible to think of anything else while concentrating on something so delicate.

"The mandala," I said.

"Nothing else?"

"There's no room for anything else."

The slight loosening of his mouth that passed for Tilik's smile let me know I had finally said something that pleased him. "You see?" he said. "There *is* a time when you have so much focus you empty your mind of all but the one thing you need to be thinking of. Now you must learn to control mental emptiness that way whenever you want to. To fill it with the lessons of the bodhisattvas instead of art. Then you will be one step further along."

It sounded easy the way Tilik put it, and I liked the look of approval on his face. But art was just so much more captivating. I didn't know if I would ever be able to shut it out of my mind in favour of the worthy lessons Tilik wanted me to learn.

When I wasn't studying, being taught, praying or practicing, Bayan took over my time. Apparently oblivious to the fact that we were novices who had to work, he expected me to play with him as though I were a willing puppy. In fact he appeared to have a lot more time on his hands than I did, always popping up with nothing to do when I was in the middle of some chore. He was very good at distracting me. He'd grab my arm and say outrageous things like 'Mongo caught Cheren masturbating in the outhouse this morning, want to hear the details?'. He tempted me with offers of extra biscuits he'd mysteriously got from the cook, in return for me making him tea while he lay around the way he used to as a lord's son. He'd get me to play a game of sheep's bones, which would end up making me late for some other thing I was really supposed to do.

Sometimes Bayan took the blame on himself. 'It was my fault,' he'd tell whichever monk was demanding the chore of me. 'I distracted him; he was just trying to be helpful.' It worked well with most of the monks, but not with my master, who expected me to be in better control of my own actions.

I was flattered by Bayan's focus on me. Even when he did things I knew were wrong and bad, and got me into trouble, I secretly liked the fact he included me. He was exciting to be around, because you never knew what might happen next. The incident with Koke's master happened just that way. We were passing their ger with no intention when Koke came out the door with an empty water bucket in his hand.

"Where are you going with that?" Bayan asked.

"My master is bathing and has asked for another bucket."

"Oh well, better hurry up then," Bayan replied, all affability. But when Koke had gone, Bayan turned to me in an urgent whisper. "Daran only has one robe. What an opportunity!" As I watched in stunned amazement, he slipped into their ger. I heard Daran give a little shriek of surprise, then a yell of anger. Bayan sped out with the robe in his arms and flung it high onto the roof of the ger, laughing like a drunken man. A purple-faced Daran dashed out of the ger a moment later, a bedcloth wrapped around himself. Bayan, his laughter turning giddy, pointed to the roof. Daran lunged, Bayan grabbed my arm, and the chase was on.

We almost ran into Koke returning with his full water bucket, which he dropped in surprise as we skirted around him. We ran through the monastery, always keeping a ger between us and Daran. I swear Bayan slowed down every time he thought we were losing our pursuer, then we'd see him rushing furiously towards us and we'd tear off again. It was a madly exciting change from my routine days and I tingled with adrenalin, flushed and sweating, until Bayan suddenly called a halt. "Enough, Dash," he called to me, and I stopped as he turned and stood, legs set apart, arms folded over his chest.

Daran roared up, his right hand raised, but Bayan was as collected as a wolf staring down a crow over a carcass. "I dare you," he said.

Daran's hand wavered back and forth. Although he must have wanted very badly to strike, he forced his fist down to his side. His whole body shook with the effort. "You are not worthy to be in this monastery!" he screamed. "Useless son of a lord's whore!"

"You're swearing," said Bayan. "That will have to be confessed in the dharma hall tomorrow. If you don't have a heart attack first; how purple you've become."

"I will tell the Abbot what you've done!"

"I have no fear of the Abbot."

Daran was breathing in short gasps. His fists clenched and unclenched as though he might change his mind about controlling them, but then he turned away. "Useless son of a lord's whore," he repeated. "In your next life you'll be a dung beetle."

As Daran turned he saw Koke, who had been standing faithfully behind his master all along. Daran cuffed him hard on the ear, causing his eyes to tear up from the sharp pain. "Get my robe down," he growled, shoving Koke along ahead of him. "And I still want that water you were sent to fetch, stupid boy."

I watched them walked away, Daran poking at his novice's back continually with a bony knuckle.

"Koke is going to get it badly for this," I said to Bayan.

Bayan rolled his eyes with disdain. "Don't be so sentimental," he said. "If Daran didn't have a real reason to hit him, he'd just make one up anyway. I haven't made any difference."

That was possible. "How did you know he wouldn't hit you?" I asked.

Bayan laughed, the easy laugh of the confident victor. "One, I'm a lot stronger than he is. Two, he's afraid of the karmic consequences of enraged violence. And finally," and here he laughed again, "I may be the son of a lord's whore, but I'm still the son of a lord."

He put his arm around my shoulder and began walking back with me. "Stick with me, little monk boy," he said. "If you have to ask a question like that, you still have a lot to learn."

Tilik knew about the episode before I'd even returned to the ger we shared. He told me, in the scarily calm voice he used for his most serious scolding, that my actions demonstrated a terrible lack of both judgment and self discipline, a disregard for others, and a worrying inclination to follow whatever Bayan got up to without paying attention to my own morals, which he hoped I possessed. As punishment I was to contemplate the importance of self-direction and present an essay on the subject to him.

His eyes bored into me as he spoke. What he said was true and right thinking, and every word erased a bit of the thrill I had just experienced, shrinking it until I could hardly remember why it had been so much fun.

But not entirely. As I struggled over my writing punishment my thoughts kept straying to the wild pleasure of running in a place where it wasn't permitted, and of Bayan's confidence, which I couldn't help but admire, whether it was right to do so or not.

Some chores I liked, and cleaning the temple in preparation for afternoon prayers was one of them. It felt special, like a secret intimacy, to be in there polishing the gold buddhas and cleaning up their temple home, as though I was doing the work directly for them. Not that I always got to polish. If I was sharing the chore with Bayan he always took that job while I swept and put out prayer books.

"Why do you always get to polish?" I complained as once again he picked up the cloth, a few weeks after the clothes-stealing incident, leaving me the broom.

"Because I'm senior."

"But you don't even like polishing."

"I like it better than sweeping." He ran the cloth idly over the statues, not even pretending that he was doing a good job but just to show me he could do it any way he wanted.

"When I'm with Koke we share. He polishes one time and I do it the next," I said.

"Koke's an idiot and a weakling. And he's not senior."

I pushed the broom around the floor in sullen silence for a while, checking out of the corner of my eye for which ones he didn't even polish at all, which ones he did inadequately. Then Bayan came over and draped the polishing rag over my head so I couldn't see.

"Go ahead, polish them then. I know you want to."

I snatched the rag off my head and kept on sweeping. "I'm busy."

"When you're done, then. I'll even put out the prayer books for you, how's that?"

It was unfair that I would now have to sweep and polish while he only put out the prayer books, but I really did want the statues to be properly polished, and by Bayan's standards the offer was a real compromise. I finished sweeping and wordlessly moved over to the alter, feigning indifference as I picked up the first statue so Bayan wouldn't mock the pleasure I got from it.

Bayan laid out the prayer books any which way, instead of neatly with the bound side always to the left so they could be opened easily.

"Do you have a date yet for your two-year review with the Abbot?" he asked.

I had been agonizing over this impending interview. At my level I got one audience with the Abbot a year, to check my spiritual progress. "In three days," I said.

"You sound worried."

"I'm afraid he'll find fault with me."

Bayan brushed aside my concern with a laugh. "How could that happen? You know a lot of dharma already, you've recited all the important mantras at least ten thousand times I'm sure, and you make beautiful mandalas. I'll bet Suren hasn't said as many mantras as you, and he certainly can't make a mandala. You had an interview last year, you know what they're like. He hardly asks you anything."

Bayan often made light of the Abbot and his position. Higher authority meant nothing to him. But Suren was a highly realized lama, our spiritual leader, esteemed enough by the monastic community to be named an abbot, even if it was for only a small monastery. I was sure that even being in the same room as Bayan's thoughts constituted bad karma. I would have to say another thousand mantras for having heard them aloud.

"Last year I was a child, but now I'm twelve so he'll expect more of me."

Bayan guffawed loudly but I ignored him.

"And I haven't been good at practicing selflessness," I continued. "Tilik says I have too much ego."

"Monks are too concerned about selflessness in my opinion," Bayan said, as though he weren't a novice himself. "Nothing interesting was ever created by selfless people. Look at Chinggis Khan for example. He would never have given Mongolia its glory without a strong ego."

"But I am not trying to conquer the world, I'm only trying to be a good novice."

"That is how Mongolia came to be under the thumb of Stalin, because we're a country full of selfless monks who won't stand up for themselves."

"You're just saying these things to test me in debate," I said, although I suspected he might really believe them. He often said shocking things. I could rarely tell whether he was serious or just trying to disconcert me.

"Think what you like," he said. He'd finished putting out the books and was sprawled out on the prayer cushions. "Why do you even care about being a good novice?"

I had never considered the why, it had been so obvious. "It's what my father expects of me. He gave up my help with the herding so I could come and learn things, and be a monk. So I must do it well, to repay him for the chance."

"So you're not here for enlightenment, then. Just to make your father proud. Maybe you should be worried about that interview."

I stopped polishing. "I didn't say that."

"You more or less did."

"I am seeking enlightenment," I insisted, hot-faced without knowing why. "I am trying."

Bayan held up his hand. "Fine, I believe you. So what do you have to worry about? You're doing well."

"My meditations are hopeless."

"There's plenty of time to develop technique on that."

"Tilik says that I have to become better at it. That if I just repeat prayers without concentrating enough to really contemplate their meaning, I'll never make progress."

"Well I'll tell you, there are masters more renowned than Tilik who would say it's useless to try to meditate without first having studied thoroughly all you need to meditate on. That you should spend ten years, or twenty, before you even try."

I liked that idea a lot. I was good at the studying part. If what Bayan said was true, then all I had to do was keep at the studying, and the capacity for true contemplation might eventually find me on its own. There was only one snag.

"But Tilik is my master, not these others."

"You see, I told you that first day you weren't so lucky to have him. The dharma is supposed to be flexible, Shakyamuni said so himself. But Tilik is rigid."

"Koke says that Tilik is demanding with me because that's what I need, with my bad fortune. He says that it's like the story of Milarepa needing Marpa. The master seemed like a torturer but his tough ways were really Milarepa's only hope for enlightenment."

"If it's torture you want, trade masters with Koke. Have you seen the way Daran has started pinching him during prayer sessions, because he can't cry out without getting punished?"

He rarely did cry out, either. "He probably deserves Tilik more than I do."

Bayan rolled his eyes. "Don't tell me: Koke has 'confided' in you that he's a reincarnate lama from some precious lineage."

I tried to hide my surprise that he knew about it. "Maybe it's possible."

"He deserves to get pinched. The more he claims spiritual superiority, the more Daran finds ways to punish him for it."

"But what if he is reincarnate? He told me he was able to visualize before he was eight years old. Now he can even visualize Avalokitesvara."

"Do you actually believe that?"

I wanted to. "He described it to me in detail," I said, defending the possibility even as Bayan's attack made me start to think it was a ridiculous boast.

I swear, if we were not in the temple Bayan would have spit on the floor.

"You're far too gullible," he said.

"But how would any of us know, really? Only the highest authorities would be able to say for sure."

"The highest authorities find incarnate lamas where it's convenient to find them, in families that have wealth to share or power to wield. They've never taken notice of Koke and they never will."

"There are real incarnate lamas, even if you don't believe it," I insisted. "Maybe Koke isn't one of them, but he's still advanced. I'm sure he does much better in his interviews with the Abbot than I'm going to."

Bayan came over and petted the top of my bristly head, something he was fond of doing. "Poor, fretful monk boy. Suren will never find fault with anyone as beautiful as you."

His words didn't make me stop worrying. The Abbot was concerned with far more than how I looked, I was sure. Bayan was just being irreverent as usual.

CHAPTER THREE

WHEN THE MOUNTAIN TIGER FROLICS, THE TETHERED DONKEY TREMBLES.

"Come, Dash, and sit," the Abbot said as I entered for my interview. The way he smiled and put his hand on my shoulder as he led me to the stool beside his chair made it feel like I was just dropping by for a friendly visit, although of course I would never do that with the Abbot. He asked me the same questions about ritual as he had in year one, and I wondered if he forgotten how long I'd been there. I thought maybe I should tell him, but I didn't.

As I recited the same sutras as the year before, he kept saying 'good, good' and patting my arm after each one as though to reassure me, even though I was calm by then because it was going so well. His hands were sweaty like they'd been on the first day I'd met him. They felt unpleasant on my skin but he was being so kind I felt I had to sit still and pretend to appreciate his affection. He asked me to talk about the Importance of Right Thinking. As I did he kept jumping in to complete my sentences with the correct ideas whether I had been going there or not, making it easy for me to get it all right.

"You seem to be learning very well," he said, having demanded less of me in that once-a-year exam than Tilik did every day. "And growing strong." He grasped my bicep in his hand, squeezing my scrawny muscle and nodding up and down approvingly. I was reminded of how my aunt used to measure my cousins and me against the main post of our ger each spring, and express delighted surprise at the discovery that we'd managed to grow taller.

The Abbot rose from his chair. "Keep studying hard. You'll be a fine monk one day. You may go now." There had been no discussion of my meditation problems, no question that exposed my failings. He probably knew all about them from Tilik already. It was evidence of the Abbot's superior compassion that he focused on my strengths instead of my weaknesses for the interview. I skipped all the way back to my ger, not even caring if anyone caught me.

My spirits were further buoyed by the start of preparations for the Tsam celebration, a big event in which we exorcised evil spirits with masked dancers and music. The monastery buzzed with extra activity. I was especially excited because I was helping to create a fierce mask for the most important character, Erlig Nomon Khan, Supreme Judge of the Dead and a great defender of dharma.

Usually my art was restricted to making sand mandalas, which were purposely temporary and were destroyed at the end of each ceremony. But Tsam masks were kept and revered for decades because deities entered into them and made them holy. The mask we were replacing had been used for at least twenty years. I imagined the new mask, the one I was helping to make, being used for even longer. New novices would see it and be amazed. Herders' children would tremble with fear. My father would be so proud.

The monk responsible for my art training, Altan, was a very good mask maker who had learned the craft at Erdene Zuu. We dipped strips of paper into a thick, slimy paste made of flour and water in which sheeps' hooves had been boiling overnight to add strength, then laid them in a tight lattice over a rounded wooden form to create the face. The paste clung to my hands like a gooey pair of gloves and when it built up enough I could squish it between my fingers and make it squirt out from between the joints. When the basic form was done we built up the buffalo snout and inserted long pointed teeth, re-used from the old mask, that Altan said belonged to a wolf. Set into deep, red-rimmed papier mache sockets, the bulging eyes shone with the flickering light of the ger so it seemed as though Erlig's gaze was following me around. I tested it from all angles, walking away and then whirling around suddenly: he was watching me, every time. Altan said I was being silly and that they were only glass, not magic.

To adorn the top we used rams' horns, curved and almost as long as my forearm. On Erlig's forehead we created a row of tiny clay skulls, like a crown, with the headdress forming a peak similar to the top of a stupa. We painted his hair orange-red and gold, and added jewels to his headdress and golden earrings to his buffalo ears. He was wonderfully scary.

After the excitement of making the mask came the dull task of extra prayers. Two full days of them, in order to purify the area to be used for the dance. Before we had even reached the end of the first day my legs were aching from sitting cross-legged. I longed to move but was afraid I'd be punished for fidgeting. Daran was on discipline duty. His eyes prowled in constant search of an opportunity to hurt us. I had fallen asleep earlier, exhausted from my hours of work on the mask, and had had my knuckles rapped hard with a stick for the infraction. The middle one still hurt.

I glanced across the aisle at Koke. Daran came up behind him and pinched the side of his neck hard for no reason at all, and scowled when it failed to break Koke's concentration. Koke was bright-eyed and intent, his eyes focused on some point in front of him as though he were talking to the Buddha in person, not directing his prayers to the incense-filled air. That was the thing about our prayers; they were a great deal of hard work but the results, unlike a Tsam mask, were not visible. You had to have faith in their effect. As I watched Koke speak so intimately with the Buddha, I was certain he was not thinking about pain in his neck or any other part of him. I envied him.

Beside me was Bayan, also staring straight ahead as he chanted, but I knew what his expression would be like. He'd have the vacant look of someone who was thinking about something completely different, something pleasurable, while his mouth made the movements and sounds required. He probably wasn't feeling any pain either, but I didn't envy him nearly as much.

I started thinking then about how Bayan bullied Koke, and how I went along with it, ignoring the part of me that knew it was wrong in order to wring a small, mean pleasure from the attacks. Was it this feeling of envy that made me do it? Could that also be what provoked Daran? Might I therefore end up like him, torturing novices who had more spiritual promise than I had?

I promptly lost my place in the scripture, my mouth shutting in mid-sentence. The words of the prayer had deserted me. My heart beat crazily, the way it did in the nightmares in which I lost my already dead mother. I looked around, helpless and panicking about the moment Daran would spot me in my silence, and then I became aware of Tilik staring at me from the opposite side. I saw his lips forming the prayer and it was as though he were speaking it into my ear, it suddenly came back to me so clearly. I began to chant again, just as Daran looked over.

The panic drained slowly from my body. I kept my attention focused forward, the way Koke did. Maybe it would even help me to ignore the aching in my legs.

The open space in front of the dharma hall had been swept and seven concentric circles had been drawn within a large square, outlining the area in which the performance would take place. At one end of the square we'd hung a huge *thangka*, a scroll painting of Begtse Dharmapala, from two tall poles. His menacing face glowered over the square to scare off any evil spirits that might have proven immune to our chanting. At the opposite end a dais was set up for Suren's throne chair, with other seats to either side of it for important visitors. Monks who would be watching took up places on the ground to his right. The orchestra—we had a pair of long trumpets, a pair of conches, a hand-drum and cymbals—sat on the left. Along the remainder of that side the common lay audience would sit on blankets or the ground.

The local population arrived in droves. I saw my father come in with my aunt and cousins but I was not allowed to acknowledge them with anything more than a quick smile. At that point in the ceremony, we monks had to stay quietly in our rows while the lay children ran around shrieking and the adults sat talking and laughing, twirling prayer wheels and gnawing on dried curd. Still, the excitement in the air was infectious. We spoke softly among ourselves about the famous dancers who had come to perform, retelling the tales we had heard about their prowess and their fabulous costumes. We tortured ourselves with longing for the sweets we would get to eat after the ceremony. Even Buqa looked relaxed. No-one was wielding a disciplinary stick.

With two monastic attendants in tow, Suren entered the area in a robe of deep golden silk with a dark red overcloak and a crested *shashir* on his head. In his right hand he held a long *beree*, its many prayer flags fluttering in the breeze. His entrance caused a ripple of acknowledgement in the crowd. Shortly after he took his seat, however, a bigger ripple occurred.

Six riders thundered up to the open gates on their horses, stopping in a swirl of dust just short of running everyone over. Suddenly all was silence; even the children stood still and gaped. Anyone who wasn't already facing the gate turned to look. The riders were Party members from the capital of our soum, distinguished by the fact that they wore army style clothing instead of the traditional dels that everyone else had on. Their leader was positioned a horse-neck ahead of the others. He was very handsome and he looked young for a leader, not much more than thirty or so, but the coldness of his expression demanded respect. He stared at Suren with the unblinking gaze of a man who knew he had the power to do whatever he wanted.

Even I knew the significance of the Party's arrival. All public displays of religious activity were forbidden. In other soums, such festivals and ceremonies had been violently repressed. But Khovor Khan was in the middle of nowhere, an unimportant outpost hardly worth bothering with enforcements. Could the officials really be here to send everyone away and tell us we couldn't go on?

I thought they might arrest the Abbot and take him away then and there. We were all frozen in mid-gesture; no-one moved or even appeared to breathe. Then Suren placed his hands together and bowed slightly to the intruder, an act of deference. It was as if this was the cue everyone had been waiting for. The Party officials dismounted, monks rushed forward to take their horses, and the men were escorted to seats next to the Abbot.

The murmurs of the locals created a quiet rustling where minutes before the air had been filled with jabbering. Their prayer wheels were clutched, motionless, in their hands. A few slipped the wheels inside their dels. No-one would risk bringing attention to themselves by twirling.

"What are they doing here?" I whispered to Bayan, who was sitting next to me.

Bayan was watching the officials with undisguised loathing. "Observing," he said. "And demonstrating the Party's generous tolerance towards Mongolian culture."

"Maybe they just want to watch the show," I suggested. After all, they had grown up with these festivals just as we had. How could their desire to watch have evaporated just because they were part of the Party now?

"You never understand anything," Bayan hissed.

Mongo turned and glared at us for speaking. The show was about to begin.

I laughed at the White Old Man as though seeing his antics for the first time. I jumped in fright when the Dharmapalas leapt, snarling, into the circle. The dancers got more frenzied and aggressive as they invoked the highest-ranking deities, for the concentration required to do that was huge, and everything depended on it. The Tsam was only effective if they succeeded in bringing the gods' power into their own bodies.

The very best moment for me was when Erlig Khan appeared in his magnificent mask. The audience gasped at his ferocity and I was filled with pride at the part I'd played in making him so. Then I quickly thanked the gods for giving me the ability to create such a good mask, for fear my selfish attachment to my own work would bring bad karmic consequences.

At the end of the performance we were allowed to mingle with the lay audience. I grabbed a few boiled sweets from the large kettle that had been set out, and ran around the outside of the square until I reached my father. I threw myself into his arms. I was still young enough to do that. He smelled as I remembered him, muttony and smoky, the scent of horses mixing with his sweat so you couldn't tell if he was man or animal.

"Did you see Erlig?" I handed him a sweet, popped one in my own mouth and gave the others to my aunt and cousins. "Did you like his mask?" I continued around the kernel of hard sugar now dissolving, gloriously, on my tongue. "I helped make that, with Altan."

"It's a wonderful mask," my father agreed.

"The Abbot gave us real jewels to use, and real horns and gold earrings. And the teeth are from a real wolf."

My cousins gasped at this impressive fact, but my father was only half listening to me. His attention was on the Party officials, who were behind me. "Do they come here often?" he asked, drawing me to him protectively.

I craned my neck around to look at them. The leader had risen, along with Suren, and they were heading towards Suren's ger. The others stayed seated while anxious monks served them milk tea and biscuits.

"This is the first time I've seen them."

"Look at how the monks grovel and serve," said my aunt. "It's pathetic. The Party men should be the ones groveling. They'll need the merit if they don't want to come back as dung beetles in their next life."

"Shush," warned my father. "They are wolves amongst the foals. Don't draw attention to yourself."

I tugged at his arm. "Come on, Ahv, can't we get tea now?"

"Yes," said my father at last. "Let's get some tea, and you can tell me what you've learned since the last time we met."

My cousins went to throw a stick with other children, my aunt went to chat with other women she rarely got to see, and my father and I squatted outside the kitchen ger drinking tea. I bombarded him with everything that had gone on in my life since I'd seen him last. We got together once every month in summer, less in winter. And even though in the two years I'd been in the monastery I'd grown used to living without him, I still felt like I was breaking a fast every time I saw him. I spoke at breakneck speed, like eating without chewing. I had a mission: having never blown the conch or sounded the tingsha as my father had wished for me the day I left, I wanted to make sure he was proud of me for the other things I had accomplished instead.

"I had a good interview with the Abbot," I told him.

"It's important that the Abbot is pleased with you."

"That's why I was allowed to work on the mask."

"Coming here was good for you," my father said. "Do you see how it allows you to create merit every day? The bad luck of your earlier years will not return; it is being replaced with positive karma."

"Do you think so?" I knew my actions fell short of creating merit every day. But it was a relief to think my father believed otherwise.

"I'm sure of it."

"But I still haven't taught you to read, as I promised," I said.

"You're a busy young man now; you have more important things to do. And what would I read, if you taught me? I'm happy just to know that you can."

I saw Bayan walking past and I jumped up to bring him over.

"Bayan, come say hello to my father."

My father stood as he and Bayan exchanged the usual polite greetings, inquiries as to each other's health and the fattening of the herds my father cared for. They'd met before, but today I saw how my father kept his head slightly bowed as he spoke to Bayan, almost as though he shouldn't be talking to him at all. And he used the formal address even though Bayan was not an adult so he didn't have to. Bayan accepted my father's use of the formal tense and used the familiar in return, as accustomed to receiving deference as my father was to giving it.

As soon as the customary greetings were done with, their exchange slowed awkwardly. I rushed to fill the gap.

"Bayan doesn't like the military men either," I said.

"Hush, little monk," Bayan said. "We shouldn't talk of these things here."

"But you did, earlier," I protested. I didn't like the way he'd called me 'little monk' in front of my father, even if he had meant it affectionately.

"Bayan is right," my father said.

Bayan looked around distractedly. "In any case, I can't stay and talk as I have an errand for the abbot." He put his hands palm together and gave a quick bow of his head to my father. "It was a pleasure to see you."

He didn't rush off as though he had something important to do, however. He drifted off to the shadow of a ger and stood watching the military men. My father didn't seem to notice.

"A fine young man," he said.

I grunted. "He was impolite, using the familiar with you."

"Oh, well," my father said, waving my concern away with one hand, "it's his station."

"He's just a novice."

"But before, I mean."

"It doesn't mean anything here."

My father studied me, measuring. "It always means something. That's how the world is ordered."

For the first time in my life I wanted to disagree with my father. I couldn't exactly, because deep down inside I understood that what he said was true. It was how things worked, even in the monastery. But whereas before I hadn't considered what it implied, I had just caught a glimpse of how that truth diminished us both. I crossed my arms over my chest, pouting.

"He's not even a very good novice."

"It must be difficult for him."

"Tilik wouldn't accept that as an excuse."

My father sighed. "Let's not argue on this holy day. What else have you been doing that's wonderful and worthy?"

"Nothing." I'd lost the mood for boasting, and was petulant enough about it that I even refused to laugh at my father's funny stories about the antics of the family dog and the horses he cared for. When it came time for him to leave, however, I suddenly realized that I was not going to see him for another month.

I clung to him as he hugged me goodbye. "I have done wonderful and worthy things," I said quickly. "I just couldn't remember any when you asked."

"I know you have, Dash. You're a good boy."

He gathered up the rest of my relatives, then he was out the gate and gone with the last of the leavers. As the gate was closed behind them I felt the weight of our separation with an aching regret for how mean I'd been. I struggled to remember why I had even been angry with him.

The monastery felt even more sober than usual after everyone was gone. Bayan, Koke and I began our task of tidying up the Tsam performance area, carrying the wooden seats from off the dais and back into the storage ger. The Party men milled around listlessly, looking eager to be off but stuck waiting. Their leader was still in with the Abbot.

Bayan carried the wooden stools in front of himself, gripping the legs tight as though he might use one as a weapon at any moment. It occurred to me that these men might have been the same ones who had killed his father, and it appeared the same thought had occurred to him, too. He went about his work with short, terse movements and a set expression that didn't invite conversation.

The Party leader reappeared, his face as blank and cold as it had been before.

Bayan stood still, watching as they mounted their horses and prepared to ride away.

"Suren made a deal," he said.

"What do you mean?"

"He's made a deal to keep the Party from bothering us too much."

"How would he do that?" asked Koke.

Bayan shook his head. "I assure you," he said slowly, "you really don't want to know."

CHAPTER FOUR

FROM SLIGHT LAZINESS GROWS GREAT INDOLENCE; FROM SMALL INCIDENTS STEM SERIOUS CONSEQUENCES.

The Party leader came by every two weeks. He'd give the bell-cord a single, hard yank, which wasn't really necessary since he was always pre-announced by the pounding of his horse's hooves. Whoever answered the door would greet him politely and escort him silently to a private audience with the Abbot, after which he left the same way he came, at full speed. Even in winter he made the journey.

Everyone got a little on edge during his visiting days. There were whispers and frowning, but I never managed to hear what was being said. I asked Tilik what the Abbot and the Party leader talked about and he told me I didn't need to know. I suggested to Bayan that maybe the leader had come for religious instruction but had to be secretive about it because of the restrictions. Bayan laughed so hard he couldn't speak for a full minute. Then he told me I was an idiot.

One thing I did understand about the leader's visits was that they reminded us there were forces outside our walls that threatened us, forces we all wanted to ignore. Mostly we lived in blessed insulation, finding out about events that seemed unreal from within our cocoon. High ranking feudal lamas, the ones with power and wealth to expropriate, were arrested and taken away in the night, never to be seen again; abbots were forced to make gifts of their finest gold statues to Party officials; monasteries were taxed to the point of absolute poverty.

We heard these things, but their effect was as muffled as a voice through the felt walls of a ger. We reacted by clinging to the established rhythms of our monastic lives, thanking Suren for whatever he was saying to the Party leader to keep our local government from attacking us in the same way.

In the winter of my thirteenth year, our monastery received a visit from a traveling lama famous for his artistic skills. Although Mongolian

Buddhism, like Tibetan, is largely monastic, our nomadic country had adapted the religion to its traveling ways. Before the oppressions Mongolia had been full of free lamas, ordained monks who had left their monasteries. Some left to pursue enlightenment out in the secular world. Others wandered around making their livings selling minor religious services—in the case of our visitor, thangkas and statues—much as one would sell cloth or utensils. It was said that some lamas were unscrupulous, conning meals and money by performing false exorcisms, divinations and other rituals for gullible herders. Others were said to have real powers. Both had been driven largely underground by communist oppression.

The one who came to us, Qara, had a good reputation. He had received commissions from a number of monasteries, including the renowned Erdene Zuu, to create huge appliquéd thangkas, banners of intricate detail that he made with silk, brocade and semi-precious jewels. Suren had called Qara to Khovor Khan to make one of these for us, and I wanted to learn as much from him as possible in the months it would take him to complete the work.

My first hurdle was to convince Tilik that in spending time with Qara I would be improving my understanding of dharma. I turned to Altan to help me come up with a good argument, and he told me what to say: that creating thangkas was like writing scripture without words; that they took discipline because they had many rules about pattern, colour, gesture and symbolism; and that my increased knowledge would be an asset to the monastery. Tilik relented, providing I didn't let my other studies suffer.

The day I was allowed to begin my work with Qara, I fidgeted all through group prayer in the morning. Prayers had been increased by an hour each day to counteract, through our extra blessings, the bad karma of the government's latest repressions. The atmosphere in the temple was subdued. Praying at happy occasions, such as celebration days and weddings, was uplifting. Praying against tyranny was hard work.

Leaving the temple that morning, my breath billowed in front of my face in the chill midwinter air. It was bright after the butter lamp dimness of the inside. My eyes burned with the sharpness of it. I wanted to run to Qara's ger, but with Tilik near I knew there would be trouble if I showed such a lack of self-control. In punishment he might even make me wait a day or more before I could go, to teach me patience. So I walked as quickly as I thought permissible, my anxious legs feeling as though they were being held back with chains under Tilik's watchful eyes.

Qara's ger was warmed by a well-stoked stove. It smelled of biscuits. He gave me one, sweet and warm and all the more delicious because I would not normally be allowed to eat it outside of a meal time. As my eyes adjusted to the light of oil lamps, I noticed that the ger was filled with a happy clutter, unlike the spare furnishings of Tilik's quarters. Even though Qara had come by horseback, he had apparently managed to load on to his pack horse an amazing assortment of unmonastic acquisitions. He had an orange silk coverlet on his bed; different colours of porcelain bowls from which to drink; a thangka as tall as me and as wide as my arms spread out, hung on the north wall; a finely painted pair of stools more elegant than any I'd ever seen; and a selection of canvas and paints and bags of fabric strips lying about on the floor. The whole place was a marvel, a completely different world packed into exactly the same kind of plain ger that I lived in myself with my master.

Being with Qara was like indulging in a game of sticks in the middle of a day full of chores. He was short and round and he laughed a great deal, even at things that weren't especially funny; he seemed to find life to be a very pleasing thing. After our refreshments, he started by sketching a composition on paper, unhampered by the dimness of the oil lamps. He first drew a faint grid to govern the precise proportions of the elements, then he began to fill in the page.

"You see me drawing all these things, Avalokitesvara here in the middle, Tara beneath him, a demon here, crazy patterns there, and you think 'what an imagination this Qara has! How does he come up with these things so easily?' Is that what you're thinking?"

I nodded.

"Haha! But I'll tell you a secret. These things, they are all dictated to me already, the order, what elements, what symbols. All I had to do was memorize thousands of rules!"

"But then you interpret them. If you didn't interpret, every thangka would be like every other."

"That's true, I interpret. But I'm not so free that I can make a thangka look like a pointillist painting, or cubist. Do you know of these things?" One look at me gave him his answer. "No I guess not. They're ideas from artists in Europe. They are not Buddhist, haha, no no."

Among my many lessons there had been one that involved studying a map of the world. Europe seemed an impossibly distant place. "You've seen a European painting?"

He nodded. "I traveled to Moscow. A man there was interested in some sculptures I make. He showed me his paintings. It was very interesting."

Qara held up his sketch and proceeded to explain the rules governing its composition. "The structure of a thangka is symmetrical. Where is the most important figure placed?"

"In the middle."

"Haha, good boy! And always the biggest. Lesser figures sit around him." He explained how to position the lotus flower, the significance of the right hand, the symbolism of the elephant, dozens of things. I repeated it all quickly, anxious to return to the exotic topic of the European paintings. It was an unexpected thrill to talk to someone so worldly.

"Since they're not Buddhist, the European artists, what do they paint?" I asked.

"Landscapes and dead things."

"Dead things? How can such an awful subject make a good painting?"

"They call them 'still life' paintings. Haha! The creatures are still, that's for sure. I don't know why they find that attractive, but it seems to be popular." He paused a moment, thinking. "They paint manifestations of the emotions and temptations of our temporal existence. Especially people. Not bodhittsatvas or other enlightened beings, just ordinary people. Often without clothes."

"Maybe it helps them exorcise the desire from their bodies, to transfer it to a painting."

"Haha! No, I don't think so. I think they just like to paint their desires, over and over again. And they sign their paintings, too, so everyone will know who made it."

This was almost as shocking an idea as dead animals and outright nudity. Buddhist art was never signed. Creating it wasn't something to take pride in for yourself, it was a tool for guiding the artist and others towards enlightenment.

"And seeing these paintings, did it make you want to do the same?" I asked.

Qara smiled at me. "I already do. I'm not a monk, like you, I am a free lama. I have a wife, for example, and although I keep a lama's vows

I don't have as many to keep as you will. So not only do I get to have a wife, haha, I can make art that is for me, as well as the art I make for the Buddha."

Up until that moment, the limits of my vows had seemed a small price to pay for a greatly improved life. I had slipped into monastic living as though it were a warm bed. But Qara's ability to choose pricked my interest.

"Which do you prefer, the art you make for the Buddha or the art you make to express yourself?" I asked.

"Oh, it's not a question of preference. Religious art helps guard against the possibility of coming back as something unfortunate in my next life. Something without arms, say. Imagine!" He wiggled his hands about in the air. "That would be very bad. My other art is a diversion which is made allowable, I think, by that which I create for the Buddha. No choice, you see? One builds up merit, without which the other might be inadvisable."

"I would like to see this other work of yours."

"Haha! I don't know what your master would say if I were to go filling your head with things that distract a young monk from his obligations. But we'll see. Yes. Maybe, I'll show you some things at a later time." He pulled a slim book out from a sack he carried with him. "But first you can learn to draw Tara. Pick a version of her from this book, then practice until you get it exactly right. And if you do a very good job perhaps you will get to paint a small thangka for yourself."

His book was a collection of iconographic drawings of the goddess White Tara. Consort of Avalokitesvara, she was born of his tears, her wisdom pairing with his compassion. Mongolians had a special fondness for her as a kind of mother deity to turn to for solace and hope. I picked a simple drawing to copy, one in which Tara was seated in the lotus position, her bare feet revealing the eyes of wisdom embedded there as well as in the palms of her hands. Peonies circled her head. Her breasts were perfect circles.

"Have you ever seen a real peony?" asked Qara.

I shook my head.

"Nor a woman's breasts, at least not for a few years, haha!"

I blushed.

"How old are you?"

"I'll be fourteen in the spring."

"Hmp. Well never mind how you might think real breasts look. Tara's breasts are more perfect. She is a deity, not a woman! You draw them just as they are here, not from your imagination, you understand?" He winked. "The peonies, too."

I tried to keep Tara's breasts firmly fixed in my mind as simple, geometric shapes on a page. Or as holy elements of a divine being. But as my hand began to draw the first unsteady curve I felt an unnerving twinge deep in my robes, a twinge that developed into an insistent erection by the time I got to the second breast. It felt as though I were trailing my pencil around the real thing. I could barely complete the shaky circle; I kept thinking her sketched-in eyes were watching me, and I imagined that she felt my pencil's indecent touch. There was no way I could make the dots that were meant to be her nipples. I kept my face, hot as Qara's stove, hunched over the drawing as though concentrating, desperately worried that Qara would notice my discomfort and guess its source.

It was the peonies that saved me. I turned my attention to them and focussed with all my might on the complexity of their overlapping petals. My erection slowly subsided. Eventually I was able, with one last, longing glance, to turn the sketch over to Qara.

"That's a good start, yes, haha!" He peered more closely. "You need a little practice with circles, though. Repeat them many times and they will become easier. And you seem to have forgotten the nipples."

There might have been a hint of smile on his face when he said this, but I couldn't be sure.

My drawing sessions of the splendid Tara turned into acts of love. I obsessed over the details lest she find me wanting in my rendering of the turn of her big toe, or the way the middle finger of her left hand curved to hold the lotus bud. I was determined to create a drawing perfect enough to earn me the reward of creating a properly painted version of her in full, passionate colour.

And was all this helping me with my understanding of dharma, as I'd promised Tilik? My powers of deity visualization were certainly strengthening. And I was gaining an excellent lesson in how powerfully our bodies are able to divert our minds from the Path. A monk in a monastery takes a vow of abstinence for the simple reason that sex is a major distraction. The Vinaya has two hundred and twenty-seven rules of behavior for ordained monks, but only four result in instant excommunication if disobeyed. Carnal knowledge of another living thing is one of them. Even the "emission of semen by design" is a serious offence. For novices and lay practitioners the rules are less strict, but we were still meant to abstain from sexual misconduct. I had no doubt that the reaction of my besotted penis to images of the bodhisattva Tara would have fit that category, even if she wasn't, technically, a living thing.

That didn't stop me. My ability to concentrate for long periods increased, but it was hardly the kind of meditation intended by my master. Any time I had the opportunity to be alone in our ger, I followed the same routine. First I took the single rag we kept for cleaning, and stuffed it inside my underclothes. Then I sat in lotus, my back straight, and began to think about the divine Tara. She would first appear in my mind as the serene being she was meant to be, poised on a lotus flower, hands positioned in a gesture of blessing that also hid her bare breasts. Then her enigmatic smile turned into something just for me. Something that hinted at lust. She moved her hands and I saw nipples, dark as burnished wood. My own hand moved too, down to massage my stiffening member. As I continued to sit still and cross-legged before her, she slid out of the lotus position as though her legs were liquid, her lower garments floating off her and away. Here my ignorance of female anatomy took over; I envisioned between her legs a fifth eye of wisdom like those on her hands and feet. It turned into a kind of soft mouth and she mounted me, divine warmth enveloping my penis. Those liquid legs held me tight in her rocking embrace until, exploding, I fell into a pit of perfect emptiness, a moment of blissful, suspended nothing.

I was accomplishing with Tara what I had failed to do in years of ritual meditation. I achieved high visualization, prolonged concentration, and even gained the place of emptiness at my climax. Unfortunately I couldn't share the good news with Tilik. I was shamed by my sessions but unable to stop giving in to them. I began to clean our ger far more than was necessary, in order to have an explanation as to why the rag was so frequently rinsed and hung to dry.

It's possible that Qara suspected. Being a free lama, he was also something of a free thinker, and might have considered it all a normal part of a boy turning into a man, even if the boy was wearing a monk's robes. He showed me portfolios of his secular work but held back certain pieces, saying that I wasn't old enough to see them. The landscapes and portraits I was allowed to look at were traditionally Mongolian in style, with just a hint of modernity. To me they looked like works of bold genius.

Qara encouraged the artist in me like no-one had before. Seeing how much effort I was putting in to learn to draw accurately, he gave me the reward of teaching me to paint a colour version of my beloved. I had a very un-Buddhist attachment to that painting. If I saw it now I'd probably recognize all its flaws, but at the time, given its subject, it couldn't be anything but the most beautiful thangka ever made.

I soon discovered I wasn't the only novice suffering from distractions. Bayan came up to me one day shortly after Qara had moved on. It was the start of spring. The air was still frigid but you could take a breath without having your lungs feel as though they were filling with ice. We were on the far side of the communal outhouse, the stench of which, even during the frozen months, tended to make it private and therefore good for novice-to-novice conversations.

"I bought a sculpture from Qara, did you know?" Bayan said in the casual tone he often used to make important announcements.

"He's a good artist," I said, equally casually, as though monks who could afford to buy art were commonplace in our tiny, middle-of-nowhere monastery. Bayan had confided in me that his father had hidden some money away for him in case of disaster. The stash gave him a certain sense of freedom, although there was little to buy around the monastery and nowhere else for him to go after the Party had condemned his family.

"Do you want to see it?" he said.

I shrugged. "Maybe." I had long since figured out that too much enthusiasm tended to drive Bayan away.

"White Tara is a part of it."

Now he had my attention, and he knew it.

"Where is it?"

Bayan grinned. "I have it in my robes. It's small. And it's not the kind of thing you leave lying around for Mongo or somebody to find." He drew it out from the folds of his inner robe slowly, relishing the suspense he was creating. He looked around furtively before exposing the statue completely, sitting it on his open palm.

There, amidst the stink of monk's shit and with the vapour of our mingled breath enveloping her like a heavenly cloud, sat a three dimensional, gold-painted version of my fantasy, except that instead of my own small member entering her divine orifice, it was the enormous phallus of Avalokitesvara, its impressive size confirmed by the way Tara had made it only partway down the shaft. His many arms were being put to good use fondling the body of my beloved while her face remained as tranquil and beatific as usual. I was transfixed.

"Good isn't it?" Bayan said. His voice had become a hoarse whisper.

I only nodded, unable to find words.

"Do you know about Tantric practice?" Bayan asked.

"A little." Tantric rituals were well guarded secrets revealed only to those deemed qualified to be initiated into them. I knew nothing about it at all.

"They use this kind of thing all the time for their visualizations."

My eyes were wide with the possibilities. "You mean they can visualize being ... him?"

"You could learn, if you practiced enough," Bayan said.

It was a powerful incentive.

"Tantric practitioners, they have sex together. It's the marriage of wisdom with compassion."

"You mean real sex? With women?"

"With anyone."

"I don't think that can be true," I argued. "The Vinaya says—"

"What do you know. Tantrics don't pay attention to the Vinaya, that's why they keep their rituals so secret." Bayan waved the statue about in front of my face. "But I have contacts. I'm even starting to learn."

Who on earth could be teaching him these things when he never left Khovar Khan? "I don't believe you."

"No?" Bayan closed his eyes and starting making thrusting gestures with his hips. "Imagine yourself, big as a pole... oh yes, there she is, Tara's coming towards me, she's opening her legs..."

I got an erection so urgent it was painful. "I have to go meditate."

Bayan's laughter, throaty and knowing, followed me all the way back to my ger.

CHAPTER FIVE

AN OLD MAN NEEDS RESPECT.
A YOUNG MAN NEEDS ADMONITION.

In the summer of my fourteenth year Altan rewarded my artistic effort by giving me sole responsibility over making the sand mandala for one of our special prayer days. I should have known I was headed for trouble when I decided on a fairly large format, a square almost as wide as my spread arms. An egoless person would have chosen a humbler size for their first solo creation.

A mandala is a symbolic sacred mansion for a particular deity, so it has to be carefully thought out and ordered according to the rules. The choice of deity was made by the Abbot, of course, but I had asked for Tara to have the honor in this one, and he'd approved because she was so popular with everyone. I spent many hours laying out a precise pattern of colourful, geometric figures, all radiating out from a central point, then filling in the intricate spaces with tiny grains of coloured sand. It was time that passed in loving communion. Because it was for Tara, it had to be perfect. The result, and I say it even now so perhaps I've learned nothing, was magnificent.

Since one good wind storm can wipe out a mandala, I worked in our temple, hidden in a corner behind a thin curtain. Only Altan was allowed to see its progress and give me guidance. On the morning of the special prayer day, everyone was gathered around the curtain waiting for the unveiling. Suren arrived, wearing a robe of the most magnificent deep purple silk with gold brocade edging. He seemed to have a new robe for every occasion, all of which inspired awe. As he came through the assembled group his steps were measured, his manner unhurried. The purple silk swished back and forth with the lilting, side-to-side movement of his fat man's walk. When he got to the curtain and paused dramatically, I had to work hard to stop myself from fidgeting with impatience. It felt like ages before he grasped the curtain with a flourish and pulled it aside to reveal my mandala to the gathered monks of Khovor Khan.

Deep orange, crimson, saffron yellow, sky blue, and vivid purples wove together in a rich and complex tapestry. The rigid lines that represented walls were balanced by the swirls and flourishes that lay within. The tiniest details were precise. There was no space unaccounted for by colour or pattern.

Suren was the first to speak. "It is beautiful. The Buddha has been gracious in giving Altan the wisdom to teach how it is done, and Dash the ability to learn. This mandala will surely generate many blessings."

"Your holiness is kind," said Altan.

I was not supposed to say anything. Since religious art is a reflection of the Buddha's wisdom, the artist is just a conduit. Still, as my fellow monks filed past for a look, I couldn't help but take their comments personally.

"It is very fine."

"What exquisite colours."

"Not bad, monk boy."

"I've never seen such advanced work by a novice."

Koke stood before it a long time before whispering to me. "You're so lucky the Buddha guides your hand. I would like to make one of these, but I will never be able."

Even Tilik was pleased. He looked at it and nodded, satisfied. "You have applied yourself well," he said.

All day long these pleasant words floated in and out of my head, flitting around the words of our prayers and the sounds of ceremonial music. I allowed myself to feast on them until I was bloated with self-importance.

But sand mandalas are transitory things. Sand is chosen as the medium specifically because the mandala's destruction at the end of the ceremony it was created for illustrates, forcefully, the impermanence of things in this life. Mandalas are a teaching tool for learning how to renounce attachment.

The destruction ritual for my mandala was left to the end of the day, when all the prayers were done. We gathered around the beautiful square for one last look as Suren spoke about the fleeting nature of worldly things. He raised his right arm in preparation. It's a simple gesture; he brings the edge of his hand down like a soft knife and cuts through the pattern in two bold, diagonal strokes, so everyone can see what was there and how vulnerable it was.

I listened to his words, I looked at my creation, I watched his hand come towards it.

Before I knew what I was doing, I took a step forward.

"Wait," I said.

Everyone stared at me in shocked disbelief. I was shocked myself, and wished instantly that I could suck the word back into my mouth.

Suren actually did wait, his hand poised just inches above the sand.

"What did you say?" he asked, although I was sure he'd heard.

"I—nothing—forgive me," I mumbled.

Suren brought his hands back together in front of himself, his ceremonial moment ruined, and glowered at me. "You intended to say something more."

I stood mute, terrified by what a single word had done and certain that I would not be saved by saying more.

"Speak!" He thundered. "You will tell me what you intended to say!"

I had never heard the temple so absolutely still. There was not a breath or the slightest rustle of robes. "It's so beautiful," I managed, very slowly, and so quietly that I hoped only he could hear it.

Suren regarded me coldly.

"Beauty," he said finally, "is the most illusory of all illusions. Of the few rare things that might merit permanence, beauty is not among them."

With that he turned his attention back to my mandala and, instead of applying a simple carving gesture, swept his entire arm through the sand, scattering it violently. Flying grains spattered the robes of nearby monks, who jumped back as though the previously blessed sand might now taint them.

Then Suren turned on his heel and strode off, the other monks scurrying away in his wake. I was left with the destroyed object of my affection, and Tilik. I could see it was taking all his discipline not to give in to uncontrolled anger.

"You will clean this up," he said, "and erase every vestige of the design off the face of the board. Then you will come to see me, by which time I will have decided your punishment."

How easily euphoria can slide into anguish. I was crying in humiliation as I cleaned up the mess alone in the temple, my nose running like a child's. Normally each grain of mandala sand is blessed by the ritual of mandala creation, and saved to scatter in a strong wind afterwards, thus distributing the good karma over a wider area. Given my actions, however, I wasn't sure what the monastery would do with the sand from this one. Probably bury it. I gathered it up, sweeping every last coloured speck into a cotton sack. The sand was everywhere, on the floor under the benches, in the seams of nearby cushions, even among the offerings on the alter. No-one entered the temple while I worked. Even Bayan kept away, leaving me to snivel alone in my labours.

After several hours I'd retrieved all that was possible to retrieve. My eyes had grown bleary from the effort. I scrubbed the lines off the board and carried both board and sack to Tilik as evidence of the deed. My arrival at his ger interrupted a steady pacing that had probably been going on since we parted.

"Sit down," he said, indicating one of the stools. He stood opposite me. "For five years I have been trying to instill in you an understanding of the principal defilements, the human flaws that prevent us from gaining the wisdom that leads to enlightenment. Can you even tell me what they are?"

"Attachment, anger, pride, ignorance, false view and doubt."

"And which of these prevent you personally from advancing in your quest for enlightenment?"

"Attachment."

"More!" he boomed, clapping his hands together with such force it made me jump. "You think you have a small problem with attachment, and that this small problem will yet be overcome without too much effort. But that's not all, no!" He was stomping around now, more agitated than I had ever seen him. "You're thinking it is your fondness for the Divine Tara that is the problem. Did you suppose I didn't know? I know. But this is not what worries me.

"You have another attachment of a far worse kind: you are attached to the idea of your self. This creates a stubborn pride. You think your miserable, individual person, in its current incarnation, is an important thing, not just the transient phase it really is. This is a false view of the reality of existence. And why do you suffer all these problems?"

I had been silenced by his tirade, so he answered for me.

"Doubt." With this word his anger seemed to evaporate into weariness, as though my shortcomings represented a failure on his part that might doom him to many more lifetimes of frustrating *samsara*, the endless cycle of human suffering, just when he thought he had been getting somewhere.

"Your motivation for becoming a monk is critical," he said. "Belief in the rightness of the Path creates a bridge to self-transcendence, without which you cannot progress. If, on the other hand, you are here for regular meals and the chance to learn—and you would not be alone—you will not become a real monk. You may be ordained, but you will not be following the Path."

"I would like to be a real monk," I said.

"What you would like has nothing to do with it, don't you see? You will be a real monk only when you *believe* that by following the Vinaya and understanding the dharma you can achieve the wisdom that releases you from samsara." He shook his head, underscoring his doubt that I would ever achieve such a thing. "That is a big problem that will take time and effort. Much effort. For now, my concern is to help you apply antidotes that might counteract the negative karma of your actions over the mandala."

"Yes, Master."

"You will first confess your recognition of the problem in tomorrow morning's prayer session. You will express your regret, which I expect to be sincere, and your desire never to do such a thing again."

"Yes, Master."

"Then you will go straight away to the refuge cave, where you will spend three days and three nights contemplating your motivation for becoming a monk. You will bring water but no food, and no sleeping mat. And at the end of these three days you will return and tell me what you've learned."

Cave retreats were not usually punishments. In fact they were a welcome break for many monks, although they were usually allowed food and a sleeping mat, luxuries I wasn't going to get. Going on retreat gave a monk extended time without the distractions of chores and the presence of others; it freed him to meditate long and hard, gaining results not possible in shorter daily sessions.

As dictated, after my confession in the prayer session I headed off to the refuge cave, which was up in the hills behind the monastery, a good half hour's trek away. I didn't dawdle; I was in enough trouble already and didn't want to risk creating any more negative karma. I felt a kind of grim satisfaction at the prospect of my task. Like a Christian flagellant who takes solace in chastising his body for the weaknesses of his mind, I thought that my three days in the cave would work some kind of miracle cure, ridding me instantly of the failings that prevented me from being a good monk.

The cave had been chosen for retreats for good reason. Big enough to lie down or sit up in, but not to stand, its solid rock surfaces kept you dry and sheltered but offered not a speck of physical comfort. That makes it sound unpleasant, but it actually had a very welcoming atmosphere. It wasn't just any old hole in the earth where an animal might take up home. It had been selected specifically because it had spiritual significance, a kind of humming vibrancy that could be felt as soon as you got close, if you stood very still and opened yourself to the feeling. The cave smelled holy, too. The walls were speckled with stubs of incense that had been burnt through the course of a thousand retreats, the smoke meant to carry merit accumulated by prayer out into the greater universe. The scent clung to the rock as a reminder of the succession of monks who had been there to pray on behalf of themselves and mankind.

Being in a contrite mood, I remained well focused the first day. There was no danger of veering towards thoughts of Tara in my meditations. The cave was so holy I feared I would be struck dead instantly if I allowed myself such an impurity there. I forced myself to spend the morning in lotus, negating my prideful self through meditation. I brought forth a clear image of myself being praised. It was tempting to stay there so it took several tries, each one slipping into a pleasant but unproductive frame of mind, before I could manage to move on to imagining the consequence: the moment at which everyone in my brotherhood, the sangha, rejected me for my awful action. I went back to the proud me and slowly made myself disappear. Such an act of negation is supposed to be useful in ridding the mind of wrongful ideas.

Hunger pangs hit me predictably around the hour when we normally ate lunch. I welcomed them as a part of my punishment that I could meet head-on and feel satisfied about overcoming. When I drank some of my water I made myself thankful for the sensation of it dribbling down my throat to my empty stomach. In the afternoon I prostrated myself to recite the confession sutra five hundred times. It was more comfortable than sitting up.

By nightfall I was pleased with what I'd managed to do on my first day, but I was starting to feel light-headed. I tried to sleep but, being used to the darkness of a ger, I was kept awake by the brightness of the stars shining directly into my face through the mouth of the cave. When I turned on my side to get away from them, my side became sore. I put my cloak over my head and missed the cushion of it under me.

By morning I was seriously hungry as well as grumpy from lack of sleep. My stomach pangs bothered me more while I welcomed them less. I was so thirsty, the only thing that stopped me from gulping down my whole water supply was the knowledge that I'd probably go crazy the next day if I didn't have any at all. I went from feeling contrite to irritated.

Despite these nagging intrusions of self, I tried to stick to the program I'd set out for myself. To reinstill my dedication to the life of a monk I recited, again five hundred times although I might have lost count once or twice, the basic mantra of the Three Jewels: *Until I reach the terrace of enlightenment I go for refuge to the Buddha / until I reach the terrace of enlightenment I go for refuge in the Law / until I reach the terrace of enlightenment I go for refuge in the Assembly.*

I meant to follow this up by meditating on the selflessness of all the bodhisattvas who remain in samsara just to help the rest of us find our way. My mind, however, refused to be still. It slipped around, as hard to grasp as a minnow in a fast river. When I considered selflessness a voice in my head reiterated all Bayan's words about the great things achieved through the application of ego throughout the ages. I thought about Chinggis Khan. I thought about Qara's wonderful artworks that he made just for his own satisfaction.

My efforts were not going at all in the right direction. Angry with my lack of progress, I got up to stretch outside the cave and have a drink, but stood too quickly and had to steady myself against the rock face. My head swam and my stomach grumbled. I considered foraging for food on the hillside. I knew which plants were edible. No-one from the monastery could see me here. But fear of greater karmic retribution, and of Tilik magically knowing I'd done so, prevented me.

To lessen the temptation I returned to the cave and sat with my back to the outside world. Then, given that concentration was proving so difficult, I began the far simpler task of chanting common prayers. The Four Immeasurables and the Seven-Limbed Prayer had worked in the past to help me focus. The more I recited, however, the less the prayers gave me spiritual guidance. They became unproductive droning. Despite all my effort and application, the momentum of the day before appeared to have vanished. I was no longer getting anywhere towards undoing the negative karma of the mandala incident. At this rate, I would be paying for it for life.

So went the whole of day two. The more I wanted my desire to be a good monk to be transformed into a pure, unselfconscious belief that it was the true path for me, the less I actually experienced it. Night came. Weary, frustrated, and disappointed in myself for lacking the simple skill of prolonged concentration so necessary for my success, I lay on the ground to await another fitful half-sleep. The smell of the earth filled my nostrils and I longed for the familiar boiled cotton scent of my thin, monastic mattress cover. Night animals scurried about the hillside, their quite scuffling as sleep-destroying as a rampaging herd of camels compared to the muffled stillness of a felt ger.

Dawn of my third day was the lowest point of my retreat. The idea that I had to face another day and night of the same torture brought on a bout of self pity in which I wallowed, lying on the hard ground and staring blankly at the pocked ceiling of the cave, until it became clear that the time was actually going to pass more slowly and in greater agony that way. I sat up, and in a slumped heap I contemplated the frustration of contemplation.

A kind of calm came over me at that point. It was the product of exhaustion and the abandonment of hope, as I had stopped thinking I might gain real insights in the cave, and now sought only to get to the end of my retreat with as little misery as possible. In giving up, I slipped into a calm, clear space in my mind with the ease of slipping into a light sleep.

While visualizing myself as ordained and wise, teaching new novices in turn how to progress towards enlightenment, I suddenly understood what Tilik had meant when he'd said that *wanting* to be a good monk had nothing to do with it. To *be* a good monk, you had to be motivated by a desire at least to release yourself from the cycle of samsara by gaining enlightenment. Preferably you wanted to release everybody else as well, by sharing your wisdom when you got it.

My own motivation was just another of those desires my ego possessed in such abundance. I was trying to be a good monk in order

51

to please my father, to impress Tilik, to gain the trappings of spirituality that would convince me, and everyone else, that the misfortunes of my early years had been wiped out by my many good deeds since.

People talk about experiencing epiphanies during meditation that lead them to deep spiritual understanding, the Path suddenly golden and perfectly illuminated before them. My own epiphany did the opposite.

I now understood that the doubt Tilik had so sadly identified in me wasn't a lack of belief in Buddhism or its tenets, but a lack of belief in myself as a vehicle for enlightenment. There was some basic characteristic I lacked. Koke and Tilik had it. It was evident in their certainty, in the way they prayed and knew there was an effect, the way they meditated and discovered something, the way they read the sutras and understood, at a deep, instinctive level, their meaning.

I had none of that. For years I had studied, and prayed, and meditated as best I could, and all I had to show for it was rote knowledge as opposed to true understanding. Playing the devoted novice had become easy enough but, under the surface, I felt there was never going to be enough to back it up. My desire to be like Koke and Tilik was as hopeless as my desire to have sexual union with Tara. A fantasy.

The idea that I would never gain true spirituality carried with it a surprising sense of release, which lured me toward it. I wasn't giving up, I told myself; I was accepting my limitations. Lots of boys entered monasteries for their education, were ordained, and continued on in the sangha. It could be a good life, useful and rich with positive karma. I could see myself in that role much more easily than I could see myself as someone like Koke or Tilik, who took his vows because he had real hope for enlightenment. I still wanted to be a monk. I was only going to stop trying to be a superior one.

With this lightening of my load, the remainder of my retreat became almost pleasant. Instead of meditating further, I passed the time watching the patterns made by passing clouds against the blue of the sky, and the graceful arcs carved by circling kites searching for prey. Instead of grasping at sleep in the night I stared at the wonder of a million bright stars against the limitless black expanse of the heavens.

Chapter Six

UNTIL THE AX IS BRANDISHED,
THE OXEN ARE AT EASE.

On the final morning of my retreat Bayan was sent up to fetch me, since a long fast can leave a person too weak to get back safely on their own. He brought me some yoghurt and biscuits, which I gulped down like a wild dog.

"You look pretty good, considering," he said.

"I'm hungry."

"I can see that. And you stink."

"Can't be helped."

"We could go back the long way, by the river," he suggested, "if you can make it that far. You can clean up better there."

It was rare that we got to swim in the river. It only happened if our turn for fetching the water that filled the monastery's barrels happened to coincide with warm weather, which was a couple of times a summer if we were lucky. At the mere suggestion of water, my skin began to itch with a desperate filth I hadn't even noticed until then.

"I can make it."

The food had given me a lift in energy, but all the same I found myself a little dizzy as we made our descent through the rocks. I drank some more water and ate another biscuit, which Bayan brought forth from the folds of his robes like a magician conjuring trinkets at a traveling show.

"I saved it from my breakfast," he said. "You're always hungry at the best of times so I figured by now you'd be famished."

When we reached the valley he gave me his arm to lean on. I hadn't realized how much walking would exhaust me.

"I'm a little weaker than I thought," I said. Bayan's arm felt powerful beneath my hand. In the years I'd been at the monastery he had grown into a solid young man, thick as a wrestler. I wondered how he'd managed to convert our meager rations into so much muscle. Although I was getting taller than he, my frame was slim, my arms half the girth of his.

Following along the base of the hills, we made our slow progress towards the river.

"So what did you think of being on retreat?" Bayan asked.

"It's very uncomfortable."

He laughed. "In your case, it was supposed to be. With a mat and some food, it's pretty good. I like to get away from the others once in awhile. From the routine, and all those rules."

"Do you meditate when you go?"

"Don't be an idiot."

I took that as a no. "I did."

"Since when did you get so good at meditating?"

"Being without food did interesting things to my mind."

"That's what Shakyamuni said. I hope you're not going to tell me you reached enlightenment."

"Don't worry."

"But you actually wasted all that freedom in deep thought?"

"Only part of the time. It was useful."

"You really are an idiot."

I didn't say anything, I just waited until his curiosity got the better of him.

"And what did you learn from all that effort?" he asked finally. "Did you ponder the defilements? Have you gained such a brilliant insight into your own shortcomings that you think Tilik is going to pat you on the head and tell you what a perfect monk you are?" His voice had taken on the belligerent tone he always fell into when our discussions involved Tilik.

"Tilik doesn't pat heads," I said. "But anyway, what I learned is that I will never be that perfect a monk." An unexpected pang that felt like bereavement pricked my heart at the words. I willed it away.

Bayan looked at me sideways. "Well what do you know," he said slowly. "Maybe you're not so stupid after all."

We arrived at the river. Patient and meandering in its path, it was a single vein pumping life into our otherwise parched land. Between a rocky outcropping and a copse of scrubby trees, an eddy in the flow had created a small pool, chest-deep at the centre. I stripped down and entered, eager for the cold water against my dry and dirty skin. I dunked my head under and felt my brain startle inside my skull at the shock.

Bayan had also entered the pool. We had never been modest about swimming together naked. It was practical to have your clothes off if you wanted to get wet.

He grinned at me. "Feel better?"

In answer I submerged again, then jumped up spouting water into the air. We had a water fight for a few minutes, spitting and splashing at each other. Then I found myself starting to shiver.

"I'm cold," I said.

"It's because your blood is still thin from fasting. Sit on the edge, in the sun."

I scrambled up the grassy bank and sat there, my feet dangling, my head whirling like the time, when I was eight, that I'd tried vodka on a dare from my cousin. Bayan stayed in the water. As he stood facing me I noticed his broad chest was slightly tanned, indicating that he'd managed to get to the river a lot more than I had.

My teeth were still chattering despite the sun.

"You're still cold," Bayan said. "I know a way for you to warm up fast. You'll like it. But you have to stay still no matter what."

I didn't say yes, but neither did I say no. I stared in paralyzed wonder, like an animal caught in the sights of a hunter's gun, as he gently spread my legs apart and lowered his face.

When he took my frozen, shriveled penis into the hot wetness of his mouth it leapt to greet him. I wanted to push him off me, to shout my disgust, but the slickness of his tongue slipping around the head of my erection sent a jolt up through my body as immobilizing as an arc of lightning, and my protest halted in its tracks. The feeling that was rushing through me now stole all control, all thought.

I came in a matter of seconds. Blood thundered in my ears, the world spun, and I felt I would shatter in a million pieces.

Instead, in my weakened state, I fainted.

I sometimes wondered, later, if Bayan had planned that event, but I think he was just an opportunist who had happened upon the right time. I'd felt awkward at the river after I came to, but Bayan was so casual and persistent he made it seem as though sharing sexual favours was as natural as scratching someone else's back in a place they couldn't quite reach. In the few opportunities that we managed to construct in the weeks and months that followed, our diversions continued. Although it was understood, without ever being said, that we would not engage in sodomy, Bayan pulled me into a physical exploration that was hard to resist and at which he had great expertise. He softened my fear of instant excommunication by rationalizing our activity with Tantric scriptures he'd gotten from I didn't know where. In short, he made it feel too good to stop, and the consequences too distant to worry about. And I let him.

As for my relationship with Tilik, that changed too. I think he recognized that I had lost the unquestioning devotion that a child has for his master or for an ideology, and I had not replaced it in full measure with an adult's thoughtful conviction. Whatever chance might have existed to help me reach enlightenment in this lifetime—which had been slim to begin with—was gone. He continued my spiritual education but it became subtly more prosaic. We concentrated on the fundamentals, such as how a mere human can effectively practice the Six Perfections of the bodhisattvas in everyday life, and we stopped discussing dharma theories that involved higher planes of being. Did it bother Tilik to accept that his pupil was not going to be highly realized spiritually? We never spoke of it, but once in awhile I caught him watching me do something right, like build a mandala or recite a perfect prayer sequence, and he would be studying me with a perplexed look on his face as though he were trying to figure out where he'd gone wrong.

That summer brought other kinds of changes as well. Japan's war with China had given Russia the excuse it needed to send thirty thousand Red Army troops into Mongolia, ostensibly for our protection against these two other arguing neighbours. It also gave Mongolia's secret police an excuse to begin arresting and executing tens of thousands of their political foes, by accusing them of being spies for Japan. Our prime minister, Genden, was one of the first to go.

It was September. Bayan, Koke and I had the job of dividing the firewood we had collected into individual baskets so each monk would receive the same small amount of fuel for the woodstove that kept his ger warm. We squatted in the dirt outside the back of the administrative ger to escape the first chill wind of the season, the wood in a pile between us.

"The Internal Ministry has arrested Genden and sixty-six others," Bayan announced. I knew it must be true because he actually looked worried, which was an unfamiliar expression for him.

"How can the Prime Minister be arrested by his own government?" Koke asked.

"Choibalsan has never answered to Genden, don't you know that? Internal Security has Russian masters."

"Maybe Genden did something wrong."

"How stupid you are." Bayan's voice was a hiss. "Do you believe the lies they tell?"

"It's just that—"

"It's just that Genden hasn't been quick enough to rid the country of us monks," Bayan finished for him. "They arrested him for spying for Japan, but his real crime in Russia's eyes is that he's been too soft on the monasteries."

Koke was quiet then. We had been ignoring, but not ignorant of the escalating frictions between the government and the Buddhist clergy.

"Why is it so important to get rid of monks?" I asked. "We're just praying and trying to generate good karma for everybody. We're not a threat."

"You only see our quiet little monastery. But the other, bigger ones have real power. They have more money than the government, did you know that? And they still control a lot of the education, which means they control what people believe. People look up to monks. Not many people look up to a Party member unless they're being forced to."

"Still, the government won't be able to eliminate every monk in Mongolia," said Koke.

"You are so ignorant it's unbelievable. Already the biggest monasteries are under threat or being destroyed. Erdene Zuu, Gandan, the most important centres, they'll be finished soon."

"But there are still many more of us," said Koke.

"I agree," I said, jumping on this optimistic view. "They've been executing high ranking lamas for years and still we keep making more. They'd have to send a whole army to get rid of us."

"That's exactly what they do," said Bayan.

Koke shook his head. "How could a soldier kill a monk? It's too much bad karma. Anyone would be able to see that."

"When your turn comes, you'll find out," said Bayan. He held up a stick. "One day you'll be here like this, and then—" he snapped the stick in two and threw it into a basket. "That's how."

CHAPTER SEVEN

AN EVIL MAN WAITS FOR AN OPPORTUNITY;
A WOLF WAITS FOR A RAINSTORM.

Choibalsan's purges of the government began in earnest after that. With a truly communist sense of equality he terrorized important people and petty bureaucrats in equal measure, so everybody could become wary of everyone else without hierarchic barriers. Most of the people he arrested simply disappeared forever, but some were openly executed as a reminder of who held the real power in Mongolia. Genden was sent off to Moscow, and it wasn't until I was an old man that his execution there was confirmed. His wife had lived the rest of her life hoping he might return.

The carnage went on for a year and a half. During that time we lived quietly, careful not to draw attention to ourselves with celebrations, not even on the holiest days. I saw my father infrequently. Few people dared visit us for the services that used to be commonplace. When they did, they arrived furtively, entering with what appeared to be a cart of supplies and then revealing the baby to be blessed or couple to be married. Even those who only wanted prayers to help an ill family member came disguised. Mongolians lived with their heads down, like dogs expecting a blow.

In the monastery we stayed within our own minds and our own world. Geography and history were part of our studies, so we understood the wider world well enough. But we viewed the current violence beyond our walls as part of the continuous cycle of human suffering. A situation that would pass, as with all impermanent things. We tried to make it pass more quickly by performing burnt offering rituals to drive out evil and by making food offerings to summon goodness. We prayed day after day. People kept disappearing and being executed all the same.

When our adult monks voiced their worries in our assemblies, Suren responded with a vague wave of his hand, as if he could swish the problems away like so many flies, and assigned enough prayer sessions to make us too tired to worry, at least out loud. He didn't come to all of them himself, and neither did Bayan. The rest of us followed orders and kept on trying.

One night in the early spring of 1939, Bayan told me to meet him at the wall behind the outhouses after everyone had gone to sleep. Early spring in our country doesn't bring much warmth, and it was still well below freezing in the middle of the night. I rubbed my hands together to stay warm while I waited for him in the darkness and hoped that no-one had a sudden need to relieve himself.

I hung back in the shadows when a figure hurried around the side of the outhouse, waiting until I was sure the bulk belonged to Bayan; then I showed myself and he came over to join me.

"Can you get over the wall?" he whispered without preamble.

It was not a very high wall at that part of the monastery, only slightly over my head. In answer I started to scramble up it, my toes scrabbling for a hold in the dried mud that served as mortar. Bayan tossed me up the rest of the way with one firm thrust of his hands on my bottom. I nearly landed on my head on the other side. Then he vaulted over, and we were standing outside the monastery. A half-moon turned the land before us into a painting of softly lit rocks and smudgy voids.

I had no idea what we were doing there. Bayan had said to come and I did. He was nineteen now, due to be ordained in spite of his unsuitability for monkhood. I was sixteen, still in thrall to his natural leadership, his rebelliousness, his sexual favours.

"I need to show you something," Bayan said.

"All right." I stood there, waiting for him to show me whatever it was, but he grabbed my arm and started to walk.

"Come on."

I followed him, hurrying to keep up with his confident strides on the rough terrain. He headed towards the path the led up the hillside behind the monastery. After passing between the two large boulders that marked the way, he began to count, one, two, three large rocks on his right. We turned right after the third one.

"You have to remember this," he said, very quietly. "Three rocks, then right. Then six rocks and left." He counted again and we turned left, then nine and right again, creating a trail of right angles along the hillside. The night quiet was so absolute that our footsteps sounded deafening. I heard every crunch under our boots and every whispered number Bayan uttered as though they were being funneled into my ears through a trumpet. We were up to thirty when we stopped. I couldn't see the monastery anymore, but I knew it was on the other side of the hill.

The thirtieth rock looked like any other, especially in the dim light of the half-moon. Bayan pushed it over slowly, grunting with the effort and being careful not to disturb the surrounding vegetation too much. Under the rock was a hole, and in it, a box. Bayan grabbed the brass handle on its lid and lifted it out.

It was a small wooden box, about as long as two hands spread wide, and half as high. He brushed it clean with his hands to reveal a fine brass inlay of a Khan Garuda, and a thick brass clasp at the front meant for a lock. It had no lock, though. There was no need when it was buried.

"This is my money," Bayan said, opening the box.

I peered inside and was astounded to see that the box was filled almost to the brim with tugrog notes. My understanding of money was negligible, but it looked like a lot to me. I had only ever seen my father handle small sums, for a single horse or a bag of flour or block of tea. Although I'd been too young to pay much attention to how much any of those things cost, my impression was that the money in Bayan's box was much more than anything my father had ever dealt with.

"There are no jewels, only money," he explained. "Jewels can be difficult to convert to cash in troubled times, but people will always take a note."

I nodded as though this were common knowledge.

"I wanted you to know where it is in case something happens to me. I'd want it to be yours in that case."

His gesture overwhelmed me. I knew it was not love or even affection that prompted him, but faith in my trustworthiness. That I would tell no-one, nor take it myself and run off, nor, especially, ever give it to the Communists. It was a great compliment.

"I will always keep it a secret," I said.

He put the box back in its hole and replaced the rock, fluffing the bits of scruffy, frozen weeds around its base.

"Have you noticed that the Party boss has not been to Khovor Khan for a month?"

I had noticed. "Maybe he was purged."

"Either he's been purged, or he feels unsafe. Either way, that's trouble for us."

His words chilled me. Like most of the monks at Khovor Khan, I tried not to think about the possibility of government repressions being inflicted on our monastery the way they had been on others.

"We should return now," he said. Scratching out our footprints with a branch, he backed away from his treasure while I started retracing our steps. We didn't stop along the way. It was too cold, and we had other things on our minds.

At the beginning of summer, shortly before Bayan was to be ordained, he approached me after group prayer one morning. It was an unpleasant day. The sky was grey and flat but wouldn't give up its rain, and the wind whipped the earth into dust storms around our legs.

He leaned close to my ear. "Suren wants to see you," he said.

"How do you know?" It was Tilik's place to inform me about audiences with the Abbot, not Bayan's.

"I just know. He asked me to fetch you."

I thought for one panicky moment that he'd found out about the things Bayan and I had been getting up to, but Bayan looked far too calm. "What have I done wrong?"

"Don't worry. You're always worrying for nothing."

"But why does he want to see me?"

"Maybe he wants you to paint him something special."

It seemed far-fetched, but of course I wanted to believe it.

"Go now, before lunch. He's in his ger."

"I can't just walk into his ger."

"I can. I'll take you, come on. He really has asked for you."

The walk to Suren's ger seemed interminable as I went through every little infraction that might have come to his attention, preparing for the worst.

We entered the silent enclosure and Bayan opened the ger door just enough to speak through the crack. "I've brought Dash."

Suren's nasal voice came floating out to us. "Come in, boy."

I ducked through the door with my heart in my throat. I had never had an interview with the Abbot in which I felt at ease. Apart from the intimidation that arose naturally from his position, there was a penetrating aspect to his beady eyes that unnerved me.

Bayan stayed outside, pulling the door shut against the wind and dust. It was tranquil inside the ger. The top flap was mostly closed against the weather, leaving a single shaft of pale light to filter down and mix with the glow of the butter lamps. Suren had been seated in his big chair, but he got up and came toward me where I stood uncertainly just inside the door. I felt much as I had the first day I met him, except that now I was tall enough to look down at him when we were both standing.

"Come in, boy, come in," he said, taking me by the arm. He wheezed a little when he walked, as though getting his bulk from one side of the ger to the other was something of a feat. "Sit down."

He remained standing as I sank onto the small stool. On the low table beside me was a plate, Chinese blue on white, on which were squares of something brown and smooth. A sweet yet pungent odor came from them.

"Would you like a chocolate?" he asked me.

"Pardon me?"

He smiled a little, enjoying my ignorance. "A chocolate. Those little things on the plate, they are to eat. Please, try one."

It would have been unthinkably rude to refuse, so I picked up a piece and placed it, tentatively, in my mouth. The explosion of taste was startling, at once acrid and sweet. It melted on my tongue and spread its impossible flavour throughout my mouth.

My surprise must have been obvious, because the Abbot began to laugh lightly. "You like it."

"It's very good, yes."

"I used to have many more interesting things to eat, given to me by special friends. Oranges, for instance. Those were rare, even in the good times. Have you ever tasted an orange?"

"No." I'd seen a painting of one, in a botany book.

"It's not possible to describe the flavour. Maybe someday I'll have one to give you."

He spoke with nostalgia regarding his lost access to these rare things, while I thought what he still had was fantastic enough. More strange to me was this sudden show of generosity towards me. It was very confusing.

"You still have an interest in art," he said.

"If it serves the monastery."

"Of course." He paced slowly, lugging himself two steps this way, two that. "I also have an interest in art. A small collection."

I sat still, saying nothing.

"I thought you might add to it."

"If that is your wish, I would of course do my best." I restrained my enthusiasm, having learned well that art created for the monastery must always be a selfless effort.

"I want something different than what you are used to doing. I think you need to see my collection first, to understand what I mean." He turned to look directly at me. "Would you like that?"

I nodded.

"Come along, then." He drew aside the thick velvet curtain that led to the other part of his ger, the part I had never seen, nor dreamed of seeing.

The opulence of his personal quarters was more than I could have imagined. At one end of the room was a low divan covered with plump cushions and yards of fine silks and velvets. Thick Chinese carpets overlapped each other on the floor. In the glow of the lamps, jewel-studded scroll paintings and dozens of gold statues glimmered and shone like a galaxy of stars.

Suren let the curtain drop and walked tactfully around me, as though he understood the immobilizing effect of his collection and knew it would take a moment for me to adjust to its presence. Picking up a lit lantern, he approached a cabinet of statues.

"You'll have to come closer if you're to see them properly."

I walked forward like a somnambulist, but was shaken into full alertness as soon as I was close enough to see them well. The entire collection was sexual in nature. Gods proudly bore erections that soared past their chins; they wielded them like swords, penetrating the vaginas and mouths and backsides of other goddesses and gods who smiled benignly.

"Do you like them?" Suren asked. Opening the glass door of the cabinet, he pulled one out. "This is a particularly clever piece that Qara made for me. Moveable parts, you see?" It was similar to Bayan's statue, except that Tara could be moved up and down the shaft of Avalokitesvara's penis.

It was well known that the acquisition of ill-omened things could cause painful disease and even death in the owner. Monks were always gossiping about cases in which this happened. I marveled that Suren could believe his powers protected him from such a dangerous collection.

"I know, as a painter you're probably more interested in seeing my other works," he went on, moving towards the scroll paintings that lined his walls.

It didn't seem to matter that I hadn't said a word since entering the inner chamber. He continued on as though we were engaging in conversation.

"I find these artworks very helpful. Stimulating." He held the lantern up to a painting in which a goddess was astride a demon, locked on to his phallus while his hands clutched at her breasts in ecstasy, the long nails of his bony fingers digging crescent moon shapes into the perfect, pale smoothness of her flesh. "Bayan tells me you are interested in the Tantric arts." I felt my insides jerk with fear. "Powerful practices, those. I'm a Tantric master, did you know that?

"I would like you to create a work like these for me," he continued. "Choose your own subject. Use your imagination. I understand it's quite a good one." He peered up into my eyes, gauging my reaction. "What do you think?"

He wasn't really asking my opinion. In my place I could only say *yes, of course Your Holiness, whatever you ask of me.* But in my utter confusion I could produce no sound.

"You are overwhelmed by the honour," he said. "Of course. I understand."

By now we had made our way as far as the divan. On the table beside it was a bowl containing two apples, which I recognized because Qara had shown me a European still life and told me the name of each exotic fruit depicted. It was extraordinary, the things Suren possessed. I had never eaten a piece of fruit in all my life. Bayan had eaten fruit here, I was sure of it. And chocolate.

I could hear Suren breathing more heavily now than before. It was ragged, uneven. I knew what that kind of breathing meant.

"And there's another honour I have in mind for you, yes. A great honour. There are not many who are chosen to assist a Master in his higher practices." He sat heavily on the divan, easing his bulk back into the waiting cushions. "But Bayan says you are an able pupil."

He pulled aside his robes to reveal that he was not wearing the customary underclothing. At the apex of his pale, soft gut and two pudgy thighs protruded his penis, pink and hopeful. Even though it was clearly erect, it stood no bigger than my thumb. I gaped, horrified.

I had performed this service dozens of times for Bayan, if not gleefully then at least in a spirit of reciprocity. But this was my abbot. I was revolted by the sight of his hideous body. His lust had a perverted, needy character to it that was completely different than the simple expediency of my encounters with Bayan. I suddenly understood what the Party leader came here for, and where Bayan had learned his many skills. Bile began to rise in my throat.

Suren stared hard at me, willing my cooperation with his sharp eyes. Accustomed to cooperation.

I turned and ran. I just had time to tear through the gate of his enclosure before throwing up my lovely chocolate, its wondrous taste now mixed with acid vomit.

CHAPTER EIGHT

WHERE THE MIGHTY QUARREL
THERE IS LITIGATION.
WHERE DOGS FIGHT THERE IS CARRION.

I went to my own ger to rinse out my mouth. Taking some water in a cup, I went outside and rinsed, spit, rinsed again, spit. If there had been ten times that amount of water to waste it wouldn't have been enough. Bayan caught up with me after the second spit.

"What are you doing back?" His voice was sharp as a slap.

"Bayan, he wanted me to—"

"I know what he wanted, idiot. You're so stupid! Did you actually refuse him? I can't believe you actually refused him!" He was holding his head in his hands and shaking it back and forth, then he stopped and glared at me and I thought he might actually cuff me, he looked that angry.

At that point the gate's bell clanged.

People rarely came to the monastery at mid-morning; it was a time devoted to chores. The bell clanged a second time and there was something about the sound, feeble yet urgent, that transmitted the desperation of the puller. Over the incessant wind came cries for help like the mewling of a famished cat, then we heard shouts from within the monastery and the bang of the bolts being yanked open quickly. We ran to see who was there.

The monk who stumbled through our gate was old and gaunt. The deep wrinkles of his face were caked with dirt and tears, and he stank of shit. He fell to his knees, clinging to Mongo, who had let him in, and tried to tell his story. Everyone crowded around but his incoherence made it difficult to hear and we had to strain to catch the details. *At prayer*, I heard him say, then he broke into loud sobs and the rest came out in garbled fits. *Soldiers* and *slaughtered* and *nothing left* came through, however, enough to terrify us all.

Tilik appeared and parted the crowd with a glower. He walked up to the monk, who was still on his knees, and put his hands on either side of the man's head, pressing firmly. He whispered a few words and the monk calmed, then rose unsteadily and allowed himself to be led away to the nursing ger.

As they left, Suren appeared. His frown could have been taken for concern over our visitor if you didn't know what had just happened in his ger.

Mongo explained what he'd heard.

"The old monk is from Arbat. He says soldiers came two days ago, before dawn during prayers." His eyes widened with comprehension and his words came faster as he went on. "They rounded up the monks. Took away their gers. Set fire to," he stumbled here, "to the dharma hall, and the study halls and the library. Destroyed the stupa, everything. Everything. This monk, he hid in the outhouse, underneath. The rest he thinks they shot or took away. All the monks of Arbat, gone."

Arbat was a larger monastery than ours, with eighty or so monks and a fine school of philosophy. Perhaps it was the school's reputation that had brought Choibalsan's fury down on it. Like his mentor Stalin, he hated displays of intellect that were not his own.

We all looked to the Abbot, hoping he would say something to reassure us.

He blanched.

"This is very bad," he said, shaking his head. "Bayan, come with me."

Bayan followed Suren to his ger, leaving behind a babble of voices pitched high with strain.

"All the monks of Arbat…"

"Do you think we could be next?"

"We're much too small to bother about here."

"Surely the Abbot's friend will protect us."

"Haven't you noticed that he hasn't come for three months now?"

"But the medical services we provide, that alone should give them reason to leave us be."

"I heard they send the strong ones to the army, where they have to break their vows by killing Japanese."

"I heard they send them to Siberia."

"But here we are too small to bother about."

"What if we are not?"

I went to the infirmary, partly to help Tilik with the visitor, and partly hoping the task would distract me from the images of Suren's exposed body, the wildly erotic statues, and the old monk's sobbing face, all of which were swirling around together in my head.

Tilik had removed the monk's filthy robes, laid him on his back on a straw pallet, and covered him with a blanket. While waiting for water to warm in a pot on the wood stove, Tilik chanted softly and ground herbs with a mortar and pestle in preparation for a medicine. The chant was as soothing as a lullaby. He handed me a towel and indicated the pot with a thrust of his chin, not breaking the spell of the sound by speaking.

I bathed the old man gently, starting with his face. His eyes were open but unfocussed, and tears slid out of them in a slow, silent stream. I had never seen anyone so inconsolable. All through my ministrations he continued to weep in this noiseless way, as though even the effort of making a full sob had become too much for him. His skinny body was limp and unresisting as I raised an arm to clean the pit or lifted a foot to get the encrusted feces off the back of his leg. His feet were cracked and bleeding, his shins bruised from his journey through strange lands in the night.

The deep herbal scent of the infusion Tilik was preparing filled the ger, and the old monk closed his eyes for a moment as though drawing relief even from the odour of it. When I finished cleaning him, which took several changes of water, Tilik gave him the potion to drink. His tears finally ceased as he fell into sleep. We applied balm to his sores and settled ourselves at the other end of the ger to watch over him until he woke.

I poured us both tea, which we drank in silence as we shared the modest comfort of a pallet. I would have liked to lie down on it after all I'd witnessed in the past hour, but Tilik sat cross-legged and straight-backed so I did the same. It seemed to me that the only sane place in the world at that moment was inside the infirmary ger with him.

"Why are you not Abbot instead of Suren?" I asked him.

"The Living Buddha did not wish it." He spoke in the same, nonjudgmental tone he used for all statements of simple fact.

"But you are superior."

"Superiority is a construct based on individual opinion and therefore invalid, because opinion, by its nature, is tainted by the human defilements that blind us against true wisdom."

"But we live in a world of opinion, whether it's right or not."

"*You* live in a world of opinion," Tilik corrected me.

I cast aside the rebuke. "Still, it would be hard to argue that you are not superior to the Abbot spiritually." I wasn't about to go into details, but I was pretty sure he knew what I meant.

"It takes more than spirituality to lead a monastery. It's a political job as much as a religious one. Maybe wholly so. Spirituality, which seeks the enlightened way, can hinder politics, which seeks the pragmatic way."

"Do you think Suren has been a good Abbot, then?"

"What is good? It's not for me to have an opinion about that. Nor for you."

This was the frustrating thing about talking to Tilik; he was full of wisdom but wouldn't give me the benefit of his judgment because he expected me to develop my own. But I was only sixteen, and felt as though I would never have enough.

The old monk moaned a little in his sleep. One hand twitched.

"What will happen to us?" I asked.

Tilik was quiet a moment before answering. "I believe we will be given a lesson in impermanence." He looked calm about this prediction. My own heart was beating wildly at the prospect.

"I heard they put the stronger monks in the army, and force them to kill people." Killing any living thing was against Buddhist precepts. The sheep whose meat we relied on for survival were butchered by someone else, and even then the animal was prayed over to ensure a good rebirth for its sacrifice.

"That could be true."

"But if a monk is forced to break the most basic of vows in that way, does such bad karma not result in many terrible rebirths for him, even though it was not his fault?"

"His intent and the circumstances of his action have a lot to do with the repercussions of karma."

"Would he still be considered a monk?"

"When a man takes his vows to become a monk, he is a monk for life. Even if he leaves the monastery. He may break his vows, intentionally or through circumstance, but in his heart the vows are still there, waiting for him to recognize them again as the truth. The wisdom of the dharma is still there. It will all be there, waiting for him to return to it when he can."

"What if he can't? Or won't?"

"Maybe he won't until another life, but it will still be there."

"And what if the monk is only a novice?"

Tilik smiled then. "You know the Path. Already when you stray from it, you understand you are straying. That is how you can be sure you know it in the first place."

The old man moaned again and Tilik got up to check his pulse. He put his fingers on the vein in the monk's wrist and listened as though the flow of blood was speaking to him. It probably was. He held his hands over the man's face, then his chest and abdomen, hovering an inch above the flesh, feeling the aura for damages.

"He is exhausted but not injured," Tilik pronounced. "I will need more *zeergene*. You must go into the hills and collect it for me tomorrow. Go at dawn; it's always best picked early in the day."

CHAPTER NINE

WHEN FLOOD WATERS COME
IT MAKES NO DIFFERENCE IF YOU SIT AT THE
DOOR OR THE PLACE OF HONOUR.

The wind from the day before had died and the dawn air was very still as I wandered the hillside harvesting zeergene, which the Chinese call *Ma Huang*. I picked only the most tender new stems. Tilik had taught me they have the highest concentration of ephedra in them, and I was careful to leave enough flowering stems that each plant could reproduce itself. The coolness of early morning was helping me to wake up, something that was still difficult for me even after all the years of practice in the monastery. I had slept on the pallet in the infirmary in case the old monk needed help, but if he stirred in the night I hadn't noticed. By the time I awoke he was sitting in the lotus position on the wood floor beside his pallet, deep in meditation. I quietly left.

When I started out, the sun was just a hint of light on the horizon. Then it rose, quickly, as it does where the sky is big and the horizon is far. It loomed huge and red, colouring the whole of the sky around it and causing the air to shimmer with energy. I always thought you should be able to hear the sun, like thunder. Instead there were just light snatches of bird song and the buzzing of insects beginning their day.

It was not a definitive sound that made me look up from my peaceful labour. It was just a sense of some impending disruption. For a moment I saw nothing, and then they were there, appearing from around the corner of the hillside that sheltered Khovor Khan from the north winds.

There must have been fifty or more soldiers, galloping towards the monastery in a whirl of hooves and dust. So many armed men for a few simple monks. I immediately lay down and flattened myself among the rocks, knowing that if I remained standing, my crimson and yellow robes would be a beacon to anyone looking upwards. I was not very far up in the hills, only the distance of two stone-throws. The steepness of the grade put me above the monastery, so peering out through the lower branches of a zeergene shrub I saw and heard much of what was going on. I wish I hadn't.

When the soldiers reached the gate I saw at their head the Party leader who had so often been our guest in the past. Everyone except the leader dismounted and tied the horses together. A pair of soldiers yanked on the bell pull. Not getting an immediate response—all the monks were still in personal meditation—the pair fired several rounds from their rifles into the wood where the bolts held it shut, splintering the gate. I saw Mongo come running out to open it, then fall back as the two soldiers kicked in what remained of the barrier. The rest swarmed in, spreading through the monastery like fire ants on weak prey.

The impatient, authoritative shouting of soldiers mixed with cries of alarm and confusion from the monks. They were roused from their meditations and rounded into the clear space in the front of the stupa. As the most sacred part of the monastery, a symbol of the Buddha that amplified the power of positive actions, any monks gathered there on a normal day would be prostrate in prayer. Now they stood before it in a tight cluster, locked in place by the shafts of a dozen rifles pointing at them.

Suren appeared, followed closely by two soldiers with their weapons trained on his back. He seemed hardly to notice them, and walked confidently towards the Party leader as though readying himself to give a rebuke for this interruption of the morning's routine.

The Party leader, still sitting on his horse, turned to Suren, raised his gun, and, without a word, shot him dead in his tracks. The soldiers left the body where it lay.

Like the bound sheep who, under the knee of the butcher, suddenly ceases to struggle, the quivering group before the stupa went instantly still. Everyone stared at Suren's body.

On an order from the Party leader a head count was taken; eighteen standing plus Suren on the ground. That would make the whole monastery, as far as they knew, for although I was not among them, the old monk was there in my place.

It only took a nod of the Party leader's head. One casual nod, the way he might say yes to an offer of bread or to a simple question.

While a handful of soldiers kept their rifles pointed at the terrified group, others went around behind and forced each monk to his knees. A loud crack sounded and Tilik twitched once, then slumped forward into the dust. The old man fell next, then the cook. The soldiers were shooting them one by one in the back of the head.

Koke started to scream, a high, girlish sound, until the thud of a rifle butt on his skull cut the sound short. They hit him several times more to be sure of crushing his skull thoroughly, not wasting a precious bullet on him. That economy was lost when Bayan leapt up and rushed the soldiers so fiercely that three of them shot him simultaneously in their shock.

I watched but did not grasp immediately what was happening. The shots, the screams, the blood: none of it seemed real. My incredulity came in part from the calmness of the soldiers, who acted not with wild bloodlust, nor with revulsion at the slaughter of fellow humans. They were just methodically shooting, calmly doing their job as though it was of no special account, while the Party leader looked on from atop his horse.

It was when the steady cracks of the rifles abruptly stopped that the reality of the scene below began to sink in. My brother monks lay crumpled and still as their blood seeped noiselessly into the earth. It wasn't the loss of them that hit me, not yet. At that moment, all I felt was terror. I was supposed to be down there, my head with a bullet in it, my life pooling red on the sand. Hiding well within earshot as I was, it still could be.

I bit back the scream that was gathering in my throat, swallowing it between short, hard gasps of breath. My teeth chattered, my body shivered, my bladder released a stream of hot urine into my underclothes. I didn't want to continue to look at what was happening in the monastery, but I couldn't tear myself away from it. And if the soldiers began to search the surrounding area, I wanted to know they were coming.

They brought around a pair of the monastery's yak carts, into which they began to load the bodies. They picked them up by shoulders and feet, throwing them into the carts as heedlessly as if they were heaving sacks of rice.

When they tossed Bayan in, his statue of Tara fell from the folds of his cloak. It was quickly snatched up by a young soldier, who laughed loudly when he saw what it was, then showed the others. A more senior soldier grabbed it from him and slapped him hard across the face. The admonition given, he then slipped the object into his own pocket.

The carts were hauled outside the walls of the monastery for the bodies to await burial in a giant pit that other soliders were busy hacking out of the hard earth to the west side. If a corpse had an open mouth or eyes, no-one closed them as they should have. The faces were not covered, nor any of the proper rites observed that might help their souls to a good rebirth.

My muscles began to cramp from not having moved for so long, and the skin of my groin and legs itched from the urine that had soaked my undergarments. As the sun rose higher my smell became more intense. Flies began to harass me, taking advantage of my immobility. Perhaps they thought I was dead. I was like a dead thing, heavy and immobile.

The soldiers ransacked the temple, throwing everything shiny onto a pile in the middle of the place where we had held the Tsam dance the first time the Party leader had come amongst us. When they got to Suren's ger I'm sure the looters pirated away many of his special works of art, even as they decried the perverted lust of monks and reassured themselves they had been right to kill them.

It took most of the day for the soldiers to pack up everything of monetary value and dismantle the monastery. At midday, army trucks arrived and the shiny things were loaded into them, as were the gers, now taken down and folded up, the stoves, the food stores, the musical instruments none of them could play, the medical supplies no-one understood how to use, and the money in the treasury chest. The large statues of Avalokitesvara from the temple and Suren's ger were more difficult to load, but the soldiers, struggling in teams of six, managed eventually. I imagined The Allseeing One locked inside the back of the truck, his compassionate gaze lost on a wall of dark canvas.

Late in the afternoon the bodies were dumped in a shallow pit. The monastery wall obscured my view, for which I am forever thankful, but I could see the occasional foot or arm or flash of crimson robe arc out above the top of the wall before hurtling down towards the grave.

In old Mongolia the nomads had a tradition of open burial. The bodies of the deceased were left, heads pointing north to the Pure Lands, out on the steppe to be eaten by wild dogs and vultures. It was an opportunity for the dead ones to make one last act of generosity, for in sacrificing their own bodies they sated the predators and thereby spared a young sheep or foal from being eaten instead. It was a bygone practice, frowned upon by 1939 when cremation was standard, but it would have been more noble for my brothers than the burial they received. When I saw them dumped and the earth hurled over top of them, I began to cry the way the old man had; noiselessly, because I didn't dare make a sound, and steadily, because there was no stopping the sorrow.

The trucks filled with gold and pillaged goods drove away. The yak carts were brought back into the compound and filled with our sacred texts, painstakingly hand-inscribed over the centuries and more precious than gold. Their fine paper and carved wooden covers burst instantly into a mass of flames when the soldiers set the matches to them. As they burned, a tank pounded our dharma hall and stupa with mortar fire until all that remained of them were chunks of stone and broken mortar, the odd piece of jagged wood jutting up out of the rubble like an arm seeking a way out.

Our stupa had contained the ashes of Khovor Khan's founding abbot for over two hundred years. Unlike Suren, he was a devoted Buddhist who had earned much merit in his lifetime. His inclusion in the stupa meant that all his wisdom and goodness were contained in the building, to pass on to those who prayed before it. I wondered where that goodness and wisdom were going now. His ashes were scattered in stone dust and dirt, his virtues flying out into the wind, abandoning us all.

The soldiers rode off. The tank rumbled away, the last to leave, trailing slow-moving billows of dust in the long, angled light of early evening. Silence descended like a cloak upon the ruins of Khovor Khan. My sanctuary, my home, embodiment of things good and wise, frail and greedy, was no more.

CHAPTER TEN

—————— ⟡ ——————

TIME NEVER STANDS STILL;
THE IRIS NEVER REMAINS BLUE.

—————— ⟡ ——————

My throat was parched and my tongue thick as I struggled to sit up after so many hours of lying still. Everything ached. I removed my sticky undergarment and managed to pee a little into my cupped hand, from whence I got a couple of meager swallows into my mouth. This may seem gruesome, but the benefit of one's own urine is well known in my country, and I can assure you if you are ever desperate with thirst you'll be happy to do the same.

I sat there rubbing my creaking limbs and staring at the bits of zeergene crushed and withered in the earth where I'd lain on them for so long. I struggled with the thought that they were no longer destined for a tincture. There was no Tilik to pound them, no stove on which to boil the water, no old monk to drink it.

Looking down at the ruins of the monastery, my heart caught as though seeing its destruction for the first time. Although fearful to go near, I knew I had duties to perform. I was the only one left to say a prayer for the dead.

I picked a zeergene stem off the ground and chewed it for strength while stumbling down the hill. There was such silence in what had been, though tranquil, a place filled with energy. It had seemed powerful, what we had created in the monastery, yet it had been whisked away as easily as a broom sweeps dirt out the ger door. Standing on the flat patch of earth where my own ger had been just that morning, I tried to comprehend that it was gone: my bed, my bowl, my tiny brass Buddha I had left in our ger in my hurry that morning to collect the zeergene. My thangka of Tara. Every one of the few possessions that represented the life I'd known for the past six years. The zeergene numbed the edges of my senses so that I proceeded in a daze, like someone who has been knocked hard on the head. I stepped around the dark, sickening stains of blood that covered the area in front of what had been our stupa, past the charred and smoldering remains of our holy scriptures, and picked through the rubble, hoping to find something left of the monastery. There was nothing. The soldiers had been thorough.

Reluctantly, I walked back out through the broken gate to the mass grave I'd purposely avoided on my way in. I prostrated myself over the soft mound of earth, my arms and legs spread wide to embrace my fellow monks, and I cried with the loud, deep sobs I'd had to stifle on the hillside. No contemplation of reincarnation could have comforted me at that moment. My brothers were gone from my life and I had no idea where they might be reborn. They were in *bardo* now, existing in a purely mental state and waiting for their rebirth. An advanced practitioner like Tilik would be able to control the circumstances of his reincarnation, but for the rest it would be a frightening forty-nine days, waiting for karma to dictate their futures. I said a prayer for each one of them to help them find the best possible rebirth. Without prayers, Bayan would return as a hungry ghost, someone who could never be satisfied. Suren would be destined for a turn in the Realm of Hell. For Tilik I prayed, selfishly, that he might be reborn into a life in which I might again meet him, and appreciate him more. For Koke I prayed that he would get another chance to dedicate himself to the Path, he who so deserved it.

I prayed aloud, in the chanting voice, so they might hear me and feel reassured. It was also reassuring to me, the warm earth against my cheek, my mind communing one last time with the others.

The time I could give myself for this communion was brief. The savagery with which the Party leader had obliterated the monastery made it clear that he intended no survivors, and such a rampage would leave behind an atmosphere of fear in which anyone might denounce me in order to spare themselves. I knew I'd have to leave this place, the region of my birth, or I would be recognized. My blood raced in agitation as I lay upon the grave and wondered how I was going to save myself. I would need herders' clothes. I would have to cover the most glaring evidence of my monkhood, my shaved head. It would take months for my hair to grow enough that I could pass as a common herder again.

My mind jumped from one desperate, half-formed plan to another. Stealing clothes from a herding family. Heading to the Gobi, where even the Party would not bother to follow. But I had no water vessel to survive a walk in the Gobi, and could not imagine myself stealing clothes, no matter how desperate I was.

Then I remembered Bayan's money. He had said that money could make people silent when you wanted them to be. I had little experience with money, but I trusted his understanding of it. Although it might not buy my absolute safety, with it I could buy clothes, and food, and a horse for travel so I could keep moving and stay ahead of suspicious minds.

Shaky with the possibility of safety that Bayan's treasure offered, I hid behind the monastery wall and waited for the dark to settle fully so I could move up the hill without being seen. I was terribly thirsty. The soldiers had emptied our water barrels and taken them away, and I would have to wait until dark before I could venture to the river. My plan was simple: retrieve the tugrogs, wash and drink in the river, then walk to my father's ger for clothes and a horse to escape on. I would leave him a large part of the money, and then I would ride away in the night to some place I wasn't known.

When night finally fell enough for me to get underway, I moved to the base of the hill and began to count, three right, six left, nine right and so on, my anticipation growing with every step. At the twenty-ninth rock of the last stretch I looked ahead through the darkness to where I knew the important rock stood. But it was not as I had last seen it.

It had been turned over and left on its side, no longer hiding anything. The square hole sat empty, its sides still smooth from where the box had recently been slid out of its place. Stupidly, I looked around, peering into the shadows, but I knew what had happened. After the arrival of the fleeing monk, Bayan had gone in the night to take his treasure from the ground. He must have planned to leave that same day, but had not been quick enough.

So the treasure, which he had been so intent to keep from the Party that he had shown it to me, had after all been snatched up in the general looting of the monastery. I was sickened with disappointment. Now I was an impoverished fugitive, unable to offer someone who might help me any incentive besides their own sense of charity.

Stumbling to the river, I drank deep of the cold water and washed my sticky skin, drying myself with my robe. It was all I could do to muster the energy to set off for my father's home, my situation was so desperate. I hugged the shadows along the base of the hills, staying clear of ger camps. All the while I mumbled prayers under my breath. The prayers kept my feet moving; if I ceased, my mind filled with images of the day and I began to weaken at the knees.

I recited to myself all the way back to my father's camp. The gers shone white under the moon, three of them now where there had been only two in my childhood. The extra one belonged to a new family the government had assigned to share the pastures my family used.

Seeing my father's ger now sitting peacefully where it had every summer, I longed to call it home again. It looked at that moment not like the rough place I had left six years ago to gain an education and regular meals, but like the most loving sanctuary in the world.

I had thought to sneak into my father's ger unnoticed, but had not counted on the family dog. He sensed me coming and started barking a warning sufficient to rouse the whole community. As he raced towards me I knew he would shift from aggression to greeting, but that was hardly less noisy as he whined and snuffled his apology at my feet. I moved forward and the grass crunched underfoot, every noise amplified in the night air. Still, no doors opened, and when I slipped into the ger of my father it seemed I had made it in without waking anyone.

"Ahv," I whispered as I pulled the door shut behind me, "it's me, Dash."

I saw him sit bolt upright in bed. "Go, spirit!" he cried in alarm.

"No, Ahv, it is truly me, in the flesh." I went and sat on the side of his bed to prove my aliveness and he fairly threw himself at me in an embrace so strong I knew he had been told about the monastery.

"My son, my son," he wept into my shoulder. "We saw the smoke. We heard from the returning soldiers…"

"I hid on the hillside. The soldiers don't know they've missed me." I explained how the old monk from Arbat had died in my place.

"The Party thinks you're dead with the others? Then we must keep it that way. To be so brutal—they didn't want anyone left alive."

"No."

"But why? Other monasteries have been destroyed, but they don't always kill the monks. Some are even allowed to come back to pastoral life, if they are too old or too young to go into the army. Why would they kill everyone at a small place like Khovor Khan?"

I had asked myself the same question, and I thought I knew the answer. "The Party leader used to visit Suren every two weeks. I'm sure they did things together that the Party would never tolerate. Physical things. Maybe, when Choibalsan started purging so many officials, the leader thought he might be exposed. And the only way to be sure no-one would tell was to kill us all."

"Suren? How could an abbot?…" he let his words trail away, shaking his head. "Nothing is as it seems anymore."

The door opened a crack and we both jumped as though caught in an indecent act ourselves. I leapt to the far side of the bed, preparing to hide myself under the covers behind him, when the voice of my aunt came through the door.

"Is everything all right?" she whispered. "I heard the dog, and your voice."

My father hesitated a moment before answering. We had been talking quietly, and the felt ger should have muffled our voices, but the dog must have set her ears to listening for disruptions in the darkness. "You should come in and shut the door, Gerel," my father whispered back. "There's something you need to know."

He got out of bed in his underwear, pulled on the pants that hung on a peg at the head, and lit the bedside lamp to a dim flame. When my aunt made out who it was kneeling on the far side of the bed, her hand flew to her mouth in disbelief.

"*Eejee*, Dash! How can it be you?"

"He was picking zeergene on the hillside and the soldiers missed him," my father explained.

She made me get off the bed so she could hug me and kiss me on both cheeks, which was when she noticed I had only my outer robe wrapped around me in the way of clothing.

"You need clothes."

"He'll need more than that. He will have to escape."

"Escape? But why can't he live with us again, like other monks have done?"

My father crumpled in on himself as he told her my theory of why the obliteration of Khovor Khan had been so complete.

"This is too terrible," my aunt said, tears in her voice.

"Not as terrible as if he were dead."

"He should have come out of the monastery as soon as the trouble started. Two years ago, he could have come back to us without a problem. But you thought he should stay."

"Give him something to eat," my father said gruffly. "And *airag*." He sorted through the single chest that held his belongings and found clothing for me, underthings and pants and an old del, matches, a sleeping roll, a flask for water and one for airag. To hide my shaved head he included a winter hat with long ear flaps. I wolfed down the remainder of the day's biscuits along with large fingerfuls of orum, and the mildly alcoholic airag softened the sharp edges of my anxious thoughts.

"You will need a horse," my father said. The herds he managed were growing well and even my father, in this hardscrabble place, had some animals to his name.

"Won't that make me too visible?"

"There's more risk in moving slowly. You need distance between you and this *soum*. On foot you will never make it fast enough." He brought a small silk purse out from under his mattress. "There is some money here. Not much, but maybe enough to help you get started somewhere else."

The thought of Bayan's box of treasure and the advantages that had vanished with it sickened me when I looked at the thin purse that represented years of savings on my father's part. "I cannot take your money," I said.

"Listen. You are my only son. Of the few animals I have, some would rightly pass to you in time, for you to establish life as a man. But you must leave. It can't happen the old way. Take the money instead. I will not let you go without it."

Relief mixed with shame flooded me as I accepted the purse from him. I took it in the formal way, with both my hands, to show my deep respect for what he was doing. Of course I would need money; it was ridiculous to think I could survive without it.

I put on the clothes. The del was worn at the collar, a little too big, and smelled like my father and the mutton-and-dung scent my own clothes had had before I became accustomed to the relative cleanliness of my monk's robes. It comforted me to be wrapped up in it. My aunt snuck back to her own ger to get more food for me, returning with additional biscuits and curd. It all felt very unnatural. I wished we were just a normal, noisy family preparing for one of its members to make a few days' trek. I wanted my father and aunt to tell me I could stay with them, that it would be safe. But I knew it wasn't.

When all was ready we went out to see to the horse. There were two tethered on ground lines near to the gers; they were the horses that would be used in the morning to go find the rest of the herd, wherever they may have found grazing for the night. To take one of these would be too obvious to the neighbour. We decided to ride out to the main herd and select one of my father's that might not be noticed as missing for a while—long enough to think up an excuse for its disappearance.

We saddled the tethered horse and I said a hurried goodbye to my aunt before untying it and mounting behind my father. I carried an extra bridle and a tether rope awkwardly in front of me along with my food supply, which hung in two sacks on either side of the horse. As we were about to set off, however, the door of the neighbour's ger opened and an older man from the new family stepped out, bringing us all to a guilty halt.

"What's happening?" he asked.

I had met him in the spring. His name was Dorj and he was pleasant enough. He had sung with us, and shared food and drink in the usual way, but he joked little and didn't take part in the drinking games that were considered normal. In short, it wasn't clear whether we could trust him. At the moment, however, with my half-dressed father, myself wearing a winter hat, and both of us loaded up on a horse at a most peculiar hour with tack and food sacks overflowing between us, we looked too suspicious to tell anything but the truth.

In the dim light of a sliver moon, Dorj's face was impossible to read as my father explained the situation.

"This is a dangerous thing you're proposing," Dorj said. "Aiding the escape of a monk has become a serious offence against the Party."

"Yes. But if it were your son, you would do the same."

Dorj stood silent for a moment and my stomach knotted up at the thought of what he could do. I might make some headway escaping, but my father would pay with imprisonment or worse. "Wait," Dorj said, holding up his hand, and he went into his ger.

"You should run away now," hissed my aunt, but my father shook his head and held firm to face whatever was coming. Not a thing breathed; the air was still as death, and even our dog, who had been trotting around us in circles, slunk to the ground in the tension.

It felt interminable but it was only a minute before Dorj returned and approached our horse. He held a small object up to me.

"If you can carry one more thing, I would like you to accept this gift. It is from Erdene Zuu Monastery, where I was once a monk myself."

An intricately carved, bronze prayer wheel, the kind you twirled in one hand, gleamed before me in the moonlight.

Now I understood why he had behaved so differently from other herders. Erdene Zuu had been a large, important monastery. Before it was closed down by the Party it had been a centre of Buddhist learning in Mongolia. Dorj must have been very well educated. I recalled what my father had said, that little was as it seemed any more. In this case, it was a good thing for us.

My father sighed with relief. I accepted Dorj's gift with a blessing. "May the rains fall in due season; may there be a rich harvest; may the world prosper; may the ruler be righteous."

Dorj bowed slightly. "I have a brother west of Arvaikheer," he said, "towards the Khangai mountains. His name is Arban. If you find him he might be able to help you."

His words gave me hope that my way might not be so hard. Maybe there were, throughout the countryside, a network of ex-monks ready to help their brethren. I thanked Dorj for his help, and my father and I rode off to find me a horse. We chose the toughest animal my father could spare, switched the saddle from the first horse and tied my few provisions to the new one. I embraced my father, knowing that it could be for the last time.

"It will take you six or seven days of hard riding to reach the place Dorj is talking about. I see no better option, and at least the land there is good. Your food will last if you're careful, so you don't need to talk with anyone along the way. You must be as invisible as possible. Do you understand?"

"Yes, Ahv."

"You are a man now. No one will pity you as a child, and few have any pity left in them for anyone anymore."

"I'll be careful."

He hugged me again, then jumped back on his horse, bareback now. There was no time for the usual milk libation or extended felicitations to bless my travels.

"Safe journey," he said simply, and rode off in the direction of his ger.

I went the opposite way, cantering north into the darkness of a complete unknown. The vast, clear sky was bright with stars. My horse and I flowed through the silence beneath them, the rhythm of his hooves against the earth marking our progress. I had woken up that morning as a novice at a monastery, and I was riding off that night as an independent man, whether I wanted to be or not. No longer under the care of my father, no longer safely a part of the Buddhist sangha, I was traveling across the land as my ancestors had done. Their freedom was not mine, however. I was a fugitive, running for my life.

CHAPTER ELEVEN

---〜〜---

NOT EVERYONE WHO SMILES IS A FRIEND; NOT EVERYONE WHO GETS ANGRY IS AN ENEMY.

---〜〜---

On my journey up to Arvaikheer I rode steadily, avoiding human contact and stealing sleep when a copse or rocky outcropping offered shelter. In the unbroken monotony of my solitary travels I learned the difference between meditation and thinking. Meditation is disciplined and objective. Even if you're not very good at it, you can usually improve your sense of control over yourself and the universe just by practicing regularly. Thinking has the opposite effect. The mind goes where it wants, conjures irrational possibilities both good and bad, and in the end leaves you feeling out of control and at the mercy of the universe.

I was just sixteen years old and I had lost my mother, been driven from my father, known evil in the guise of goodness, and seen all my monastic brothers slaughtered. I'd missed having a fortune by a matter of hours, and gained being alive by a matter of minutes. I had become a monk to have something to eat, whereupon life in the countryside had improved to the point that food was no longer an issue. I had remained in the monastery, only to end up in a position where I was not able to be either monk or herder.

Possibly my charmed period of positive karma had been revoked. It was true that I hadn't been entirely worthy in my actions, but if the misadventures of my teenage ego and hormones had been so bad, why was I still alive when better people were not? This was incomprehensible to me, the fact that only I had been spared. I gnawed at the unanswerable question the way a dog gnaws at a hard bone, never managing to swallow it but never letting go.

They traveled with me, the others. A point of dharma would occur to me and I'd think to ask Tilik about it before remembering I couldn't. Bathing in a stream, when my head broke the surface for air I expected, for a second, to see Bayan squirting a stream of water at me. My loneliness increased with each of these tricks of the mind.

There were moments when I managed to appreciate the pleasure of being on the move. It felt natural, like an instinct long suppressed, to be galloping across the steppes, reminiscent of the old days when we moved camp and my cousins and I rode ahead of the slow yaks with their heavy carts, hurrying on our swift horses to the next camp ground.

The further north I got, the more lush everything became. The palette of my homeland was made of weak browns and dry greys, leaves that couldn't quite get to green, and only the occasional burst of colour after spring rains. It was scruffy and hard and parched by the Gobi. As I ventured north, grass began to wet my horse's mouth when he chewed. There were colours here. The ground was a carpet of soft green. At dusk, the vast steppe sky, bigger somehow than the sky above Khovar Khan, exploded into a wild kaleidoscope of pinks and purples, punctuated by the fiery orange of the setting sun.

But those moments of appreciation were rare. Mostly I was beset by worry about the future and memories of the past. By noon of the third day, when I paused in the lee of the hills to eat and to rest my horse, my sense of solitude was acute. It had rained in a brief, hard burst that morning and now the sun was shining as though the storm had never occurred. I hung my wet del on a tree to dry and sat at the base of it to eat a biscuit and dried curd. So many times at Khovor Khan I had sat like this to eat, cross-legged on the ground, but surrounded by the other monks. I saw them all around me now. My chipped blue bowl was in my hands, filled with salty milk tea. Bayan was to my left and slipping me an extra piece of bread. Koke was on my right and looking straight ahead as though he didn't notice. Mongo slurped his tea, hunched over the bowl, while Tilik sat upright and drank noiselessly.

For years I had lived in company. Praying, eating, working, learning, painting, sleeping; I had done nothing by myself except meditate. Overcome by loneliness, I put down my food, closed my eyes and began to pray.

Entrusting in the Primal Vow of Buddha,
Calling out the Buddha-name,
I shall pass through the journey of life with strength and joy.
Revering the light of Buddha,
Reflecting upon my imperfect self,
I shall proceed to live a life of gratitude.

I heard Koke sound the tingsha, pure and perfect and utterly real. With a rush of joy at being back in the temple where I belonged, I opened my eyes.

The steppe spread before me in an uninterrupted sweep. A warm breeze ruffled the arms of my hanging del. My horse stamped his foot against a fly. I sat there and wept, as inconsolable as the old monk, for everything that was gone.

Nearing Arvaikheer I increased my caution; towns were strongholds of Party faithful. That morning I had had to ask directions of a lone herder and he had answered cautiously, staring at my winter hat and knowing, I was sure, that it hid a shaved head.

Arvaikheer was a tiny, dismal town consisting of a couple of concrete buildings and a handful of gers set in the flat of the open steppe. It served as a way station for post and for travelers needing to change horses, but in earlier times it had served a nearby monastery. I knew the monastery had been destroyed two years before, and despite the danger something in me needed to see the ruins. When night came I rode to the monastery at a quiet walk and hobbled my horse to the other side of it, away from the town, approaching the ruins on foot.

Even in the murky darkness of a new moon it felt like a familiar scene. Although it had been a more significant monastery than Khovor Khan when it stood, the pale shards of its rubble were much the same. I thought I caught a faint smell of char still hanging in the air, and I imagined their prayer books going up in smoke as quickly as our own had. Whirling the prayer wheel that Dorj had given me, I walked the perimeter. I could find no telling mound. Whatever had become of these monks, they were not buried here.

In front of what appeared to be the ruins of the stupa, I prostrated myself and began to chant, breathing the words softly into the ground beneath my face, my forehead touching the earth. I thought about how the prayer might reach the souls, in reborn bodies or their old ones, that had once inhabited this monastery. It would reach them like the touch of sunlight or a light rain, not as words but as a sensed blessing, the way prayers go out into the universe from a whirling prayer wheel. The thought soothed me. The ruins had not given up their holiness entirely. I could feel their force surrounding me in a way I hadn't experienced since leaving Khovor Khan. Would it stay, I wondered, or did holiness drift off little by little, like the smoky residue of the fires that had consumed the scriptures?

I wanted to curl up in the rubble and stay there. It had only been a week but I was tired of running, of hiding, of being a fugitive for the benign offence of having been a novice monk. I turned my head so I was resting, no longer praying. How easy it would have been to let myself fall asleep in the warm embrace of residual bodhicitta. But I started to think about how someone might find me there in the morning, and the fear of being sent to prison or the army—or simply being shot—drove me back through the darkness to retrieve my hobbled horse. I put my arms around his neck and hugged him to feel the heartbeat of a living thing but he just stood there, mute and uncomprehending of my need. He had been grazing, and I had interrupted him.

I let him eat a while longer before mounting again and using the night to keep heading towards the Khangai mountains. At dawn, herders began emerging from isolated groups of gers to collect their animals for milking. The mountains were clearly visible now. It was time to ask someone exactly where Arban lived.

Riding in the opposite direction at a leisurely pace was a young man. He rode in a Mongolian saddle, not the Russian cavalry tack I had noticed a few people using, and he was wearing a del, not army clothes, which I took to be a sign that he was still a part of the old ways. I cantered over and greeted him.

"Do you know where to find the ger of Alban, brother of Dorj?"

"I do," he replied, staring at my hat. "Who are you?"

"My name is Dash."

"Where are you from?" he asked, without giving me his name in return.

"South of here."

"Why are you wearing a winter hat?"

"It is my only hat."

"A man needs more than one hat."

"Perhaps that's so, but this is my only one."

He nodded but said nothing.

"Can you tell me the way?" I asked again.

"If you follow me, I'll show you."

"You don't have to go to the trouble."

"It's no trouble. I'm already going that way. Follow me." He trotted off. "My name is Ariunbold," he said over his shoulder.

I fell in beside him. "I thought Alban lived close to the mountains."

"He moved."

Anything was possible in those days of change. We began to talk. I asked if his family's herds were fattening nicely, which was the polite thing to say to a herder, and he gave me quite a story about how well their herds were growing, and what experienced herdsmen his father and brothers all were. When he asked about me I told him I was the middle brother of a poor family, and was traveling to my cousins north of the Tamir in the hope that they would take me in because there was no future for me where I'd been.

"Unusual to have cousins so far away," he commented.

"They were more adventurous than my father," I said, wishing I'd created a story that didn't make my father sound so uncourageous.

He seemed to accept my explanation, for he didn't ask me anything more but continued on about himself. I didn't care what he talked about, I was just happy to be with somebody congenial after eight days on my own. Once we had gone an hour or so steadily north-east at a fast trot, however, I began to wonder how Dorj's brother could be so far from where I had been told to look for him.

"Where did Alban move to?" I asked.

"Bayan Ulaan."

That was a town, with a Communist-sounding name of the kind the Party liked to give places now. I stiffened with a sudden anxiety. "But Alban is a herder."

"Not anymore. A lot of people are moving to the towns. It's progress. More modern than this backwards pastoral life." He glanced sideways at me, a sly smile on his face. "Don't you agree, that Mongolia needs to throw off its old ways?"

"Maybe a little," I ventured cautiously.

"Like the monks, for example," he said. "The monasteries were full of corruption and decadence, filling the common people with superstitious nonsense, stealing alms from the poor to fatten monastic coffers, and all the while fornicating and drinking amongst themselves. Thank goodness Choibalsan is finally doing what should be done. The sooner they're all dead, the better." As he finished speaking, he looked straight at me.

His intention was suddenly clear. Arban was not in Bayan Ulaan, unless he was in jail there. This man knew what I was. He was bringing me to town so he could turn me in and gain favour with the local officials.

I wheeled around on my horse and took off in the opposite direction at full gallop, with Ariunbold right behind me on a mount much fresher than mine. As he drew alongside me I thought, panic-stricken, that he was going to pull out a gun and shoot me, or shoot my horse. But he did not have a gun.

He was laughing maliciously. Then he shouted at me, his words cutting through the wind in my ears.

"Run, filthy monk! Run until your horse drops dead, you will not save yourself! No-one will help you here. They will hunt you down and give you what you deserve!" He pulled up abruptly. "Arban is dead!" he yelled, and his horrible laughter echoed in my head as I galloped back towards the mountains.

I didn't dare talk to anyone else as I rode back, loosely following the course of a large river but keeping my distance from ger encampments and any other riders. At midday I ate my last biscuit. Four rectangles of curd were all that remained of my food supplies, which I had hoped to replenish when I met Arban. Now I had no destination and almost no resources. The coins in my purse were useless if it wasn't safe to approach anyone to buy food.

In Ariunbold I had experienced for the first time in my life the assault of hatred, all the more stunning because I had been enjoying his company before he revealed his true self to me. If one ordinary man met at random could wish me dead with such intensity, there were bound to be others like him. I had no choice but to hide in isolation until I looked like any other Mongol herder. That would take months.

Seeking shelter in the nooks and crannies of the Khangai mountains seemed to offer the only possibility of safety. They rose before me with a quiet grace, the green folds of foothills rising to thick, dark forests the likes of which I had never seen. I continued north, the mountains on my left, until I found a broad valley that led to the interior.

At the top of the valley, just before the steppe grass gave way to a wall of larch forest, sat a small, solitary ger. Smoke curled from the chimney hole. It was late afternoon. I was tired, not having slept the night before, and hungry. Mongolians have a tradition of hospitality that dates back centuries, a tradition in which no one is turned away from a ger no matter how little food is available to share. Now, with hatred and fear in the air, I could no longer count on that tradition. I stopped my horse within shouting distance of the ger and stared at it, trying to decide if I could even risk going past it to gain the mountain pass, let alone approach its occupant for help.

As I stared, the door opened and a figure ducked through it and out into the late afternoon sun. It was a woman, white-haired, bent with age and tiny to begin with, so that when she stood she was scarcely taller than the low lintel of the door. She beckoned for me to come forward.

Her del was a worn, pale memory of once-blue cloth, belted at the waist with a strip of rawhide wrapped several times around and hung with fragments of mirror. Her eyes sat like black pebbles in a face of crinkled leather, around which her luminous hair billowed freely instead of being tied back or held in a scarf as was customary.

"Why do you not dismount?" she asked. Her voice was raspy, as though she suffered a perpetual thirst. "Are you afraid of an old woman?"

She was a little fearsome, but it was not knowing who else might be inside the ger that had me ready to flee.

"There is no-one else here," she said. "You must enter my ger and take refreshment. It is quite safe."

The thought of food and drink made my mouth begin to water. We had exchanged none of the usual polite phrases of greeting. In fact I hadn't spoken at all. It felt like sleepwalking as I got off my horse and began to hobble him for a short stay.

"Your horse will feel better if you let him eat," the old woman said. "He's had a long day."

I shifted his bridle to remove the bit from his mouth, removed the saddle, ground tied him so he could graze, and followed the woman into her ger.

The light inside was dim and the air hung with the pungent smoke of juniper, which was often used against evil spirits.

I took my place on a stool and she began to bring me things; first salt tea, then bowls of orum, biscuits and sweet, crumbly *tos*. I ate what she offered in famished silence, ravenous for the generosity as well as the food.

"I saw you coming," she told me after I began to slow down.

"How did you see me from inside your ger?"

Her laughter sounded like a dry cough. "I saw you in my mirror."

I finally understood. She was a shaman, rare in these parts but not unheard of. Her belt, with its mirror fragments to ward off evil, was all that indicated her special status. Shamans were also being oppressed by the Party; unlike Buddhists, however, they had no scriptures to burn or monasteries to destroy, so they were harder to stamp out.

"You can take off your hat here," she said. "No-one will come. Stay and eat with me, and tell me about your monastery. Then you must sleep, for I can see you're very tired. In the morning I will tell you where to go."

I took off my hat and she came around behind me and clasped my head between her hands, pressing gently but firmly in the same gesture Tilik had used with the old monk. All my sorrows seemed to flow into her hands.

"You are full of loss," she said. I didn't deny it. With her hands upon me, however, my weariness lifted and my breath became deeper, as though I were in meditation. When she removed them I felt refreshed.

"Tell me about your brother monks," she asked.

"They are dead," I began, then stopped. Just saying the words brought a tightness to my throat that made it impossible to go on.

She nodded. "Yes. So let us speak about their lives. Were there other novices?"

Tentatively at first, then gathering strength as I discovered that my need to talk about them grew with every tale, I told her of Bayan and his noble birth, how he was not a good monk but had always been good to me. I told her of Koke and his spiritual certainty. I told her of Tilik, of his wisdom and his unwavering self-discipline.

"He was descended from a great shaman, my master."

"He was a true master, then! How lucky for you." She grinned, her mouth full of gaps from missing teeth. "Do you know how many of your Buddhist ceremonies have come from shamans? You think they've given you only acts of superstition, don't you? Circling an *ovoo* three times when you come upon one; venerating the sky and mountains, fire and water; flinging libations in the Ten Directions so the gods can drink before you do. Superstitions. But not the sacred rites of Buddhism."

"Buddhism came to Mongolia from Tibet, in the time of Kublai Khan."

"Ah, but it's like water, your religion. It takes the form of whatever vessel it's in, so it can quench the spiritual thirst of any kind of people. Even shamanist people."

She told me how the pantheon of fearsome deities known as the *dogshid* were Shamanistic in origin, as were the burning of dough *sor* to destroy evil spirits, the *dalaga* arrow ceremony for summoning prosperity, and many others. She spoke of her trances and communication with the spirit world, and how similar it was to a lama's communication with the Buddha while in deep meditation. I learned many things. As we talked her ger grew dark, but she lit no candles.

"Now you must sleep," she said eventually. "But first drink this, which will be good for your spirits."

It smelled like vodka but more aromatic, as though it had been steeped with herbs. "What will it do?"

"It will help you sleep by ridding your mind of its troubles."

"I wasn't allowed such alcohol at the monastery. Only airag."

"You won't be able to keep all your vows. Your gods won't mind. This is good for you."

I drank it, and lay down on the bed across the ger from the shaman woman's. It was only seconds before I dropped into the welcome blackness of a dreamless sleep.

In the morning I felt completely rested, but that wasn't enough to overcome my despondency at having to leave. I knew shamans lived in isolation, that I couldn't stay, but it was hard to leave the one person who had showed me true kindness on my journey, when all that lay ahead was loneliness. We stood outside her ger in the weak morning light. My horse was saddled and ready, but I couldn't bring myself to mount.

"It's not so difficult to be alone," she said.

"You have more experience than I do."

"You have to learn to speak to the spirits who are all around you. They'll keep you company."

"I don't have that skill."

"Everyone has it. You'll see." She handed me my sacks, which she had refilled with food and water. I offered to pay, but she wouldn't take my money.

"Go up this trail through the larch forest," she said.

"I've never been in a forest before." It looked foreboding to me. The densely clustered trees crowded the edges of a narrow track, swallowing the light. I thought I might not be able to breath in such a closed place.

"There's no need to fear. Before nightfall you will come to an open plateau with eight lakes and a waterfall. Do not linger there. You must leave your horse and go on without him so he doesn't give your hiding place away, or get attacked by wolves while you sleep."

He was the only living thing to have shared my lonely journey north. I couldn't imagine letting him go.

The shaman looked hard at me. "You will want to take him further, but you must leave him at the lake, because from there he will return to the steppe and find a new home. To keep him with you will doom you both."

I nodded. "I'll leave him there."

"From the plateau, walk north three days. There you will find the shelter that is meant for you. There are caves. You will find your way—it has been told to me."

Her words lent me just enough confidence to depart. "Thank you, Great Mother. Spill fat."

"Such a common salutation from a holy man. Give me a proper blessing, monk."

"I'm not ordained."

"You're still a monk."

"By the power of the Buddha may all evil omens and untoward circumstances, the ominous cry of birds, the malign conjunctions of the stars, and evil dreams be undone."

"That's a good one. I hope it works."

"But what is a Buddhist blessing to a powerful shaman?" I asked. "You must command more potent invocations than I do."

She smiled, her few teeth shining yellow in the morning sun. "In difficult times, I believe it's wise to accept whatever kind of blessing people are willing to bestow on you."

CHAPTER TWELVE

TO A FRIGHTENED MAN,
EVEN DRY DUNG IS MOVING.

I found a cave as the shaman foretold, near a rivulet of flowing mountain water and facing south, like the entrance to a ger. In the shelter of trees whose strange, pressing closeness still felt oppressive to me, I lived like the hermit forest monks Tilik had once told me about. Isolated from the world, without even my horse for company, I had only my own resources for finding enough food to sustain my body and enough discipline to sustain my sanity.

The vegetation was different from that of the region that I knew, and many times I wished for Tilik's encyclopedia of edible plants as I foraged for food. *Gichgene* I recognized, and ate nothing but the roots of this plant for so long that even today I cannot stomach it. Many animals shared the mountainside with me. I saw my first marmots, large rodents common to the Khangai but not found in the dryness of my home province, as well as plump gray hares. Kites and eagles soared above, hunting them with great skill. I thought many times about trying to trap one for myself, but the thought of killing any creature with my own hands had become intolerable. The animals therefore grew fat while I grew thin.

But physical hardships—the hard ground and the scarcity of food— paled in contrast to the emotional ones. I foraged only in the barely light hours at dawn and dusk, so I wouldn't risk discovery by the odd person who came through the area: hunters, people gathering rhubarb or looking for stray animals, travelers using the pass below. The Khangai are traversable mountains dotted with valleys, terrain easy enough that a strong horse can take you through them in a couple of days. My cave was up high enough that no-one had cause to venture there, but there was still a chance I would be seen if I wandered around the hillside during daylight.

At first I spent a lot of my time near the mouth of the cave, crouched in the shadows with the furtiveness of a fox in its den, to scan the area for human presence. After a week or so of watching, two men on horses appeared down in the valley. I wondered if they might be sympathetic to a fugitive monk. I strained my ears to hear sounds of talking, of laughter, but they were too far away. I thought about the food they might have with them and my mouth began to water. Then one raised a rifle to shoot at something in the hills, and I jumped at the sound as if I were the prey they were hunting. It was too dangerous to make contact.

For weeks I tortured myself by searching for people and imagining what they were like. If there was more than one of them, I thought about the conversation they might be having. Were they telling stories, talking about a girl they had their eye on, discussing a horse one of them wanted to buy? I imagined what they'd eaten for breakfast, what prayers they said in the privacy of their own gers, what they argued about with their families, what their favorite food was, whether or not they had a dog. All the details of the lives that I made up for them, no matter how mundane, seemed infinitely fascinating in my loneliness.

Most torturous of all, I thought about how any one of them might have enough compassion in him to lead me back to the world of men. But how could I be sure? Once a traveler in the pass below came close enough that I could hear dim snatches of a song he was singing as he rode along. Someone who sang so joyfully must be a good man, I thought, and found my heart beating fast in anticipation of finally showing myself. But as the words reached me I realized it was a bawdy song he was singing, something about a girl and horse. He laughed to himself at the end of the tune, and it sounded so much like Ariunbold that I slunk back into the recesses of my cave until the man was out of sight.

So it went for several weeks. Then I stopped spending so much time looking for salvation from the outside and started to search within. The Buddhist phrases "I take refuge in the Buddha / I take refuge in the Dharma" became a deep truth for me. The spiritual quest I had been so willing to compromise while at Khovar Khan became my sole aim, the thing I clung to for hope and sanity.

To keep the prayers from slipping from my memory I decided to write them down, using chalky stone on the walls of my cave. It was hard going compared to the ink pen and fine paper I was used to. The writing stone was inconsistent in its chalkiness and didn't always leave a clear mark, and the unevenness of the cave walls meant I often encountered a crevice or a bit jutting out right in the middle of a word like a hiccup.

Then I would wipe the phrase away with the hem of my del and start again, planning it to fit within the flaws of the rock.

Soon the dark walls were transformed into a pale sea of scripture. To the rear of the cave Avalokitesvara sat suspended in waves of prayers. Demons and protectors created a halo around the mouth of the cave. Words swirled around crags and crevices.

Within this makeshift temple the rituals of meditation and prayer began to shape my formless days. I rose in the predawn to look for food, bath in the stream and drink. With my few miserable roots and leaves before me I then meditated, applying an almost fanatical discipline to consistently find the quiet place within, because without those calm moments I thought I would lose my mind. Afterwards I ate, very slowly and thoughtfully, while studying the sky and its infinite changes and thinking of nothing but that. Later still I read the prayers from the wall, left to right, prostrated myself and recited others I remembered, and read the wall again from right to left. After a nap, I spent several hours contemplating specific dharma subjects as though preparing for a debate with Tilik.

These things kept me going, but by the fourth week of my hiding I realized that I missed the physical focus of writing on the walls now that I had run out of space and could only squeeze in the odd phrase here and there. I decided to construct a mandala on the ground instead. I began hunting for small stones of different colourings when I foraged for food. These I meticulously sorted, pulverizing those that lent themselves to it, and organizing the others by shade and size to use as they were. The result of my efforts was rudimentary, more like a beggar's hut than a symbolic home for the gods. The colours were limited to earth tones, the lines were rough, there was no finesse. But it was a project that had no end. Working on it gave my days fresh purpose.

At the end of each day, however, I faced the prospect of sleep and the terrible nightmares in which I watched my brothers killed again and again. I'd wake up in a sweat, just as the soldiers discovered me on the hillside and aimed their rifles at my head. I ached for human comfort so badly that I whispered into the darkness just to hear a voice, even if it was my own. The shaman woman had told me to talk to spirits. I talked to a pantheon of bodhisattvas.

As summer waned, my weight dropped and the hair I was so desperately trying to grow came in slower as I grew more malnourished.

It was only half a finger long, still a giveaway, and now the hollows forming in the frame of my body, skinny to begin with, were an added suspicion. Most Mongolians look fattened by the end of summer, like their horses. Months of eating dairy fills in the flesh that winter tends to take away. I looked the opposite. I had kept myself clean and my single knife had served as a razor for my thin beard, but my del hung on my bony shoulders and my face surely bore gaunt witness to a couple of months of inadequate food and fitful sleep. The nights became cold and chilling rains began. It would not be long before approaching a ger camp would be less risky than trying to stay alive where I was.

On the afternoon of my fifty-fourth day in the cave, having finished adding a new room to the mandala, I sat in lotus to contemplate the completion of my labour. In a relaxed state I tuned my awareness to the physical situation around me. The weather had previously been fine, but I sensed the arrival of a storm slipping over the top of the mountain from the north. The singing of birds stopped suddenly as they flew to cover. I heard the raindrops come, one plop, then another, then suddenly a torrent. I smelled the air change from dry and dusty to the iron odour of water on rock.

As I took all this in with my eyes closed, something else filtered through the pounding of the rain on the mountainside. I heard a scrabbling sound, like a large animal working its way up the rocks. Too noisy for a wolf. A stray horse would stay in the valley. The deer and mountain goats of the area knew I was living there and never came close. Could it be a man? My eyes popped open. Who would be coming up so high off the pass? What could they be looking for? The sound continued to come closer through the driving rain.

The cave was quite open, only one place towards the back where a slight outcropping in the curve of the wall provided a darker shadow in which I could flatten myself, standing, and hope the intruder did not investigate too deeply. I jumped up from my meditations and hurried to the shadow.

The sound of laboured breathing and the slapping of a water-soaked del against someone's boots confirmed my worst fear. What had I been thinking to try to hide there? I would have been better off in the company of a wolf, for a man who rushes to a cave to escape the rain and then finds himself surrounded by a work of manic art, the walls covered in script and religious images, the floor half taken up with an intricate stone mandala, is going to investigate fully.

I heard an intake of breath sharp enough to be audible over the rain and imagined the intruder noticing, as he looked up from shaking himself off, just what he had stumbled into. There was stillness then. I did not breathe. My ears felt stretched out, big as a fox's, as I strained to discern what he was doing. I heard feet treading softly on the floor, two steps taken stealthily towards the west wall. His eyes would be adjusting now to the dimness of the cave's interior. He wouldn't understand the Tibetan words as scripture, but the drawings made the subject clear. The footsteps moved along slowly, inching towards the back and the nook in which I was hiding.

I had no plan for the inevitable moment of my discovery. Lacking a weapon or, for that matter, the will to use one, I could only make myself still and hope that whoever it was lost interest in the rambling scripture, or that the rain stopped as suddenly as it had begun and he could leave the cave.

But the intruder stepped to the right, around the edge of the outcropping towards Avalokitesvara, and there we were: face to face.

She did not scream. A soft-faced girl no older than I, she seemed paralyzed by her discovery, her eyes wide with fright.

We stared at each other as our mutual alarm hovered in the air between us. I saw her calculate my emaciated face and my too-short hair.

"*Om mani padme hum,*" she whispered. The mantra of universal compassion.

Her voice sounded like a song from the God-realms. I fell to my knees before her and sobbed, shamelessly, into the rain-laden folds of her del.

CHAPTER THIRTEEN

―――――――――――

THE PERSON WHO HAS SUFFERED
MAY YET KNOW HAPPINESS;
THE STRAY DOG MAY YET GROW FAT.

―――――――――――

I believed that Erdene's appearance in my cave that rainy afternoon was karmic. She had been searching for some young horses that had broken from her family's herd when she'd spotted the cave, thinking nothing of it until the rain suddenly started and she'd decided to scramble to its shelter.

The morning after she found me, she returned. Even though she'd promised to, I'd spent the night sleepless with worry that she wouldn't, or that a Party official would arrive instead. My relief on hearing her voice outside the cave was profound.

"*Sain bain uu*?" she called out. I didn't clutch at her clothing when she entered the cave this time. The very memory of such desperate intimacy caused me some embarrassment now that she was back.

"I've brought you food, and a sheepskin for warmth." She knelt on the ground and I did the same, opposite her, as she placed her gifts between us. It was the proper way a woman would offer something to a monk: not directly, which risked the possibility of touching, but in the space between. "There is yoghurt, and boiled mutton, and biscuits."

They were wrapped in a square of rough fabric, knotted at the top. "Thank you," I said, "for the things you've brought. And...and just for coming back." I began to work at the knot. It was hard to resist ripping at it, I wanted the food so badly. My hands trembled in anticipation, and Erdene looked discreetly at the floor.

"You should eat the biscuits first," she said. "My grandmother told me it would make you sick to eat the meat first if you've been starving."

"You told someone about me?" My hand hovered over the biscuits, fear overcoming hunger.

She looked at me then. "Please don't worry; my family would never harm a monk."

There was no reason to mistrust her guileless face. She had returned, with food and warmth. I grabbed the biscuit and bit into it. Possibly it was no better than the biscuits I had been eating for years, but at that moment it was the most delicious thing I'd ever tasted. I was acutely aware of the way it crumbled on my tongue, of the butter enfolding bits of flour, of the way sweetness mixed with a hint of salt – even though I took but half a second to swallow the first mouthful. I gobbled the rest of the biscuit up and reached for another one immediately. When I brought a third one to my mouth I stopped in mid-bite as I realized how I must have appeared: a crazy person, savage with hunger. Maybe even frightening.

"Excuse me." I wanted to regain some composure, to show more of the restraint expected of a monk. But my hand hovered before my mouth with the biscuit, unwilling to go so far as to put it down completely.

"You must be very hungry," Erdene said. "Go on, eat. You need to."

And so I did. I ate eight biscuits, leaving the remaining three in order to have something for tomorrow's breakfast, and used my fingers to scoop half the cool, creamy yoghurt out of its leather sack, after which my shrunken stomach felt utterly bloated.

"I should leave the mutton until this evening," I said, although the thought of it sent my saliva running afresh.

"Yes, it would be best to wait." She wrapped the leftover food up again as though saving me from the temptation. "My father has a plan for you."

"You told everyone in your family?"

"What could I do? I cannot save you alone."

"Forgive me. I am—" I didn't finish.

"Frightened?" She leaned towards me a little. Her hands shifted in her lap and I had the idea that she might have reached out and touched me if I had not been a novice monk. I wanted her to. "We are a Buddhist family," she continued. "Avalokitesvara has brought you to us, and we must respond. We will make you safe."

"How can you?"

"You can join our camp, as a herder. My uncle and his family will take you in; they have one young son, so you would be a help to them." She was excited about the plan, explaining it in a rush. "We will say you are an orphaned distant relative of his wife, no longer possessing a family of your own."

101

Perhaps mistaking my stunned silence for reluctance, she carried on. "A poor relative," she said. "That would help explain your, hmm, thinness." She looked down as she said this last thing, her voice trailing off. One did not talk about the body with a monk.

"And your uncle has agreed?"

"Yes, of course, why would he not?"

After what I had experienced in the previous months, I could think of many reasons. Had they not considered the risks? Their generosity was great, yet she presented it as something anyone who could use an extra hand might agree to. My emotions were still so raw I had to struggle not to break into tears again as the miracle of what she was offering seeped through to me.

"My father said that if you agreed, I should come tomorrow with an extra horse," she said, "so you would look as though you came on your own, and I only rode out to greet you. Not for our family, you understand, but in case anyone else should meet us along the way."

I looked around the cave that had contained my existence for so many months, took in the weight of its unbearable loneliness, glimpsed a vision of this comforting future she offered in its place.

"Thank you," was all I could manage to say.

The next day she left the two horses tethered in the pass below and climbed up to get me.

"Are you ready?' she asked, as though I'd had things to pack. And although I didn't in the tangible sense, I felt an unexpected anxiety.

I looked around at my scripture, the crude mandala, the smooth spot towards the back where I had slept. I wished I could pack them all up with me, like the contents of a ger.

"You will make a new home, and we will help you," Erdene said.

I nodded, but there was a lump in my throat as I left the scriptures behind and followed her down the hill to the horses. The sun had risen above the highest trees; it would be hitting the second prayer from the left about now. I repeated the words to myself in farewell.

We mounted the two strong horses and followed the pass down to the valley, which soon opened up to rolling steppe. The sky was once more the broad sweep of blue I used to know, not a narrow thing hemmed in by hills and branches. My lungs filled involuntarily with air in the expanded space.

Erdene and I rode side by side, moving at an undemanding trot. She talked of the weather and their livestock, of the land we were in, and told me about the family members I would soon be meeting. Her voice flowed easily, like a gentle stream. I had been so long without the pleasure of another human voice that I was happy to listen.

"Have you been thinking about what it will be like, living with us?" she asked.

I had been thinking of little else. I worried about whether my new family would like me, whether they really wanted me to join them or saw me as a charitable obligation, an extra mouth to feed. I wondered how I would ever repay their generosity, and whether I would be able to earn my keep as a herder, having left the life so young.

"A little," I said.

"Are you worried?"

"A little."

"My family is kind. Even though they are my family and so of course I'd say that, it's still true."

"They must be kind, to take me in."

"If you think of good things it will help you not to worry. What are you most looking forward to?"

I frowned as though thinking hard, but I already had an answer. "Drinking tea."

Erdene laughed, a sound as light and soothing as a hand bell. "There will be plenty of that. What else?"

"Eating biscuits when they're hot out of the cookstove. And mutton broth."

"All food! What else?"

"The sound of the wind on the *other* side of the ger wall, while I am warm and dry inside."

"That's a good one."

"Sleeping in a bed."

"My uncle snores; he might keep you awake all night, even in a comfortable bed."

Tilik had always made a slight, raspy noise in his throat as he slept. I thought about the way the sound had comforted me for all the years I'd lived with him, reassuring me if I woke in the night. In the cave there had been no such comfort, and much need of it. I would happily endure a dozen uncles snoring directly into my ears, just to know that someone else was there in the darkness.

"I will not mind," I said.

The valley eased out into the wide steppe, vast and inviting before us. I kicked my horse and he leapt into a gallop, flying across the steppe with Erdene and her horse keeping pace. I could accept whatever lay ahead. What mattered was that we were thundering away from the past, with its memories that clung to me like the ache of a lost limb. I couldn't gallop fast enough.

Just before the midday meal we neared the family camp. I heard a girl call out to the others about our arrival. By the time we got to the hitching line to dismount, a gaggle of curious relatives had gathered to inspect me. Their expressions were first curious, then shocked, then purposefully blank like people who are trying not to stare. I must have looked dreadful.

A man about the age of my father stepped forward. Fit and handsome, he had an air of authority about him.

"Welcome, Dash. May you be happy here," he said, bowing to me slightly with palms together. "I'm Gan, Erdene's father."

I bowed lower, in deference, and then the others all began to introduce themselves in a riot of names and faces I couldn't keep straight. There was a brother, someone's wife, Erdene's mother. A tiny old woman came forward at one point and held a braided rope of yak's hair towards me with trembling hands.

"Will you bless this? We have a sick calf."

There was a belief that tying blessed objects around the neck of a sick animal could help to cure it. I did as she asked and gave it back to her.

"Would you like some tea?" a woman in a soft yellow del asked me.

My yes came out like a kind of sob before I could control myself. She took me by the elbow and started to lead me away to a ger, shooing the others away with a flick of her hand. "I'm Tuli," she said. "You'll be living with my husband and I, and our son Tabin. You look like you could use a moment of quiet."

The ger was plain but cozy, adequately furnished and neatly kept. Tuli led me to a stool and served the tea in a simple white bowl. I held it in both hands, savouring the steaminess of it, the smell as reassuring as an uneventful day. I took the first sip and a profound warmth spread through me. My lower lip began to tremble. Tuli knelt beside me, taking the tea gently from my hands and placing it on the other stool. She wrapped me in her arms. I heard the soft sound of a lullaby, felt the warmth of her body, her living breath next to my ear, the gentle rocking motion of her embrace. I let my tears flow. The Buddha had bestowed upon me the greatest of gifts, human compassion, and my relief was too overwhelming to contain.

CHAPTER FOURTEEN

―――――――∽∾∽―――――――

IF YOU DRINK THE WATER,
FOLLOW THE CUSTOMS.

―――――――∽∾∽―――――――

Cholon and Tuli seemed genuinely glad to have me join them. I was nervous over lunch that first day, like a guest who's not sure what's expected of him. But Cholon put me to work right away afterwards, repairing tack, gathering stray sheep, and chopping logs into stove wood. I felt more at ease that way. By dinner time I was more tired and hungry than nervous.

I drank several bowls of salted tea again before starting in on the food.

Tuli looked on with a smile. "I can see you will be easy to please."

Erdene came in with biscuits from her ger, which were being traded for some of the mutton stew Tuli had made, in the tradition of all herding camps.

"Did you have a good first day?" she asked.

I nodded.

"The rope you blessed, it worked," she said. "The calf is already much better and drinking again."

"I'm glad," I said, "but maybe it would have recovered anyway."

"Grandmother is certain it was the blessing that made the difference. She says that even as a novice you are a holy person, possessing powers from your knowledge and practice."

I said nothing. Monks like Tilik had powers; my blessings were feeble gestures of hope in comparison.

"But I suppose if we are to keep you safe, we have to stop treating you as a monk. You're a herder now." She smiled at me with a look, girlish and shy, that made my face redden instantly. Appearing not to notice, she took her bowl of stew with a cheerful goodbye and returned to her own ger.

"Dash," Tuli said as she served me my stew, "with all your education, do you think you could teach Tabin how to read and write a little? A herder's son doesn't get much schooling. He's almost nine and he barely knows the characters."

"I'd be happy to," I said. It seemed the least I could do to repay their kindness in keeping me.

"As long as it doesn't prevent him from getting his chores done," said Cholon.

"There will be extra time come winter," said Tuli. "And some math? He knows a bit about counting, and adding and subtracting, already."

"What does he need with more math?" asked Cholon.

"Just some practice," countered Tuli. "So it comes easier. And what if he has a big herd to keep track of one day? He'll need to count to more than ten."

"I can help with that," I said.

Tabin eyed me with curiousity. "Do monks only study?" he asked. He knew my past life as a novice was a strict family secret, and that made it intriguing to him.

"We did many chores as well."

"What kind of chores?"

"Hauling water, collecting firewood, cleaning the temple, making tea and keeping the stove warm."

"Some of those are girls' chores."

"Tabin!" scolded his mother.

"It's all right," I said. "There were no girls there, so we shared the work, all of it, between us. When we weren't praying or studying."

"Did you ever get to play?"

"Not as much as before, when I lived in a herding camp like this one."

"Do you know how to play *shagai*?" Tabin asked, putting his food bowl on the floor and scurrying over to the drawers at the foot of his bed. He pulled out a small, leather sack with a drawstring top and shook it. "I have a really good set."

Shagai are small bones from the ankle of a sheep, which are used in a variety of games. The most common is to throw them down on a hard surface, then try to pick up all the ones that have landed on a particular side without touching any of the others.

"Maybe a monk doesn't play such things," said Tuli.

Tabin looked confused. "But Dash isn't a monk anymore, he's a herder, that's what Erdene said." He turned to me. "Aren't you?"

I found I couldn't answer his simple question.

"Yes, he is," said Cholon. "After we have finished eating, we'll all play."

Tabin was the best at shagai, quick to spot the ones that had landed on the "horse" side, and nimble with his fingers. By the end of the first week my playing had improved somewhat. Other things were less easy to get used to.

For six years my rhythm had been that of the monastery, with its balance of work and prayer, the relative peace of its days, the opportunities for personal meditation. My solitude in the cave, although a torture, had further habituated me to time spent alone and in contemplation. Life in a herder's ger was noisy and relentlessly social by contrast.

Hardest of all was finding time to meditate. My nemesis at the monastery had become my refuge in my isolation, and an impossibility in the ger camp. We worked together, ate together, played games, told stories, went to sleep. After a week of trying fruitlessly to snatch an hour from the day without interruption, I woke before dawn one morning, moved quietly to the floor and put myself into lotus there. It was hard to get to the still place in my head; my mind wanted to go back to sleep rather than focus. It took so long that by the time I was there, things started happening around me. Filtering first into my consciousness was Cholon lumbering out of their narrow bed with a groan and shuffling out the door to pee, his footfalls on the wooden flooring feeling like an earthquake to my motionless body. Then came the long creak of the stove door as Tuli opened it to stoke the fire. She was probably being specially careful to make as little noise as possible, but my senses had already been infiltrated. I kept my eyes closed but was no longer meditating in any way as their morning drifted in through my ears and nose: water being poured from a canister into the kettle; the kettle clunking onto the stove; tendrils of dung smoke wafting out into the room, Tuli waking Tabin with the grating hiss of a whispered 'Wake up, cricket!'; Cholon coming back in with a prediction of late morning rain.

I opened my eyes to find Tabin staring at me.

"What's it like to meditate?" he asked.

"Peaceful."

"Is it easy?"

"No."

"I'm sure it can't be very easy trying to meditate in here," said Tuli. "Do you miss having a quiet place for your rituals?"

I thought of the purse of money my father had given me. It was enough to buy a small ger for myself, but I didn't want to. When I woke in the night, terrorized by my nightmares of death, the soft, steady breathing of the family was an instant reassurance. Their very presence confirmed for me the existence of a normalcy I no longer took for granted.

"Only a little," I said. "I'm happy to be here." And for the most part, I was.

Soon after my arrival, we migrated to the winter pasture. I had just gotten to know the land, whose relative lushness was so different from my homeland. Rather than camels, my new family kept the yak-cattle hybrid *khainag* along with sheep and horses. I'd barely learned where best to graze them, where to find them when they went off on their own, where the river was easiest to ford, where it was best to drink, and then it was time to pack up and start again. Erdene's father Gan made the announcement one evening and by the next morning we were hauling the tarpaulins off the gers and taking them apart for the move.

I had almost forgotten how ingenious a ger is, it had been so long since I'd packed one up. The felt walls rolled up, its central poles came down, the accordion sides folded to slim rectangles, the wood floor came apart like a puzzle, and the whole thing was strapped on to a single yak cart by the end of the morning. The sparse furniture and iron stove went in a second cart along with the family chest, the contents of the kitchen, and a couple of battered suitcases sufficient for personal effects.

The winter pasture was a prime spot that must have been in the family for a few generations. It was not far from the river and tucked into hills that sheltered us from the worst storms while allowing enough wind to blow the snow off the frozen grass that sustained the herds through winter. There was a corral with a low stone wall to protect the animals and give us a concentrated supply of dung to dry as fuel for the stove.

We had barely set up home when a traveling Chinese merchant arrived to sell us any goods we might need for the long winter ahead. Despite the distances and lack of population in Mongolia, word managed to travel fast. The merchant seemed to know we had moved almost before we knew it ourselves.

Erdene's mother, whom everyone just called "Maa," served the merchant tea and biscuits. Tuli brought over orum and yoghurt, and the adults settled down for a brief gossip while the younger generation sat restlessly awaiting the big moment when the merchant would reveal the contents of his cart.

Finally, after he'd exhausted his news of births and deaths, marriages and horse race results, we got to go out and see what he'd brought. The cart was packed with a dizzying array of items: barley flour, soap, candles, oil for lamps, needles and thread, mirrors, hair combs, bolts of cloth and some ready-made clothes. It was as though he had unveiled a small carnival.

Everybody bought something, mostly utilitarian but also small luxuries like a new knife with a carved camel bone handle for Gan and a scarf for Tuli, pretty pink hair clips for Erdene and her sister Dadal, and a set of four coloured crayons for drawing with a pad of coarse paper for Tabin. The family was moderately well-off by Mongolian nomadic standards, being able to purchase such items once in a while. Prices were negotiated loudly with much playacting by the merchant, who wrung his hands theatrically and claimed they would be the ruin of him.

I hung back, watching. I was growing out of my old boots, and I needed a wool del because the summer one I had from my father was already insufficient for the weather. But I had never bought anything in my life. Clothed in my aunt's homemade dels and then by the monastery, dirt poor to begin with and then divested of worldly goods, I had no idea how to choose from the vast array on offer before me.

As the transactions of the three families began to wind down, the merchant looked at me.

"What about you?" he said, examining me with a squinty eye. "You're new to this family."

"He's my cousin's son," said Tuli, sticking to our story. "Orphaned in a family with too many mouths to feed, so he's come to live with us."

"Well, does your cousin's son need anything?"

"I need boots," I managed to say. "And a wool del."

"Just the cloth," corrected Maa. "We'll sew it for you, like everyone else in the family."

And with that Maa and Tuli took over, arguing over the bolts of cloth the merchant brought forth for me.

"This blue is the best colour for him."

"The grey is a better quality. Heavier."

"Grey, for Dash? He's too handsome for grey, it's an old man's colour."

"But with an orange sash—"

"If it's not too expensive—"

"The blue one," said Erdene, cutting in. "Which goes well with the purple sash he already has. We'll make him a sheepskin for extra warmth." She stepped forward and held the fabric, the colour of a summer sky at dusk, up against me. The effect must have pleased her, for she smiled. I flushed.

"I believe you're right," said Maa. "It does look best."

"Boots?" said the merchant.

Those I picked for myself, along with a thick pair of socks. I was counting out the money to pay him when he pulled a wooden crate out from one side of the cart and lifted it with a grunt to the top of the heaped clothing.

"Here's something else you might be interested in," he said, pulling the canvas cover aside to reveal the contents.

They were books.

"It's not a very good selection," he continued, pulling out some samples. A Russian novel translated into Mongolian. A small book of medicinal plants, illustrated. A child's primer of Asian geography.

"He has no need of those," Gan said quickly. "He can't read."

"As you like." The merchant covered his wagon up again, took our payment, snapped his yak to attention with a whip and rode away to the next ger camp.

"Spies," muttered Cholon. "They're everywhere."

"He knows it's only the monks who can read," said Gan.

"But you can, too," I said. Gan had a handful of books in his ger that had been passed on to him by his father.

"The Chinaman knows how I learned. He knows everyone's story and was probing for yours. He's not to be trusted."

"Well, nothing was revealed in the end, so all is well," said Maa.

We returned to our respective gers, slightly subdued by the incident but still buoyed by the excitement of our purchases, in the passing way that new things bring. Tuli was to cut the cloth for my new del and I couldn't resist fingering it, embarrassed by my own eagerness but wanting to know what it was Erdene had seen when she'd pictured it on me. Tuli got up from organizing the sewing supplies she'd bought.

"Let's see how that looks again." She fiddled with the cloth, draping in over my shoulders to get an effect more like a finished del, then fetched the hand-sized mirror and tried to show me by holding it up far enough away that I could catch a glimpse of my whole self. My image in the murky light of the ger was hard to make out. What I could see was that I was bigger than I'd thought. I'd filled out a bit already and I looked taller. More like a man, with the blue cloth hanging cleanly off almost-straight shoulders, not drooping away from the neck like it does with a half-formed adolescent.

"*Ai ho*, that was a good choice Erdene made," Tuli said. "You'll look like a Mongol prince."

I allowed myself the vanity of a smile. Reluctantly, I removed the cloth and folded it back up again. The women would not start cutting and sewing it until the next day.

Tabin, unconcerned with how I looked, was struggling to draw a convincing horse with his new set of pencils. There were only red, yellow, blue and black. He had put the bright colours aside in favour of the more credible black for his creation.

"Dash, do you know how to draw, along with all the other things you know?" he asked.

I hadn't done anything creative since my rescue from the cave. I was already feeling out of place, my intellectual aptitude no match for the raw, physical competence expected of a herding man. To portray myself as an artist would only widen the gulf, it seemed to me.

But when I took a look at his horse, the too-short legs, the too-long neck, I had to help. "To draw realistically you have to understand proportion." Making a quick grid on a second piece of paper, I superimposed a better horse on top of it. "Look at the squares and see what parts of the horse fall into what squares. Then you'll be able to imitate it."

"That's a very good horse," Tabin said. He held it up to his father and mother. "You see how good it is?"

Cholon glanced briefly at the drawing. "That is pretty good," he agreed, then went back to repairing a bridle. "Not that knowing how to draw a horse is going to help you raise them."

Soon it was time for the autumn ritual of culling animals judged too weak to make it through the winter, so that precious pasture wouldn't be wasted on those unlikely to be sustained by it. Our camp already had enough male hands for the work, so I was sent to a neighbour's to help them out.

I knew these people from our summer pasture. Our two groups were quite close, sharing stallions, ram and bulls to keep the bloodlines fresh in our herds, so it was only natural that we would also share labour. The father, Jaran, had a cigarette perpetually dangling between his lips. It never fell, even when he talked. His son, Bat, was a year older than I and built as tough and thick as a bull, a perfect body for the kind of work that needed to be done. They had already selected the doomed sheep and corralled them separately before I arrived. I was given the requisite welcome of airag, then we got straight to it.

My heart quickened with trepidation as Bat picked a sheep out of the panicking group and dragged it by means of a rope around its neck to its place of death. It knew perfectly well what was going on, bleating its panic and desperately fighting Bat's forward movement. At the appointed spot Bat flipped it on its back, then Jaran took the rope and sat on the ground, bracing his feet against the sheep's shoulders to stretch out its front half. I held the back legs, my foot against its backside, leaving the belly clear for Bat to wield the knife.

I was grateful not to be able to see into the creature's eyes because it would have been the undoing of me. As I held the legs I silently prayed for a favourable rebirth for the sheep, and forgiveness for myself. I might have closed my eyes. Bat knelt over the sheep and slit it open effortlessly, reaching in for the heart within seconds to kill it fast without losing any blood. The back legs twitched once, violently, in my hands, as though delivering to me its fleeing soul. I saw again the twitching limbs of the monks of Khovor Khan as they fell under the soldiers' bullets.

"You can get up now," said Bat, and I realized I was still holding tight to the dead legs. I scrambled to my feet.

As Bat removed the internal organs into a pail, Jaran started walking towards the corral. "Come on," he said to me through his cigarette. "Let's get the next one."

I fixed my eyes on the ground before me as we walked, trying to overcome my revulsion. There were eight others in the corral waiting for the same treatment.

"Raised in a monastery, were you?" Jaran asked.

I didn't know what to say.

"I noticed you were praying over the sheep. Your lips were moving." The was no rancour in his voice. Just a statement of fact.

I nodded.

"You'd better get used to killing your own food now, boy. You don't want to let others see you praying. They might not always be understanding."

When we caught the next sheep, Jaran handed me the rope. "You take her over."

As I pulled the reluctant load along I mentally sent my prayers through the rope, careful to keep my lips shut tight. Jaran walked beside me, sucking thoughtfully on his cigarette and ignoring my tug-of-war with the frenzied sheep.

"You can stay at the feet today, though," he said. "Best get used to slaughtering again before you handle the head."

The next day a census man showed up at our camp, in a jeep whose strangeness and noise sent the dogs into a barking frenzy. He was dressed in the army-style shirt and pants that Party bureaucrats favoured, over which he wore a Russian soldier's coat a size too large. Its insignia had been removed, leaving dark green patches of protected wool against the worn khaki of the rest. He kept a clipboard held tight to his chest as though the contents were too important to let anyone glimpse, and he didn't smile, not even when accepting tea from Maa.

When all of us were gathered in Gan's ger to verify our existence, the man began to check off the names on his list.

"We just had a census taken," said Gan.

The man just kept checking his list and looking at each of us in turn, matching bodies to names.

"I see one extra male here who is not on my list from the last census," he said, looking at me. "What is your name?"

"Dash."

He wrote it down. "Patronymic?"

This was a new thing, to want two names instead of just one.

"Chuluuny," said Tuli quickly. Son of Chuluun, whoever he was.

The man looked at her, then at me. "Is that correct?"

"Yes," I said.

"What camp are you from?"

"I'm from Kovd."

"He is the son of my cousin," Tuli said. "Orphaned and come to live with us."

The man pursed his lips, clearly displeased. He was writing in his clipboard notebook, many more things than my name and birthplace.

"You should have registered with the soum when you arrived," he said.

"I'm sorry. I didn't realize."

"Age?"

"Sixteen."

"Responsible adult?"

Cholon stepped forward and presented himself reluctantly.

The man drew himself up to his full height but was still a hand shorter than the person he was about to badger. "As the responsible adult it was your duty to register this boy. If he is not registered he cannot receive the many benefits our benevolent government has planned for all the people, namely: the care of a doctor when he is ill, and education, and productive employment, without which Mongolia will forever be a backward nation." You could tell he'd given the speech many times.

This lesson delivered, he took down the numbers of animals in our various herds, then gave another little speech about how, although herd counts were the highest ever in Mongolia's history, our leaders in their infinite wisdom had set for the country a goal almost ten times greater. I wondered how the land was going to support all those animals.

Then the man snapped his book shut and left, trailing dust, black exhaust and barking dogs in the wake of his jeep as we stood outside the ger watching him go.

Cholon shook his head. "Blow blood! What a lot of nonsense about education and health benefits. How would anyone out here get to a school or a doctor anyway? It's not government benefits that sent him here, it's that cursed Chinese trader." He spit onto the ground.

"They'll be starting a file on you now, Dash," said Gan, "so be careful. They don't need a real offense to be suspicious anymore."

CHAPTER FIFTEEN

FOR A WISE MAN, TWO EARS
ARE NOT ENOUGH; FOR A FOOLISH MAN,
ONE TONGUE IS TOO MANY.

Autumn passed into the short, crisp days of winter, a season when life gravitates towards the hearth stove at the centre of the ger. We concentrated more on indoor tasks, which in my case included teaching Tabin. Although he fidgeted constantly on his little stool as we went through sums and practiced writing Mongolian script, he had no shortage of intelligence. For writing practice we made a blackboard by cutting a log into thin planks about a palm in width, coating them in tallow and leaving them to dry in front of the stove, then applying soot from the cooking pots to make the boards black. A pointed stick dipped in ash was our writing tool. That was the practice board; Tabin's reward when he had perfected each new letter was to draw it in ink on fine Chinese *muutuu* paper. By the end of the winter he had a respectable collection of the entire Mongolian alphabet.

The three households often passed the long winter evenings together, playing checkers and shagai games. The best evenings, however, were those passed in storytelling. Gan's father had been such a good storyteller that their feudal lord had kept the family as one of many adjuncts in service to his court. This post would have been passed on to Gan had the lord not fled the country when he was dispossessed of his goods in the late 1920s.

It was at this court that Gan was taught to read as an aid to memorizing the lengthy texts. Whereas Cholon, the younger of the brothers, had shown himself adept at keeping the lord's herds, Gan had been quick to start telling stories as a boy. Recognizing the talent, his father taught him many traditional folk tales and he even became skilled at reciting the grand hero epics that could take several days to perform.

Now his only audience was his family, but we were no less spellbound than the aristocrats for whom he had once recited. Gan had an instinct for what we needed to hear. Folktales generally depicted meek, ordinary people who triumphed over power or strength by their wits and moral fibre. Hero epics, on the other hand, immersed us in fantasy; heroes with superhuman physical and mental gifts, breathtaking consorts and fantastic horses won massive battles against all odds and triumphed easily over evil. The epics were chanted rather than spoken, and Gan's poetic modulations were like music, booming here, soft as a whisper there, pulling us in to the story with the hypnotic power of a magician.

Just prior to *Tsagaan Sar*, the lunar new year, Gan embarked on the *Geser* epic that would fill the three evenings before the main celebration.

> *Han Hormasta Tenger's white oldest son,*
> *Master of the peak of a high jutting mountain,*
> *With the power of the tornado,*
> *With a horse brown as a hawk,*
> *He who poisons the poisonous and has revenge on evil,*
> *Who sees good and stops evil,*
> *Was Zasa Mergen Baatar.*

I often kept my eyes closed as Gan told the story, in order to better visualize it. When I opened them it was to watch Erdene discreetly, on her side of the ger with the women. If she happened to glance my way I quickly averted my gaze, fooling myself into thinking she hadn't noticed.

I adored her. Having saved me from solitude and hopelessness she had become almost a mythical figure for me, like the epic heroine Erjen who was capable of bringing the dead back to life. My previous obsession with the bodhisattva Tara had done nothing to prepare me for the complexity of caring for this real, flesh and blood girl. Erdene, her sister Dadal, and other girls from neighbouring camps were affectionate and flirtatious in an easy way that the local boys hardly seemed to notice but I found completely unnerving.

I searched for signs of particular favour from Erdene, soared with happiness at the touch of her hand on my sleeve or at a smile I believed was just for me, then crashed back down to earth when I saw her do the same to Bat or some other boy. I didn't know what she felt for me.

I hoped it was not pity.

Early in the spring I began, with counsel from Gan and Cholon, to acquire a few animals with the little money I had from my father. When I turned eighteen the following year I would be expected to behave like a man and develop some wealth of my own, and the only wealth that counted for a herder was livestock. This was when Communism was still in its "gradual" phase, when markets were controlled but we still owned the herds we kept.

I started with two ewes, in addition to the gelding I already had. Now, with the birthing season close at hand, I had arranged to buy a pregnant mare from our neighbour Jaran.

"She's a good mare," Erdene's father said to me as I was saddling my gelding to ride over to Jaran's camp. "Not fancy, but durable. She'll give you a strong foal." Neighbours knew each other's animals well.

Erdene came rushing out of her ger, holding an extra bridle and fixing her hair back in a bright yellow scarf at the same time. "Let me come with you," she said, knowing I would. "And I'll ride her back."

The mare could more easily be led back, but I grabbed the ready excuse for Erdene's company. I mounted my horse and she sprang up behind me, quick as a grasshopper. We departed at a walk, with Erdene's hands holding the tall back of the wooden saddle. As we moved away from the camp, however, she slipped her arms around my waist and gave me a squeeze.

"You've filled out nicely on our good cooking," she said.

I was glad she couldn't see my hot red face. She seemed to know what her affections did to me though, for she laughed in her light way.

"Come on, Dash, let's gallop."

She didn't need to ask twice. My horse leapt forward at my kick and Erdene clung tight, her chest flush to my back and her arms around me.

"Faster!" She shouted into my ear, and I urged the horse forward until we were flying along the steppes, whooping with the exhilarating freedom of it. Like this I could handle her nearness. It was communion without the awkwardness of speaking, intimacy without the tension of intent. I would have galloped like that until the horse dropped, if I could have.

But Jaran's camp came into view. I slowed the horse, and Erdene pulled away from me again to sit primly upright. My back felt cold without her there. She slipped to the ground as soon as we halted.

I tethered my horse. The mare was tied there, too, but it wasn't polite to start looking at her yet. First we had to drink tea and airag and eat a little of whatever was offered. As a prelude to getting down to business, Jaran made predictions about the coming summer and the favourable state of the post-winter pastures. Then he got to the horse, extolling her steadiness of disposition, her consistent foaling record, and her ability to survive harsh winters. When it came time to name a price I saw him glance quickly at Erdene, who was pretending to chat quietly with Jaran's wife but was really listening carefully.

He quoted me a reasonable price and I accepted, with the unspoken understanding that the mare would prove equal to the inspection to follow.

Once we'd sealed the deal with a sip of vodka taken three times back and forth from a communal cup, Jaran lit a cigarette and we all went out of the ger. As he and I looked over the mare at the hitching line, out of the corner of my eye I noticed that the brawny Bat had drawn Erdene into an animated conversation by the side of their ger, too far away for me to catch their words.

Jaran opened the mare's mouth to show me her teeth. "Ten years old, eight foals, seven of them still alive," he said. "Straight legs, see? All four, straight and strong."

I was only half listening to him. I heard Erdene's laughter and wondered what Bat had said to win himself such a reward.

Jaran picked up the mare's near front hoof. "Tough hooves. No problems. Never lame."

I nodded distractedly and examined the mare's back, not because I needed to but because it afforded me a view of Bat and Erdene. He was touching her, an exaggerated, theatrical stroking of her hair where it fell down her back from beneath the yellow scarf. Stroking her hair! I couldn't imagine ever doing such a thing, especially not with such ease. Was this why she had wanted to come, not to ride with me but to see him? I could see the side of her face, the roundness of her cheeks as she smiled for him. She threw her head sideways, not to get away from his hand, but to make the hair swing about, teasing him.

"Are you happy with her?" asked Jaran.

It took me a moment to realize he was talking about the mare. "Yes." I counted off the tugrogs we had agreed on, and put the spare bridle on her.

"Bat," called out Jaran, "they're going now."

I kept my gaze averted when I handed Erdene the reins, afraid that I would see happiness in her eyes from her encounter with Bat. She sprang up bareback as I mounted the gelding. It was emasculating for a man to ride a pregnant mare.

Returning at a walk, we spoke little at first. I was caught up in wondering how Bat was able to flirt with her so effortlessly. I feared she was caught up in replaying the delights of their conversation. Finally, when I could stand my self-torture no longer, I blurted out what was on my mind.

"What was Bat saying that made you laugh?"

Coming out suddenly like that, without preamble, it sounded petulant and peevish. The knowledge shamed me but it was too late to take it back.

"Is that what you've been thinking about in your silence?" she asked in return.

"Of course not," I lied. "Not the whole time." I glanced at Erdene just long enough to catch her frown.

"He was only saying silly things."

But they'd made her laugh. I wanted to be able to say them too. "Like what?"

"Oh, things about my scarf. He thought it was pretty against my hair."

"And that was funny?"

She sighed loudly, as though I was being especially thick. Which I was. "He said he wanted to steal the scarf so he could have something to keep that had been against my hair."

"Besides his hands."

I hadn't meant to say it. It just popped out, deepening my humiliation.

Erdene gave a snort. "You're even sillier than he is."

Stricken, I rode on in silence.

"Are you jealous?" she asked eventually.

I certainly was. Of how effortless it all appeared. Of Bat's confidence. But did Erdene want me to be jealous? I didn't know whether she would be pleased or irritated. "I envy how easily he talks to you," I said.

"But he never says anything important."

"He makes you laugh."

"Anyone can do that."

I couldn't. At least not nearly as often as I wanted.

"If you want to talk to me," she said, "tell me all the things you know."

"That would bore you."

"No it wouldn't. You're educated, Dash. I want to learn."

I didn't want to be her teacher. I wanted to tell her she was lovely, to whisper things in her ear, to make her smile. I fell silent again, unable to do one and unwilling to do the other, as stubborn and witless as a yak.

The spring rains promised to bring Jaran's prediction of good summer grazing to fruition. We moved camp again, back to where I had first joined the family, and where we would remain until fall if the pasture held up. The days lengthened and Arkhangai became lush again. My new mare gave birth to a good, strong colt.

"Now you have the start of a proper herd of your own," said Tuli at lunch that day. "The kind of herd that will attract a good wife."

"He's only seventeen," said Cholon through a mouthful of biscuit.

"That doesn't mean he's not thinking about it." Tuli looked at me expectantly, but I was too embarrassed to respond.

"Can a monk marry?" asked Tabin.

I shook my head.

"But he's not a monk," asserted Tuli.

"Have you ever kissed a girl?" asked Tabin, screwing up his face. "Kuki kissed me once when I was seven. It was yucky. And if you get married you have to kiss your wife all the time."

Cholon and Tuli both roared with laughter. I forced myself to laugh along. It was funny, but I was mostly thinking about one thing: this little boy had more experience with girls than I did.

One morning not long after, I was sitting on the ground outside our ger mending tack when I saw Erdene walk down to the river by herself to do the family washing. I gathered up the bridles and went to join her.

She was kneeling at the river's edge, plunging the clothes in one at a time and scrubbing, then laying each garment out on the grass to dry. Although the sky was clear blue and the sun warmed the ground, it was still earlier enough in the season that the water was frigid, making Erdene's hands and forearms bright red.

"Aren't your hands cold?" I asked.

"It's easier than hauling water to the ger."

I sat next to her, facing in her direction so I could work on the tack and still watch her.

"Your mare's foal is growing fast," she said. "He'll be a fine horse."

"And my lambs are healthy. I've been lucky."

"Like your name." She wrung out an under-tunic and laid it on the grass. She was quick and efficient in her movements, snapping the material straight then bending to lay it out in a single, fluid motion. A bit of hair escaped the bun she'd pulled it into and fell over her right eye. I wanted to tuck that bit of hair behind her small, perfect ear. Her skin there, at the edge of her hairline, would be soft, like the belly of a new lamb. There would be a hint of dampness from her exertions.

"How big is Russia?" she asked out of the blue.

"What?"

"Russia. I want to know how big it is compared to Mongolia." She came back and knelt in front of me, ignoring her washing.

"Many times bigger. Why?"

"When I was little, Ahv always talked about how we had finally thrown off the Chinese yoke. Now he talks about Russia and how we are under a new one. And I wonder, why do we keeping bearing the yokes of other countries?"

"If Mongolia is the size of that small scarf," I explained, pointing at the clothes she'd laid out, "then Russia is the size of three dels. China is two dels."

Erdene shook her head. "Mongolia feels so big to me when I ride on the steppe or look out from the top of a mountain. It's hard to imagine Russia and China being that much bigger."

"But it's not just the size of their land that makes them stronger," I said. "They have many more people. China has hundreds of millions of people, and we only have eight hundred thousand or so."

"I don't know what those numbers mean."

"I'll show you." I took her hand and pressed it, palm down, on the grass under my own. "Imagine that the number of blades beneath your hand is the number of Mongolians."

"Your hand is nice and warm," she said.

"Yes, uh, it hasn't been in the river," I said, then felt like an idiot since that was quite obvious. Tentatively I lifted her hand and put it between both mine to warm it. She let it stay there.

"So," I continued, struggling to remember what I'd been explaining, "look at the small amount of grass that was under your hand."

She looked.

"And compare it to all the grass from the river to our gers, and you'll understand how many Chinese there are compared to us. Russians are fewer. Maybe as many as from the river to where the dog is standing."

Erdene sat looking at the spaces and evaluating the difference. "But if they're both so big, and have so many people, what do they want with us?" She wriggled her other hand in between mine. I desperately wanted to stop talking of China and Russia, and instead say something endearing–having no idea what that might be–but she was concentrating, looking at me intently, and I also wanted that to continue.

"They don't trust each other, and we lie between them," I said.

"So Mongolia is a shield for whichever country controls it."

"Exactly."

She smiled happily and I was butter in the sun. "Now you've told me about something you know, and it didn't bore me." She let her hands stay wrapped in mine and studied me, her head to one side quizzically as though she were waiting for more. But what kind of more? Was I supposed to teach her a new lesson, or do something with her hands? I stared at them, at their redness, at the stubby nails chipped from work. I wanted to bring her chapped fingers to my lips and kiss them back to smoothness, but the very thought of such contact paralyzed me with fear. What if she didn't feel that way about me at all? I was living like a member of her family. She probably thought of me as a brother. Or maybe still as a monk; the family continued to turn to me for prayers and special blessings to remedy all kinds of ills.

As if in answer she gently slid her hands back out of mine. She returned to her washing, quiet now, while I agonized over what might be going through her head. For my part, as I went back to mending the bridles, I was thinking how the imprint left by her cold fingers on my palms felt so inexplicably warm.

After that I made a point of finding opportunities for lessons and the possibility of physical contact they might give. I drew maps in the dirt with a long stick to teach her geography, and guided her hand with mine when it was time for her to recreate them herself, my fingers burning with the memory for days afterwards. We learn mathematics with small stones that I would place in her hand although it would have been easier to put them on the ground.

One warm evening we lay on our backs on the ground so I could teach her about the stars. She started off a hand-width apart from me and somehow over the course of showing her the Azure Dragon and the Black Tortoise the distance had been closed. I felt her arm along the length of my arm, her hip touching mine, the heat of her thigh. The start of an erection made me sit up suddenly in embarrassment. I couldn't look at her. After a minute of awkward silence she sat up too, and told me it was time for her to return to her ger. I mumbled my agreement.

And so it went. In the process of telling Erdene the things I knew, I still couldn't tell her how I felt. I couldn't even stroke her hair.

CHAPTER SIXTEEN

———————————✦———————————

A PUPIL'S KNOWLEDGE COMES
FROM HIS TEACHER;
A LAMP'S LIGHT COMES FROM ITS OIL.

———————————✦———————————

With the longer days of summer I had more time to ride off after supper to a quiet place for the meditation that had been so difficult to accomplish in the family ger. At a particular spot I liked best of all, at the top of a hill overlooking the winding course of the Tamir river, I hobbled my horse and sat in lotus looking out across the valley. The sky was streaked with broad swaths of pink, like the strokes of a fat paintbrush, and I let myself take in its beauty while saying some simple prayers. I thanked Buddha for his compassion in saving me and finding me a true home. I asked that I be worthy by following steadfastly the Eightfold Path. I asked compassion for all others who still suffered. For the thousandth time, I begged forgiveness of Tara for having defiled her purity in my younger years.

The praying gave me a great sense of calm and centering. So much of the day was spent in dealing with life, and so little of it was spent like this, I knew my spirituality was slipping steadily away. The depth of faith that I had felt in the cave seemed almost dream-like now, it was growing so faded. Had it all been no more than a product of my desperation, easily knocked aside by the demands of herding life? Or was it the allure of those demands that was confounding me? The currency of my new life was strong herds, a swift horse to ride, a wife, children. Attachments and possessions. I wanted them. Had I learned nothing about their inherent impermanence?

I closed my eyes and concentrated on the serenity of no distracting sounds, just the play of an evening breeze against my skin. Eventually I silenced my questions and found the quiet place within, and there the light that reconnected me to my past and to my faith. In that place, it seemed to me, I balanced the day's myriad violations of my vows. There it felt as though what Tilik had said could be true: that having been a monk, the Path would forever be clear before me, if I only took the time to see it.

I stayed on the hill until it grew dark, clinging to the comfort of meditation and wishing I could keep the feeling with me throughout the day. If I had found it hard to be a monk, I found it harder still to be an ex-monk groping his way, clumsily, to being a herding man.

That summer we went as a group to the *Nadaam* festival at the nearest town, Ikh Tamir, a few hours' ride away. It was the first time I'd been to the festival as a layperson since I was nine. Now I was eighteen and there was no other way to attend the festival, since the Party had banned all prayers and blessings at the event.

Still central to festival, however, were the traditional competitions in the three "manly sports," oddly named since of the three—archery, horse racing and wrestling—it was only wrestling that didn't have women competing. We arrived mid-morning to a lively chaos, with the Party's opening speeches over and the horse race about to start. Dismounting and tethering our horses, we joined a large milling crowd, some still mounted while those on foot dodged hooves and struggled to catch a glimpse of the departing racers. Amidst a lot of shouting, two dozen horses, many of them bareback, charged off with their child jockeys. A thick cloud of dust trailed after them. The course was so long that they wouldn't appear at the finish line until after lunch.

"We have to go watch the wrestling now," said Dadal, grabbing Erdene by the hand. They hurried along, calling to the rest of us who were dragging behind.

"Come on!" cried Erdene, "What if we miss him? Hurry!"

When we got to the wrestling ring, it was thronged all around with spectators. Dadal and Erdene found a friend among them, Jaran's niece, Bulgaa.

"He's won his first two matches," Bulgaa said immediately, forgoing greetings in her excitement. "You're just in time to see his third."

We maneuvered ourselves into a position to see the wrestlers in the ring. The match was just beginning, with the two opponents circling each other, flapping their arms like eagles to boast of their strength. They were beefy and muscular as a pair of oxen. I recognized one of them with a jolt.

"That's Bat," I said.

"Isn't it exciting?" asked Dadal. "Our neighbour could be a champion."

"He's very good," said Bulgaa, proud of her position as his relative.

I watched the match and resisted looking at Erdene. Bat was good. His opponent was slightly larger than he, but not as quick or decisive in his moves. They grappled a few times without result and then, all of a sudden, Bat flipped him onto the ground. I didn't even see how he'd done it.

Everybody cheered around me and I forced myself to do the same, not wanting to appear churlish. Bat did his victory dance. He seemed to be looking especially at Erdene, and she seemed to be smiling at him in response, but from my angle of view it was hard to be sure.

"That was a clever move," said Cholon.

"He's quick," agreed Gan.

"He downs a sheep just like that, too," said Cholon. "Doesn't he Dash?"

"He does," I admitted reluctantly.

"A useful kind of man for a herding camp."

"Or for a husband," said Dadal, elbowing her sister and erupting in a fit of giggling.

Soon the wrestlers' break was over and Bat was back in the ring. His new rival was better matched; neither of them was finding it easy to get a good hold on the other. There were several times when it appeared as though one of them would see victory, then the other managed to regain his feet. The girls cheered Bat on, confident his muscles and his cunning would make him the winner.

Then, just as Bat had done in the previous round, the challenger found a moment in which he could seize the upper hand. He forced Bat off balance to a point of no return. The girls gasped and held their breath. Bat went down with a loud thud.

The family sighed with disappointment.

I was elated.

"He'll win next year," said Bulgaa.

"He was looking like a champion," agreed Erdene.

"He did very well," said Gan. "Three matches. Very impressive."

The girls turned away from the ring, their interest gone now that their champion wasn't competing.

"Let's look at the market stalls," suggested Erdene.

I was quick to agree, happy to get away from the wrestlers, any of whom could have flipped me in less than a second.

Ikh Tamir was not much of a place. The town consisted of a handful of gers, a couple of which were stores, and a wood chopping factory. When Nadaam was on, therefore, the resulting expansion of the market was a welcome chance to see new things. A dozen or so vendors set up stalls to sell their handicrafts. There were knives with handles worked in silver or out of sheep or camel bone; snuff bottles carved of jade and onyx; embroidered purses from China, covered in tiny beads in jewel tones; saddles embellished with silver medallions and leather tassels; fancy whips and horse gear of every type.

As we strolled among the market stalls I positioned myself beside Erdene, and felt inordinately proud just to be in her company. No matter that the entire family trailed along with us; I liked to think that she and I made a striking pair, I in the new purple del Tuli had made me for summer and Erdene in her emerald green one, with her hair drawn up under a silk pillbox hat. The atmosphere in the market was festive. Children ran around frenzied by too many sweets, their mothers paying no heed; there were pretty new scarves to look at, and tempting jewelry. The air was filled with the babble of people who hadn't seen each other in months.

In the last stall there were paintings for sale; small, affordable works on wood, silk and leather, depicting Mongolian landscapes and everyday pastoral life.

"*Burhan miny*, Dash, is that you?"

I hadn't noticed the vendor, having been drawn first to the art.

"Qara?"

With his longish hair and unremarkable, sand-coloured del he could have been any slightly unkempt, nomadic artist. He rushed from the stall to envelop me in a bear hug, then held me at arm's length for a quick inspection.

"Look at you! Almost a man, and a fine one at that. Skinny but good looking, just like when you were a young boy." His smile fled as he looked around, suddenly furtive, and spoke with a quiet urgency. His searching eyes were so close to mine I could smell the airag on his breath. "I heard, you know. About Khovor Khan. Terrible, so much more brutal than the others. I thought you were gone with the rest of them."

"I was on the hillside when they came," I said, and was surprised how quickly a lump formed in my throat. It had been so long since I'd spoken of that time. "I hid."

"That's good. Very good. Your name, you see? It's true."

We were huddled like spies, completely forgetting my adopted family who had gathered around us, instinctively sheltering us from onlookers by inspecting, with real or feigned interest, Qara's artworks. He noticed the others with a start.

"Haha! Who are all these wealthy patrons you've brought me?" he said, giving Erdene and Dadal a distinctly unlamalike appraisal.

I introduced them all, describing Qara simply as a great artist from whom I had once been fortunate to learn a little. They complimented his work lavishly, and Maa and Tuli each bought paintings on leather hung from sticks, which could be rolled up and easily transported in the nomad tradition. Qara wrapped them up, happy.

"I'm very pleased you like my work, but how can you have any more space for art in your gers when Dash is living with you? He must have filled your walls by now."

The family stared at me blankly.

"He drew me a horse once, to teach me how," said Tabin.

"Just one horse drawing?"

Tabin nodded.

Qara looked at me in amazement. "What happened to your art, boy?" He checked the end of my arms to make sure my hands were still there. "They still work, don't they?"

I was squirming under the double scrutiny of Qara and my family. "There's been little time for art since—"

Qara cut me short with a hand, his eyes darting back and forth to check for untrustworthy eavesdroppers. "Say no more. But you should develop your style now, you really should. The Party is very fond of artists."

"It is?"

"If they paint the right subjects, yes. Haha, yes! I even heard they're starting a program to send talented young artists to Moscow to learn western techniques."

"I don't think I could paint for the Party."

"Well, you think about it. At least start back at it. What a waste if you don't! You make some paintings like mine, make a bit of money, buy yourself some animals while the Party still allows free enterprise. No telling when they'll change their minds again." He poked me in the ribs. "Make yourself into a fine marriage prospect, haha!"

He rummaged around under the little table that held his artworks, eventually pulling out several leather pouches and an assortment of vials which he laid out before me on the table. Powdered pigment, linseed oil, brushes. A slim book about perspective.

"Everything you need. And for you, an exceptional price!"

It was as though he'd laid out lost scripture books instead of art supplies, the way the sight of them and the smell of the linseed brought memories of Khovor Khan swirling into my head. My first drawings of Tara. Alban's careful instruction. The catastrophic mandala. The absolute peace I felt when absorbed in the process of creation.

Erdene nudged me gently.

"Buy them, Dash," she said.

"What?"

"I've seen what you can do." She lowered her voice, leaning in to me. "In the cave. Qara is right, you have to buy these." I saw the light in her eyes , the faith she had in my abilities, her eagerness for me to do this.

I bought them. I couldn't refuse her. Or myself.

The first thing I painted was a miniature Tara in the Buddhist style, on a piece of wood no bigger than my palm. A size you could hide easily. I painted secretively in the dim light of the ger, hiding my criminal activity from the outside world. There was no lust in my painting of the goddess this time. I painted her with the reverence she deserved, and with the thought that it was only right to start with her. I recalled from memory the appropriate symbols and proportions. Painting that first miniature felt the same as drinking the first cup of tea I'd had when Erdene had brought me home from the cave. It unleashed an appetite that I had forcibly suppressed.

The family, of course, knew what I was up to. Like many herders, having been brought up Buddhist they kept shrines secreted away in cabinets placed on the north wall of the ger, the place of honour. Gan wanted a Tara miniature like mine. Cholon wanted one of Avalokitesvara. These I gave away, as it would have been wrong to accept money for them.

One day in autumn, when I was riding near the edge of our pasture lands, Jaran came cantering towards me.

"Sain bain uu," I said in greeting.

"Sain. Are your animals fattening well?" he asked.

"Yes, thank you."

"And the colt?"

"He's very strong. A good colt."

Jaran nodded and lit a cigarette. It seemed odd that he'd come over just to exchange polite greetings, so I waited. "I understand you paint well," he said at last.

"I have painted a bit, but I can hardly be the judge of it."

He lowered his voice as though the khainag were spies. "My wife would like a thangka of Tara."

I nodded.

"Little, you understand. Something that could hang at the back of a closed cabinet, say." He peered at me through the veil of smoke in front of his face. "Can you do that, in the traditional way?"

"Yes."

"How much would it cost?"

"I could never charge for that."

Jaran grunted, satisfied. I knew I would see some favour returned in the future.

"Greetings to your family," he said, and cantered off again, his mission accomplished.

Over the winter I began to broaden my artistic scope. Translating my skills from the two-dimensional techniques of the religious art I knew to those required for realistic landscapes and scenes, however, proved challenging. Qara's little book had five brief sections, each with a single page of explanation and another of sketches to illustrate the principles discussed. The first two sections dealt with perspective and proportional division. As they were mathematical concepts I found them quite straightforward, so I made myself a blackboard like the one I'd made for Tabin and practiced a few examples. But when I looked outside, I realized that the cubes and rectangles of the illustrations bore no relation to the curved hills, gers and rivers that I saw.

The remaining sections explained overlap, scale, and the way colours fade in objects further away. These were complex subjects for someone accustomed to arrangements that were dictated symbolically, not by how the eye perceives. When I made a thangka, Tara was always the largest object because she was most important. Even a pagoda would be shown smaller than she. Oriental landscape paintings, also familiar to me, followed a similarly stylized approach, with mountains always drawn bigger than houses, which were in turn bigger than people or horses, regardless of whether they were meant to be in the foreground of the scene or miles away in the background. But in Qara's book it was all different. A mountain in the distance, for instance, was to be drawn smaller than the horse in the foreground, even though the mountain is actually much bigger. That is how the eye perceives it.

My other artistic challenge was choice. Liberated from the Buddhist strictures of how to render my subjects, I was at first lost in a wilderness of possibilities. Then, throughout the course of that year, I learned how to frame the scenes of my days. Watching Tuli milk a khainag, I moved a few paces to the right and could see how it made a more pleasing composition. While holding a wriggling sheep for Cholon to shear, I pictured us from the outside and imagined how the elements—Cholon, myself, the sheep, the hills in the distance, the fleece—could make a painting. I learned how to see things differently just by thinking about them in this way. My imagination, the bane of my existence as a monk, became an asset.

It took a lot of practice to learn this new way of seeing things. I wore out several blackboards over the course of the winter. And because my herding chores always had to be done first, I found myself stealing time from my meditations. A few times I got so caught up I neglected to meditate altogether. Then I would say a few hurried prayers before going to bed, and promise to make up for it the next day.

I told myself that a slight fall-off in religious observance was inevitable. I was a herder now, after all, no longer a monk. I couldn't be both.

After dozens of attempts over many months, I finally had two pastoral scenes, painted on leather, that I thought good enough to hang from the ger poles. Shortly afterwards, a traveler came through our area and stayed with us for the night. He complimented me on the paintings and bought one of them for a tugrog before he left.

Tuli was so excited by the deal that she went and told the other ger families. Erdene came over immediately to congratulate me.

"Your first sale!" she said, clapping her hands together in glee. "It's wonderful."

Even Cholon was nodding. "Maybe there's something in this after all," he allowed.

"You should make more, and take them to Ikh Tamir to sell in the stores there," said Erdene.

"That's a good idea," agreed Tuli. "They would be sure to take them."

"I don't know," I said. "It's taken so long just to make the two I hung."

"But now you know how," said Erdene. "The next ones will be easier. You have to try."

I loved the way Erdene looked when she was excited. Her face shone and her eyes widened as though my meager talent were a marvelous present she had just unwrapped. Her enthusiasm started me thinking that maybe I could make something of myself through art. I wasn't good at flipping sheep or wrestlers, but maybe this gentler talent could be equally attractive.

That possibility spurred me to keep at it, so that by summer I had a handful of paintings to take to Ikh Tamir. The town had changed in the few years since I'd arrived in the area. A dismal concrete building now housed government offices. A couple of Russians had taken up residence, a doctor and a man who had been sent to expand the wood chopping factory. Their white faces looked odd amidst our own and they had built unusual houses of logs, which were quite a novelty.

Ikh Tamir's two general stores were still run out of gers at the time. Both of them agreed to display my paintings alongside the sacks of flour, rolls of felt and wool, kitchen implements and bottles of Russian-made vodka. When I went back two months later, five paintings had sold. With much bartering back and forth between the stores I managed to consolidate my earnings, after commissions, to a full brick of tea.

I rushed home to split the brick between the families, placing Erdene's chunk in her hands with all the reverence of someone who has just laid a block of gold at the feet of his beloved.

CHAPTER SEVENTEEN

———

EVEN THE SEA NEEDS SALT;
EVEN A GODDESS NEEDS A HUSBAND.

———

In 1942, when I was nineteen, Tuli turned my world upside down with an announcement. It was a year in which other awful things had happened; Moscow, for example, had executed yet another Mongolian prime minister and put their man Choibalsan in the position. But Tuli's news was an even greater disaster to me. We were eating dinner in our ger, escaping the wet chill of a rainy autumn day. The room was filled with the greasy smell of smoke and mutton dumplings.

"Maa says Bat has asked to marry Erdene." She glanced at me when she said this, then looked away.

Cholon sucked the fat off his fingers before responding. "That's a good match. Bat will have a large herd from his father, even with the Russians demanding half the stock to feed their war."

I watched in stunned silence as Cholon, Tuli and Tabin casually stuffed slippery blobs of fatty dough in their mouths as though the world had not just come to an end. The pot clunked on the stove, broth was slurped, their conversation continued. Was mine the only heart that had stopped?

"But he's so stupid," said Tabin. Now that he was literate he was feeling superior.

"He knows everything he needs to know to be a good herder," Cholon said.

The sudden dryness of my mouth had turned a bite of dumpling into a clogged wad that threatened to gag me. With an effort I swallowed it, feeling the hard lump work its way painfully down my esophagus.

"What has Erdene said?" I managed to ask, although I had so little breath I could barely voice the words.

"She hasn't given an answer."

"I don't know what she's waiting for," said Cholon.

I wanted to rush over to Erdene's ger and beg her to marry me instead. There were two reasons why I didn't.

The first was that it was pouring rain outside. A feeble excuse, perhaps, but it meant that when I got to her ger I would either have to make my plea and declaration in front of her family, or drag her out into the privacy of the downpour for the occasion. Neither seemed likely to help me win her.

The second reason was harder to overcome. I looked at myself as a marriage prospect and wondered what I had to offer. Love for her, yes, but in the harsh reality of a Mongolian life how would that keep us sheltered or put food on the table? I knew what poverty and hunger felt like, and wanted much better than that for Erdene. The government had just taken five of my fifteen sheep to feed the Russian troops fighting their Big War. How could I present myself with a paltry ten, plus four horses, against the hundreds of each that Bat had?

I spent the night agitated and awake, hopeless to come up with what I might offer her to compete as a suitor. The chill wind that beat at the side of the ger towards dawn brought with it the most devastating possibility: Erdene might actually want to marry Bat. Of course she would want the security he could bring her. Who wouldn't? But maybe she also liked his muscular confidence, his obvious suitability for the kind of life we led, his comfortable acceptance of the parameters of that life. He was not hampered by religious obligations, or a useless education he had to hide, or artistic desires.

When I made my declaration of love Erdene would, in her gentle way, let me know that when it came to husband material he was clearly the better choice.

By morning I was a wreck. After our breakfast tea, when Cholon had gone outside to start his day, Tuli leaned close to me and said in a low voice, "If you don't want to lose her you have to go talk to her now, Dash."

I looked into her face and found reason for hope.

"Do you think?"

"Never mind what I think. Just go!" She shooed me out the door.

The rain had stopped, leaving behind crisp air that made clouds of my breath against the orange and blue of a barely waking sky. Erdene was just leaving her ger, yawning. Bits of her hair were slipping out from under a woolen cap and she was sticking them back in, frowning a little as though they were unruly children. I thought about how, if she married

Bat, I would never see her in this fragile, sleepy morning state again.

I walked up to her and mumbled a greeting. She didn't answer, but looked hard at me as if daring me to say more.

"Will you walk with me awhile?" I asked.

"I have to do the milking."

"It could wait."

Dadal came out the door behind her. One look at my miserable face and she said, "Go ahead, Erdene. I'll get started."

And so we walked, towards the hills and away from the camp.

"I heard some news from Tuli last night," I said.

"What news was that?"

I was going to have to actually say the words. "That Bat has asked to marry you," I croaked.

"So he has."

I cleared my throat, trying to rid it of the massed tightness there. "And will you?"

"Should I?"

"Do you want to?"

"A woman needs a husband, and I have no other prospects."

"Maybe I could be another prospect."

Erdene stopped and turned to me with the look she usually reserved for difficult yaks. "Are you, Dash?"

"I'd like to be."

"You haven't shown it."

"I've been unsure. Not about you, I don't mean. Never. But about myself. I have very little to bring to a marriage. Almost nothing in the way of wealth."

"Do you think that matters so much to me?"

Did her words mean I had a chance? "If not to you, then to your father perhaps," I said carefully. "He will be expecting a gift of livestock from whoever marries you."

"I cannot believe a monk is telling me I, or my father, should be concerned with material wealth."

"I'm not a monk. I'm not even a lama. I was never ordained."

"Well you certainly act like one." She cocked her head to one side, examining me as though I were some strange biological specimen she was having trouble fathoming. "Why don't you ever touch me?"

I reddened. "Touch you?"

"Yes. You're standing here talking to me about marriage, but you've never shown me that you're interested in the things that go on between a man and a woman who are married."

The perfidity of my years as a monk would have been a revelation to her. But those acts of lust had contained no tenderness, no preamble, no gentle seduction. Nothing to show me how to begin.

"I've wanted to, always," I said. "But I've never known where to start." It sounded pathetic, even to me. I was sure Bat would never have a problem like this.

"Really? That's it?"

"What if you said no?"

Erdene frowned. "Idiot monk," she said.

I was sure I had lost her. But she grabbed the collar of my del and pulled my head forcefully down to where she could plant her mouth on mine.

Her lips were as delicious as my startling encounter with the chocolate years before. Soft but firm, with a hint of butter biscuit. Unfortunately my response was inexperienced and stiff. I had never kissed anyone before.

Erdene shook her head, but her eyes were loving. "You spent too many years in a monastery."

"I can learn," I said, kissing her again, a little more confidently this time. "Teach me."

CHAPTER EIGHTEEN

―――――――⟋⟍―――――――

A STONE THROWN UPWARDS
FALLS ON ONE'S OWN HEAD.

―――――――⟋⟍―――――――

We set our wedding day for the third day of the Blue Dog month. We took it as a good omen that the day was bright and windless. As Erdene walked down the white felt path towards the door of Cholon and Tuli's ger, I felt as though we were receiving a princess in her fine golden del, dangling earrings and beautifully embroidered hat. Tuli made a libation of milk and Erdene was brought into the ger with great formality.

In the old days a lama would have blessed the nuptials before family members recited their own felicitations for our future happiness, fertility and prosperity, but now no-one would dare come forward to offer such services, even if we had dared to look for them. The ger was crammed with family and neighbours drinking and eating the fancy foods the women had been preparing for days.

Bat seemed pragmatic about having lost his suit for Erdene to me. He embraced me in congratulations, then spent most of his time talking to Dadal.

Erdene leaned close to me. "You see how Bat has recovered? And I believe my sister looks very happy for that."

Dadal was glowing with the attention. "She does."

"She will be a perfect wife for him," Erdene said. "He only asked me because I'm the eldest. Now he is free to make the right choice."

When the feasting was over, we were led in a procession by Erdene's parents, along with Cholon and Tuli, to a new ger just for us. Erdene squeezed my hand as we ducked through the door together. It was her first time seeing what I had been working on for weeks, and I held my breath as she looked around.

The ger was simple, with a plain wooden floor and without any silk to hide the lattice of the walls, but I had carved the central poles with demon-chasers and painted them in bright orange. We had one narrow bed with drawers at either end, and a low table with two stools, all of which were also painted with traditional floral motifs that made the ger quite cheerful. In the place of honour against the north wall was a small standing cabinet with double doors, inside of which I had placed the thangka of Tara.

"It is perfect," said Erdene, and I breathed again.

We lined up wood chips in the hearth area, poured butter on them and lit them, both hands together on the match. The assembled parents recited more felicitations to bless our ger. I said a prayer of thanks to Avalokitesvara for my very good fortune, and I never meant it more than on that day.

The intimacy of married life unfolded like slow moving miracle. I was constantly amazed that Erdene was mine to hold and kiss and make love to. The first brush of my hands on the smooth, perfect skin of her body, unlike any other thing I'd ever felt, and the abandon with which she opened herself to me, were unimaginable until I experienced them. All I'd known about sex before Erdene were the hurried, focused acts at the monastery. Their expediency wasn't remotely comparable. With Erdene, our physical explorations were bridges to deep places within ourselves, places of utter trust. I felt at those times both intensely inside my body and also outside of it, in hers, our separateness eliminated.

Often I would lie awake at night and simply listen to her breath, in and out, in and out, such simple but powerful evidence of her existence in my life. It seemed the power of my name had finally returned.

Now that we had our own ger, it was easier to keep up meditations and prayers at the start of the day. In fact, Erdene insisted on them. She was quiet as a stone while I meditated, and often joined me in the prayers, sitting quietly beside me as I chanted. We were still as much a part of the collective work as always, and we still ate with Gan and Maa or Tuli and Cholon, as the camp families all shared in the making of the meals anyway. But at the end of the day and at the beginning, our time was luxuriously, sweetly our own.

Having our own home came at a price, however. The money I'd brought with me from my father was almost gone. Our small herds were healthy and growing, but not yet enough to sustain us, let alone allow us to think of having children. I therefore began a new wave of painting. I kept to the subjects Qara said were popular, scenes of everyday life painted on rolls of cloth or small pieces of wood. From an artistic perspective they were not very gratifying. I wanted them to convey the inner life of herders; the reverence for nature that came from having your whole life depend on it; the patience required with a difficult animal; the generosity shown to passing strangers; the selflessness needed to live communally. I'd seen enough of European art to know it was possible. Without a teacher, however, I lacked the techniques needed to breathe such life into my work.

Erdene still thought my paintings were wonderful. Other people seemed to agree, for most of what I brought to Ikh Tamir sold. Tsagaan Sar turned out to be a particularly popular time for buying scroll paintings. We entered the new year with money for an additional ewe, and requests from the stores in Ikh Tamir for more paintings like the ones they had just sold. We hoped for children. I planned a trip in the spring to see my father, thinking it might now be safe, to tell him all my good news.

That spring, the census man returned in his noisy jeep.

He had apparently gone up in the world; this time he had the luxury of a driver, who stayed behind the wheel throughout the entire visit, as though one of us might leap in and make off with the vehicle if he should leave it. As if any of us knew how to drive.

The census man moved fastidiously, taking care not to dirty his coat as he climbed down from the jeep. It was the same coat, but this time he had no clipboard. He stood very straight, clearly impressed with his own mission as he prepared to announce his purpose to everyone who'd assembled outside the gers when they'd heard him coming.

He looked around at all of us for a moment before fixing his eyes directly on me. "Chuluuny Dash?"

"Yes."

"Are you the person who created the paintings being sold in the stores of Ikh Tamir?"

I nodded, wondering what edict I had broken in doing so. We all hung on his words in anticipation of the worst.

The census man bared his teeth suddenly, making him look as though he might attack at any moment. When he held his face like that for a few seconds longer, however, I realized it was meant to be a smile. "A word in private," he said to me.

I invited him into our ger, where Erdene served him tea and a biscuit before leaving us alone, giving me one worried, backward glance as she ducked through the door. Our guest consumed our offerings swiftly, with great slurping sounds and noisy, wet chewing. I sat opposite him and waited.

"The mayor of Ikh Tamir is impressed with your painting skill," he said once he'd finished.

I tried not to let him see my relief. "That is very generous of the mayor."

"Our town is expanding, thanks to the foresight and hard work of the Party. It is their desire to have industry so that everyone may be gainfully employed, schooling to free Mongolia of illiteracy, and a hospital where everyone may benefit from the services of properly trained doctors and nurses."

"Those are very worthy goals," I said, unable to see what any of this had to do with my paintings.

The census man pursed his lips and brought his fingertips together, a sign that he was getting to the important part. "The mayor believes that towns of significance have, besides these things I've mentioned, strong cultural programs as well. Music. Theatre." He paused. "Art."

"If the mayor thinks my small talent can be of any benefit, I'm very flattered."

"The mayor would like to be able to demonstrate that a local artist can produce work at a level that competes with the artists of other, larger towns. Perhaps even Ulaan Baatar."

"I really am not at that level."

"We know." He let this sink in before continuing. "But the mayor believes that all you lack is instruction. To that end, he is prepared to send you to Ulaan Baatar for eight months to receive instruction from the art school there. Then you will return and create, for the glory of our community, the kinds of paintings and sculptures he would like you to create. The State will pay you for this art."

The flattery of the offer was negated by the price I would be paying. The thought of living in Ulaan Baatar was bad enough, especially since I knew they would expect me to leave Erdene behind while I studied. The idea was made even worse by knowing my reward upon returning would be to create art that glorified something I didn't believe in, a movement that slaughtered monks.

"It's very generous, but I think there must be someone else who deserves this honour more than I."

"You mistakenly assume you have a choice."

"We are free men in Mongolia, the last I heard."

The census man got up from his chair as though pondering this statement, moving towards the cabinet that held the illegal thangka as he did so. He stood before it, touching the door with his hand. "A very attractive cabinet," he said.

He didn't have to open the door to show me that he knew what was inside.

Hidden shrines like mine landed people in jail—even people who were not ex-monks with false identities. My heart started pounding in familiar fear.

He turned back to me. "It would be best if you were to embrace the worthiness of the Party's objectives. Freedom is found through contributing to the Party's goals, not by resisting them. Men who do not understand this often find themselves in situations that have unfortunate consequences not just for themselves, but for their wives and families."

His face was devoid of expression. Neither threatening or friendly, just stating the facts. I thought of the soldiers who'd come to Khovor Khan; they'd had the same disengaged air about them.

"Do you understand?" he asked.

"Yes."

"Then I assume I have the pleasure of telling the mayor we have an agreement."

I nodded.

"You're literate?" he asked.

"Yes." There was no point in pretending otherwise.

"That will prove helpful. In two weeks a vehicle will arrive to transport you to Ulaan Baatar. Accommodation will be provided at the school. You will return here only when you've completed your studies."

He flashed the bared-tooth smile briefly, then headed for the ger door. We went outside without a word, and he climbed back into the waiting jeep.

"Two weeks," he said, then the jeep roared back to life and they were off in a great swoosh of dust and exhaust.

Everyone had been gathered expectantly outside, waiting for us to emerge. Erdene rushed up and threw her arms around me.

"*Eejee*, Dash, I thought they were going to take you away."

I explained how it was they intended to do just that. She burst into tears.

The rest of the family began to talk all at once.

"So far away!"

"It's a horrible place. Crowded, dirty, smelly."

"Propaganda, that's what they want you to make."

"What has this country come to?"

"Are you really going to art school?" It was Tabin.

"Apparently."

"Eight months in a real school, learning how to paint." He was the only one of us who was smiling. "That's exciting. You'll be so good when you get back."

CHAPTER NINETEEN

IN THE LAND OF THE BLIND, DO AS THE BLIND; IN THE LAND OF THE LAME, DO AS THE LAME.

The army truck that took me to Ulaan Baatar looked like the one they had used to take away our statue of Avalokitesvara when they destroyed Khovor Khan. It was wide and squat, with a canvas-covered back area that had been fitted with two rudimentary wooden benches for passengers. I traveled with five young soldiers whose captain rode in the relative luxury of the front cab. The soldiers and I spoke little. They had been trained to be a fighting team and were wary of a civilian. I kept wondering if they had killed any monks. Just being in their company made me feel sick to my stomach.

It was my first time in any kind of motor vehicle, but I wasn't impressed. The trip took two bone-jarring days over a wide, rutted track, each bump reverberating through the hard benches and up our spines. The canvas sides lifted up, so we could have our choice of stifling airlessness or perishing wind, choking dust and diesel fumes. I left the endless manipulations up to my fellow travelers. We stopped at least once an hour to patch tire punctures or to pour water into the engine from a metal tank we kept in the back with us. It would have been faster, and more comfortable, if all of us had ridden horses instead.

We were in the month of the Red Hare, a few weeks before my twentieth birthday. I noted, when the canvas was open, the subtle signs of spring. In sheltered spots the weary ground wore the slightest haze of green, as hard to discern as the fuzz of a young man's first beard. Herds had the exhausted, unkempt look of survivors of an ordeal, which they were. Still, here and there rams and bulls were energetic enough to mount their females, which I liked to think of as evidence of their optimism for the future. I was sorry I would be missing the summer in Arkhangai. Its steppes would soon be lush and green, it rivers full and rushing. Erdene would grow brown as a nut in the sun. She would make delicious yoghurt from the milk of freshly fattened ewes and have no husband to eat it. She would reach for me in our bed, her knowing fingertips seeking my skin, and realize she was alone.

I tried to distract myself by reciting prayers and some of Gan's stories. But the one that stuck in my mind was about a young married couple separated by war, and it only heightened my loneliness:

I wish I were the warmth
Of the sun in the sky,
So that my body could warm
Altansuhe, my beloved.
I wish I were the wind
Which blows as it will through the wide world,
So I could accompany
Altansuhe, my destined love!
I wish I were a cloud
Gathering in the heaven above,
So that I could be the shade
For Altansuhe, my beloved.
I wish I were the moon
Of this turning world,
So that I could watch over my dear one
Through the depths of the dark night.

As this ran through my head, memories flooded in as well – the tenderness of her hand stroking my cheek; her warm breath and lips, soft as down, at my ear; the way her body rose to meet mine; that quick, mischievous look that came upon her at the most unlikely times, just before she turned to me and slid her hands inside my del. As much as I couldn't have imagined these things before I had them, now I couldn't imagine myself living without them.

By the time we neared our destination I was weary and morose. As we crossed the Shar Khov pass through the last of the hills to the west of Ulaan Baatar, the soldiers lifted the canvas to get a better view. This must have been their first trip to the capital too, for they were craning their necks excitedly for their first glimpse of the big city.

What a sight it was. Smoke stacks spewed grey plumes that rose into the air above, then spilled out over the valley like a colourless fungus on green grass. To one side was a sea of gers, each one enclosed in a square of tall wooden fencing. These belonged to people who had moved to the city for steady work but hadn't been able to secure an apartment in one of the new blocks that were going up. To the other side was a sprawling army camp with more gers, but also huge buildings with curved roofs and rows of tanks. In the countryside we had felt the existence of the Big War only as the Russian army's insatiable appetite for our livestock. We had heard it referred to as World War II, but believed Mongolia to be a neutral nation. Here in the capital, however, our true involvement was more evident. I wondered if the barely-men who traveled with me would soon be fighting.

In the middle of these two suburbs was the city proper, and as we entered it I was bombarded by noise and stink. The main road was paved in tarmac that smelled like poison. With it mingled the odour of uncollected garbage. Cars and jeeps dodged the occasional horse and rider that shared the road, along with groups of parading soldiers and hundreds of bicycles with bells that seemed to ring constantly. There were buildings on all sides, stifling to me in their verticality. Many of the buildings were very grand, with huge columns on their facades, and gardens—clipped, tended gardens, an incredible idea—at their entrances. Other buildings were less prepossessing, made of grimy stucco with tin roofing and nothing but worn patches of lifeless earth in front of them. There were electrical lines and factories, low apartment blocks that looked like places to keep prisoners, innumerable small stores and, everywhere, people. It was like a Nadaam crowd, but they were hurrying along, not lingering and chatting they way they did at the festival.

We passed beside a long, high wall, inside of which I glimpsed the familiar roof-lines of Buddhist temples. Gandan monastery, the seat of Buddhism in Mongolia, had been a beacon of Buddhist philosophical and scientific learning. It had been closed a year before they came to destroy Khovor Khan, its monks dispersed, disrobed or killed. Gandan had had a copper statue of Avalokitesvara twenty-five metres tall. Like ours, it had been hauled away. We drove past the main gate, locked tight against intruders, and I wondered why the whole thing had not been razed to the ground like so many others.

We drove down a narrow lane where a pack of wild dogs was scavenging through piles of garbage. The driver honked and tried unsuccessfully to hit them, then pulled to a stop outside one of the grimy stucco and tin constructions. The army captain came around the back to fetch me.

"Here you are, boy," he said. "This will be your home in Ulaan Baatar."

I grabbed my one suitcase and clambered out the back of the truck.

"Ever been in the city?" he asked.

I shook my head.

He clapped me on the back. "Well, enjoy yourself, then! Lots more to keep you busy here than in the countryside."

I thought he might leave then, but he accompanied me through the gate, to the door of the building. I wondered if he had orders to make sure I was received before he let me out of his sight.

"*Solongo ee guai!*" he called out, rapping on the door as one would never do at a ger.

A short, stocky woman opened the door after a minute or so. She looked as though she could easily upend a Nadaam wrestler.

"This is Dash, the new boy," the Captain said. "Dash, this is Solongo, the building manager. She'll take care of you from here. *Bayartai*." He turned and left.

The building manager eyed me briefly, taking my measure. She ushered me in, then closed the door behind me and bolted it. "Follow me," she said, proceeding up a set of narrow stairs. "Where are you from?"

"Arkhangai."

She grunted. "First time in Ulaan Baatar?"

"Yes." It was also my first time on a staircase. My small, battered suitcase thudded against the wall with each step.

"You'll get used to it." She stopped in front of a door, one of six along a dim hallway. "This will be your room. You share with Guyuk." She opened the door to a room in which there were two iron beds with taut sheets and wool blankets of a dull brown, a low shared nightstand, and a plain wooden chest at the base of each bed for belongings. The beds were so close together you could touch one without getting up from the other.

Shooing me in, she remained in the doorway for lack of space. "Down the hall you'll find the toilets, sinks and showers," she said, then cocked her head to one side, examining me more closely. "Have you ever used any of those?"

I shook my head, embarrassed by both her question and my

answer.

"I'll leave the demonstration up to Guyuk. Don't waste the water; you get two minutes a day." Turning to a switch on the wall, she flipped it up and an overhead lamp burned with a feeble light. "Electricity. Don't waste that, either." She turned it off again and the light sputtered out with a fizzling sound.

"Your art school's a few blocks from here. Guyuk will show you." She looked at her watch. "He should be back soon. Breakfast is at seven in the morning, dinner six at night. Curfew is eleven o'clock. If you're late to meals you don't eat. If you miss curfew, you sleep on the street—not to mention the trouble you'll get in. Do you have a timepiece?"

"No."

"Best follow the others, then." She paused for a moment, as though doubtful I was taking this all in. "I'll leave you to settle now. Yours is the bed on the left."

She left the door open. I listened to the creak and groan of the wooden stairs as she plodded her way down them. When she reached the bottom I moved to the only compelling thing in the room: a window, from which I caught a glimpse of distant green.

I was so homesick at the beginning of my time in Ulaan Baatar that every time I saw a man with a horse I fantasized about buying it and galloping back to Erdene. Not that I could; I'd be jailed, or worse, for disobeying a state order. Then I fantasized about writing Erdene and having her join me in the capital, knowing that it would not be allowed either, we couldn't afford it anyway, and she would be miserable if we could.

So I had no choice but to navigate my new situation without her. Living as an art student in Ulaan Baatar was so different from any Mongolian life I had known that it felt as foreign as a distant continent. There were wonders, to be sure, and every one of them I longed to tell my wife about at the end of each day. The marvel of hot, flowing water in the shower, even if it lasted only briefly before shifting unexpectedly to freezing cold. Lights that came on with the flick of a switch and didn't fill the room with any smell at all. A toilet that flushed away human waste. Most of the time. The multitude of large, ornate buildings of stone and cement, with glass windows and stairs and many rooms all under one roof.

I longed to share all the new experiences with Erdene. Not being able to do so took much of the magic out of them, turning them from exciting adventures into sad reminders of what I was missing. At night my loneliness was unbearable. I'd try to fall asleep quickly so as not to have to bear for long the cold feeling of being alone in my bed. But then I'd awake to another's breathing and it would take a moment for me to realize that it was not my beloved's but belonged, instead, to my roommate Guyuk. The disappointment was as fresh and stabbing each time as though it were the first.

Guyuk, a weedy, awkward young man with a pock-marked face, was manic in his enthusiasm for the Party's cause. His relentless zeal, characterized by longwinded speeches that required no reciprocal input from me to fuel them, made my head pound. I'd met deep belief before, in Koke and Tilik. What made Guyuk's different was his obsession with having me agree with him. At the monastery we'd been encouraged to debate. Guyuk didn't want debate. He wanted absolute conversion. He had been educated at a Party school in his home soum and had accepted without question everything they'd told him.

Although Guyuk was happy to discuss politics anywhere, he was at his most vocal at a small bar we went to at the end of each school day. The bar's main attraction was the cheapness of its watered-down beer. I'd never had beer before, but I found I liked it very much after I got used to the bitter side of its taste. The bar was a dark and airless place, with smoke as thick as fog hugging a handful of tables that never stood evenly on the beer-warped wooden floorboards. Every evening the two corner tables were taken up with silent old men playing checkers or card games, while at the middle tables younger men talked loudly about horses, girls, and the virtues of communism. I never heard a dissenter voice his opinion in public.

For these outings, Guyuk always wore the hideous red tie that identified him as a member of the Young Pioneers. Whenever he put that thing on he walked with his chest stuck out as though the tie were an advance guard sent out to impress people about the person behind it. I found it embarrassing, but other young men in the bar often tipped their hats to him in recognition. Most of them wore army style clothing similar to Guyuk's. I always wore a del, having nothing else to put on, looking more in keeping with the old men than the ones my own age.

"Most of the lamas were not holy men at all," Guyuk began with the first sip of his beer one evening, and I knew he was about to launch into one of his favorite topics: the dissolute monastic system and how important it had been to free the country from its yoke.

"Especially the more powerful ones," he continued, as I tried to avoid looking at the tie. "They kept concubines, did you know that? The so-called Holy One had women. How can a monk, the most important monk, have women?"

He was speaking of the eighth Jebtsundamba, our late king.

"And it didn't stop there," he kept on, not needing an answer. "Many monks, even those considered most holy, fornicated amongst themselves as well. Their bad behavior is well documented. The monastic system was more dissolute than the aristocracy. It was very right of the Party to destroy the monasteries, don't you agree?"

I stared into my beer and said nothing, so he began with a fresh list of monastic sins, as though I might be convinced through sheer volume.

"Maybe as a boy you were taught to revere monks. But I'll tell you, they were bad. They drank to excess. The streets of Ulaan Baatar were filled with drunken monks wandering back and forth from the monastery. Filled. Half the men of working age in Mongolia were lazing around like this, feeding off the workers and contributing nothing. What's more, the monks who had positions of trust embezzled funds from their treasuries regularly, making the greediest of them hugely rich while the workers suffered in poverty. No wonder Mongolia couldn't progress under the weight of so much corruption."

"Not all monks were like that," I said quietly so as not to draw attention to myself.

Guyuk leaned towards me confidentially. "That is just what the monks wanted the people to believe. You're not the only one who was fooled; don't feel badly. How could you know what they were really up to behind the monastery walls?"

You have no idea, I wanted to say, but I just looked at the table, not trusting myself to meet his zealous eyes.

He was winding up. "Fornicating, drinking, embezzling funds. These are not holy behaviors. So can you tell me, how is it that men who have taken vows could behave in this way?"

I had considered that question quite a bit myself. "They were human. Who among us has no weakness?"

Guyuk patted me on the shoulder. "You are too innocent, my friend.

Always thinking the best of people. But if one is weak, it's better not to make vows that will not be kept. The Party understands that. They don't expect everyone to be able to do the right thing all the time. So they help the people overcome their weaknesses by always reminding them how to behave. It's for everyone's good, you see?"

I thought about the Party soldiers firing bullets into the heads of monks both weak and strong, and could not see how that had been for anyone's good. Better a few bad monks than none at all. There had to be merit in at least trying to follow the Path, even if one failed. How else could there be any hope in the world?

There was no point in discussing this with Guyuk, however. He was already on to his next diatribe. I drank the rest of my beer and let my thoughts drift to Erdene. She was the one I wanted to be talking with. Or not talking with, and enjoying that too. I wished I were back in her arms, where all questions ceased to matter.

Depite the proselytizing, Guyuk was the closest thing I had to a friend in the city, and he was a tireless guide. He dealt with the prosaic, such as where to get essentials like soap or a razor cheaply, and with the impressive, showing me the columned grandeur of the state theatre and other Soviet-orchestrated testaments to progress.

On one of our days off, when we were wandering around in the central square, a loud voice began to make announcements.

"People of Ulaan Baatar," the voice boomed, "this afternoon at the state theatre the Mongolian People's Party is pleased to offer a new shadow show, *Sukhbaatar; Hero of the Nation*."

Guyuk got very excited. "A new shadow show! Have you ever seen one?"

I had no idea what a shadow show was, but I was more perplexed by where the voice was coming from. I looked all around the square but saw no one. The voice continued on, telling us what time the show was starting and how it cost nothing to attend, thanks to the generosity of the Party.

"Who is speaking?" I asked.

Guyuk started to laugh. "It is the radio," he said, then laughed some more when I still looked blank. "Everyone from the country has the same reaction. Soon they'll have a radio like this in Ikh Tamir too, you'll see. There is a building on the other side of the city, where Party members make announcements into a microphone. The sound travels over wires to that speaker box over there," he said, pointing to a wooden post with a speaker on the top.

I wondered if Guyuk had asked the same question when he had first heard it. He was clearly enjoying his superior knowledge now.

"I suppose you don't know what a shadow show is, then," he said.

Although I was irked to display my ignorance twice in a row, I had to shake my head.

"You'll love it. You sit in a dark theatre and moving pictures are projected on a big screen in front of you, to tell a story. You see it all happening as though it were real, with all the sounds, and even the people speaking."

It sounded amazing, but I wasn't going to give him the satisfaction of my saying so. "My imagination does that on its own."

"We have to go see it. I can get us seats, I'll bet, so we don't have to stand with the crowd at the back."

"How will you manage that?"

He pulled on his red tie and grinned. "I have connections. If we go to the Revolutionary Museum now there may be someone there who will help us."

Off we went. The Revolutionary Museum was one of Guyuk's favorite places to visit, although it was small and the displays never changed. It was a celebration of all he held dear and he always entered the dull cement building reverentially, lowering his head slightly and speaking softly as though entering a temple.

"You stay here," he whispered when we were in the main room. "I'll go to the offices upstairs and try to find my friend."

Listlessly I looked around at what he'd taken me to see many times before. A handful of other people studied the exhibits intensely, and for the few words they uttered to each other they used the same hushed tones as Guyuk. Some took notes on small pads of paper. The display cases were perfectly clean and polished, with neat hand-written signs glued to each one: do not touch the glass. The room still smelled faintly of the vinegar that was used to keep the glass pristine. Among the exhibits were photos and statistics of the pre-revolutionary situation in Mongolia— that is, what the Revolutionaries felt they were saving us from—and materials explaining the organization of our new government.

I looked at this Party version of the old Mongolia and wondered how much was actually true. There were shocking statistics about the poverty of the people and the wealth of the monasteries and feudal lords. An example of confiscated wealth from a single lord had been set out so people could get an idea of what had been "hoarded" by these masters before the revolution. 1,422 horses, 2,046 sheep, similar numbers of other livestock, 45,000 tugrogs, 136 bolts of silk, 12 wooden boxes inlaid with gold, 93 necklaces and bracelets of gold and jewels, 27 golden Buddhist statues, and more. It was almost incomprehensible compared to the handful of things that could have been listed from my father's home of the same time, or even the relatively secure one I had now.

Some samples of confiscated luxuries had been laid out in a display case. A finely engraved silver striker and knife lay beside a jade necklace and an onyx snuff bottle. There was an inlaid wooden box with brass handles not unlike the one in which Bayan had hidden his money, and I wondered if any of these other things had belonged to his family. The Revolutionary Museum wanted to portray people like him as monsters. But although he had behaved as a lord, even at the monastery, he had never seemed like a monster to me. He had been my friend.

Guyuk came back grinning broadly with success. Sidling up to me like someone trying to sell contraband goods, he showed me the tickets in a quick flash.

He glanced at the display cases in front of us. "Terrible, wasn't it, what the wealthy kept from the rest of us? Such inequality." Then he pocketed the tickets without a trace of irony, and led the way back out on to the street.

Coming from life in the middle of the untouched steppes, it was hard to fathom going into a big building and watching people and places unfold on a huge screen in front of me as though they were real life. But that is just what happened at the shadow show. The story was about Sukhbaatar who, in his role of ousting the Chinese Revolutionaries and the opposing but equally rapacious White Baron, had become a national hero. Never mind that in using Russian Red Army help Sukhbaatar had accidentally ushered in Moscow's own brand of oppression. He had died within the first year of their government, which made him the perfect hero, unassailable for the murders, disappearances and appropriations that followed his noble actions.

The film didn't dwell on any of the bad things. Watching it was like having one of Gan's epic stories come to life. Although it was in black and white, my mind filled in the colours instinctively. When Sukhbaatar raised his banner to lead his troops into battle it was so stirring that I almost leapt up to follow him myself. When the cavalry galloped across the screen to the sound of pounding hooves and blasting rifles I was ready to dive for cover. When the music came on at the moment Sukhbaatar took his place in the new Mongolian People's Party, it made me want to cheer for his victory.

The medium's power lay in its seamlessness. It melded into my head so I lost track of what was being presented and what I was imagining, like having a machine feed you the sensations you might get from a fantasy. Even while I understood it was propaganda, I found myself wanting to believe every bit of it was true.

It was a wondrous thing, and it scared me.

CHAPTER TWENTY

THE FOREST HAS TREES BOTH
TALL AND SHORT; THE MULTITUDE HAS MEN
BOTH GOOD AND BAD.

The Art Academy was a Moscow-directed institution whose Russian teachers, their strange complexions as pale as fish bellies, followed a strict political agenda. I was very excited to have real experts teach me, but I bristled at the way we were always made to emulate the Soviet style of socialist realism. In our exercises we could venture towards early modern concepts such as impressionism, but the only time we were shown anything as extreme as a cubist painting was to make sure we understood how ridiculous it was. Our teacher explained socialist realism's objectives by quoting from the Russian Literary Gazette: *The masses demand of an artist honesty, truthfulness, and a revolutionary, socialist realism in the representation of the proletarian revolution.*

The studio where we painted was on the second floor of the plain, square box that was the Academy building. It was roomy for the fourteen students in our class, and bright with light that flooded in from windows at our back. Our tall wooden stools were positioned in a neat row, an easel in front of each one. We were not allowed to move them around. I was assigned the third stool from the left.

A few weeks into our classes we had a lesson on chiaroscuro techniques. We had been instructed on the idea by examining Caravaggio's *The Calling of Saint Mathew* and I was excited to try it, for I felt that it would solve the problem of flatness that made my scenes of daily life dull. The day before, we had been given squares of cardboard with a scene outlined on them already, and had begun the process of filling it in with oils in a way that would demonstrate our understanding of the lesson.

Everyone worked on the same scene, of a family inside their ger taking possession of a radio. The father had just pulled the device out of a box, while the mother and two children looked on excitedly. An old woman sat to one side on a bed. All the faces were penciled in, but in the process of painting we were to bring them to life. The light source was, naturally, the hole at the top of the ger, but we could take artistic license and angle it a little to our own taste.

By the end of the second day my painting was taking shape well. I had set the light so it shone mostly on the eager faces of the mother and children, lit the father's proud face from the side, and left the grandmother in dimmer light in the background. I paid no attention to what anyone else in the class was doing, concentrating only on my own work. Towards the close of the session our teacher, who had wandered among us the whole time but offered little direction, had us all stop.

"All right class," he began in his Russian accented, but precise, Mongolian. "Let us look at some of the work that has been done today." He stopped at the easel of one of the better artists of the group and peered at the painting through little half-glasses that were perched partway down his big, straight nose. Then he held it up so everyone could see. "Cheren here has made a good start. The light comes in at a strong angle, he needs only to intensify it a little. He could shine it more on the faces of the children, for example, which are a delight." The boy and girl wore beatific expressions, as though they were in a state of religious bliss.

He moved to mine, and I felt a surge of pleased anticipation.

After studying it intently for a moment, however, he frowned. But he still held it up to show the others. "This is a fine example of too much technique. Dash has applied chiaroscuro forcefully but has failed to communicate the central idea. Technique means nothing if it doesn't bring the emotion of the scene to life. Here, in fact, the chiaroscuro is getting in the way of the story."

My face burned with humiliation and anger as the teacher continued. "The father looks pleased, but the deep pride he would feel on bringing home a marvel like the radio is obscured by the way the strong light glances off his face. And his family, are they happy enough?"

Everyone in the room guessed the answer and shook their heads on cue.

"The light is washing out what are, to begin with, expressions that do not quite hit the mark," the teacher said. "Then we come to the grandmother. She lies in shadow, forgotten. Quite unacceptable. What kind of decent herding family treats their grandmother like that?"

He handed the painting back to me distractedly while casting around the room for a better example, and set his sights on Guyuk's easel. Guyuk was easily the least able student in the class, and this work was no exception. He had positioned the light directly overhead so that everyone received equal illumination, completely missing the technical idea.

"This work may lack a little in the application of chiaroscuro, but it is more than makes up in the emotions of the characters." I looked at it, disbelieving. The family had the vapid but mesmerized expressions of idiots watching a carnival, with the father as the barking showman. They were crudely rendered, as well. "You see how overwhelmed everyone is at their good fortune," our teacher continued. "And we can see it because they all get some light. Chiaroscuro is not a technique to use for the sake of it. In this softer application, no one is left in the shadows. Look here at the grandmother. You can almost feel for yourself how happy she is to have lived long enough to see her family join the modern age." He nodded, satisfied. "Good work, Guyuk."

Later, over beer, Guyuk couldn't stop talking about it. We were in our usual place where the old men played cards. Guyuk had grabbed his favorite table, the one smack in the middle of the room where he could be seen by everyone. Having a beer with him was the last thing I felt like doing at that moment, but he had insisted. He was like that; clingy and always wanting to do things together. I could never seem to just go someplace by myself.

"I couldn't believe it when the teacher picked mine," he said.

I was in complete agreement, but he was so obviously pleased I didn't want to say so. It didn't matter; he went on anyway.

"I spent a lot of time thinking about the light, in fact. How with it coming from the top it would be equal for everybody, which seemed right to me."

I nodded my head without conviction.

"And the happiness of the family, I was glad that came through. Do you think it did?"

"Yes."

"That's good. I was especially pleased about that."

I took a few good swallows of beer.

"Of course, you're much more talented than I am. Anyone can see that. But in class today, the teacher addressed an important issue: communication." Guyuk hit the table with his fist for emphasis.

"I was communicating," I said.

157

Guyuk shook his head in the special, patronizing way he had when he felt I was just not getting something. "But *what* were you communicating? Your own ideas? That's not the point. Our art has a job to do. That's what counts."

I was getting a feeling I'd been here before. "It has to be selfless, you mean?"

"Yes, that's it exactly! For the benefit of the people. Not for our own satisfaction."

"Guyuk, don't you ever just want to express your own views?"

He looked truly astonished. "But I am."

It's impossible to argue with a zealot.

"You think about it," he went on. "It's important to understand the reason for painting. It will come up again and again."

And he was right. A few weeks later we began portraiture. This I found fascinating, and practiced all the time, even outside of class. I was particularly interested in the eyes and how much they revealed about personality and emotion. What we were exclusively directed to convey, however, was a nobility of expression that came from dedication to the Cause. You couldn't show sadness, weariness or, worse, bewilderment. The result was that we produced portraits of every petty bureaucrat in the city, and they all looked as though they shared the same mind. Which, I suppose, might have been the case.

I tried delving into their eyes to bring them to life for myself. One day we had as our sitter the Deputy Chief of Civic Cleanliness. He was newly appointed, fresh out of school and had never organized anyone or anything before. It showed in his fleshy, soft face. He wore a studied expression of authority that spread itself too thinly over his plainly visible lack of confidence.

My portrait of him showed exactly that. I captured the hesitation in his eyes, and the tiniest downturn of the mouth where it would, in a confident man, go straight across.

When we had finished our work, the teacher asked for a show of hands. "Which of your works do you think most reflects our esteemed Deputy Chief?" he asked, going around the easels one by one. "Cheren?" Three hands. "Bourtai?" One hand. "Guyuk?" No hands. "Dash?" Eight hands. The majority of our group.

"That's interesting," said the teacher. "And Honoured Deputy, which one do you prefer of yourself?"

The Deputy looked around uncertainly at the many images of himself that dotted the room. Finally he settled on Cheren's.

"This is the one I like best."

The teacher smiled and the Deputy looked vastly relieved, as though he had just passed a critical test.

"And does anyone know why?" asked the teacher. No one raised their hand.

"Because it shows the real man within," he answered for us. "The leader. The man who will be." The Deputy smiled and nodded at our teacher, pleased with this interpretation. "Portraiture," the teacher went on, "is not photography, it is a creative act. We use it to show what is important to know about a person, not what we might think we see."

Another lesson learned.

Frequently during my dutiful conjuring of idyllic communist scenes I thought of Tilik. It was ironic that after all his attempts to rid me of my attachment to my own art, the Party was managing to accomplish what his efforts had not. But he would not have been happy about it. I corrupted what I knew to be the truth with every painting. Yet what could I do? The census man had made it clear that a lack of co-operation would be dangerous not just for me but, more importantly, for Erdene.

When I asked myself what Tilik would do in the same situation the answer was bleak. He would never be in the same situation. He would never have fallen in love with a woman and promised to take care of her. He would never have sold his soul for a vague promise of artistic recognition. He would never have let fear compromise his principles.

In fact, he would never have left the cave.

From the beginning, the confines of the city stifled me in a way the walls of Khovor Khan had never done. You could see over the top of Khovor Khan's walls, for one thing, to the endless blue sky and the hills and plains. In Ulaan Baatar the buildings hemmed everything into too tight a space—the people, the walls, the motorcars and army jeeps, the eye's freedom to see.

So I began to walk out towards the hills that surrounded the city. The first time I went out it was our weekly day off from school, a beautiful, sunny day that wasn't too hot. I made the mistake of mentioning at lunch that I was thinking of going for a walk and Guyuk, ever my shadow, jumped right in.

"What a wonderful idea," he beamed. "Such a good day for a walk. Exercise, yes, that's what we need to keep us from turning into flabby artists! I know exactly where to go."

"I was just going to follow my nose." I wanted to go alone, not with company.

"Oh, but it's too easy to pick the wrong path and end up somewhere less pleasant. I know them all. I'll show you."

I tried to get out of the house while he was going to the toilet, but he caught up with me outside.

"Trying to escape me?" he asked cheerfully, as though he never suspected that was exactly the case.

"I didn't know where you'd ended up," I lied.

"Never mind, I'm here now. Come on, this is the best way." He led me up into the nearest of the hills but soon began to complain about the effort. We were only halfway up when he started campaigning to go back home, and grew so annoying that I finally agreed.

Thereafter he continued to come with me, even though it was clear he didn't want to. It didn't matter what kind of subterfuge I tried, he always appeared at my side before I'd reached the end of our street. When I took advantage of the lengthening evenings and skipped dinner in order to walk, he skipped it too, then ruined the peace of my outing by complaining about his hunger. When I got to a spot I liked I'd stop and sit, still and comfortable, and look out at the view I'd gained. Guyuk hated sitting still. He'd pace around and suggest we leave a dozen times before I'd finally get tired of arguing and start back in grumpy silence. It was intensely irritating the way he clung to my presence like a foal that can't separate from its mother.

After a few weeks, again on our day off, he said he really wanted to go see the circus at the state theatre. Thinking this was my opportunity, I told him I was going to walk to the top of Chingeltei, one of the four holy mountains surrounding the city. It was a trek that would take all day and involve missing lunch. He tried to talk me into the circus, but I stood firm.

"Well, I'm sure a walk is better for us anyway," he said with a sigh.

"But there's no need for you to give up the circus. I can find my on way up the mountain now."

He put his hand on my shoulder in a friendly clasp. "I wouldn't hear of it," he said, but I could see he was really disappointed. "I feel responsible for you here, like an older brother."

"I'm fine on my own."

"No, I want to come with you."

I could not shake him. We were not even half way up the mountain when he stopped, using his need for a drink from his water flask as an excuse.

"Look at this view," he said, exaggerating his words as though he were trying to convince a child of something special. "It's spectacular, isn't it? You don't even have to go all the way to the top to see many beautiful things."

Ulaan Baatar sprawled below us with all the grace of a drunk who has collapsed in the street, its limbs flung out with no sense of purpose. Beyond it stood the three other holy mountains, and soft rolling hills, but the foreground of the city was what struck the eye.

"It will be much better from the top," I said. "From there you can see out the other direction too, away from the city."

He looked around at the sky. "I don't know, Dash. Those clouds look like they could bring in a downpour, and I'm not dressed for it."

A sudden downpour was always a possibility in Mongolia, but it seemed unlikely to me.

"Why don't you go do what you want?" I said. "If you go back now you can still catch the circus. I can manage fine. I know my way around now."

Instead of jumping at the opportunity he began to fidget, glancing around nervously as though there were spies in the bushes when we were actually very much alone.

"I should really go with you."

"You don't need to." I looked at his fretful face and the way he wrung his hands together. It finally dawned on me why he was there. "Have you been assigned to follow me?"

Guyuk looked so crestfallen I knew right away that it was true. I was appalled, not just by his capacity to do such a thing, but by my own gullibility in mistaking spying for friendship, as irritating as his companionship might have been.

"The Party asked me, as your roommate, to keep an eye out for you. To help you integrate, you see. Help you understand the virtues of Socialism and all the wonderful things it's doing for Mongolia."

"You mean they didn't want me doing anything foolish, like running away or encouraging discord."

"It's understandable enough that the leader of your soum wants to make sure he gets his prized artist back."

"I thought you were my friend. What an idiot I've been! How often do you report to the Party?"

Guyuk's eyes looked anywhere but at mine. "Twice a week. But I am your friend. I've only said good things."

"That's because I haven't done anything that could be said against me." Not that it made a difference. People denounced others with total fabrications in order to get ahead themselves. It was common knowledge.

"The Party," began Guyuk nervously, "you won't tell them you know?"

"What would they do if I did? Do they pay you for this service? Will you lose your beer money?"

"Much worse: I'll lose my position at the art school. I'm not lucky like you, with real talent and intelligence. I was only allowed in because I agreed to do this kind of thing for them." He looked pathetic.

"Don't worry. I won't tell them. And I won't run away or do anything stupid. I have no desire to create trouble for myself."

"You're a good man, Dash." He grinned like an idiot in his relief.

"But you have to stop following me."

The grin disappeared. "How can I do that?"

"You can make your reports from when we go to the school or for a drink, and when we're at the boarding house. But when I walk you can't come anymore. That's my condition."

"You don't think they'll get suspicious if I no longer report any walks at all?"

"Make one up once in awhile. Say only positive things, mind you. If they pick me up to question me, the first thing I'm going to tell them is that you failed to keep your mission a secret from me."

Guyuk nodded furiously. "Positive, yes, only ever positive."

"So," I said, gesturing down the mountain towards the city, "you can go back now." He stood rooted to the spot, incapacitated by the risk involved in his sudden freedom. "Go on, it's all right. I won't do anything foolish and I promise to tell you all about my walk when I get back."

He left then, reluctantly, and I continued up the mountain with a lightness of spirit that felt as though I had been carrying him on my back up until then. The climb focused my thoughts. I felt each welcome pull of air into my labouring lungs, and the steady rhythm of my steps. I became acutely aware of what was underfoot; crunching stone, a springy bed of aromatic thyme, a patch of soft, silent sand. As I climbed higher the great blue sky grew wider and the earth revealed itself all around me in an endless sea of rolling hills.

How I had missed my prayers and contemplations since coming to the city. My brain had become cluttered, like a box accumulating junk that badly needed sorting through and throwing out. It contained letters to Erdene of the kind I would not be able to write, the only safe letter being a dull one; technicalities of the art I was learning to create; fears of the future and what might be asked of me; longing for the serenity of the countryside; worry about how I was beginning to forget whole passages of prayers through lack of use.

These things and many more slowly dissipated like mist under the sun by the time I reached the top and turned to face the Pure Lands to the north. In peaceful solitude I sat upon the holy mountain and turned my troubled mind to the Noble Truths and the light of the Path that still strove to shine, however dimly, in the core of my soul. I went deep inside and saw it there, like the fading flicker of a cooling fire. I made promises to Tara that I would not be able to keep; promises about meditation, conscientiousness, and right action. I let myself believe these promises contained karmic power. But right intention is not the same thing as right action. In Buddhism, as in life, right intention means nothing at all.

Chapter Twenty One

FLEEING FROM THE FIRE,
ONE FALLS INTO THE WATER.

After a few weeks in which he wrung his hands over every fake report he filed, Guyuk began to warm to his compositions. He went from fretting to boasting about his cleverness in making up things we had supposedly done together.

"Read this one," he said of his latest. "I'm really getting the details now." He pointed out the parts he felt were best, jabbing at the page with his finger. "Here, look: *Subject stopped in square to sit on bench. Subject looked melancholy. Discussed virtues of socialist progress. Subject became lively in debate. Rain ended conversation and we returned to residence.* Or this part here: *Subject had one beer and paid with small change.* You see? I add specifics, like *one* beer and the fact that you used coins rather than a bill to pay, and that gives it realism. Maybe I should take journalism courses instead of art."

As he grew more confident in his fibbing, I grew more confident about my freedom of movement. I went to visit the closed-up monastery of Gandan Khiid. No one was allowed inside; the surrounding walls were high and the big wooden gate was barred. I circumnavigated the place as though circling a very large sacred ovuu. While I walked, I studied the tops of the temples and dharma halls that still rose above the outer walls.

It was dusk, and the streets were almost empty. Inside the monastery, sparrows and pigeons flew from one building-top to another, the only residents of an institution that had once housed one of Mongolia's largest and brightest monastic populations. The occasional chirp or coo was the only sound. I stopped at the entrance, taking in its beautiful upswept rooflines, its many menacing demons—who had not managed to protect the monastery from closure—and the rich decoration of the façade. The double wooden doors, painted deep red, were shut tight, with not even a tiny hole through which to peer inside.

Barred as I was from entry, physical or visual, I still felt Gandan call to me. I pressed my forehead to the wood of the gate and put my palms flat against it. The music of a thousand sutras floated into me, the smell of incense and butter lamps filled my nose. My lips began to move as I fell into quietly chanting along with what I heard clearly in my head.

In the midst of my soothing commune with the ghosts of Gandan Khiid, I felt a hand grasp my shoulder. Military police! All images of the monastery flew from my head as I froze in place, paralyzed with fear as I waited for the barked orders: *hands above your head, turn around slowly, what are you doing here, you are under arrest.*

But the voice that spoke was quiet, almost tremulous. "You should not be here, my brother."

I turned cautiously to see an old man, thin as a wisp of smoke and dressed in a threadbare del that might once have been the same deep red as the monastery gates. He smiled serenely.

"What you were doing is very dangerous," he said.

"Yes, Master. I couldn't help myself."

"That is all well and good, but there are safer places for this. Even now, it is possible." He looked around, not furtively, but it was clear he had become accustomed to checking. "Why don't you walk with me awhile?"

"I have only a short time before curfew."

"A short time is sufficient. Which way are you going?"

I told him my direction and we began to walk together, looking like any grandfather and his grandson making their way home at the end of the day. It was just as well, for what we discussed was highly illegal.

The old monk's name was Dampildorg. He was part of a group of four who had been resident at Gandan and had been considered too feeble at its closure to bother with execution, jail or army service. In a very unsocialist manner they had simply been put out on the street to find their own, new way. It was through the kindness of common Mongolians that the monks now lived together in a ger in the sprawling suburbs west of the city, where they kept sacred texts stuffed in mattresses, prayer wheels under the floorboards, and Buddha statues in flour bins.

They prayed, every day, keeping the same schedule they had for decades.

I told him of Khovar Khan, its terrible end, and how I now lived as a lay person. I told him how difficult it was to maintain regular prayers and meditations with all the daily work of a herder and he nodded, not saying anything, which made me feel ashamed to have given my faith so little effort.

We came to the corner at which we had to go our separate ways and stood facing each other. I didn't want to let him go.

"A master needs a novice," he said, as though sensing my own need.

"But I am a married man now."

"Are you still a seeker?"

"I still seek." My heart was wild with hope but I tried to present the disciplined face of a worthy pupil.

"Do you know the ger camps to the west, beside the horse market?"

"I know where they are."

"If you should come there, ask anyone where the four old men live and they will tell you how to find us."

I practically wept with joy. "Thank you, Master."

Dampildorg bowed slightly to me, palms together. I bowed lower, and we parted. I rushed back to the dormitory with the excitement of a child who has found a precious missing object under the bed. It seemed my promises to Tara were already having an effect. I was careful to hide my feelings from Guyuk, however.

"Where did you go this time?" he asked when I returned to our room. "I have to make my report." He liked to have some facts before he started his fictions.

"I walked around the city, examining the architecture in the evening light. It gives a kind of chiaroscuro effect that is useful to study," I said.

"What a good idea. I'll say that we did that together so it looks good for me, too."

"The theater is particularly grand with its large columns. I just noticed that for the first time tonight, how powerful it looks." What I really noticed is how easily I lied. I would have to send special prayers to Buddha after the lights were out.

But Guyuk was thrilled, believing my words were proof that I was beginning to embrace the marvels of Soviet domination.

"You see? I know it's taken some time. The big city is hard to get used to at first, but then you start to see just how great our progress has been since the Party began bringing us forward." He nodded his head up and down, agreeing with himself. "I'm very pleased. My report will be so easy today! I won't have to make anything up."

The next evening I went directly to find the monks' ger after classes were done, telling Guyuk I was going for one of my long hill walks. I went in the direction Dampildorg had told me, west of the horse market, and came to a neighbourhood where high wood fences partitioned off yards of bare earth with a single ger in the middle of each one. Children played stick games in the long, dusty laneways that ran the length of the fences. Most of the gates into the enclosures were open, and through them I saw families doing all the things they used to do in the countryside, before they came in search of jobs: pounding felt out of wool, weaving rope from yak hair, repairing tack, playing cards. The smell of open latrines hung in the air.

"Good evening, revered mother," I said to an old woman who was leaning against her gate jamb, idly watching the children play. Behind her the family dog barked at me and strained wildly at the rope that tied him to a stake in the ground. "Do you know which ger is home to the four old men?" I shouted over the din.

She looked me over as though assessing my trustworthiness, then threw a stone at the dog to silence him. He skulked off to lie beside the ger at the farthest reach of his rope. "Everyone knows the four old men," she said at last. "Go to the first lane that crosses this one, turn left, and walk over three lanes. Turn left again. Theirs is the second ger on the right."

"Thank you. Spill fat."

There was no dog at the enclosure of the monks. "Dampildorg!" I called out as I passed through their gate. "*Nokhoi khor!*"

After a brief period of scuffling inside the ger, Dampildorg stuck his head out the door. As soon as he saw who it was, he smiled broadly.

"Dash, how good to see you. Come in, come in."

Their ger was sparsely furnished with four Soviet-issue iron beds, a low table but no stools, a single kitchen cupboard, and a small, battered traveling trunk. Dampildorg gave me tea and introduced me to the other monks, who were sitting on the floorboards of the ger.

"Chinua, Delger, Tumen." In their thin, wizened states they looked remarkably similar to one another. I sat down on the floor with them.

"We were just discussing how it is possible to contemplate the self versus the not-self while in the fourth *dhyana*, since being there implies

167

a state of non-being in the first place," said Chinua.

"I am not advanced enough to participate," I said. "I will listen."

And so I did. It made me aware of how much I had been drifting spiritually since the loss of my master at Khovor Khan. It takes many lifetimes for a monk to become enlightened, and it's not a journey one can accomplish alone. The more highly realized monks guide those who are still finding their way along the Path. For a novice, trying to gain enlightenment without a master is like trying to cross the ocean without an understanding of the stars. I had been lost, drifting through a secular life that was gratifying my human desires but was far from the course I had set at Khovor Khan. In listening to the four old monks I felt I had stumbled back onto it.

For the next few weeks I continued to visit them. They began to test me, as good masters do, and I gained confidence in my answers back to them as my early lessons reasserted themselves. With every visit it began to feel more normal, the atmosphere in the ger a salve against the reality of arrests and oppression outside their gate.

"Do you not fear getting caught?" I asked them one day.

Dampildorg shrugged. "When they closed Gandan Khiid we thought we would be sent to prison, or killed, but we were not. We have already faced the worst possibilities, and yet we are still here, able to continue our prayers. So we must."

"One cannot predict the future," said Chinua, "except to know that we will not last forever. But each day that we wake up here is a gift we must not squander. To worry is fruitless."

It seemed so simple when he said it that way, so obvious. Tilik had also tried to teach me to exist in the now. I still had much to learn.

The next day I brought with me a tiny block of wood I had secretly prepared with gesso, and my oil paints.

"I am going to paint you a small thangka," I announced. "Who would you like on it?"

They gathered around my supplies excitedly.

"Can you paint White Tara?" asked Delger, the quiet one. "She has always been my favorite."

"She is my favorite, too," agreed Tumen.

"It should be Avalokitesvara," said Chinua.

"I suppose there is not enough room to do both," said Dampildorg.

"What if I paint Avalokitesvara first, and then, when I get another chance, I will paint Tara," I suggested.

"Oh, yes," they all agreed, "that is an excellent idea."

Their softly chanted prayers were a perfect accompaniment while I gave myself over to painting the miniscule thangka, happy to be able to give something back to these monks who had given so much to me over the previous few weeks. Occasionally, when they were chanting a prayer of which I was particularly fond, I stopped painting and closed my eyes to concentrate on the words. I felt a serenity I hadn't experienced in years.

After a few hours, when they had completed their prayers, I stood up. "I must return before curfew," I said. "The thangka is not quite finished, but this layer needs to dry before I can add the details."

They gathered around to inspect my work..

"It has been so long since we've seen a thangka," said Delger, close to tears.

"It is very fine," said Chinua.

"Avalokitesvara will be so pleased," said Tumen.

Dampildorg put an arm around my shoulders. "We will need much patience to wait for your return to finish it."

When I returned to my rooms a letter from Erdene was waiting for me on my bed. It had been opened, of course. The Party didn't bother with the subtleties of steaming and resealing, preferring the intimidation of openly reading people's mail. The time it took for their spying, as well as the slowness of getting letters to the post in the first place, meant I always got them weeks after they'd been written. The Party knew all the family news from past letters: that Dadal was to marry Bat before the end of summer and that she would go live with him at his family's camp, that my wife's favorite mare had produced twins, that her grandmother was sick.

"Have you read it, too?" I asked Guyuk, who was sitting on his own bed studying.

He shook his head. "I'm not allowed. I'm only supposed to follow you."

I pulled out the letter and my heart warmed at the familiar sight of Erdene's writing. Her dogged practice had made it as precise and fluid as any monk's. It was a short letter, right to the point.

She was pregnant. The ardent unions of our final nights together had created our first child. If I studied well, I could be home in time for the birth.

A piece of flotsam drifted in on the river of joy that flooded me. The flotsam was fear. Now I had an extra reason to do whatever the Party wanted, and the Party knew it too. Suddenly my sessions with the four monks felt recklessly dangerous, not the soothing, uplifting encounters I had thought them to be. What had I been thinking? I couldn't possibly continue to see them now that so much was at stake.

A couple of days later I returned to the monks' neighbourhood. I would finish the thangka I'd started, then tell them I could no longer risk being a part of their prayers, no matter how much it had come to mean to me.

As I walked through the alleys between the ger enclosures in their neighbourhood, I noticed there was none of the usual bustle of children playing. The few adults I saw glanced at me and quickly turned the other way. There were whispers and worried glances. The old woman who had first given me directions, and who was often hanging about her gate watching the laneway, peaked at me through her ger door and then slammed it shut.

When I arrived at the monks' enclosure, their gate was off its hinge and propped against the outside wall. Inside there was no ger. All that remained was a tell-tale circle of worn earth. I stared in disbelief.

"There's no need to come here anymore, Dash."

The speaker stepped out from the gate of the enclosure across the way. He was dressed in military clothes. I didn't recognise him.

"Who are you?"

"A friend of your mayor. A concerned friend." He came towards me casually, as though there was nothing unusual about our meeting.

"You've done very well, leading us to these treacherous monks. The Party is grateful to you."

His words were like a kick to the gut that left me gasping for air. The man took my elbow, perhaps to support me, but also to lead me away in a manner that made us appear to be chummy collaborators.

"It's very important that you comport yourself wisely, Dash. The mayor would not look kindly on having his cultural investment fail on him. That would go badly for everyone."

I was too stunned to do anything but let him lead me away, my mind reeling with questions I knew I couldn't ask about the fate of the four kind, wise monks who had given me so much peace. In going to them I had thought only of my own needs, concerned only with the risk I was taking for myself and my family. My selfishness had betrayed them as surely as if I really had been a Party spy.

Silent, wide-eyed children poked their heads out from the safety of their gates to stare as we went by. When we passed the old woman, she came out of her ger to scream at me.

"Traitor!" she shrieked. "May evil spirits torment you through infinite lives!"

We kept on walking. A stone hit the back of my head with a sharp stab of pain and I lurched forward from the impact, but the military man just kept pulling me firmly along with him. I imagined the monks being herded along this same lane. Had they been marched out at gunpoint for all to witness, or had they been thrown into the back of a closed truck? I felt a trickle of blood dribbling down my neck from the cut at the back of my head. Would they kill the monks, having spared them once? Would they be separated and sent into exile in Siberia? I couldn't decide which fate was worse.

Just beyond the edge of the neighbourhood we rounded a corner and a jeep was there waiting for us.

"The lodging house," the military man barked to the driver when we climbed in.

As we sped away, I wondered what had become of the unfinished thangka.

When I returned to the lodging house, Guyuk's things were gone and his bed linen had been changed and smoothed flat. No-one in the house said a word about him; it was as though he had never lived there at all. The next day his place was taken by an exceptionally dull young man of similarly modest artistic talent but tremendous tenacity in following me around. We hardly spoke over the five months that remained of my time in the city. There were no more trips to the cinema, or beers after class ended for the day, or spirited lectures on the many benefits of socialism. There was only the monotonous repetition of study-eat-sleep, and his silent, oppressive presence that trailed behind me everywhere like a dark cloud.

I focused on performing well enough to be allowed to go home before my child was born. I took no walks and never meditated. In the classroom, my sudden devotion to perfecting the socialist realism style was received with the guileless confidence of the true believer; better to accept it as happy evidence that I had finally come to my artistic senses, rather than question its authenticity. My growing mastery of the style earned me many enthused claps on the back from our teacher. He might as well have been sticking me with a knife, the way my essence seemed to trickle from the wound of every whack.

In the Red Mouse month, scant weeks before Erdene's due date, the school decided I was ready to be released. I was driven back to Ikh Tamir, this time in the front of a truck whose payload was supplies instead of people. The driver was a garrulous type who apparently enjoyed having some company on the trip, for he talked incessantly even after I stopped responding in the hope of some silence. As we got closer to home my longing for Erdene grew until I could barely contain my excitement. I imagined seeing her big round belly for the first time, imagined feeling the kicking life within, touching her skin, drawing my fingers through her hair, breathing in the scent of the chamomile that she used to keep it silky. But when we reached the place where the driver had to turn south, he continued along the dusty road.

"You must go across the open country here to reach my ger," I said.

"Oh, but the mayor said I was to bring you first to him. He will receive you while I unload my supplies, then we will carry on to your ger."

It would only be a brief interruption, but by then I had become so anxious to see Erdene that my disappointment was intense, like a baby who has had a sweet ripped from his grasp just before it gets to his mouth. My training in patience completely deserted me. I drummed my fingertips on my knees, I huffed and sighed. We reached Ikh Tamir and stopped outside the town hall, an uninspired cube of grey cement, two stories high, with mean little windows and absolutely no decoration. Soviet grandeur was apparently not to be wasted on the provinces.

I got out of the truck. "Bring your portfolio," said the driver. "He wants to see your work."

Dutifully I got my portfolio out of the back and went inside the town hall. The mayor's office was on the first floor, guarded by a middle-aged woman who wore the pinched expression of the perpetually miserable. She was banging away slowly on a dusty black typewriter—I had first seen them at the school in Ulaan Baatar—with three alternating layers of carbon and white paper extruding from the machine.

"Sain baan uu," I said politely. "I am Dash Chuluuny. The mayor has asked to see me."

She continued to type without looking up or responding; a decisive bam on one of the brass keys, pause, bam bam, pause, bam. She re-read what she had just written. Then she looked at me with squinty eyes. "I will check when he can see you," she said, and got up from her chair. A arm's length away was the door to the mayor's office, which she opened just enough to stick her head around. "Sir, the artist is here."

The mayor said something I couldn't hear, and the secretary extracted her head and closed the door. "One half hour," she announced. "You may sit on that stool there."

I sat on the stool, the lone piece of furniture in the corridor beside the woman's desk and chair. She was not wearing a watch, and there was no clock to be seen. I wondered how anyone would know when one half hour was up, then I realized that it would be up whenever the mayor decided he had made me wait long enough.

The typing machine banged on, making it impossible for me to go to a quiet place in my head to search for patience. I closed my eyes and tried to concentrate on my breathing, in and out, and not on the irregular clacking and the loud ping as the end of each line was finally reached. Eventually there was another sound, a dreadful sharp buzz from inside the mayor's office.

"You can go in," said the secretary.

I picked up my portfolio and entered his office, a large room whose relative emptiness dwarfed the mayor and his furniture, which consisted of a plain wooden desk with a closed back, two wooden chairs for guests, a padded but well-worn chair for the mayor, and a black metal filing cabinet with many dents.

"Welcome back," said the mayor. "Your report from the art school is very good. I have always had a good eye for talent of all kinds."

I wondered what the school had said about me. The students didn't get the reports, only their sponsors did. "Thank you, sir."

"Did you enjoy it?" he asked, which surprised me a little because I didn't think enjoyment was part of what they expected me to get from my studies.

"It was very stimulating," I said, uncertain how he wanted me to answer. "I think I learned a great deal."

"Your teachers believe so." He paused for a moment, and then when it became clear that I wasn't able to guess what he wanted me to say, he supplied the words for me. "It was a great opportunity for you. I hope you appreciate your good fortune."

"Yes, it was indeed a great opportunity. I hope I continue to be worthy."

That seemed to please him. He nodded. "Let's see your work, then."

I opened the portfolio and laid the six paintings I'd brought with me out on his desk. Two were portraits, one a landscape of the hills around Ulaan Baatar, and the other three were socialist realist scenes of proletariat life. The mayor was smiling openly, looking at each carefully, standing back and then examining them up close.

"Good, very good, yes, well worth the investment," he said. He looked up at me. "You may leave these here and go to your home now."

Leave them? "I had hoped to show them to my family."

The mayor chuckled and shook his head at the same time. "Dash, comrade, these are not for you, these are the property of the Party, surely you understand. Payment for the investment we've made in your education. If you want to show your family what you've done, I'm sure they will be able to see some of them on public display next time they come to town."

I should have realised they would not let me keep them. "I understand."

"You will be paid for future commissions. Your portraiture, I see, is quite worthy. We will contact you when we want something painted. We will supply materials for those commissions. Meanwhile you are free to sell what you like to others, if others want to buy. Only the allowed themes, of course." He looked at me sharply. "You know what's allowed by now, I hope."

"Yes."

"Good, then. You may go."

I went back out to the waiting driver, who was sitting in his truck smoking a cigarette.

"Is your boss happy?" he asked as he started the motor.

"Yes," I said distractedly. I had never thought of the mayor as my boss, but that was precisely what he had become.

"It's good to keep the boss happy," the driver said, and off we went.

I saw the white outlines of our gers in the distance and leaned towards them instinctively. "There," I said, pointing. "My home is there." My voice broke.

The gers grew larger. I could see people now, and others coming outside as they realised I was arriving. Then we were there, and there Erdene stood, her hands on the small of her back, ripe and round as the fruit in a Dutch still life. We were barely stopped when I flung myself out of the truck and ran towards her, stopping just short of toppling her over. I touched her belly with wonder, I touched her face, I ran my hands through her hair. "My love," I said. We wrapped our arms around each other, her belly warm and full between us. I was home. She was my home, and I had returned at last.

CHAPTER TWENTY TWO

―――――〜∾〜―――――

THE DRAFT FROM UNDER THE BED
MAY PROVE WORSE THAN THE COLD WIND
FROM THE RIVER VALLEY.

―――――〜∾〜―――――

A year after my return from Ulaan Baatar, when I had settled, mole-like, into the secure tunnel of living as husband and father, herder, and socialist painter, the authorities reopened Gandan Khiid monastery in Ulaan Bataar. A dozen obedient monks were hauled from captivity and installed to lend credence to the pretense of religious tolerance. The government played with Buddhists the way a cat plays with a mouse. The prey, made desperate by its knowledge that the worst is likely, snatches at every brief glimpse of hope. I thought of the four old monks and wondered if they would consider it a wonderful opportunity, even if it were a sham. It was idle thinking. If they were alive, they would certainly not be chosen. They were too devout.

Erdene could not understand my lack of enthusiasm at the news. "Wouldn't you like to go there, to experience a prayer service in the company of monks again?" she asked.

"It's too far."

"But if it weren't."

"It's all for show, so it wouldn't be the same," I said.

"The Party may consider it a show, but for the monks involved maybe it's real."

"The Party would never let it be real. It's a trap to lure the true believers."

"I can't imagine them arresting everyone who walks through the gates of Ghandan Khiid."

It wasn't everyone I was worried about. I looked at my family: Erdene stirring a roiling pot full of mutton, the steam clinging to her face and making it glow in the dim light of our ger; our daughter Tsetseg in abandoned sleep on the bed, on her back with her mouth slackly open, oblivious to everything but her own dreams. It was hard to believe that the destruction of Khovor Khan had led me to them. I could never risk trouble.

"I have a different life now. A happy life, with you and Tsetseg. I'm not a monk anymore."

"No, you're the Party's local artist." Erdene looked at me hard, then turned back to her pot. "I know your painting brings us money, but I don't see how that can be so important that it overshadows all of your earlier life. I think you still are a monk somewhere inside. A free lama, at least. I hope you are."

I thought of the promises I'd made to Tara on the mountaintop outside Ulaan Baatar. How impossible they'd become to uphold, how pointless it had been to make them. "It's dangerous to practice Buddhism these days. Have you forgotten what happened to the four old monks in Ulaan Baatar?"

"You have to stop thinking that was all your fault."

"But it *was* my fault. I was reckless, I didn't take enough precautions in coming to see them. I shouldn't have gone to them at all, I attracted trouble."

"They were happy to have you, though."

"Much less happy when it led to their arrest, I imagine."

Erdene turned to face me. She held the wooden spoon in her hand as though she wanted to whack some sense into me. "*Eejee*, Dash, I can't believe what I'm hearing. You told me yourself they accepted whatever the future held. Teaching you was a last gift for them to give, and now you act as though you never received it."

"We pray daily, and keep a shrine. I'm still Buddhist."

"Like any couple who was raised with faith, yes, we do these things. But you were raised for more than that. You hardly meditate at all anymore. You don't even accept requests to create thangkas for people. All you create are paintings the Party will approve of. Shame on you."

She was absolutely right. And I absolutely did not want to hear it. "It's more important that I do whatever must be done to keep you and Tsetseg safe."

"After six years of studying dharma in a monastery, you don't know the principles of karma? If you want to keep us safe you should be collecting merit from Avalokitesvara, not from the Party."

"These days one has to do both."

"And just how are you doing both?"

I had no good answer for that. It was a monk that Erdene had saved when she first met me in the cave, and I suspected it was the part of me that still commanded her deepest love. Yet I was helpless to ovecome the fear that kept that man in hiding.

"Maybe you should go visit your father in the spring," she said.

"You want me to go away?"

Erdene put down her spoon then, and came to sit beside me on the bed, slipping her arms around me and pressing the damp, mutton-scented softness of her cheek against mine. "I don't want it; I hate it when you're gone. But your father has waited a long time to see you again. First it was fear for his safety that kept you from him, then your trip to Ulaan Baatar, and then Tsetseg. It's time to let him know you're well."

It was true I had been remiss, always planning to return to my homelands and then finding a reason not to. I wanted to see my father, so why hadn't I?

"Go soon," she said, "before we move to the summer pastures and the lambing and foaling begins. We can manage without you for a couple of weeks."

So I traveled back through the lands I'd traversed in terror five years before. This time I had a better horse, but more importantly I had the ability to travel the way a Mongolian ought to: not keeping to himself, but expecting and receiving hospitality in whatever ger is close at hand when evening approaches and he stops for the night. I brought with me a number of small landscape paintings on silk to give as presents to those who put me up and fed me. Nothing religious.

When I started out, the steppes of Arkhangai were beginning their transformation into vast, springtime sweeps of wildflowers and sweet-smelling herbs. I had become accustomed to their lushness, so as I traveled south to the parched lands of my birth it was startling to see how impoverished everything was. There were spring flowers, but they were small and desperate-looking by comparison. The men looked more bent than I remembered. They spoke wearily of sparse rain and winter livestock losses. Seeing the difficulties of the herders in the area I was glad I was bringing with me a purse with a few tugrogs for my father.

The site where my family had wintered since we first started herding for Khovor Khan eventually came into sight, three white gers clustered like mushrooms in the lee of the hillside as they had always been. I spurred my horse to a final gallop. I was eager now to see my father after so many years, imagining the look of joyful surprise that would spring to his face on seeing me, and how it would feel to hug him again.

Reining to a halt outside the gers, I tied my horse to the central hitching line. A young woman with a baby balanced on her hip emerged from the doorway of the middle ger. I strained to see vestiges of my youthful cousin in her face.

"Dzaya?" I asked.

She looked at me quizzically. "My name is Khongi."

I began to wonder if somehow I had the wrong camp site. Flustered, I kept my identity to myself. "I am looking for the herder Ogotai. I have been sent to find him by my mother, who is a distant cousin."

"I'm sorry, but Ogotai died last year," the woman said.

All the breath went out of me, and for several moments all I could do was stare at her wordlessly. Eventually I managed a whisper. "But he was still young."

"I did not know him." She paused, peering at me. "You look ill. Would you like some tea?"

I nodded my thanks, wanting to sit down more than I wanted the tea. Inside the ger was an older woman, short, fat and with frown lines so deep it looked as though she hadn't experienced laughter for decades. She brought me biscuits, frowning all the more at the trouble, while Khongi organized the tea and explained that I had been looking for "the old man" regarding some family matters.

"He is beyond concerning himself with family matters now," the older woman said.

"And the woman Gerel who was also of this camp?" I asked, trying not to reveal my emotions.

"Gerel has gone to live with some cousins. Her brother was dead, her daughter married and moved to the camp of her new husband, the son went to Ulaan Baatar to find work in the factories. There was no one left here for her."

There had also been Dorj when I had fled; as a former monk he would not have left my aunt without resources. "But Dorj and his family, were they not taking care of her?"

The woman narrowed her eyes. "That man has been gone for four years. It brings evil to speak of him."

"Pardon me." There was only one explanation. He had exposed

his past as a monk, or it had been exposed for him, back before the re-opening of Ghandan Khiid, when the tolerance for faith had been zero. I shivered at the thought of what had become of him, and grasped my tea cup hard with both hands so my trembling would not show.

"We came to share this winter site with Gerel and Ogotai when the other was taken away," the woman continued, refusing to use Dorj's name. "We told Gerel she could stay after her brother died, even though a widow woman who is not a relative is a burden, as everyone knows. She chose to leave. It is my husband's brothers who live here now."

"I see." And I did; I saw the covetousness in the woman's eyes. I saw the smug satisfaction of having gained a fine wintering site due to her cleverness in taking advantage of the misfortune of others. I wanted to know how my father had died, but the thought of hearing the details from such a person filled me with grief. Instead I got directions for finding my aunt. Leaving as quickly as I could, I rode the rest of the afternoon to reach her.

The herds were being brought back to water and corral for the night when I arrived at her camp. At the second ger I found her, alone and stoking her stovefire in preparation for the evening meal. I didn't need to identify myself. She took one look and launched herself at me for an embrace that bore all the pent-up force of long absence and a terrible loss that should have been shared but wasn't.

"Your father," she began once she'd finally let me go.

"I know. But how?"

"A stomach cancer took him. It was long and painful. He prayed for your return, but it was not to be."

How I wished then that I had set out on even one of the occasions when I had thought to. "I couldn't," I said. "There were so many reasons. Did he know that?"

Gerel took my hands in hers. "He didn't blame you." I longed to believe her. But in her voice and eyes there was the damning presence of forgiveness.

"I couldn't," I said again, and a sob came up on the wake of the words, then another, and another. I fell into my grief and wept like a child, face down and sobbing on Gerel's bed.

She let me go on, stroking my back gently until I was spent, then brought me airag to soothe me.

"I met the people who are living at our old camp," I said. "Did they drive you away?"

"There was nothing left for me there with all my family gone. Who can live with strangers? Here I'm with people of my own blood."

"And Dorj, what happened to him?"

Gerel shook her head sadly. "He met some other monks at a camp a half-morning's ride away. They began to hold prayer services among themselves. Then they blessed a newborn baby and were denounced by someone at the ceremony. Foolish, so foolish, to take a risk that way. They were all imprisoned, and lies were spread about them to make people think they had been doing vile things.

"The State took what little Dorj's family owned," Gerel continued. "His wife moved back to be with her people, who did not want her because she was tainted by the Party's bad favour, but where else could she go, poor thing? Dorj never returned."

Despite the many sadnesses we had to share, our reunion also held a quiet joy as we talked well into the night. With the lamp turned down low and our voices soft in the cocoon of her small ger, I told her about my flight to Arkhangai, the cave, and my new life with Erdene and Tsetseg. She was thrilled to hear we had a child, and said she would count Tsetseg as another of her own grandchildren.

I asked about Khovar Khan. I didn't intend to see it for myself; I was not at all ready for that reunion yet. Gerel told me the walls were being eaten away slowly by the hungry, dry wind. She said a group of herders had tried wintering their animals there, since the positioning offered good shelter, but they had suffered many deaths of both animals and humans in the course of their first season and had not returned. It was said the ghosts were too numerous and fierce, and would not let anyone defile the sanctity of the place by living there without the sangha.

After a few days I began to long for home, so first thing the following morning I packed to leave. We agreed that I would write, since one of her nephews had been attending school and was reasonably literate. I gave Gerel the best of my remaining landscape paintings.

"It's our summer pasture lands," I said. "The Tamir river, our gers, the Khangai in the background."

"It's so green," Gerel said. "Is the grass really like that?"

"In the early summer, yes."

"You must be happy there. And now I will be able to picture where you are." She hooked the painting on to the lattice wall, then walked over to the hutch that stood in the place of honour.

"I also have things for you. Your father asked me to keep them in case you should return one day." Pulling a small bundle wrapped in blue silk from the hutch, she came and placed it on the bed beside me. "Look inside."

The bundle contained my past rendered in objects. There was the silver-backed brush engraved with a running horse, which had been my mother's only luxury. As a child I had often taken it from our hutch and stroked its smooth silver back, imagining what she might have looked like—always beautiful in my thoughts—as she pulled the brush through her long hair. Also in the bundle was my father's favorite horse whip, the one I had watched him weave from leather. There was his onyx-handled knife set and flint, the handle carved by him to resemble a ram, and a set of playing cards, his favorites, that he had painted with bright geometric designs now faded and creased with use.

Then there was the silk thangka I had made for him when I was fourteen. It was of the Bodhisattva Tara, then the object of an attachment I'd thought inextinguishable. He had been so proud of that gift. It was evidence that his sacrifice in sending his only child away to Khovor Khan had been worthwhile.

After casting a quick glance outside to ensure no one was around, Gerel closed the door to her ger

"There's something else," she said, and began hauling a battered brown traveling chest away from its spot near the bed. I helped her move it. She got down on her hands and knees and lifted one of the floorboards that had been covered by the chest, then reached into the space below and pulled out a different bundle. This one was wrapped in plain burlap. She handed it to me and I started to unfold it, but stopped abruptly when I recognised the deep burgundy of monastic cloth.

"What is this?"

"Go on, keep going," my aunt said, gesturing impatiently, oblivious to my alarm and anxious for me to see the treasure within. "It belonged to Dorj," she whispered, "who gave it to your father for safekeeping, who gave it in turn to me. Now it's yours to protect. That is the right thing."

Reluctantly I continued to unwrap it. Inside the burgundy cloth was a classic, rectangular Buddhist scripture book, two narrow blocks of wood with sheaves of paper pressed between them, penned in Mongolian script.

"It's one of the books Dorj transcribed himself, from the Tibetan into Mongolian so he could teach those who only knew our own language," Gerel said. "He was only able to save one book, but on the final page he drew a map showing where other sacred items have been buried for safekeeping, close to Erdene Zuu."

I opened the wooden cover of the book and began to read. The prayer, a familiar call for the blessings of Avalokitesvara, sounded inside my head like the singsong chanting of an entire sangha of monks. As I leafed through each page I was once again in Khovor Khan's assembly hall, Bayan and Koke beside me, Tilik keeping one stern eye on me even though he seemed to have his eyes closed, incense smoke mingling with the smell of butter lamps, the sweet ping of the tingsha. Once again I was the novice newly arrived, before Bayan, before Suren, before art, when it all felt holy and undefiled, and my own attainment of enlightenment still possible.

Then, like a ghost melting into the shadows, it slipped away. The scripture was unfinished, with writing turning abruptly to blank pages waiting for a hand that would never write in them again.

"I can't keep this," I said. "It's too great a risk for my family."

My aunt was astounded. "Who doesn't live with risk these days? You're a monk, Dash. It's only right that you should protect this precious thing."

"I'm not a monk anymore. Just a husband and father. A herder. An artist. Not a monk."

"I'm glad your father can't hear you say such a thing. He believed as Dorj did, that to be a monk is forever, even when you're not able to live like one."

And look where that thinking got Dorj and his family, a voice inside me said. It was a shameful voice, but it possessed me. When, under the stern eye of my aunt, I bound the scripture book tightly to my stomach inside my del, it felt as dangerous as a pot of oil set next to an open fire. The only way I could bear its terrible weight was to reassure myself that I would bury it someplace safe along the way.

Gerel also gave me a blue prayer scarf from her collection of secret things. That I tied to the first tree I came to, as travelers often do, leaving the silk to flap in the wind and disperse its stored blessings to anyone who still had the capacity to receive them.

Chapter Twenty Three

WORDS SPOKEN TO AN UNCOMPREHENDING MAN ARE LIKE PEARLS CAST INTO THE ASHES.

Several times during the first day of my journey back I thought about burying the scripture book, but couldn't find a place that felt right. The people who took me into their ger that night seemed sincere and open, and as I stealthily kept the book hidden from them I wondered if they would kick me out or embrace me were they to know I had it. The times were like that; no-one revealed their beliefs. The second day went the same. On the third day I came to a place that seemed sufficiently special, a small hill that arose on an otherwise flat plain, as though the earth at that point yearned for the Great Blue Sky so intensely that it had managed to pull itself towards it.

I rode to the top and hobbled my horse as in a common travel break, ate some curd, drank some airag, and scanned the landscape all the while to make sure there was no-one close by to enquire as to why I was digging in the earth. Kneeling, I took out my knife, the only tool I had for the job, and began picking at the ground. It was gravelly and loose and came away quite easily, so before long I had a shallow hole big enough to accept the book.

I sat with crossed legs and removed the bundle from inside my del. My stomach felt immediately free, my breathing deeper. I took the book in both hands and prepared to pray over it before putting it in the hole. Instead of prayers, however, what came into my mind were visions from the past. I remembered when, as a still-new novice, I had been allowed for the first time to wrap the cloth around the prayer books we had just used that morning, and put them back in their allotted cubby-holes. It had felt like the most important job in the world. I remembered Tilik instructing me in how to turn the pages using the barest of touches, so the fine paper would not be ruined by sweaty fingers. I saw again all my slain brothers being tossed into the hastily dug hole that was their mass grave, felt again the horror of it, the way it defiled their spirits and weighed forever on me for not being able to do anything about it.

I began to cry, with deep, ravaging sobs that shook the book in my hands. I clutched it desperately. How foolish I had been to think I could bury such a treasure. I would never be able to leave it to moulder in the ground, its blessings uselessly discarded. Not even in earth that rose to meet the sky.

As I neared the Khangai mountains I knew there was one other stop I had to make. Nestled in the lee of the hills, the shaman's ger was much as it had been five years before; a silent, solitary white mushroom in a grassy slope edged with poplars. As before there was no hitching line, so I tethered my horse to the ground in preparation for staying awhile.

I realized how much I had been looking forward to seeing the old woman when no one came out to greet me. When I peeked inside the open door all was still, but there were clues that the shaman still lived there and would be back soon; ritual objects such as a skull and a shaman's drum were on the hutch. The same vivid red velvet bedcover was on the wooden bed and a brick of tea sat on the plank that served as a kitchen counter.

Being tired from my travels I drank some of the airag I'd brought with me and lay down in the grass to wait. It felt good lying there with the late afternoon sun on my face and the new green smell of spring grass filling my nose. I dozed off from the comfort of it, only to awake with a start when a hot, moist and foul smelling breath of air hit my face.

At my left shoulder, close enough to touch, a wolf sat calmly examining me the way one of our dogs might have sat watching a sheep being butchered; a little expectant, but patient. I had never seen a wolf so close up that had not been safely dead. Despite my fear, which kept me frozen lying down before him, I couldn't help notice that his eyes held a deep intelligence. I thought he might speak at any moment. Instead he uttered a short, whining sound and licked his chops. At that point a shadow fell over me from the right.

I had not even heard her approach. She might have been floating for all that her footsteps sounded on the grass, or perhaps I was just so distracted by the wolf that I didn't register her presence. What was clear, however she had gotten there, was that it was not the old woman. Her del was pure white and her leather sash held not only shards of mirror but also shining silver discs and bells. Besides this she wore an apron of many colourful cloth strips that wriggled in the breeze like a rainbow of snakes. A cascade of black hair fell forward and framed her face as she leaned over to look at me. One of her eyes, startlingly, was pale blue, but she was not unhandsome.

"You were right, Tegusgal, we have a guest." She was addressing the wolf as she looked at me.

"I came to find the old shaman." I felt ridiculous lying there as I spoke but I was afraid of how the wolf might react to any movement.

"You can rise. Tegusgal will not attack you."

When I stood up the woman put her hands on either side of my face and peered hard into my eyes. "And what does a powerful monk need with the advice of a shaman?" she asked, then dropped her hands from my face and burst into raucous laughter as though her insight were a clever joke. "Never mind. My grandmother is dead, as we all must be eventually. But her gift survives in me and that is what you've come for."

She went to her door in a jingle of bells and silver so melodious I couldn't believe I had not heard them when she'd first approached. The wolf padded after her like a docile puppy.

"Enter, enter," she said, gesturing for me to come. "You cannot be turned away."

She lit a juniper twig first, to keep evil spirits at bay, then stoked the fire for tea. Besides being a supplicant I was also a traveler and needed to be refreshed before anything else. Throughout these activities, she didn't speak, and nor did I. Tegusgal lay like a sphinx on the floor in front of me and made me the sole focus of his unnerving attention.

"So, monk," the shaman said once she'd served me a bowl of tea and sat down on a stool opposite, "I ask you again, why have you come?"

"I wish you wouldn't call me a monk."

She nodded. "I see. That is not a bad reason."

"No, I mean –"

"I know what you meant. And I know what lies deeper." She jangled the mirrors at her waist. "The mirrors see everything, inside and out, the visible and the invisible. You are a monk who does not want to be seen as a monk, which is a difficult thing to be."

"I only came to see the old shaman because she helped me once. I was traveling nearby. I wanted to thank her and let her know I was well."

"But you are not well."

I frowned and thought I caught the hint of a sly smile in response.

"If you are not a monk," she continued, "why do you bear scriptures at the center of your being?"

Instinctively I felt for the scripture book that was still bound fast against my navel.

"You may hide from yourself but you cannot hide from me, monk."

"I hide not from myself but from a world that punishes the faithful."

She rose from her stool and fetched her drum from the hutch. It was small and oval, an iron band stretched with thin goat skin and fitted with a handle over which were strung nine small iron rings that clinked as the drum was struck. For a beating stick she used a thin rod covered in snake skin, with coloured ribbons coming out of the end like a serpent's tongue. She sat on the floor beside the wolf and began to beat the drum in a slow, steady rhythm over which, in a voice pitched low like a man's, she began to chant.

"Odqan Talaqan Mother arose
When Khangai Khan was still a hill
When the elm-tree was still a sapling
When the falcon was a fledgling
When the brown goat was a kid
When Mount Burqantu was still a hill
When the willow was still a sapling
When the lark was still a fledgling ... "

Her chanting, combined with the growing scent of juniper smoke, was hypnotic. Tegusgal closed his golden eyes. After a couple of minutes, the shaman suddenly stopped and sucked in three breaths very quickly, like someone coming up for water after being submerged for a long time. Tegusgal's eyes popped open.

"You are marked by loss." The shaman looked into some unknown distance as she spoke. "Death and loss; they cling to you like shadows."

My heart constricted. "In the past, yes. But in the future?"

"All life is transient."

"There are some losses I don't think I could bear."

"And the loss of the Path, does that not count among them?"

I didn't answer.

"You will have the chance to regain it. I see it in the future."

Rather than bringing me joy, the idea made me fearful of its consequences.

"So much fear. Too much." The shaman pulled her focus from the future she was seeing and looked at me directly.

"Your master always told you attachment would be your downfall."

"There are attachments I believe to be worthy."

"You have sacrificed your own spirit, hoping to protect something you believe to be even more valuable. But nothing is more valuable than your own true spirit, monk. I don't have to be a Buddhist, or even a shaman, to see that."

I was about to deny her words but she held up her hand. "Your father named you well. You will have a chance to regain your spirit in the future, which is a great good fortune. But it's only a chance. Don't let fear squander it."

"But my family? What of them?"

"All life is transient. You should know that better than anyone. Just as there are many forms of attachment, there are many forms of loss. Death is only one way to lose a person you love."

I hurried home after that, blindly hearing only the possibility of loss in the shaman's words and anxious to be reunited with my family. There was an awkward moment when I first arrived and Erdene hugged me and felt the scripture book between us, and I had to let her know with my eyes not to say anything in front of the others. The fewer people to know, the safer for them.

I picked up Tsetseg, held her tight—she was too little to note anything amiss—then kept her on my hip while I told the others my sad news. They gave me words of comfort, touched my arm and face, Erdene put her arms around us both. They were my family now and I was grateful to have them.

I kissed Tsetseg's pink cheek. "I've brought some treasures back with me, little one," I said, although at one year old she couldn't really understand me. "Would you like to see them?"

"Treasures?" asked Erdene.

"A few things my father left me."

Gan offered to take care of my horse so we could go into our ger and have this moment to look at my inheritance. With Tsetseg on my knee I took the brush out of the traveling bag first. Erdene exclaimed at its beauty and Tsetseg grabbed for its shininess, all smiles when Erdene brushed her hair with it. They explored the playing cards, looking at each one to find the small differences my father put in the pictures as a kind of game. I knew them all but only gave them hints if they were really having trouble.

I handed Erdene the thangka. She put her finger to Tsetseg's lips to show her this was something just for us, then put it in our secret shrine in the cupboard. Tsetseg got a hold of the riding whip and put it in her mouth because she was teething, then I bounced her up and down and she held it like she was supposed to, already learning how to ride at the same time as she was learning how to walk. The last of the treasures was the knife and flint set, which Tsesteg was allowed to touch but not hold.

Eventually she tired of all the excitement and was ready for her nap. It was only then I was able to tell Erdene what the bundle in my del was. With our daughter securely asleep and the ger door closed, I removed the book and showed it to her.

"This belonged to the man named Dorj, who gave me the prayer wheel when I fled my home. He was translating the Tibetan scriptures into Mongolian, but was caught blessing a baby along with some other monks and was taken away."

Erdene was examining the book with wonder, holding it as reverentially as a holy relic. She didn't seem to have heard the part about Dorj being taken away.

"It's a marvelous thing," she said. "I can read it. Is that why he translated it, so ordinary people could read it?"

I began to get irritated that she didn't understand the peril she was holding in her hands. "Probably. But you see here, where the writing ends abruptly?" I said, rudely flipping the pages the way one is never supposed to, "Dorj was arrested and never returned, and now his wife lives in penury. We are going to put the book under the floorboards along with the prayer wheel and not speak of it."

Erdene closed the book slowly, with a look of sadness that was more painful to me than any words she could have spoken. She gave it back to me. Chastened, I handled it respectfully now as I wrapped it up, first in its burgundy cloth, then the burlap.

"I know it's beautiful, this book," I said. "And I'm sorry we live in times that don't allow us to keep it in the open. Even under the floorboards it's a great risk. The four old monks, Dorj, and others, who knows how many, have all disappeared. The threat is real. I have you and Tsetseg to take care of. We must be very careful."

Erdene just nodded, her mouth a thin, terse line. I put it in the niche under the floorboards. We did not speak of it again, not for a very long time.

CHAPTER TWENTY FOUR

---~~~---

A PERSON BURNED BY HOT MILK WILL BLOW ON YOGHURT WHEN HE DRINKS.

---~~~---

The following year, 1945, Erdene bore a son. We named him Tilik, even though from early on it was clear the child had none of my master's capacity to be still and quiet. For us, Tilik's arrival was the most important event in a year of many momentous things. Our active alliance with Russia in World War II led to Outer Mongolia's international recognition as an independent country, free from the lingering claims China had maintained. It was for this Sukhbaatar had started the revolution so many years ago. Everyone celebrated having finally achieved it.

The thrill was dampened, however, when our government announced the Mongolian alphabet was to be replaced by Russian Cyrillic. Despite our newly-declared independence, our bond with Russia was proving every bit as tenacious as the feudal hold of China had been. A period of chaos ensued as those who had been struggling to gain literacy, as well as those who already were literate, scrambled to decipher their language by a whole new set of symbols. Gan and Tabin, the only other literate members of our camp, came to our ger once a day and we all practiced together to try to master this strange way of writing and reading.

During the postwar period, as the country rebuilt its economy with Russian help, I had frequent painting commissions, thanks in part to having developed a style of socialist realism that borrowed heavily from the much-esteemed Russian artist Boris Vladimirsky. I began to focus on portraits, where I could veer from my art school training enough to imbue my work with a bit of truth, at least compared to the idealized scenes that were typically requested of me. I became quite good. Even Cholon admitted that my profession was at least a secure one, although he continued to see painting as far less important than herding, and grumbled about the loss of hands every time I had to take myself away from camp work to fulfill a commission.

Unlike Buddhist art, I was encouraged to sign my paintings so everyone would know where the works had come from, earning credit for Ikh Tamir as well as for myself. I have to admit, I liked the praise I got. My master Tilik had never managed to completely remove my pride from my work. Now that I was in the lay world it grew, feeding on itself while I made only half-hearted attempts to keep it in check.

One day a messenger drove in to our camp to inform me that he was to take me immediately into town to paint a new portrait. I was being driven in order to save time, as the sitter was very important and would not accept the delay of me riding there.

Dutifully I packed up my painting supplies—oils, as the Party always stipulated oil on canvas for high level people—my bedroll, some food, and a change of underclothes for my stay in town.

"How long are you gone, Ahv?" asked Tsetseg as we went outside to say our goodbyes.

"Not long. One sleep, maybe two." I picked her up and whirled her around me, which always made her shriek with delight and forget whatever was bothering her. Then it was Tilik's turn, toddling towards me on unsure legs, to be tossed in the air.

I kissed Erdene, climbed into the jeep and we drove off.

Traveling by motor was not necessarily faster than by horse, given the fact that most of the trip was over roadless land. It was, however, considerably more comfortable than riding in the early spring weather. The air was crisp, the wind harsh, and we passed through a sudden squall of hail less than halfway to our destination, the hailstones clattering deafeningly on the metal roof of the jeep.

Ikh Tamir had grown in the past few years. Despite the evils I associated with the socialist movement, it had also brought about many improvements. There was a reasonably reliable postal service, health care, and the start of a national education system. A new school had been set up in a ger, with extra gers for weekday boarding of the herders' children who lived too far away to make a daily trip. Industry in the area had also increased. Along with the wood chopping factory, there was now one producing dairy products that were becoming famous throughout the region for their superior taste. It was work that offered an alternative to the insecurities of nomadic life, and it lured many people to the town.

The driver took me to the town hall, which was one thing that had not improved over the past decade. As new demands were placed on the building, rooms that had once been spacious were divided up and then shared. I had the use of a second floor room, which was usually the domain of the local librarian but was given over to me when there was a portrait to be done. Its single window let in good, diffuse northeastern light, which is why I got to use it. With the librarian's desk pushed to one side there was enough room for my easel, a chair for the sitter, and a narrow space in between to lay out my bedroll for the night. A good portrait could not be done in a single day.

The eminence of the sitter was apparent by the fact that someone had bothered to heat the room in advance. The chemical smell of the petrol burner lingered but the apparatus had been removed lest I get the idea I could hang on to such a luxury. I would only see the heater again if the sitter complained of growing cold. While I waited for my subject to arrive I set out my things. A canvas, already stretched and prepared, had been left for me from the carefully regulated supply kept by the government. It was quite large. This portrait was evidently destined for an official building.

When I heard footsteps clicking down the corridor, I stood straight and faced the door in order to present the best appearance to the dignitary. The mayor's voice, obsequious and rushed as though he feared being cut off in mid-sentence, echoed through the empty hall.

"I'm sure you'll be very pleased with the results. He's a fine artist, very fine indeed, truly gifted in portraying a flattering likeness, as you've seen for yourself."

There was no response from his companion. The mayor's fawning continued.

"Although we are not the biggest soum in Arkhangai, we do not lack for cultural talent, no indeed."

When they arrived at the open doorway the mayor's beaming face appeared first. He began his introduction before my sitter had even gotten round the corner. "Here he is, our own D. Chuluuny. Dash, you have the great honour of providing a portrait of Arkhangai's new governor, Mr. Badrakh. I need not say more."

The governor walked through the door with a slight nod of acknowledgement towards me. It was just as well he wasn't interested in talk, for I was suddenly so short of breath I could not have uttered a word.

The unforgettable coldness of his eyes had not changed a bit since the day eight years earlier when he'd given a similar nod to order the destruction of Khovor Khan.

To have him there before me was to face my most terrifying nightmares. In my mind's eye I saw him raise his arm coolly to shoot Suren dead, and I was seized with an animal instinct to flee. Sweat broke out on my forehead and I wiped it away with my hand, then worried that I looked too nervous, like I had something to hide.

"The portrait is to hang in the *aimag* headquarters building in Tsetserleg," I heard the mayor say. "I'm sure you understand what an honour that is for all of us, Dash."

The blood was rushing through my brain so violently I thought I might faint.

"Yes, I can see from your surprise that you understand." He turned to the Party leader. "Your importance has cowed our humble artist. But he will recover, I assure you."

The mayor was beginning to look worried that I might not. The new governor glanced at me disinterestedly, as though the whole thing had not been his idea and if I fell dead from shock it would matter little to him.

Wringing his hands, the mayor began to do what I should have been. "Sit here, please, sir," he said to Badrakh, then turned to me with a pleading look. "Dash, please instruct our esteemed guest on how to best sit for his portrait."

With leaden movements I directed the governor to shift his body until I found the best angle for catching the light on his features. As I did so he began to study me with a keener eye. The beads of sweat returned.

"Have you not painted senior officials before?" he asked.

My voice stuck in my dry throat briefly before anything came out. "Some, sir," I managed to say.

"And yet I make you this nervous."

I nodded, hoping he would take it wholly as painter's nerves.

"Where did you learn to paint?" he asked. My hands began to tremble with the fear that he knew me as the artist at the monastery. I could not think of a reply; my mouth just opened and shut.

The Mayor, still standing uncertainly in the doorway, spoke into the void. "He studied at the College of Art in Ulaan Baatar. One of the top in his class." He looked at me hard, perplexed by my strange behaviour and willing me to come to my senses in order to save his own face.

"Dash, is that the final angle you want for Mr. Badrakh?"

I put all my effort into a reply. "A little towards the window," I said, then escaped to the other side of my easel. The barrier, although only thin canvas, gave me a moment of respite from my panic.

"Is everything fine now then?" the mayor asked, doubtful. "Shall I leave you?"

Badrakh dismissed him with a small wave of his hand and turned his eyes to me. "I'm ready."

A detached part of me noticed that he was still very handsome and that the light caught the planes of his face beautifully. But when I began looking at him deeply, as I always did before beginning a portrait, I was bombarded by horrid images: his cool nod; Koke's scream and the mush they had made of his head; Tilik and the old man slumping to the ground; the dark stains of their blood in front of our ruined stupa. I felt I might throw up at any moment.

My whole body began to tremble so much I had to hide further, scrunching as small as possible behind the canvas. I sharpened my already-sharp sketching pencil, I rattled the brushes around in their tin. Anything to help gather my wits. Then I heard my master's voice teaching me my first breathing lessons. *Draw the air deep into the pit of the belly*, I heard him say, *then out through the top of your head. Slowly. Over and over*. I saw him in my mind's eye, serene and patient. I took a few breaths this way and felt some small measure of calm come over me.

With the return of my wits I realized that Badrakh probably had no idea who I was. Why would he? He had never given a moment's notice of anyone other than Suren during his many visits to the monastery. This small hope was enough to help me begin again. I made myself look at the surface of his face only, the way I would approach an inanimate object in a still life. It was the only way I could bear to look at him.

One pencil mark followed another, then brush stroke after brush stroke, like walking through a killing desert one step at a time. The painting I made of him over two awful days portrayed a handsome man with the stern but benevolent gaze of a strong leader. He liked it very much. The mayor was thrilled. I was exhausted.

When the jeep dropped me off at my ger that evening, even the joy of Tsetseg and Tilik greeting me with the enthusiasm of puppies was not enough to lighten my heavy mood. Erdene saw it right away.

"The sitter was the man who used to visit the Abbot at Khovar Khan," I told her. "The one who—" I couldn't finish.

"*Burhan miny*," she breathed.

But the children were oblivious in their excitement. "Come, Ahv, you're just in time for evening prayers," said Tsetseg, for whom this evening ritual was filled with magic.

"We'll talk later," Erdene whispered to me, as Tsetseg already had my hand and was leading me to our cupboard to open the shrine. Tonight, more than ever, I welcomed the consolation of it.

I took the handle of the right-hand door and Tsetseg took the left, her eyes aglow with anticipation, then on my nod we opened the doors together. She loved this part, peering inside at the shrine's contents each night as though she'd never seen them before. They were secrets only for the family, she knew that well already, and that made them more precious. There was our thangka that I had painted when we first married, and beside it now the smaller one I'd made for my father. There was a butter lamp, a little brass incense holder of a kind commonly sold by Chinese merchants, round in shape and engraved with demon-chasers, and a handful of incense sticks wrapped in a piece of silk and tied with string.

Tsetseg's job was to unwrap the incense, select a stick, put it in the holder, and wrap the remainder back up again. It was a ceremony she took seriously, always thinking carefully about which stick to select for the honour, although they all looked the same. Then Erdene lit the incense and the butter lamp and we all sat on the floor cross-legged to pray.

The ritual was always soothing, binding us together in a moment in which nothing else mattered but our togetherness and our thoughts focused as one on the Buddha. Even Tilik sat still in Erdene's lap, riveted by the tendrils rising from the incense in the flickering light of the butter lamp.

I always started us off with a prayer in Tibetan, changing my selection to suit the season and our situation. Tonight I chose one to bless the family. I needed to believe they were blessed. Usually my concentration was complete, but this time I kept being interrupted by the cold face of Badrakh. I stumbled so badly that Erdene noticed, even though she didn't understand the language, and glanced at me worriedly.

When I made it to the end of mine, Erdene said a prayer in Mongolian from the handful she knew. I listened to her sure, solid voice and hoped her faith would make her words come true.

Then Tsetseg, in her own words, asked Tara to take care of us, with an innocent acceptance that Tara would make it so. Our prayers were the last thing we did in a day, so when the children went to bed their heads were filled with blessings and the image of the divine Tara watching over them.

After they fell asleep, I lay wrapped in Erdene's arms in our narrow bed, soaking up the comfort of her embrace as we talked in low voices against the soft breathing of Tsetseg and Tilik on the other side of the ger.

"This portrait was exhausting," I said.

Erdene stroked my head the way she stroked our children when she was soothing a hurt. "It must have been terrible."

"It all came rushing back to me, the killings, his nod, the blood, the screams."

She continued to soothe me.

"At first I was terrified he would recognize me, but of course he had no idea who I was."

"No, he wouldn't."

"His name is Badrakh. He is now the governor of our province, and he is ruthless, entirely without a heart."

"Many of the governors are like that."

"I had to make him look noble. It's always my job to make them look better than they are."

Erdene was silent.

"I am no longer a free man."

"That is true."

"Not that anyone is truly free," I rationalized. "A monk is bound to the sangha. A man to his wife. A child to its parents. All of us to the whims of the Blessed Blue Sky, whether it gives us rain to fatten our herds or impoverishes us with drought."

Erdene paused in the stroking of my head. "But all those bonds are made from a person's own will. A monk can leave the sangha, a man his wife, also a child his parents when he grows up, and a nomad can change his life for one that is not dependent on the sky if he doesn't like what it has dealt him."

Erdene always knew the truth. I could never fool her. She understood that my bond to the Party was that of a slave to his master, not at all the same as these other ties.

"Do you know the story of Syakhindya and Prince Bambur?" she asked.

"He was a great Khan and she was his young daughter-in-law."

"Against the laws and customs of his people he wanted her for himself. But when he tried to force his love on her, saying that as a great Khan he could make any kind of rules he wanted, this is what she told him: 'Rulers change and die, but the laws and customs of the people are eternal. They are stronger than power. They die only with the people.'

"Maybe faith is like that, too," Erdene said, "and as long as there are people to keep it alive, power will not be able to kill it."

I wanted to agree with her. Having to paint Badrakh had been a karmic slap in the face, and should have been enough to make me see wisdom. But all I could think of was how every time I had encountered someone who was trying to keep Buddhism alive, they had met a dreadful fate.

How easily resolve can be undermined by constant fear, so that faith is snuffed out not by a single blow but by endless small snips to the wick, until the flame gutters quietly into darkness.

A week later, I screwed up my courage and went to visit the cave. I had not been back since my rescue, although I had dreamt of it often. In my dreams I didn't enter, but rather found myself to be in it already, a pleasant discovery that felt like a coming home of the spirit. All my writings were there, and the mandala, but more beautiful and perfect than they had been in reality. I sat serenely drinking them in until, without warning, a malevolent spirit with a face like a Tsam mask materialized from the rocky outcropping at the back of the cave, and my tranquility was replaced by terror. At that point I awoke. It was the same every time.

I rode off to the cave alone, following the pass until I began to recognize the views I had stared at for so long in those days: the opposite slope with the oddly twisted larch at its summit, the slab of rock that jutted out in the shape of a ram's head, the tiny waterfall to the east side of the cave. I tied my horse and climbed the last of the way up, as Erdene had once done to escape the rain.

Standing on the ledge outside the cave I paused, my heart beating frantically as though it couldn't distinguish if this place was friend or foe. I took a couple of steps forward, straining to see the dark interior after the bright light of the afternoon sun. Now I wanted to see the scripture I had written and my drawing of Avalokitesvara, but it was hard to make anything out. I ventured the rest of the way in and let my eyes adjust.

Where once there had been a record of three months spent deep in prayer, there was now a grayish smear. Someone had taken the trouble to roughly erase the entire thing until not a single clear line remained. Avalokitesvara, the demon-chasers, the script, it was all a dull smudge on the dark rock. Even the mandala had been swept away, leaving only a few stray pebbles off to one side.

Closing my eyes I tried to sense a lingering atmosphere of spirituality, but found none. I ran my fingers over the wall where Avalokitesvara had been, and a damp, chalky residue came off on them. I picked up a pebble hoping to recognise where it might have been in the mandala, but it gave me no clues. I felt winded, as though I had been dropped on my back from a great height.

There are many forms of loss.

Of the most intensely spiritual time of my life, there was no longer a trace. Tucking the pebble into the fold of my del, I left the cave and headed back down the hill. I could not bear to stay, not even for one prayer.

CHAPTER TWENTY FIVE

———————— ∼∿∼ ————————

IT IS BETTER TO BE THE HEAD OF A FLY
THAN THE TAIL OF A TIGER.

———————— ∼∿∼ ————————

The early 1950s saw an explosion in Mongolia's industrialization. Russia poured money into the transformation of our economy from a pastoral to an industrial-agricultural one. The Party was successfully dragging us into the twentieth century, though the population was still mostly nomadic at heart.

"I heard they opened a factory at Tsetserleg," complained Cholon as we were playing shagai in his ger. "Imagine a herder working in a factory. What do they think we are? I'd feel like I was in prison."

"At least the pay is pretty good," said Tabin, who was now almost old enough to go to work, and which made his father look up sharply in concern. "It would be worse to be an agricultural worker. They're trying to grow wheat on the steppes, that's what a traveler told Bat last month."

"Mongolians using a plough?" Cholon was appalled. "That's work for the Chinese."

"Why?" asked Tilik. He was just beginning to be able to play, and in doing so he soaked up the adult conversation around him. Shagai games were a boy's introduction to a man's world.

"Because they have been tilling soil for thousands of years so they're good at it," I said.

"It's demeaning work for a nomad. We have more pride than they do," said Cholon, correcting my answer. "Anyway, they'll never grow wheat on the steppes. The land doesn't want to be tilled, but the Russians will never understand that until they've failed for at least ten years."

One thing modernization brought that everyone liked was the radio. I bought one, and our extended family crowded regularly into our ger to listen to transmissions from Ulaan Baatar. There were many political speeches and newscasts, but occasionally traditional Mongolian music or a new play was broadcast. Although Gan's stories were more interesting by far, the radio gave us previously unavailable daily knowledge of what was happening in our country.

Another welcome addition to our lives was the cinema. Ever since my first viewing in Ulaan Baatar I had been fascinated, and now shadow shows arrived from time to time even in hamlets as tiny as Ikh Tamir. The Party had organized a mobile version—a movie projector and a large rollout screen—that toured the soums in order to extend the reach of the Party's propaganda. None of us cared that the content of the films was biased. The entertainment was worth it.

Just as when I went to Ulaan Baatar's cinema with Guyuk, these movie events, and the occasional television transmission for which the mayor opened Ikh Tamir's one black and white, fuzzy set to the public, followed a hierarchy for the six rows of seats they set up in the town hall's public meeting room. Important officials and well-connected bureaucrats got front row seats of course, but beside them, for one show only, were workers who'd received awards for factory production, mothers who'd achieved awards for the production of many children, and Youth League or Pioneer members who were being rewarded for some job especially well done.

As the resident artist of Ikh Tamir I was given four places in the last row of seats, so that my family and I didn't have to stand in the cramped area at the back. I had become a kind of pet for the mayor, his cultural pride and joy. He never asked me to join the Party—there was an unspoken agreement between us—but he did expect cooperation from me. If I wanted to continue earning my living as a valued artist instead of, say, a bottler of yoghurt or a log cutter, I had to play the role of model citizen.

One afternoon at the completion of a film called 'The Railway!', the mayor approached us.

He greeted me with a familiar hand on my shoulder, Erdene in a polite and formal way, then turned to the children.

"That was a good film, wasn't it?" he said jovially. "Did you like it?"

It had been a rousing tale of everyday heroics in building the railway line that would one day link east to west. The children both had the sense to nod vigorously, much to the mayor's satisfaction.

"It's a great thing the government is doing for our country," he said. "And the help we've received from Russia for this project! Where would we be without them? We'd still be in a backwards condition, that's where."

More nods from the children, although by now it was unclear whether he was still talking to them or just talking in general. He turned to Erdene and me.

"These films are educational, but there's so much more you could be doing for your children," he said. "We have a new teacher at the school here in Ikh Tamir, you know. One who is certified and qualified from the teacher's school in Ulaan Baatar. And he brought supplies with him, so now there is paper, and enough pencils for everyone. Erasers, too. And a chalk board for the teacher."

The schoolhouse was a ger, and up until then the education had been useless as the instructor could barely read and write himself, and knew nothing except propaganda. It had been a struggle to convince anyone to attend, since for herding families it was not compulsory because the children were needed for chores at home.

"That's very good news for the community," I said. "But we don't live near, so I've been teaching our children at home. They are still young, but we cover math, reading and writing in Cyrillic, geography, all the official things." I didn't add that I also taught them the outlawed Mongolian script, or that they learned the history of our country through Gan's epics.

The mayor put his arm around my shoulder and I felt Tsetseg's hand seek out mine and hold it fast. "If they came to proper school," the mayor said, "they would also learn other important subjects, such as history. Besides, it would be a boost for this project that is important for the community, but which requires the actions of enlightened people like yourselves to convince others of its merit."

Erdene spoke up at that point. "Yes, Dash, I agree this is an important topic and we should discuss it at home," she said. I knew where she stood on the issue, but the mayor did not and therefore took her words as hope.

"Ah, women and their wisdom. They are the light that pulls us forward," he said, and took his leave of us.

Erdene whispered to me when we were out of earshot. "I can't stand that man. He's so false."

"It's his job to be false. If he didn't do it well, he be laying railway ties like the people in the film."

The four of us went outside, got our horses and rode back home, where we did not discuss the important topic at all because we were already in complete agreement that we should keep our children out of the school for as long as we were able.

We managed to put it off for a year. We argued that Tsetseg was only eight and Tilik six. We couldn't yet part with them. They were needed at home for chores. We used the same excuses every herding family was using. The mayor tolerated it until 1952, when several things conspired to make it impossible for us to say no any longer.

First of all, the Prime Minister Choibalsan died in January and Tsedenbal was appointed in his place. Like any change of leadership within a closed political system, this entailed many purges of Party members who had previously been loyal to the old leader. Our mayor must have felt he was hanging on to his job by a very thin rope and needed to demonstrate how well he had everybody under control. Adding to his urgency was the completion of a new, concrete school building. Having inaugurated it with much pomp, the mayor was now expected to fill it with children.

At the end of summer Erdene sat Tilik and Tsetseg down on stools by the hearth stove.

"Your father has something important to tell you," she said. The children sat expectantly, hands folded in their laps. Tilik twirled his index fingers around one another incessantly, as he always did when forced to sit still.

"As I mentioned in the spring," I began, "a new school has been built in Ikh Tamir, and a trained teacher has been hired." Tilik stopped twiddling his fingers. "Your mother and I have decided it would be best for your education if you were to go to this school."

Tsetseg dropped her expectant gaze down to her lap. "We'll have to live there, won't we," she said to her knees.

"It's too far to travel every day, yes. During the week you'll live in the dormitory with children from other herding families, but you will be home for weekends, all holidays, and for the summer months."

"I don't want to be educated," she said.

Tilik's brow was furrowed with thought. "Who will milk the yaks and gather the dung when we're not here?"

"Everyone else will help get the chores done. And on the days when you're here, you can do a little more to make up for it."

"What would we have to do at school?"

"Reading and writing, math, science. The basics."

"I already know how to read," protested Tsetseg.

"When would we start?" asked Tilik.

"Next week."

Tsetseg's shoulders began to shake, then tears spilled into her lap. As Erdene crouched to put an arm around her, I noticed she too was weeping.

"What if we don't like it?" asked Tilik.

"I'm sure that won't be the case."

Tilik turned to his sister. "Maybe it won't be so bad. We'll get to read instead of doing chores."

"I like our chores," Tsetseg sobbed. "Why do I have to go?"

Erdene, tear-stained and miserable, looked at me as though she was wondering the same thing, despite the fact we had discussed it many times.

"A good education is a valuable thing, even for a herder," I said. "Times are changing, and it will be useful for you to know something besides herding."

"But I don't want to know about anything else."

"I'm afraid there is no choice," I said. "It is the way of things now."

"They won't let us pray," Tsetseg said.

"That's true, you must not be seen to pray when you're there. That's very important." My heart constricted with both fear and guilt at my own instructions.

"We can pray more on weekends," said Tilik, "right, Ahv?"

I nodded slowly, and hoped it was enough.

Our children rode to Ikh Tamir at the start of each week regardless of the weather, stayed there for four nights, then returned to us to catch up on news and chores. Tilik soon became eager to be back off to school at the end of every weekend, and when he was home spoke of little else. Even Tsetseg seemed to find a bit of unexpected confidence with her independence, although she remained a quiet and contemplative girl. As for Erdene and I, the extra chores we now shouldered in our children's absence gave us little time to miss them, although in the evening hours our ger felt far too large and tranquil without them. We told ourselves a good education was worth the pain of separation.

Then one day in mid winter Tilik came home and stunned us with a question.

"Ahv, are we proletariats or are we peasants?" he asked over mutton broth and dumplings one evening.

I'd heard such terms from Guyuk, but I never expected to hear them from my own child. His eight-year-old voice sounded far too young to be using them. "We're just herders," I said.

He screwed up his face, unsatisfied with my answer. "Don't we have to be one or the other? Since we're not bourgeoisie or imperialists. Sukh says that only workers in factories are proletariats, and that people who live in the country are peasants. But you have paid work too, even though it's not in a factory, and I'd rather be a proletariat because those are the people who get to lead the revolution."

Tsetseg jumped in. "The revolution is over, stupid. Peasants only existed when there was an aristocracy. Anyway, Ahv is an intellectual. Which makes you the son of an intellectual, even if we live in the countryside."

"Our teacher hasn't said anything about those," Tilik said uncertainly.

Erdene was ashen-faced. I probably was too.

"Who's Sukh?" I asked.

"He's a boy in my class. His father is a manager at the dairy factory, and has received many awards from the Party for his good work."

"Sukh doesn't board at the school during the week, then."

"No, his family's ger is in Ikh Tamir. Sometimes he takes me home with him for dinner so I can have a better meal than what we get at the school."

"That's very kind," I said, but I worried about how much Party ideology the family was feeding him as well.

"He's a proletariat," Tilik said, as though kindness and being a proletariat were two sides of the same shiny coin.

"Does it matter what we are, if we're good to others and work hard at whatever we do?" I asked.

"Yes it does," answered Tilik. "The proletariats are the only ones who ever get a front row seat when the cinema comes to town."

He was right about that. He had a child's keen eye for how the system worked, which made it difficult to convince him of any other point of view. Unlike his sister, who appeared to take anything learned at school as part of a trial she simply had to get through, Tilik took it all to heart.

"Why do we keep our prayers a secret?" he asked one evening after we had finished our usual ritual. The rest of the family had the tranquil air we usually felt after the ceremony, the secure feeling of a bond re-established. Tilik wore the look of someone whose mind is working out a problem.

"Because the people who rule Mongolia at this moment don't like the Buddha."

"Why not?"

"Because the Buddha is more powerful than they are, and that makes them frightened." I looked around our ger in the still-dim light that made everything soft. Erdene and Tsetseg were setting things out for the next day's breakfast and I wanted to concentrate on the simple, predictable pleasure of that, but Tilik was not to be quieted.

"But we like the Buddha," he said uncertainly.

"Yes."

"Does anyone else?"

"Yes, but it's hard to tell who because our current rulers, the ones who are frightened of Buddha, punish people who do."

"What kind of punishment?"

I didn't want to frighten him, but he had to understand the importance of silence. "They put them in prison."

Tilik thought about that one for a moment. "Can the Buddha get a person out of prison?"

"The Buddha has spiritual power, not physical power. But every action, bad or good, gets repaid at some point. The Buddha leads us to good actions so that good things happen in return."

Tilik frowned. "But going to prison isn't a good thing. So if praying to him is a good thing, why does a bad thing happen as a result?"

Erdene and Tsetseg stopped what they were doing to listen to my answer. I tried to figure out what my old master would have said. "Buddha has a bigger idea of time than the one we have in our short lives. Sometimes it takes awhile for him to overcome the bad things people do to each other, but he always wins in the end."

This wasn't good enough for Tilik. "I don't see how the Buddha is more powerful than our rulers," he said with perfect human logic. "They can put a person in prison. And the Buddha can't get them out."

He got up then. "I need to pee," he said, and went outside. He'd come to his own conclusion. As far as he was concerned, there was nothing more to be said.

Erdene and I talked a lot about the situation after that. "These questions of Tilik's are getting more and more difficult," she said. "And he hardly breathes a word during prayers anymore."

"He's confused about what's right. The Party presents him with the world as it is right now, the physical world. It's difficult to teach him about his inner world when they're talking to him about things that are easier to understand."

"The Party has a chance to persuade him every day. They could convince him that their way is better than the Eightfold Path. We need to instruct him more."

"It would be dangerous to talk to him too much about dharma. What if he starts asking questions of the Party the same way he asks questions of us? We would all be found out."

"Then he needs to see it for himself, through example, that the Buddhist way is best."

"What more can we do, in the two days we have?"

Erdene was silent for a moment. "We need to move closer to Ikh Tamir, so we can all live together again."

"Last time we talked about that, you couldn't bring yourself to move. This is your home. It is my home now, too. And the children's, when they are here. How can we leave?"

"How can we not?"

We applied for permission to move. We waited four months for a response, during which time we were like the wind blowing this way and that, caught between wanting them to say yes and wanting them to say no. When we finally got our answer it was hard to know whether or not we should be happy. The Party agreed to our request on one condition: As part of the after school program for Ikh Tamir's young pupils, two afternoons a week I was to teach art.

I knew what themes I would be expected to teach my students. I knew how I would be expected to channel their creativity to fit Party ideology. I sensed the lasso around my neck but, like a well-broken horse, I let myself be caught and led. It was all best for the family, I told myself.

We moved at the end of the summer, in time for the start of the school year. The other families at our new camp begrudged our entry into their area. Their pastures were already overgrazed, mostly due to poor management. We culled our herds but it was still a strain on the land. Although we brought a good stallion with us to inject new blood into their horses, our new neighbours clearly wished that we, and the rest of our animals, did not come with him.

When we first arrived they greeted us as tradition demands, and welcomed us by giving us lunch because we were busy erecting our ger. But there were indications even then.

"You can put your ger there," their lead man, Natsag, told me. It was the windward side of the camp, whereas a polite person would have offered the leeward side. "And you should keep your herds to the north, there," he said, pointing to the barest grazing in the area. I told myself this was a camp with less than what we had at home, so they had to be a bit stingy.

The next day we slaughtered a sheep and brought them stew to demonstrate our willingness to share. Tsetseg took them over a large bowl of it at dinner time.

"The people in this camp are mean," she said when she returned. "They gave me three tiny biscuits in return, not even enough for all of us, and they're yesterday's biscuits, and I saw they had many fresh ones by their stove." Her face was red with insult.

"They don't have much, they have to be careful," I said.

"I think Tsetseg's right," said Erdene. "Today, when you three were out with the herds, I went over to their ger to do my sewing with the other women, and they hardly said a single thing the whole time I was there. I finally left because it was so uncomfortable, and as soon as I got up to go they started chattering away to each other as women normally do."

"Well, we will just have to keep being pleasant and hope they become more friendly."

Instead, I found the same thing. When I tried to interest the men in a game of cards or shagai they made excuses as to why they couldn't. When I came upon them playing without me, they told me they were just finishing. Even their children rarely played with ours.

One weekend about a month after we arrived, Erdene and I were sitting quietly in our ger. She was mending clothes and I was working rawhide into a new lasso. The children were outside gathering dung for fuel with the neighbours' children when Tsetseg came rushing through our door, her hair flying out from under her headscarf, her eyes panicked.

"Ahv, come quickly, Tilik is in a fight."

I ran outside to find my son astride Natsag's boy, who was older and bigger but whom Tilik had pinned to the ground. Tilik was trying to stuff dung into the boy's mouth.

"Better a Party spy than a filthy, dung-eating peasant!" Tilik shouted. "You're worthless! Stupid and worthless!"

Natsag came around the back of his ger and watched as I dragged Tilik off his son. He was frowning the way someone does when they see the horse they bet on coming in well behind the leader. The boy scrambled to his feet, spitting brown gobs out of his mouth as he retreated to a safe place behind his father.

"What is this all about?" I asked, holding Tilik tight in my arms until his fists stopped swinging.

"Bold said we're Party spies sent here to keep an eye on them," he said. I felt him shaking slightly as his fighting adrenalin started to wane.

"Boys say all kinds of things they don't really mean," I said. "The wise man ignores such things."

"But he did mean it, Ahv. Everybody at this camp thinks so."

I was shocked.

"Go wash your mouth," Natsag said to Bold with a dismissive flick of his hand.

"Is this true?" I asked. "Is this what you all believe?"

"We see what we see. Bold says your boy is favoured in class."

"If Tilik is favoured it's because he works hard."

Natsag gave a sharp snort of disbelief. "He's favoured because he panders to the Party. Just like his father. Personally, I would rather be the head of a fly than the tail of a tiger."

"We're not the tail of anything. We're herders, just like you."

"You are not at all like us. You want to move close to the school and the Party says yes, even though there is not enough pasture for you here. And it's not as though you need your herds, anyway. You are offered an easy job at the school, when you already have work making paintings, if you can call that real work. You even get seats at the cinema." With a weary shrug he walked away, as though the matter of our favour was just one more unfairness forced on him by the Party; inevitable, outside of his control, and not worth discussing further.

I turned with Tilik to go back to our own ger and found Erdene and Tsetseg standing outside the door, witness to the conversation. I felt their forlorn expressions as a silent remonstration. What Natsag had said was true.

Inside our ger I sat Tilik down and stood before him.

"We all understand that Bold's accusation was terrible," I said, "but your reaction was even worse. Do you understand why?"

"The dung could make him sick."

"Even without the dung, you did wrong."

Tilik sat in sullen silence, looking at the floor.

"Anger doesn't resolve anything. It only feeds negative karma."

"But what he said was bad. He'll get worse karma than I will."

"You only have to worry about your own."

"If I didn't do anything after what he said it would be cowardly."

"Better cowardice than violence."

Tilik's stony expression made it clear that he was unimpressed. Looking at him I saw myself sitting in front of my master years ago, and thought that perhaps if I had listened better then I would have a better idea of what to say now.

"Right speech and right action are two important precepts of the Eightfold Path. No matter what he said, you were wrong to call him stupid and worthless, and you were wrong to act violently."

"Yes, Ahv," he said stonily.

"I want you to promise me you'll try not to lose your temper over words that way again, and never speak untrue words yourself against another person."

"I promise Ahv." He looked up at me. "I haven't finished collecting the dung. Can I go back out now?"

"Yes. If Bold comes out, tell him you'll finish the job by yourself today."

His face betrayed nothing of his thoughts. He got up and went out the door without a hint of remorse.

It was not long before the Party taught Tilik a lesson he found more compelling than mine.

When it came time to move to winter pastures, Natsag and his family did not come with us. They packed up one day with a terse announcement that they were being relocated, along with Natsag's parents. Natsag would not say more. Only his brother and cousin remained with us. They needed to remain close to Ikh Tamir as some members of their families had part-time jobs in the dairy factory.

After they left, Tilik told us he'd complained to his teacher about Bold's accusations.

"I told the truth," he said. "And I didn't show any anger, just like you said. I even admitted about the fight." He was proud of himself, eager to show us he'd done things the right way.

"Now I understand," he continued happily, "that it's better to let the Party punish the bad people rather than trying to do it yourself. That's what they're there for, after all. To take care of us. My teacher told me so himself."

Erdene looked to me, horrified. "Tilik," I said, "it's not always a good thing to go to the Party. They can be perhaps too quick to punish people."

Tilik's face was crestfallen, then angry. "But you said!"

"I said to tell the truth, yes. But complaining to the Party cost these people their camp site and their livelihood. It's terrible for them."

"They were bad!"

"People make mistakes, including each of us. We cannot judge others so harshly."

"The Party can. The Party knows what to do." He scowled at me and I knew what he was thinking: *they know better than you do*. His lips tight, he stomped over to his school books and put his face deep into the first one he came to, instinctively using it as a shield against me. I had never imagined that education could become between us, but I was beginning to see it could be so.

In my own work with the art program, I saw how good the school was at getting their ideas across. Pioneer and Youth League volunteers had been brought in to help me, just as they helped the main teacher during the regular school day.

While presenting a lesson one afternoon on drawing faces, I asked the students to try to draw someone they recalled well from memory, such as their mother or father. One of the Pioneers, Gombo, a sallow-

211

faced young man with a falsely sweet manner, interrupted me.

"Trusted comrade, I have another suggestion," he said, and pointed to a large photograph of Tsedenbal—the Prime Minister who had replaced Choibalsan—that hung prominently on the front wall of every classroom. "Some of our pupils might find it easier to work from an image that is already in front of them, don't you agree?"

"The idea was to draw from memory," I replied. "Children tend to remember what their parents look like quite well."

"Of course, you're the instructor. And it is always good to honour one's parents. But maybe a choice should be offered? After all, who could be a more fitting subject for a portrait than our beloved leader?"

After some humming and hawing, most of the children chose Tsedenbal as their subject. For every one who did, Gombo and his comrade made a point of speaking to each of them in a confidential way, smiling and commending them, delivering reassurance, carefully nurturing their trust. When I tried to do the same for the others, however, I was quickly interrupted to deal with some trumped up question. Delivering trust was the territory of the Young Pioneers. I was only supposed to deliver the lesson.

I began to realize that the pattern was always the same. Whenever I began to speak to any of my pupils individually, even if it was only to correct a technical problem they were having, an assistant always appeared at my side as if by magic. Even with Tilik I was not allowed to hold a private conversation during my lessons.

I also noticed how the children responded to this attention from the assistants. They glowed with pride when they were singled out for praise and smiled with shy longing whenever a Pioneer approached them, as devoted as dogs to an adored master.

And my son was no exception.

CHAPTER TWENTY SIX

IT IS USELESS TO GROPE BY NIGHT AFTER SOMETHING LOST IN THE DAY.

For several years we lived like lost souls in extended bardo, seeking a new life but unable to find a way out. Any choice we dreamt of having in the matter was eliminated when a law was passed requiring all children to attend school. We watched Tilik participate less and less in our family prayers to the point where he was there only in body, and we were powerless to stop his withdrawal. We watched ourselves grow tired with frustration and bored with the long winter evenings that were no longer filled with Gan's stories.

So when my old friend Qara appeared unexpectedly at our door in the early spring of 1957 we welcomed the distraction of his visit. He had moved with his wife to Ulaan Baatar to become the editor of a magazine about the arts in Mongolia. When my name had come up as an artist to feature, he had been happy to use the opportunity to seek me out.

The children were at school when he arrived. While Erdene prepared him tea, he bounded around the confines of our ger like a penned bear. The polite thing was to sit and wait to be served, but he was far too excited for that.

"You're politically perfect for the magazine, my boy, haha! A respected artist who has not forgotten the rewards of a herder's hard work. A true man of the people. A socialist ideal!"

"I really don't see myself that way."

"No matter. It's a government magazine. It's what they see in you that counts, and I'll make sure they see the things that please them."

I saw Erdene frown.

"And your art pleases them, oh yes. Tsedenbal himself will be asking you to paint his portrait if you play your cards right."

Erdene placed the tea on our low table and Qara was forced to restrict his bulk to a stool in order to accept it. He had always been a large man, but he'd grown in the years since I'd seen him last and now he would have outweighed two of me. Balanced on our stool he reminded me of a newspaper photograph I'd seen of a Moscow Circus elephant performing the same feat.

"So that's what you do now, make up this magazine?" I asked.

"This will be my second issue." He squirmed a little. "I started as the photographer. Do you know how to use a camera? I should show you one day, you'd find it interesting, oh ho! My job was to shoot the photos of featured artists, Party officials opening new plays and art exhibits, that kind of thing."

"And now you're the editor? Congratulations are in order."

"I'm still the photographer, but yes, now I'm the editor too." His usual joviality had ebbed. He leaned towards me and lowered his voice instinctively although there was no one but Erdene in our ger to overhear him.

"I don't really know what I'm doing. My former boss, the previous editor, was a highly competent man. But he was invited to participate in the special Conference of Intellectuals organized by the Party Central Committee."

"What's that?"

Qara looked surprised. "You really are far away from the capital here, aren't you? The Russians have been defaming Stalin now that he's dead. When the new come in, the old go out. So Tsedenbal did the same with Choibalsan, denouncing his "cult of personality" and so on. The Party even started talking about reform, and in that spirit they asked a group of their favourite intellectuals to offer their opinion of the Party's policies. Off the record, of course."

"No one would speak the truth otherwise."

"But here's the thing. The talk of reform passed, and anyone who was foolish enough to have criticized Party policies was exiled to the most remote places shortly after the conference. Including my boss."

"But had the Party not promised there would be no repercussions?"

"They had. You see? Nothing changes. You cross the Party and that's it for you." He shook his head. "So that's why I'm editing the magazine now. It's far too visible for my liking. One or two bad choices and I'll find myself being re-educated in Siberia for intellectual confusion. But I have no choice."

"There isn't any danger for me in being a featured artist, I hope."

"No, no. Don't worry. You don't even have to say anything if you don't want to. I can make up quotes that won't get you exiled."

"What difference would it make, really?" It was Erdene, speaking from the bed where she had been sitting quietly throughout our conversation. "If Dash spoke his mind, I mean. We already live in exile."

"Here?" asked Qara, looking around.

"We're finding it difficult," I explained. "Away from family, with neighbours who are not friendly. And we're not happy with what the children are being taught in school."

"Siberia would be much worse," Qara said. "They don't send people there together, either."

"There are things to be thankful for, no doubt," I said. Erdene was silent, her eyes averted from us both.

"So, about the article," Qara continued. "My sources tell me you studied art in Ulaan Baatar for eight months, where you were one of the top pupils in your class."

"Technically, perhaps. But the teachers always faulted me for not having enough affection for the subject matter."

"I heard that, too. But you got over it, I understand."

I winced. "Who is this source who knows so much about me?"

"Ah, Dash, still an innocent. If someone in the Party asks me to feature a People's Artist, you can be sure they have done their research first."

"Then why do you need to talk to me?"

"For authenticity, haha! And to take your photograph. But most of all because it allows me to make this pleasant journey to see an old friend."

"That last one is not a bad reason."

Qara smiled. "More facts: the mayor of Ikh Tamir is your patron?"

"Most of my work is for the Party, through him."

"Portraits of notables. 'With a keen eye for bringing out the inner man,' that's what I was told."

"They like to think so."

"And do you still sell paintings to the common man?"

"People buy landscapes on silk or leather from time to time. The stores in Ikh Tamir carry my work."

"You can't be charging very much for those."

"Painting the landscapes soothes me."

"Quite so, yes. I also enjoyed it," Qara said, nodding, then he leaned close as he had done earlier. "Are you making any thangkas?"

I glanced at Erdene. "No," I said.

The former lama looked relieved. "That's good. Best to stay away from that kind of thing these days. Really. You never know who might leak a secret under duress."

He asked me a few more questions, then we went outside to take photographs. He slipped in one of Erdene and I together, along with all the ones of me he had to take. When he finished the roll of film he took the camera apart to show me how it worked.

"When I get the photographs developed, I'll send you some," he said. "You will be the only herding couple in Ikh Tamir to have photographs of yourselves."

Qara stayed with us one more day, interviewed the mayor and the storekeepers about me, then returned to Ulaan Baatar to make the next edition of the magazine. True to his word, within a couple of weeks two photographs arrived in the post. There was one of me alone, and one of us standing together in front of our ger. They were the first photos we had ever seen of ourselves. In both of them I was smiling in a strained way that showed my nervousness in front of the camera. Erdene looked beautiful but startled, like a forest doe that has just raised its head at a suspicious sound.

It was fascinating to see ourselves, but after we had studied the photographs for awhile and shown them to the children, Erdene put the pictures in the drawer of our cupboard, tucked under documents. The last thing we needed was another visible sign of our privilege.

Two months later a copy of the magazine arrived, a dozen pages printed in black and white. Most of it was occupied with art exhibits in the capital, and the latest unveilings of civic statues in various town squares across the country. I was in the middle spread, the "People's Artist" feature. There was the same photo of me that Qara had sent us, one of the mayor, and a couple of portraits I had painted. One of them was Badrakh's.

The family gathered around me excitedly to see the article.

"Look at how good your father's portraits are," Erdene said. They rarely got an opportunity to see them, apart from the one that hung in Ikh Tamir's town hall, because I painted them away from home.

"That man looks especially important," said Tilik, pointing to Badrakh.

I wished Qara had chosen any other painting. "He is the governor of Arkhangai."

Tilik was delighted. "My Ahv has painted the governor of Arkhangai," he said. He would be telling everyone at school the next day.

Tsetseg had been reading the text. "Did you really say those things about making art available for people who can't afford it?" she asked.

I started reading where she indicated.

A true man of the people, still living in the traditional herder's way, Dash Chuluuny doesn't let his fame separate him from the proletariat. He makes sure the local stores keep a good supply of his well-loved landscape paintings at affordable prices, and has been known to give them away to those who can't afford even those low charges. "Anyone who has a thirst for culture should have access to it," he says. "Art is not just for a wealthy few. It is for the people."

"No, I didn't say that."

"But it's a right thought, anyway," said Tilik. "And this part here is very good, about not feeling the need to live in a fancy way even though you could, and how proud you are of the local school and how well Tsetseg and I are doing there. Our names are there in the magazine, see Tsetseg?"

"But if Ahv didn't say any of this, how is it good?" asked Tsetseg.

"I'm sure he thought it, at least," said Tilik. "Can I take the magazine to school tomorrow, Ahv?"

Erdene had turned away; she'd had enough of the article.

"I don't think you should take it," I said. "That would be bragging, and that is not a right action."

"But no one will believe me if I can't show them."

"They do not need to know."

Tilik needn't have worried. The mayor made sure his copy of the magazine made it to the school so that the children could tell their parents he was a "patron" of art and that their after-school art instructor was someone notable. Tilik was thrilled with the attention and wanted to talk of nothing else. Erdene, however, forbade everyone in the family from speaking any more about the article. I never saw it again in our ger. I suspect it ended up in the stove, but I could never bring myself to ask.

The following spring, Tilik and I were outside splitting firewood when a lone horseman came trotting towards our ger. As he halted by our tether line I recognized him as Gombo, the sallow young man who had inspired my art students to use Tsedenbal as their portrait subject. He had since graduated from Young Pioneer to full-fledged Party member. Tilik recognized him too, but with more enthusiasm.

"Gombo!" he cried, running up to help him tie up his horse, and receiving a warm clasp around the shoulders for his trouble.

I welcomed the young man as civilly as I could.

"I'm here to tell you about an important new resolution that has been taken at the Thirteenth Party Congress," Gombo announced. "Faithful Party members are being sent out to every herding household with the news. When I saw Tilik's family on the list I asked to have the pleasure of being the one to tell you." He placed his hand affectionately on Tilik's capped head. I wanted to swipe his hand right off, but instead I invited him to enter our ger, as I knew I must.

Tilik pulled a stool into the place of honour for him and Gombo sat, praising Erdene for the quality of her biscuits and the neatness of our ger. His comments came out not as compliments, however, but as judgments he felt qualified to make on her performance. It was particularly patronizing given that he was still very young, perhaps twenty. Erdene scarcely acknowledged his words. I'm sure she was glad Tsetseg was off visiting a friend in another camp and was not there to hear them.

I had the feeling he was looking around hoping to find flaws; a sign of excessive wealth, some inappropriate luxury, a religious artifact left lying about. But as the magazine article had attested—its one truth—we lived simply. And our few religious articles were well hidden.

Once Gombo had drained his tea, he got straight to the point. "The Mongolian People's Revolutionary Party has decided that, for the future development of our country, the transition to a socialist economy via collectivization of the herders has become essential."

"But the Party tried that already, in the thirties," I said. "It didn't work, and they reverted back to private ownership."

"That's because our economy was not yet ready, and the people were too ignorant to understand. But we are much further ahead now. And to help the people understand, we are going like this, ger to ger, so that no one might suffer ignorance in the matter this time."

I noticed Tilik sitting on the bed listening intently. His eyes were fixed on Gombo as though he expected gold to pour forth from his mouth. Erdene was also sitting on the bed, but she looked as though she expected serpents.

"I thought animal production was increasing in line with targets," I said. "Why change something that's going well?"

"Because the old policies have resulted in inequalities among the herders. Differences in capital accumulation allow the exploitation of poorer herdsmen."

Suddenly Tilik jumped in. "Only through collective ownership of the means of production can all herdsmen be truly equal, Ahv."

"You're absolutely right, Tilik," said Gombo, seizing the moment as he had done in art class. "And by ending the separation of herdsmen into different groups, we end exploitation."

Tilik beamed with pride. Erdene put her arm around him but he squirmed, wanting to be an adult in the conversation. She removed her arm.

"I don't believe we have been exploiting anyone," I protested.

"Then you have much to gain and little to lose."

"Besides what herds I have."

"You will be allowed to keep fifty head for your personal use. With all due respect, Dash *aa*, you are a noted artist of the Party. You do not need large herds to live well."

Fifty head of anything was negligible, and worthless if you wanted to keep a variety of animals. "And what becomes of the rest?"

"The government will buy them at reasonable prices, whereupon they will become the property of the people. Herders will be organized into cooperatives, or *negdel*, to look after specific breeds of animals. By specializing in this way each negdel will maximize their knowledge."

"But our whole system of agriculture is based on raising a variety of animals, all complementary. The horse for riding, cattle and sheep for milk and meat, the wool for felt, the leather for clothing, and so on. How are we to provide ourselves with these things if we can only raise one kind of animal?"

Gombo smiled at me the way adults do when they hear children say things that are laughably ignorant. It made me boil with anger but I kept my face still.

"You describe the agriculture of Mongolia's past," he explained carefully. "We can develop successfully only by combining such traditional skills with modern scientific and technological achievements, and these can only be offered fairly to all through a socialist economy."

He went on to describe how each cooperative would contribute the products of their particular animal, and the products would then be shared among different cooperatives so that everyone got what they needed. Likewise the work we currently did all together in our ger camps would be divided up into specific jobs so that each person learned one skill well and had the rest done for them. It seemed like a crazy idea to me. I glanced at Erdene and she was shaking her head, clearly thinking the same thing. A herder was successful because he mastered many skills. If you needed soup you could make soup. If you needed felt you could make felt. What kind of benefit was it to have a system in which you were not allowed to make for yourself the things you most needed?

"I don't think it will work," I said when he had finished. "The herders will not accept it."

"Are you saying you yourself do not accept it?"

Tilik was hanging his head with shame that his father should doubt the intelligence of the Party. "I'm saying only that last time the Party tried to collectivize herders, they resisted," I said. "And I don't think things have changed so much that they will not resist again."

"Of course collectivization is entirely voluntary," Gombo said. "There may be some who fail to grasp the importance of doing their civic duty, but we will do our best to convince them, and I'm certain we will prevail."

I understood him perfectly. "What is the timing of all this?"

"We will establish the first negdel in Ikh Tamir this spring, for cattle. It will be a very important one. Since it's in your district, you will be encouraged to join."

"And for the rest of the country?"

"The Party has set a goal of three years for the transformation, but we feel sure the industrious people of Mongolia will work to achieve it faster than that. Great leaps forward are often best achieved in a single burst of effort, don't you agree?"

I did not agree, not with any of it. But like the other half a million herders in Mongolia, my lack of agreement meant nothing to a Party determined to collectivize its animal husbandry.

The herders did resist, as I predicted, by delaying their entry into the cooperatives, selling their livestock first to anyone who might give them a better price than the low one set by the government, slaughtering and eating in an unseasonable fashion those they could not sell, anything to prevent the cooperatives from gaining what was theirs. In some regions they went so far as to destroy pastures. It was all useless against the will of the Party. In the space of one year almost one hundred percent of the country's herders had been collectivized, voluntarily or otherwise. Gombo must have been very proud.

We kept thirty horses, for a Mongolian without a horse feels incomplete, and a household cannot be without its own airag. We also kept four khainag and four cows for milk, two yaks for hauling, milking and for their hair, and ten sheep for wool and eating. But fifty animals is a hobby, not an occupation. All those years we had lived as herders because we liked it, even though my income as an artist meant we didn't need to herd to live. We did so because we liked the peace of it, the way it made us feel part of the land and seasons, for the variety of the chores and the sharing of the load among families. All that was disappearing.

By handing our herds over we automatically became a part of the cooperative near Ikh Tamir. We tried to make a place for ourselves there, but it was too strange. Russian technicians introduced milking machines to increase production, and young female Pioneers dressed in army uniforms like men tried to teach experienced milkers like Erdene how to use the machines instead. When Erdene first put the sucking tubes on to a cow's teats, she jumped in surprise at the way the connecting hose jolted when the suction began. The young instructor sniggered and Erdene refused to return.

I only lasted a week before I gave up my position as a herder. The herders knew more than the bosses, but were beaten down by the rules and by people denouncing each other in order to get ahead. It was called a cooperative but there was little cooperation compared to how we had kept our animals in the old way, with our families.

CHAPTER TWENTY SEVEN

EVEN ROUGH CLOTH FROM
YOUR HOME GROUND SEEMS SMOOTH.

Towards the end of the summer we went to visit Erdene's family. They had also been collectivized, and were breeding khainag. Like everyone else they were displeased, but they still lived in the lands they loved, there was no factory to go to, and they had each other for comfort. Tabin, now thirty, was married, and Tsetseg was pleased at the chance to help look after his two toddlers. Tuli doted on Tilik like a grandmother, while Cholon tried to make sure the boy hadn't lost the ability to do a man's proper work or—almost as important—play a good game of shagai. Gan and Maa welcomed us into their ger, where Erdene slipped into her old household routines as though she had never left. Every day her parents still opened their cupboard on the north wall to say a prayer before the thangka I had made for them years ago.

In the evenings, by a bonfire, we listened to Gan's stories and sang the old songs just as we had before we'd moved. I watched Erdene listening to her father's stories; her eyes were gently closed, her face serene. She was more peaceful than she'd been for a long time. Frequently I caught her just standing and staring at the gers or the familiar hills.

On the third day of our visit she insisted that the two of us ride to the place at the foot of the hills where, sixteen years earlier, she had agreed to marry me. We hobbled the horses and sat on the grass. The afternoon sun, pure yellow in a blue sky, cast voluptuous shadows of the hills upon the steppe. With her arms wrapped around her knees, Erdene looked across the plain towards the ger camp that had been her summer home all her life until we'd moved to the outskirts of Ikh Tamir. It was only a half-day's ride, but it could have been another country altogether.

"Tsetseg has finished middle school," Erdene began. "She doesn't have to go anymore."

"Does she not want to continue?"

"She has suffered school because she had to. Now she wants our old life back."

"As do we all. But it's gone. Even here, things are not as they were."

"Still, here there is some comfort."

I recalled the way Erdene had looked by the bonfire the night before. "Moving closer to the school has been good for the children, though," I said.

"For Tsetseg. She needed to come home to her family every day. But Tilik?" She was silent for a moment. "What influence have we had, Dash? Being with him every day these past few years, has it made a difference? I think many times he finds us embarrassing because we don't embrace the political ideals he believes in."

"It is a difficult thing, to influence him against the teachings of the Party. I've been doing my best."

"But it's not working. We are all being tortured for the sake of a battle we are losing."

"We cannot leave him to Gombo," I said.

"In another year, he won't give us a choice."

Tilik would graduate middle school the following spring, one year younger than Tsetseg because he'd started sooner and learned faster. He had been talking about going to Russia to continue his education. Many bright students were sent there, especially the eager socialists. Gombo would surely arrange to make it happen.

"Then I have one more year to make a difference in his life."

Erdene said nothing. Perhaps she doubted that I could do so. Perhaps she just doubted her own ability, or Tsetseg's, to withstand another year in exile.

"Maybe you and Tsetseg should move back here, with our ger," I said. She didn't jump to say no, and that told me everything. "You can take the animals; Tilik and I will only need a few horses. I will buy a small ger for us to stay in during the week, when he goes to class and I teach, and at the end of every week we will come back here for two days just as the children did at the beginning."

"To break up the family is not good," said Erdene.

I took her face in my hands. Although at thirty-five she already wore Mongolia's climate in a tracery of deep creases fanning out from her eyes, to me she was as beautiful and perfect as the day I first saw her in the cave. I realized in that moment how much Ikh Tamir was crushing her with its lack of community. She needed the comfort of her full familial group. I had to let her go back.

"It's the only way", I said. "Five days a week, from autumn through spring; that's all. You and Tsetseg cannot go back to Ikh Tamir. It was bad enough living with strangers when we still had our herds. Without them it is intolerable. We must move back to what we know and those we love. It is only that you and Tsetseg are going first."

She let me convince her, which is how I know it was what she really wanted. I have never been able to tell Erdene what do to.

The first debate I had with Tilik on returning to Ikh Tamir in the autumn concerned where to live. Now that we had no animals except our two horses, he wanted to move to one of the fenced enclosures that had been set up in the town. I wanted to stay in the countryside.

"Everything is easier if we live in town," he argued. "We can walk to the school and to the stores for food. There is even a man who brings water in barrels for a fee, so we don't have to borrow a yak and go to the river."

"I like going to the river."

"Then why do you often send me? And in the winter that is not a pleasant chore at all."

"We have always lived in the country."

"Then it's time to try a new way."

"I do not want to try a new way. Those enclosures are like prisons. I cannot live in one of them, and we will not."

We set our new ger where the old one had been, but Tilik was grumpy and uncooperative the whole time we were erecting it, and he complained every time he had to go for water, so that I couldn't forget his point of view.

With the extra time I now had from not keeping animals, I created more small paintings to sell at the stores and came to the school at the end of every day in order to be closer to Tilik. My plan was that when he and I were not busy with our work we would do things together. In particular I wanted to take the newly freed time to teach Tilik Buddhist dharma, but instead he joined the athletic and chess clubs that had started up at school. His wiry frame made him quick on his feet and his quicker brain won many chess matches, which made them call on him all the more. I went along to watch, a ghost hovering in the background of his life.

One day in late autumn, a Russian who liked my paintings and had bought several to take home as gifts invited us to Tsetserleg to see his airplane. An airstrip had been set up there to take cargo and the occasional person back and forth to Ulaan Baatar. In a country where the horse was still the major form of transportation, airplanes were a marvel. Both Tilik and I were thrilled at the chance to inspect one with someone who knew about them.

We met the Russian at the airfield, and he brought us over to see the plane where it sat tethered against the wind with ropes and large heavy blocks, not unlike a horse that has been ground-tied. It was a small plane with the wings attached at the bottom of the body, and a single propeller at its nose. Inside, there were two forward seats for the pilot and co-pilot, and two more behind. The rest of the interior was empty, with nets and ropes for holding cargo in place during flight.

"Can you show me how to work the ailerons?" asked Tilik. "And the rudder, and the wing flaps? Is it the ailerons that make it turn, or the flaps?" He was using Russian words for the mechanical parts. I didn't understand what he was talking about.

The Russian laughed. "You know a lot already."

"We learned a little in school about how planes fly."

"Very good! Come to the cockpit. I will show you everything."

While I looked on from one of the passenger seats, Tilik sat with the pilot and learned how to use the joystick. Back for up, forward for down, side to side for turns.

"Look out the window, there behind," instructed the Russian. "See how her flaps move when you move the stick like so? And the foot peddles, they make her rudder move, see?"

"And what do all these gauges mean?" asked Tilik after he had mastered the intricacies of steering.

"I do not know how to explain in Mongolian. Too technical."

Tilik glanced at me briefly, then turned back to the Russian. "Speak in Russian. I can understand."

They carried on a rapid conversation, some of which Tilik translated for me until it became clear I didn't understand the physics fully in any case. This too was part of our divide. Tilik had studied not just Russian but also modern subjects, while I had studied Buddhist philosophy, religious art, astronomy, botany, herbal medicines, and the Tibetan language.

Tilik switched back to Mongolian and begged him to take us aloft, but it was not allowed.

"You go to school, learn for yourself," said the pilot.

"I'd like that," said Tilik. His hands were on the stick, moving it this way and that as he looked intently through the windscreen, already airborne in his mind's eye.

The Russian turned to me. "Your son is a natural pilot!" he said, grinning.

I tried to smile back, but it probably wasn't convincing. I was seeing something for the first time: that my son inhabited a completely different world from mine. His was the new one. I would never keep up.

It wasn't much of a surprise when Tilik came home wearing the dreaded red tie and military clothes of a Young Pioneer. To commemorate the occasion he'd been given a beautiful, leather-bound book of Tsedenbal's speeches. He saw my displeasure but knew I was powerless against the state-sanctioned beliefs he embraced. We didn't pray together after that. In the evenings he read his book of speeches, memorizing every word. I stared at my father's thangka and tried to address Tara, but each turn of the page in Tilik's book tore through my concentration and left me mumbling the prayers, fruitlessly, to myself.

Chapter Twenty Eight

IF YOU'RE AFRAID, DON'T DO IT.
IF YOU DO IT, DON'T BE AFRAID.

Shortly after Tilik became a Young Pioneer, the neighbours who still remained after the dung incident received a new member into their household: an aged uncle. They all seemed nervous about his arrival and were not at all pleased to have him there.

He arrived on a yak cart rather than riding on a horse, buried under several layers of sheepskin against the winter cold, and I noticed as they helped him into their ger that he babbled continuously under his breath. I assumed he had dementia. When I went to their ger the next day to bring them a block of tea in return for a couple of bowls of their stew, however, he raised his voice on seeing me and I heard him clearly.

He was reciting Buddhist scripture in Tibetan. My surprise must have signaled to him that I understood, for he immediately addressed me.

"You understand the words of the Buddha?" he said in Tibetan.

I nodded slightly, nervous about divulging my capacity with the rest of the family watching us.

"Compassionate Avalokitesvara has answered my prayers at last," he said, again in Tibetan, and began to weep. His old lips kept moving even when he stopped talking, as though they had become so accustomed to it they could no longer hold still.

"Please excuse my uncle," said my neighbour. "He is not in his right mind. All day long he speaks in the language a lama taught him many years ago, back when there were such things. But of course he doesn't practice religion anymore."

"Of course not," I said. Since they were convinced Tilik and I were spies, a notion amply confirmed when Tilik had their relatives sent away, they must have been in terror to be housing a scripture-babbling old monk next door to us.

"My father could not keep him, he drove the household crazy with his constant talking."

"I understand. But someone has to take him in. You are doing the right thing."

My neighbour looked greatly relieved. It was more likely the old uncle had been sent away because he was a risk, not an irritation.

My neighbour's wife handed me our two bowls, now filled with stew. I thought it best to leave right away.

The old man spoke again as I opened the door to go.

"Thank you, Compassionate One," I heard him say. I glanced back. His eyes were closed. He was smiling softly and nodding his head up and down, up and down, content.

The following morning as I sat painting a winter landscape in the cozy warmth of my ger, I heard at my door a voice so faint it might have been the whisper of a ghost. I wasn't certain I had even heard it.

"Is someone there?" I asked.

"It is I, Arigh," the voice said more clearly now.

I opened the door to find the old monk. He bent down to enter but he was scarcely straighter once he was in, he was so stooped with age. I offered him tea.

"Not too full a cup," he said, showing me hands that trembled uncontrollably. "These old hands spill too much."

As I prepared the tea he shuffled over to inspect my painting, peering at the work on the easel. He was not mumbling.

"Do you know how to make a proper thangka?" he asked.

It felt very odd to be speaking openly about such things with someone I'd just met. "I have done."

"I would very much like to see one again." He turned from the painting to look at the source of the light that was shining on it. In addition to the usual, dim oil lamps I had purchased a real luxury: a battery-operated flashlight that shone a relatively powerful beam of light directly at the work surface. I had strung it up on the roof poles with some twine. "How does that work?" Arigh asked.

I took it down and showed him, pulling out the batteries. "These wear down, like the butter in a lamp," I explained. "Then you have to buy more. The bulb also has to be replaced from time to time."

He nodded. "Like the lights in town buildings where they have electricity."

"Yes." I put the flashlight back together. "Please, sit and I will bring you the tea."

"Do you have more of those batteries?" he asked as he maneuvered himself carefully onto the stool.

"I keep a small supply."

"That's good, because we will need much light for our work."

"Our work?"

I gave him a half-bowl of salty tea, which he accepted with two hands and struggled to bring it to his mouth without spilling. He drained his bowl and set it down on the table, then reached into his robe and brought out the familiar form of a wood-bound scripture book, holding the sacred object out to me with his trembling hands.

I hesitated.

His hands wobbled more. "Take it," he said, "Before I drop it. The Buddha would not be happy if it fell on the floor."

I took it from him and forced myself to open it. Inside was a familiar sutra, but it was not in the Tibetan in which I had learned it.

"It's in Mongolian," I said. "In the old script."

"Translated, yes. There was a time when all our scripture was in Mongolian, did you know? It is important that we have proper translations of our own, Mongolian Buddhist traditions. The new Mongolia will not understand Tibetan, so we are translating all the scriptures. That is our work."

In my mind's eye I saw the unhinged gate of the four old monks and the flattened circle of earth where their ger had been, their existence erased. I knew where this kind of work led. I closed the book and tried to give it back to him, but he kept his hands obstinately in his lap until I gave up. "The new Mongolia will not understand Mongolian script, either," I said. "It would have to be in Cyrillic."

"That would be wrong."

"The Party does not allow scriptures, in any language."

Arigh shook his head. "That will not last. All human constructs are temporary, you know that. And when it changes we must be ready. I repeat the scriptures to myself aloud so that I don't forget them before they're written down."

"Which your family takes for madness."

A mischievous smile crossed his wrinkled lips. "It is perhaps better if they do not understand."

"Surely there are already Mongolian Buddhist scripture books buried in safe places, or taken out of the country."

"Perhaps there are. But perhaps there are not, or they will not be found. How can I, who have the capacity to do this work, leave it for others? Each individual effort is another assurance that in the time of freedom, which will come even if it is centuries from now, we have the means to rebuild our faith."

I thought Arigh must actually be mad, to be working at something so risky, impossible and unnecessary. But as he sat there in his patient monk's way, waiting serenely for me to respond, it occurred to me that perhaps it was his very effort that counted, not the necessity or lack thereof. Throughout a time of great oppression this feeble monk had been quietly exercising his beliefs in the most selfless way possible—preserving them for future generations—while thousands of others, like myself, had allowed themselves to be beaten down. Arigh's small act of courage made my own cowardice all the more shameful.

"The scriptures are many," I said. "Too many for one man. Are there others involved in this work?"

"Fewer all the time. Some younger ones were imprisoned or executed along the way, and some death has claimed naturally. When we left Erdene Zuu, we were twelve. Now we are half that, so far as I know."

Erdene Zuu. I thought of another scripture book from a monk of that monastery, translated by his own hand into Mongolian. A book that had seared my stomach over a long journey and now lay under the floorboards an arm's length away.

"Dorj was one of you," I said.

Arigh's eyes lit up. "You knew Dorj?"

"He came to live at my father's ger camp after the destruction of Erdene Zuu. I knew him only briefly, and I was not there when the authorities came for him."

"But he told you of our work."

My heart beat fast with a familiar rising fear. I had been happily painting a landscape when this monk walked in. I didn't want to get involved. Just knowing what he was doing was risk enough for me. But there he was, his face shining with joy to think he'd found a link to one of his lost brothers, and I felt myself being dragged into his dream despite the voice that screamed in my head to show him politely to the door.

"Dorj never spoke of the work," I said. "But he left something for me to keep safe." I moved the chest of drawers at the end of the bed, lifted the floorboards, and removed the book from where it lay with Dorj's prayer wheel.

Arigh caressed the cover like a mother stroking the cheek of child returned from a long absence. He opened the book and began to look through it, turning each page slowly until he got to where the writing abruptly ended. He looked up at me.

"But why have you not finished it?"

His innocent question was like a sudden slap to my face as I realized that the idea of completing it had never even occurred to me. Back when I had been alone in the cave after Khovor Khan, the need to remember and write scripture on every wall had been so powerful it could not be contained. But with time that need had become as indistinct as the emotion of a long-past dream.

"My memory of the scriptures is poor," I said. "I was never ordained."

It was a pathetic excuse. His nodding acceptance made me feel worse for having uttered it.

"Then I will help you, and you will help me. My task was to transcribe the Short Discourses, but I remember many scriptures besides those entrusted to me. My mind is still clear; it is my hands that betray me." He held them out in front of him, watching their spasms as though he were trying to figure out how he had ended up with such useless tools. "I have been praying for a year for the Buddha to send someone to write for me. And now here you are."

You will have a chance to regain your spirit in the future, the shaman had said. *Don't let fear squander it.*

Arigh was smiling at me happily, not imagining for a moment that I could have doubts about such a worthy enterprise. "Has the Buddha been so kind as to send me someone who also has a good supply of fine muutuu paper to write on?" he asked.

I nodded weakly.

"*Ai ho*," he said, "the Buddha is doubly compassionate." He leaned toward me. "And now will you show me that thangka?"

Arigh wasted no time, appearing the next morning as soon as his relatives had scattered to their various jobs. With him, however, was his nephew's wife, the matriarch of the ger.

"I'm very sorry to disturb you," she said. "But the old man insisted you had invited him to come watch you paint. I'm sure he must be wrong, but he wouldn't be quiet until I agreed to come over and put it to you myself."

I looked from the impatient wife to Arigh, his expression all innocence. I was already having misgivings and thought about telling her she was right, he had not been invited. I would come back as a dung beetle in my next life for such a thing.

"It's all right," I told her. "I did in fact invite him to watch, as he seemed to need entertainment and you seemed to need a break. He's welcome here any morning he wants."

The woman looked at first stunned, then delighted. She turned to Arigh. "Behave yourself now," she said, waggling a finger at him as though he were four years old. "No blathering on and disturbing the kind man." She looked at him for a moment, frowning as though she doubted his behavior would allow her this freedom for long. Then she turned to me. "Thank you," she said simply, and went back to her own ger.

We started with the completion of Dorj's book, with Arigh dictating what came next and me writing it. That first morning I worried constantly about being found out. I thought I kept my fretting to myself, but finally Arigh brought it up.

"Do you know how many times you have glanced towards the door since we began?" he asked.

"Am I doing that?"

"About once for every sentence written. Do you think someone is going to swoop in and arrest us both?"

I did.

"This is your ger," he reassured me. "They will call out first."

I was pretty sure they hadn't bothered to call out to the four old monks. They had swooped. With Dorj they had been more polite before taking him away for ever. The result was the same either way.

"Just write." He gestured with his hand to keep the words flowing. "The script becomes more beautiful that way."

"My writing isn't fine enough for this work," I argued. "I'm out of practice."

"Well, if you keep at it, soon you will be back in form," he said, and waited for me to begin again.

My script did become more beautiful after several weeks. Little by little I began to enjoy the process and worry less. The flowing symbols married well with the Buddhist prayers, producing a harmony between my hand and the sounds it was depicting, like making a kind of music.

I remembered lines I thought I had forgotten, phrases often popping unexpectedly into my head when Arigh couldn't recall some part or another. With practice this ability grew, as though the scriptures had been locked in a dusty cabinet in the back of my brain, waiting for someone to prise open the creaking door. Arigh invariably knew more than I—he had been in a monastery almost fifty years before Erdene Zuu was destroyed—but the fact that I had not lost everything I'd learned encouraged me.

Mid-morning we always took a break for tea. The woman of his ger started sending him over with a few biscuits.

"See what my keeper has given me to bring you today?" he said the first time he came with them. "She's so anxious for me to keep coming here that she's willing to part with food." He started laughing. "Our actions are already producing positive karma, you see? That stingy woman is learning generosity!"

We set the biscuits on the hot iron top of the stove to keep warm, and when it was break time we sat ourselves on stools to either side. We talked of our experiences as monastics.

"It's a good life, being a monk," Arigh said, as though we were merely on vacation from our monasteries and they continued on in our absence, waiting for our return. "The schedule, it gives discipline to your day."

I nodded. "Although it took me a long time to learn how to wake up that early."

"That can be difficult. But there are compensations."

"Like the first moment of chanting, when the low hum rises like a bird taking flight."

"Oh yes, that is a lovely moment," Arigh said. "And the single note of the long trumpet. We had an old monk, Sube—he would be dead by now—who loved to sound that instrument. He would play extra notes, even when they interfered with prayer words, just to hear the sound." He laughed, remembering.

"Was he not disciplined by your Abbot?"

"Never enough! The Abbot gave up trying, saying that Sube existed as a test of his capacity for patience, and so he must leave him be."

"For some, not everything can be renounced."

"For most, in fact."

We told many such stories during our sessions together. We never spoke of our monasteries' destruction, or our own survival.

A few weeks into our efforts, Arigh startled me with a question.

"Why does your son wear a soldier's clothes and the blood red scarf?"

"It is a symbol of his membership in the Young Pioneers."

"Does he not know it is bad karma to wear red around your neck?"

I hesitated. "He does not believe in karma. He believes in the Party."

Arigh's lips were working, his nearly toothless gums chewing at my answer as though it were a difficult piece of gristle. I had chewed on it a long time myself and could have told him it would not go down.

"Did you not instruct him?" he asked.

"I instructed him. He was often the one to lead our family prayers when he was younger. Before he started going to school." I could feel myself bristling, rising to Tilik's defense. Or mine. "A Party school."

Arigh nodded.

"I instructed him in the Eightfold Path. About right view and right intention. We had many discussions about right speech and right action, right livelihood and effort. Perhaps less on right mindfulness and concentration, as he was not practicing meditation. But it was useless against what the Party taught him every day."

Arigh continued to nod thoughtfully, neither condemning nor accepting my claims.

I sighed. My defenses were pointless in the face of the truth. "I was too busy protecting my son to guide him well. I had seen so much death. I wanted to spare him. I didn't foresee the cost."

"How can we know?" Arigh said. "After all, we are not enlightened beings."

Although my work with Arigh gave fresh purpose to my days, it was still for the weekends at home that I lived. Every time I saw Erdene again I felt the same combination of relief and joy, like a blessing not fully deserved. Tsetseg was blossoming, happy to be living at home and working as a milker for the cooperative. I noticed that neighbouring boys were starting to ride by regularly, hoping to catch a visit with her.

The weekend before Tsagaan Sar our whole camp was dizzy with activity in preparation for the festivities; slaughtering sheep, making sweets, dumplings, and special pastries shaped like a *gabj* wheel, polishing silver strikers and knife sets to wear with dress dels, collecting and making small gifts to give. Even Tilik seemed completely swept up in the activity, and for once not looking as though he wished he were back at school. As Erdene fitted him for a new silk del for the occasion to replace the one he had outgrown, I watched and thought how much better he looked in traditional dress. I had forbidden him from ever wearing his uniform and tie home. It was bad enough when he had told Erdene about becoming a Young Pioneer; I didn't want to upset her further by having her see the uniform. Here like this, preparing for Tsagaan Sar, it was as though we were still the traditional herding family we used to be.

Later that evening we managed to send the children out to the other gers to play and visit, giving us some time to ourselves.

"I have something to tell you," I said to Erdene when they had gone. "Something good, I think."

She looked at me quizzically. "You think?" She sat on our bed and patted the place next to her for me to join her.

"An old monk has come to live next door to us at Ikh Tamir," I said.

"A monk? Openly?"

"Not openly. But he revealed himself to me. He has been translating scripture into Mongolian script, like Dorj. Part of a network of monks who are doing this work in secret, each one with responsibility for a different set of scriptures. To save the words for future generations who won't understand Tibetan."

"That's noble work," she said. "And courageous of them."

"I am helping him."

Erdene's open-mouthed surprise made the risk of it all come rushing forward again.

"I don't know why I said yes, it's so foolish," I said, my words tumbling out in an effort to reassure her. "We try to be careful. I tried to refuse but I just couldn't. His hands no longer write, he's afflicted with trembling. He believes that Buddha sent me to him."

Erdene touched my face gently to stop my torrent of words. "Perhaps," she said, thoughtful, "it is the other way around. Buddha sent *him* to *you*, Dash. It's what you should be doing."

"It's dangerous."

"It's important."

"You want me to continue?"

She kissed me. "Yes," she said, then smiled, then kissed me again more deeply. "My handsome monk." She pushed me back on to the bed and sprawled on top of me with a playful ardour she hadn't shown for a long time.

"I should draw the curtain," I mumbled into her hair, breathing in the familiar, heady smell of her.

"Cholon said he would play shagai with them. They won't be back for a long time," Erdene said, and her hands slipped between our bodies to untie my sash.

CHAPTER TWENTY NINE

THE MAN WHO HAS NOT
TAKEN CARE OF HIMSELF WILL NOT BE ABLE
TO TAKE CARE OF OTHERS.

For Tsagaan Sar we got a few extra days of holiday, days spent in celebration, feasting and games. I found it more difficult than usual to ride back to Ikh Tamir when they were over. To compensate I threw myself into the scripture writing with renewed vigour, often continuing on after Arigh had gone back to his own ger, or starting before he arrived, when I could remember enough of the text to do so.

"What good progress we are making," Arigh said near the end of one morning's efforts.

A half dozen pages were laid out on the floor of the ger to dry before we bound them to make the fourth book. "We're getting each book done much faster now," I said.

"Your writing is improving too, don't you think? These pages look better than the earlier ones."

All of a sudden the door flew open. Having imagined such a thing obsessively at the start of our project, I had slowly forgotten to fear it. But when I saw a figure bursting through the door unbidden, my heart leapt immediately to my throat.

"Ahv, I have the most wonderful news."

It was Tilik, home early from school. As he pulled the door to behind him I felt my jellied heart sigh with relief. Then I saw his eyes adjust to the dim light, to Arigh, to the sheaves of scripture now scattered about from the blast of winter wind that had flown in with my son.

"Sain bain uu," he greeted Arigh, politely. But his face had shifted from looking excited at his news to looking suspicious. Arigh and I were frozen like illicit lovers who had just been caught in bed. Tilik bent to pick up a sheaf.

"What are you doing?" he asked, then began to read. "*Eejee*, it's scripture," he exclaimed. He dropped the page as though it had burnt his fingers.

"Arigh, you should return to your own ger now," I said. He shuffled out without delay.

When he had gone I explained to Tilik what Arigh's mumbling was really about, and what we were doing.

"How could you put us in danger this way?" he asked, horrified.

"It is important work."

"More important than the family? I came to tell you my good news, but it will never happen if the Party finds out that my father is making scripture books with some crazy old monk."

"Tell me your news."

A little of Tilik's previous excitement returned to his face. "Gombo has arranged, through a very important friend, for me to attend the scientific school in Tsetserleg."

I wanted to share his happiness but found myself struggling. "The scientific school?"

"The one I've been talking about; the one that allows you, if you do well, to carry on to the Russian higher school in Irtusk. And there I could study aeronautics. I might even be taught to fly."

He was rushing forward in time, forgetting the scriptures that lay about him as he dreamed of the possibilities. I had forgotten the scriptures too; I was grappling with the idea of him going to school in Tsetserleg, the capital of Arkhangai, instead of in little Ikh Tamir.

"When?"

"Gombo says that because my grades are very good I could transfer right away. Then, by the end of next year or at the very most two years, I might be ready to go to Russia."

"Right away?"

"Yes, Avh, yes." I could see he was getting frustrated with my slowness to embrace what was, to him, an unquestionably thrilling opportunity. "It's very special that I'm being offered this."

"Of course it is. Because you are such an able student. I'm proud that you've done so well."

"So I can accept?"

"But the capital is such a long way from home. It would be more than a half day's ride for us to get back at the end of the week."

"They have a dormitory there."

"You mean you would go without me? And stay there?"

Tilik gave a quick, impatient frown. "Gombo will look out for me. He's been promoted to teacher's assistant there, you see, and he asked that I come with him as his best student."

I started to shake my head. "We've talked about this before."

"But now I'm fourteen. I'm old enough. And," Tilik continued with an air of someone about to pull a winning card out of hiding, "I'll have protection. Gombo's important friend lives in Tsetserleg too, and would act as my sponsor, like a guardian. He would be a very good guardian."

"Who is he?"

"He's the governor."

I felt faint. The governor had survived more than a dozen years in his position, consolidating his provincial authority despite changes of leadership in Ulaan Baatar and the subsequent Party purges.

"Badrakh," I said.

"The one you painted, yes." Tilik beamed, sure of his card. "You see?"

"No, Tilik, I cannot let you go into the care of that man."

The sudden confusion on Tilik's face turned quickly to anger. "What do you mean? How could you not?"

"The governor, he has done unspeakable things."

"How would you know anything about him? Gombo knows, and he says he's very respected in the Party."

I struggled to figure out just how much I should tell my son. "He ordered the murder of many innocent monks at a monastery called Khovor Khan," I said.

There was a split second in which a flicker of concern crossed over Tilik's face. Then it was replaced with fresh certainty.

"The governor was doing his duty. The monasteries were dissolute and enslaved the people through false beliefs."

I looked him in the eye. "I was one of them. I was a novice there and those monks were my brothers. They were all executed, and only I escaped."

Tilik's mouth opened and shut a couple of times before he could find his tongue again. "You were a monk? *Eejee*, it gets worse all the time. They'll never let me go to the school if they find out."

"Tilik, did you not hear the part about executions? Those monks were innocent."

"They misled the people and kept them in ignorance for their own gain. The monasteries had to be destroyed. It was all explained to us at school."

I exploded. "They were murdered! These people telling you things, they don't know. They weren't there. I was there."

Tilik was shaking his head. "Monks make trouble. Look at Arigh, he's old and he is still doing so. Everything was fine until he came along and you started doing all this with him. I'll never be able to go to the school with a father who is writing scripture books against the law."

"Enough! Arigh is exercising his beliefs, and they are also my beliefs. They are the result of many centuries of meditation by wise men, not a few decades of experimentation by power-seeking revolutionaries. I am proud to be helping in this work."

"But it's wrong!"

"It's the Party that is wrong, and I'm not going to let them teach you any more!"

Our heated words had raised the level of tension in our ger so that it seemed to replace the oxygen, leaving the air stifling. We were both breathing heavily. Tilik's face twisted this way and that, and for a moment I thought he might cry. Instead, he bent down to the floor and in one quick motion gathered up a sheaf of the drying scriptures. He tore them in half, then in half again, casting the bits around the room in a last, violent gesture before rushing out of our ger, leaving the door open behind him. He raced over to his waiting horse and leapt on. As he galloped away towards Ikh Tamir his body was hunched and furious, kicking his horse into a maelstrom of flying hooves and dust.

I closed the door. Our ger was a mess of scattered fragments and whole pages littering the floor, but I didn't have the energy to pick them up. I opened the shrine cupboard and sat amongst the debris to ask guidance of Tara.

For most of the day I stayed there contemplating what I should do. I didn't go to teach my class and Tilik didn't return. I knew he would be with Gombo or the family that often fed him lunch. People who were right-thinking in his view.

The school was undeniably a wonderful opportunity for him. I had left home far earlier to gain an education, and if my father had managed to let me go for the chance at a better life, why couldn't I do the same for my son? Was I wrong to force my beliefs on him if he chose to take another path? Was the brief phase of my influence in his life truly over, and I was being blind to it? All children must go out into the world at some point.

I remembered how, when he was six, he'd asked to lead our prayer session because he had memorized a Tibetan scripture and was proud to show it off. I had let him, because in truth I was proud also. Proud! I could practically hear my master yelling at me over the lost decades for that obstinate flaw. I hadn't realized, as my son mastered more of the scriptures, that it was the mental challenge that intrigued him more than the prayers themselves. I should have caught it in his voice. He recited, he didn't pray. I hadn't heard it then because I hadn't wanted to.

And when he started going to school even those recitations waned as he replaced the learning of scripture with more compelling things. I gave myself excuses: his lack of time at home; he could only keep so much in his young head at once; he would come back around to the scriptures once the novelty of his new subjects wore off.

I could give myself excuses no longer. Tilik was on his way to becoming a man, and I'd had so little influence on his beliefs that he might have belonged to another family altogether. But he was still my son, my flesh and blood. He had worked hard to be asked into the Tsctscrleg school and he would make the most of it. I couldn't hold him back from such a prize even if I were able, which I was beginning to doubt.

What then was to be done about Badrakh? His sexual leanings were one concern. Clearly he liked men, and if he had the same tastes as the Abbot he might he also find a boy of Tilik's age attractive. The Abbot had probably started training Bayan that young. How could Tilik defend himself if Badrakh approached him in such a way?

That was dangerous enough, but in many ways it was Badrakh's ruthlessness that worried me more. Up until now Tilik had been influenced by people like Gombo, whose philosophy was ignorant, in the way of young men who have embraced an idea without thinking about it much. Badrakh's philosophy, on the other hand, was considered, calculated, practiced, and utterly without heart. How could I possibly balance his influence in Tilik's life if I had been unable to balance Gombo's? And if Tilik got close and then displeased him, what terrible thing might he do?

Tilik didn't come home that night. I wasn't surprised; he was stubborn like his father and was no doubt thinking about how he was going to come back home without losing face. I planned out what I was going to say to make him understand things. I cleaned up the ger, burning the torn bits and noting which scriptures they were so I could try to do them again before Arigh had the misfortune to see that they were missing.

The next morning I had barely got out of bed when the door opened and Tilik walked in. He must have been up with the first light. I wanted to hug him, I was so relieved to see him, but he didn't look ready for that.

"Good morning, Ahv *aa*," he said with a formality we never used.

"Good morning. Would you like something to eat?" I poured water from a bucket into the kettle and put it on the stove.

"No, thank you." He was still standing just an arm's length in from the door, and made no move to remove his outer coat. "I'm only here to tell you something, and then I'm going back to school."

Something strange in his voice, a kind of forced calm over crackling tension, made me drop what I was doing and focus all my attention on him. "I'm listening."

"Gombo and the governor are modern, right-thinking men," he said carefully, as though he had practiced the words many times. His hands were clenching and unclenching at his sides in his nervousness. "I will go to school in Tsetserleg as they have suggested." He took a fraction of a second to swallow. "And you will give your permission, because otherwise I will denounce the old monk for his activities."

I was too dumbfounded to speak and he didn't wait for me to recover. As he turned to walk out the door again he paused only for a moment. "I told them you were sick yesterday. But they are expecting you back at the school this afternoon."

And with that he got back on his horse and trotted off, calmly this time. I wondered if he hadn't threatened me directly because he knew it would be more effective to use Arigh instead, or whether some vestige of a filial bond prevented him. At that moment he seemed capable of anything to get what he wanted.

I had worried about Badrakh's influence, but in fact the damage had already been done. My own efforts to guide him had been too feeble, my lack of courage too palpable, my faith too inconsistent. And while I dithered the Party had made him into someone willing to sacrifice an old monk for his own gain.

There are many forms of loss. All those years, and I had been afraid of the wrong thing.

Later that week I tried to tell him about Badrakh. Our conversations were stilted to begin with, with me not knowing what to say and Tilik working very hard to pretend nothing bad had happened. When I sat him down and began to explain what I knew about the governor, Tilik interrupted me.

"I think the monks at your monastery were making up stories," he said.

"No, Tilik, monks do not make up stories. What I'm telling you is true."

"It must have been another person. You can't be sure it was him."

"I could never forget him."

Tilik shook his head. "Anyway, that was a long time ago and it doesn't have anything to do with me."

"It could have," I insisted. "What I'm saying is Badrakh could approach you in an inappropriate way, and if that were to happen you would have to get on your horse and come home right away, because otherwise you'll find yourself in a very dangerous position."

Tilik stared at me as though I were trying to convince him that the world was flat. "Why are you trying to make me think the governor is a bad man? I'm going to the school, it can't be changed now."

"I'm trying to make you understand what is true, so you can protect yourself."

"I already know what is true," he said with utter surety. "I won't need to protect myself, because Gombo and the governor will take care of me. They told me so."

I put my hand on his arm, desperate to get through to him. "Tilik, I'm your father, so I have more reason to take care of you than anyone else in the world. Why do you believe them and not me?"

He slipped his arm quietly out from under my touch. "They understand what I can do. They let me do exciting things. You just want to keep me safe, and then I don't get to do anything at all."

That was how the world looked to him. He was fourteen and confident of his progress through life. What had my years of protection given him? Looking at this person before me who believed nothing of what I did, I didn't even want to answer that question for myself.

He picked up his school book and pointedly sat on the bed by himself to read. He knew what he wanted. It was not me, or my beliefs.

When the weekend came we traveled to our home camp for the dreaded prospect of telling Erdene what Tilik was about to do. She wouldn't want him so far away, and the suddenness of it would make things worse. After this weekend he wouldn't be home again until the summer. We agreed to get it over with right away, so when we were barely off our horses and inside with our tea, Tilik rushed through the details with a mixture of excitement at the future and nervousness over his mother's reaction.

Erdene listened calmly until she found out he was going the following week. Her teacup practically fell from her hand and she set it down hastily, the tea sloshing over the rim and onto our little table. Tsetseg fetched a rag to wipe it up.

"So soon?" Erdene said. "I thought you were talking about the next school year."

Tilik fidgeted on his stool. "There's no point in waiting if I can go now."

"I don't know," she said vaguely, searching for reasons for him to stay. "You're still so young."

"The dormitory is full of boys my age. I have Gombo to take care of me, and he has—" Tilik glanced at me "—important adult friends who can also act as guardians."

"You're certain this is what you want?" she asked him, although he had made that clear enough. She looked back and forth between us.

"For many years, *Ehj*."

"Will you take your horse? It's a long ride back home."

"It's only half a day. But yes I can take my horse."

She continued on with all the worries a mother keeps in her pocket; for good food, keeping warm in winter, having a decent bed, and for each one he had a reassurance. Finally she turned to me. "And you think this is a good idea?" she asked.

"Ahv said I could go," Tilik said quickly. Erdene cocked her head at me, still questioning.

"It's a great chance for him and he's worked hard for it." My voice was tight because all the other things had not yet been discussed, and Erdene caught it. She looked at me hard; I knew that look. "Children," I said, "Your mother and I have to talk between ourselves."

As they got up to leave I heard Tsetseg say under her breath, "You've really done it this time." Tilik glanced worriedly over his shoulder as he ducked out the door, then closed it carefully behind him.

"The guardian he speaks of is Governor Badrakh," I told Erdene. Her face went pale.

"Badrakh? Our son will be under the protection of a murderer and sodomist?"

I nodded, unable to look her in the eye. "I told Tilik everything so he would know to be careful."

"And you think your words will protect him?" She started to rise from her stool, agitated. "How could you possibly have agreed to this?"

"I had no choice."

"That's what you always say!" She jumped up, looking towards the door as though she was about to rush out and tell Tilik he couldn't go.

"Erdene, he saw the scripture books. He threatened to denounce Arigh if I didn't agree."

Erdene looked as though she had just been slapped in the face. She crumpled back down to the stool and sat silently shaking her head. When she finally looked back up at me, there was such misery in her eyes I thought my heart would break. "Our son would denounce an old, holy man? How could he?" she asked in a tiny voice.

"He believes it was right to have destroyed the monasteries. He believes everything the Party has told him, that monks make trouble and the monasteries were dissolute, a threat to the people."

"How could we have a son who believes that?"

"The Party has given him a more compelling view of the world than I have. And I've been too weak and too blind to prevent it."

She didn't disagree, and her wordless confirmation of the truth saddened me. One of my first lessons at Khovor Khan had been about giving. My master Tilik had told me that the first Perfection is generosity, but one must think carefully about the gift. Only if it brings about true benefit for everyone is it worth giving. If not, it is false generosity. I had been giving my son Tilik protection, but the gift he'd needed from me was unwavering belief.

"He's chosen the way of the Party," Erdene said sadly.

"Right now he's young and grabbing at all they say. When he gets older he might gain another perspective."

"Perhaps," she said without conviction. She turned to me and I folded her in my arms as she wept, shaking, into my shoulder. There were no words that could comfort her. I just held her silently, soaking up her sorrow as though that could somehow ease the inconsolable pain. It was hopeless, I knew. I had helped create the pain, and I could not erase it.

While Tilik and I had been breaking the news to the family, Gombo had been making the final arrangements for leaving. The morning after we returned, therefore, Tilik paced our ger impatiently, his bag packed, waiting for Gombo to come for him.

"I hope, now that you've made your decision, everything goes well for you at the new school."

"Thank you Ahv," he said distractedly.

"Always study hard."

"I will."

"And if there should be any kind of problem, any kind at all, you know we're only a half a day away."

"I know. But there won't be any problems."

"You'll write and tell us all about your experiences?"

"Every week. I promised Ehj."

"I have a small thing to give you," I said, and took the packet, wrapped in brown paper, out of my del. Tilik stopped his pacing and turned to me, surprised, tentatively putting out both hands to receive it in the respectful way.

He opened the package. "Grandfather's playing cards," he said, and a trace of his old affection came into his face as he ran his fingers over the familiar design. We had played with those cards many evenings over the years.

"I retouched them a little. I thought you might want to use them in the dormitory."

"Thank you. I'll take special care of them." He smiled shyly at me then, the first smile I'd had from him in a week. I wanted to hug him, was about to hug him, when Gombo called outside the door to announce his arrival. Tilik turned from me to go open it.

Gombo greeted me politely, then spoke to Tilik. "Are you ready?"

Tilik nodded.

"Don't worry, Dash *aa*," Gombo said to me. "We'll take good care of him. And in the summer, he will return to you in the country for a month. We can't let him get too soft leading an academic life, can we? It's important to remind ourselves about the real work of the people once in awhile."

I bit my tongue.

"Come on, Tilik, get your bag," Gombo said, and led the way out to where the horses stood, tied to our hitching line. Their breath formed billowing clouds in the crisp, still winter air. Tilik's horse stamped his foot as though impatient to be off. I stood by uncertainly as Gombo secured Tilik's bag to the pack horse.

"Take care of yourself," I said to Tilik. We embraced briefly, awkwardly, our arms nor sure how to express themselves anymore. With Tsetseg and Erdene his hugs had been long and fierce. I envied the strength of their affection even at the brink of this contentious separation.

The neighbours came out of their gers to watch the departure. The matriarch brought out a ladle of milk, which she timidly handed to me.

"For the libation," she explained. "No-one should go on a journey without it."

Tilik and Gombo were mounted now. I was certain Gombo was not a man who believed in the power of a libation, but nevertheless I took the milk and sprinkled a bit on each of the horses, then to each of the four cardinal directions.

"Safe journey," I said.

"Thank you, comrade," Gombo replied over his shoulder, already on the move.

Tilik's face was a mixture of excitement and trepidation as he trotted off. He did not look back. I stood until I couldn't see him anymore and wondered if, even for a moment, he imagined me standing there, watching him go.

CHAPTER THIRTY

SNOW WEIGHS DOWN THE
KING OF MOUNTAINS.
AGE WEIGHS DOWN THE PRECIOUS BODY.

With Tilik gone my small ger was silent as a tomb, and I found I couldn't bear to stay there after the first sleepless night. Mongolians aren't meant to live alone. My obligation to the school would last until the summer, but it was easy enough to ride back and forth from our home camp for the two afternoons I had to work. I went home the following day to consult with the family, and returned with a plan.

I called Arigh to my ger. My easel was packed up, the flashlight no longer strapped to the roof pole. He looked around, sighed with the prolonged exhale of someone accustomed to disappointment, and sat on his stool while I brought him his half-cup of tea.

He took the cup with two trembling hands, as he had done at the start of every session we'd had over the months we'd been working on the scriptures. This time, however, he didn't drink right away as he usually did. "You're leaving," he said. He looked up at me with hurt in his eyes. The tea sloshed around chaotically.

"I'm not a monk. I can't live without my family."

He nodded, bringing the tea to his lips and struggling to hold it there until he'd consumed it all. Getting the cup up and down for many smaller sips was too challenging.

"But you'll continue the work," he said when he had finished. There was questioning in his voice.

"I can't do it alone." I sat opposite him. "Arigh, I've spoken with my family and we would like you to come live with us. To continue the work. We have a large ger, there would be room enough."

His eyes were wide with surprise. "Live with you?" he repeated.

"Yes. There are four gers at our camp and everyone is related, like in the old days. We are Buddhist. We will still need to be cautious, but among the family no-one will deny us our work."

"I will live with Buddhists," he whispered, almost not believing. "I won't have to pretend to be mad."

"No, you can quote as much scripture as you like, in either language."

He started to smile as the possibilities sank in. "Does your family pray?" he asked.

"Every day."

Tears welled up and trickled down his face. He was nodding his head up and down, weeping and smiling at the same time. "I will live with Buddhists. Yes, with Buddhists who pray every day." He reached out a trembling hand and touched my arm. "A thousand blessings on you and on your family," he said.

And indeed, I felt more blessed in that moment than I had in years.

Arigh's relatives readily agreed to the move. If they wondered why I would make such a crazy offer, they were not about to jeopardize the deal by asking. They gave me a yak and cart to move Arigh and the few things we were taking away. I arranged to give my ger and most of its contents to the authorities in Ikh Tamir for people in need.

Back at our family ger camp, the old monk slipped into our routines as quietly as a sigh, our lives adjusting to his presence in many small and soothing ways. Our daily prayers were graced with formal blessings and small rituals I'd forgotten over time. Other family members dropped in to ask for blessings and interventions, shyly at first and then with a dawning confidence that this was once more a regular, enriching part of our lives. Arigh's face took on a look of peace, not unlike the statue of Avalokitesvara we'd had at Khovor Khan, so that just to look at him would make your worries fade.

As herders, it was a time of other, less pleasant transitions. Now that the family was part of a collective, our days were less diverse. We specialized in the breeding and milking of khainag. Other specialists did the slaughtering, brought us felt for our gers, and provided us with sheep products beyond the small amount we produced from our own. Herding had gone from being a self-sufficient life to being a job that depended on other jobs, done by other groups.

In the first two years of collectivization, half the people who had been herding for a living stopped doing so, and instead flooded the towns and cities in search of more promising livelihoods. Our family group began to reflect that change. Our nephew moved to Tsetserleg to work in the dairy factory. Our niece married and moved to Ulaan Baatar. Like many other young people, they turned their backs on the herder's life. It was only Tsetseg who stayed.

These changes allowed Erdene and I to tell ourselves that Tilik's departure had been inevitable, although that did little to ease our sense of loss. His first visit home was fraught with tension. Arigh went to stay with Gan so Tilik could have his old bed back with us. The bit of distance was a good thing, because Tilik refused to acknowledge the monk's presence, neither speaking to him nor answering unless I forced it.

The only thing that mattered for my son was school, that shining new universe he now inhabited. He didn't seem to be in any jeopardy, but if he had been we certainly wouldn't have heard about it. He only spoke about the positive things: the various technologies he was studying, especially airplanes; the many intelligent people he was meeting, all of whom were extraordinary and superior; the modern conveniences such as running water and electricity that he lived with daily.

By the second meal, Tsesteg had grown irritated by his excited talk. "You've become boastful," she complained.

Tilik looked confused for a moment, as though a negative response to his report were unimaginable. Then his brow furrowed in the way it always did when he was readying himself for a fight.

"At least I have something to be boastful about," he retorted.

"So do we," Tsetseg said. "We raise good, fat khainag to feed Mongolia. And the Party would be the first to tell you how important it is, if you had the ears to listen."

"Of course," said Tilik, smirking. "Hairy khainag are just as important as advanced science to Mongolia's future."

"Feeding a growing nation is critical," I interjected. "However, boasting is unnecessary talk."

Tilik rolled his eyes. "Not Buddhist 'right thinking'?"

"You know that."

"The world follows a different Path now, Ahv."

"Not in our house," I said.

"That's why I live at school." He said it under his breadth, face towards his soup bowl. But it was loud enough to be clear.

I recalled how my master Tilik had struggled to correct my pride, when I was about the same age as my son was now. I wished I had the strength of my master, but I did not. And my son did not have the willingness of a novice.

"When you are at school," I said, "you will no doubt behave as you believe best. But when you are here you'll respect our beliefs."

Tilik glanced at Erdene, who was staring hard at him with a heartbreaking mixture of authority and sadness. "As you wish," he mumbled.

He did his chores sloppily and without enthusiasm, putting bridles in a heap and not checking them, not chopping wood quite small enough to fit easily in the stove, not bringing in quite a full load. He rationalized the many hours spent with his books by insisting he had to study. By the time he left, after just two nights, he didn't promise to come again in a month the way we had originally planned.

"There's a lot of school work I must do if I'm going to get to Russia," he said.

There was always studying, and Party events, and other opportunities in his rich new life. So many that, despite Gombo's promise to send him home for proletariat training in the summer, in fact Tilik hardly spent any time with us again before heading triumphantly to Irtusk, as had wanted, by his sixteenth birthday.

And his letters home, ever fewer, never did lose their boastfulness.

Tilik's estrangement, and my own culpability in having made it so, weighed on me. I turned to Arigh, leaning towards his belief the way a dog leans towards your meal; with longing underpinned by the misery of knowing that it isn't his. I watched how Arigh meditated every morning now that he was in a place in which he could. I envied him.

One morning, on rising from the lotus position—which he held as easily as if he were a young man—he asked me why I didn't do the same.

"What do you do while I'm meditating?" he asked.

"Chores." I nodded towards Erdene, who was rolling dough for biscuits, her forearms covered in flour. "Like my wife."

"Then when do you meditate?"

"I haven't done so for a long time."

"But you have the capacity?"

I recalled the many fruitless attempts of my youth, and how they had been transformed into the only thing that had saved my sanity in the cave. Then the practice had slid away from me again. "I had the capacity. But I lost the skill through lack of practice."

Arigh looked around my ger and I knew what he was seeing: it was quiet, private, and with no intrusive neighbours wondering what you were up to. What kind of excuse did I have?

"While you were living here, like this?" he asked in astonishment.

"I was … afraid." I was aware of Erdene, suddenly motionless in the midst of her work. Listening.

"Of the police?" He looked perplexed. "But who in your family would denounce you for meditating?"

"No one." He didn't know about Tilik's threat, but ultimately that was beside the point. It was true I'd been afraid of the police. My real fear, however, had been even more potent. So potent I had never let myself admit it.

Arigh sat down on his stool and motioned for me to sit opposite. He didn't speak, so we sat there, each staring ahead and contemplating this question he'd asked. Erdene was rolling her dough with almost imperceptible motions, as though she feared too much movement might scare the discussion away.

"I have not always been consistent in my actions as a Buddhist," I confessed. "I have compromised myself with many acts of negative energy."

Arigh nodded slowly. "That is a very human problem."

In the hierarchy of Buddhist rebirths, the best we can aspire to as unenlightened beings is a precious human life, that being one in which Buddhist practice is possible. If you're born into one of those, your duty is to ensure practice happens and conditions are maintained for it. I had that kind of life. It had been thwarted by the monastic massacres and oppressed by politics, but these were only excuses.

"The truth," I began, speaking to myself as much as to Arigh, "is that because of my negative acts, I grew afraid that I would sink into my inner place one day and find there was no longer any flame glowing there." I felt grief well up in me. My voice shrank. "I was afraid there would be only empty darkness, with no sign at all of the Path."

Arigh continued to nod, thinking about the problem. Then he stopped, looked at me kindly, and spoke. "But did you look to see if that was so?"

His question stunned me. It was so simple, so obvious, yet something

I had not dared to do. "I did not," I said.

"We will look together for your flame. You'll see, it's still there. I wouldn't be here in your ger if it were not."

"I have been given a precious human life and I have been squandering it."

"But you are still young," Arigh replied. "Dash. Your father named you well. You have many years left, and I am here to help you while I can. What could be better fortune than that?"

Out of the corner of my eye, I caught movement as Erdene began cutting up the biscuit dough with her usual brisk chops. I looked over and saw that she was smiling, content.

Arigh did help me, leading me to see how the tiniest ember can yet be fanned to a solid flame. My meditations became regular, deep, and rewarding. I began the slow process of forgiving myself.

When summer came I painted Arigh a thangka: White Tara on a tiny coin of wood, like the one I'd started but never finished for the four old monks in Ulaan Baatar.

I gave it to him one afternoon when we were seated outside our ger door, soaking up the warmth of the late afternoon sun.

"I made you something that is like carrying sunshine with you all year round," I said, presenting it wrapped in a wisp of blue silk, holding it out with two hands.

He took it slowly, graciously, in the way of a monk who needs nothing—then beamed like a child receiving a New Year's gift when he opened the cloth and saw what it was. He held it first between thumb and forefinger, peering at it to discern the details, but his hands shook too much and he had to place it on his knee where it could be still.

"How beautiful her expression!" he exclaimed, leaning over it intently. "Her hand, the flower – how lucky for me Buddha has let you be the conduit for his wisdom in this way."

I smiled. It had been a decades since anyone had reminded me about the origin of art. "For a long time now people have let me believe I'm the artist."

Arigh brushed the idea away with one hand. "Ridiculous. I'm sure you were taught correctly. Buddha moves through you."

"I had many lessons in that, yes. I'm not sure I learned them well. Or at least I've been content to forget them."

"It's not easy to keep the Path in the secular world."

"Is it really so wrong to feel proud of creating something beautiful?"

He looked at me keenly. "If you must believe that you create your paintings, at least don't believe it of the religious ones. Only divinity can create divinity."

"Yes, Master." I said it without thinking, surprising myself with how easily it had come to my tongue.

Arigh laughed so hard the thangka almost fell from his knee, but he grabbed his prize before it dropped, holding it fast in his fist. "Yes, that is true isn't it? Even though you are no longer a novice, I no longer look like a monk, and we have no monastery." He shook his head in wonder, peeking at the coin in his palm, then closed his eyes and turned his face to the sun. "Ah, Buddha, what power he has. A beautiful thangka, a great blue sky, a master for a pupil, and a pupil for a master." Bringing his hands to his forehead, he bowed in thanks. "Life is wonderful."

As a master he was not demanding; he simply kept pointing to the Path and inviting me to walk along it. For five more years we transcribed the scriptures, and then he was so old and frail he could mumble only a few words from his place on the bed, willing me to remember the rest for him. I did my best.

When his heart stopped, it did so peacefully at dawn on a crisp spring day. The family paid their respects and accompanied me with his body, borne on a stretcher strapped to a quiet pack horse, as far as the foot of the hills. The rest of the journey I needed to make with Arigh alone.

Slowly I climbed to the highest point, leading the horse behind me through a rocky and meandering trail. The sun rose bright and hopeful, the air was windless and quiet but for the soft thud of unshod hooves on hard ground and the occasional cry of a circling hawk. At the summit, in an open place of stunted grass and lichened stone, we stopped.

Arigh had asked to be laid to rest in the old way. I cut down a tree from the forest edge and removed its branches one by one, chiseling and notching them so they all locked together to form a raised pallet. It took a few hours, and in that time I thought of all the monks I had not buried, as well as the one I was able to give a proper ceremony. Each branch I notched for a different brother: for my master Tilik and for Bayan, for Koke and Mongo and the rest, even Suren; for Dorj; for the four old monks of Ulaan Baatar; and lastly for the monk who'd brought the best of their teachings back into my life, when I thought they'd all been lost to me.

His body was light as a child when I lifted it off the horse and laid him on the pallet. He was not shrouded. He lay with his serene face open to the great blue sky above, his head to the sacred north. Animals would feast on his body and that would be his final gift to sentient creatures, sustenance for their current lives. That was the old way.

I lit incense at each of the four cardinal points and sat on the ground to pray for his spirit, and the spirits of the others in whatever lives they now led. I meditated on their acts of goodness and their shared wisdom, at one with them again until the sun began to set in a pink-tinged sky. Then it was time for me to leave them to their worlds and return to mine.

As I led the horse back down the path, a fox appeared on a ledge of rock to our left. I stopped to watch him raise his nose and sniff the air from the summit. He looked at me, studying me calmly for a few seconds, then trotted off up the hill. The gift was there for him, and he was wise enough to take it.

CHAPTER THIRTY ONE

ONE'S HAND CAN DEFEAT ONE MAN;
ONE'S HEAD CAN DEFEAT A THOUSAND.

Soon after Arigh's death, my memory came to its last page of retained scripture. Remembering the words I'd learned so long ago, which were only a small portion of the hundreds of sutras and precepts, had been like searching for coins tucked away for safekeeping. I had turned out every pocket, opened every musty drawer, and now the last, shaken tin lay empty. The finished books, enough to fill two suitcases, constituted about third of a complete set. The ones that remained to be done were the most advanced. The ones I had never had the chance to learn.

Knowing there were other monks with whom Arigh had worked, I set out to find them. Erdene agreed there was no choice in this. I had started on the task and it could not be left half done. It wasn't fear of what pathetic kind of creature I might be in my next incarnation if I didn't see the job through to the end, although that might have been justified. I simply, deeply needed to finish the whole set. To write them without Arigh's wise collaboration already felt like there was a gaping hole in my days; I made to ask him a question a hundred times, turning to see the empty stool, before I understood he was no longer there. To no longer be writing them at all would feel as though I had been sentenced to spend the rest of my days in darkness.

I had a handful of names and the towns they once lived near, from Bayankhongor aimag all the way to Kentii. It took me two days to ride to Delger, only to find that contact had died. The same thing happened in Tsakhir, and once again I returned home with no result. But near Kharkhorin, close to the old monastery of Erdene Zuu, I found the man named Chamuka. Since no-one would dare speak of a mission such as mine with a stranger, I used the code established by the first transcribing monks, saying I was looking for a white yak that had escaped my herd. He correctly replied that my yak had indeed joined his. A group of perhaps twenty animals dotted the thinly tufted steppes in front of us.

Chamuka took them in with a sweep of his arm and declared that mine had, unfortunately, turned brown to fit in with the rest, then laughed loudly at my obvious confusion, slapped me on the back, and invited me to his ger to see his scriptures. It was the first of many small practical jokes he played on me over our time together.

I had to accept that creating a complete set of scriptures would require a perfectly Buddhist exercise in patience and delayed gratification, involving sneaking around the country for decades tracking down a small but dedicated group spread over many *soum*. They had sutras and prayer shawls and small golden statues, hoardings kept for years in remote caves and secret floorboard nooks. When I met them they brought forth these things with a shy reverence, as though each time they revealed the divine object, its presence in their lives felt like a fresh miracle. Particularly powerful was a tingsha whose gentle ping I heard in the dense air of a felt ger for the first time in twenty years. It made me sigh for the lost serenity of the chanting sangha, something I had taken for granted in the monastery and occasionally even resented it as a tedious chore. Time had worn the memory to an experience purely sweet and greatly missed.

Together the monks and I copied volumes I was missing. I created copies of mine in return, transporting volumes back and forth so that several complete sets could be produced. We were a secret society, hunched over our clandestine words while Tsedenbal's modern Mongolia raged on above our heads, like one of the new trains that roared over the unnoticed activities of ants between the tracks.

My fellow transcribers were older than I by as much as thirty years, all of them ordained well before their monasteries were destroyed. Like Arigh, they were the devout and the practiced, masters yearning for a pupil and I, the orphaned novice, clung to them as adoptive fathers.

Juchin was practiced in astronomy. When I visited him I had to be prepared, on any clear night in all but the coldest weather, to go outside and lie on my back on a bed of furs beside him while he taught me the constellations, determined to pass on his knowledge. He was seventy-eight when I first met him. He teased me when I decided I would only come to see him in summer, pronouncing me soft.

Yeke was a philosopher, still lively in debate until his last breath at eighty-three. Progress on transcribing was always much slower with him because so much time was spent in discussion instead of writing. It was an inefficiency I cherished.

There were no other artists. The thangkas I made as gifts were received with sighs of such poignancy and longing, emotion never expressed over my secular paintings, that I finally began to understand how it is that Buddhist art is not about the hand that renders it, but the spirit that moves that hand.

Our activities were not without risk. Sometimes volumes had to be hastily relocated in the dark of night. A relative would ask a dangerous question, a traveler might cast a sideways, suspicious glance. If we were overcautious it was because we knew the consequences of discovery. There was a particularly nerve-wracking incident in Moron when officials, tipped off by snooping neighbours, took one of our members away for questioning and ransacked his ger. His scriptures had been moved just two days earlier. Because no more evidence could be found he was eventually released, deaf in one ear from the continual, maddening cuffing he'd received as part of his torture. We moved all activities out of towns and into remote herder camps after that.

Still, while other dissidents suffered work camps or were executed to silence their rebellious voices, we remained luckier. The members of our group grew old, they shrank and died as bodies do, the thangkas and scriptures passed into the hands of the still living. Perhaps we were less bold, but I came to appreciate that it is not only the openly heroic who can make a difference. It is also through the willingness of the essentially unheroic to do what's right, and to do it so quietly that they are never sung about as heroes, that regimes may be toppled. Country grocers left food out their back doors for activists, herders misplaced horses for the use of the disfavored, sympathetic families hid and fed perpetually nomadic enemies of the state.

Over three decades we, a small group of pacifist monks as timid as mice, completed three full sets of handwritten sutras and precepts in the Mongolian language, in the unwavering belief that someday they would be of use.

In 1990, quietly and without bloodshed, the Mongolian people shook off the yoke of Party power. As the USSR disintegrated, the Russians abandoned their control of our country and we blinked awake, like coma victims unexpectedly regaining consciousness. After seventy years of autocratic rule, we decided to hold a democratic election.

No matter that we elected the MPRP back into power. This time it was our choice, and there were legitimate opposition parties to temper them. Newspapers flourished with a fledgling freedom to print their own opinions. Economically, Mongolia was in a state of chaos following the rapid flight of Russian capital. Our future recovery, however, finally lay in our own hands. On the happy yellow horse day in the black tiger month of the water monkey year – the middle of February 1992 - the government announced a new constitution that would ensure the Mongolian people democracy, freedom, justice and equality.

It was a clear blue day of the same year, the kind of day when winter's frigid air has made the subtle shift that carries with it the possibility of spring, when a lone horseman came trotting towards our ger . I was untethering my own horse from the tie-pole, to let him search for bits of grass beneath the snow. "Sain bain uu!" the rider called out when he was barely within hearing, waving an arm and breaking into a canter. Just as I thought he might run me down he pulled up his horse and leapt from the saddle all in one motion. I had a split second to catch a glimpse of him beneath the furry hat, earflaps down, before I was enveloped in a bear hug.

It was Chamuka's son, Munlik. He had been involved in many of his father's Buddhist activities but I hadn't seen him in almost a year.

"Welcome," I said. "Are your animals still fat? And how is your father?" I held him at arms length and took in his broad grin. "Clearly he must be well, since you're in such a happy state."

"He is well. Unable to come himself at eighty-six, but I have good news he wanted me to bring."

Erdene, overhearing the commotion, stuck her head out our ger door. "Munlik, welcome." She knew almost everyone I had worked with, having insisted on traveling with me frequently despite the danger. "You need tea. Come in, come in! The stove is warm and we have biscuits."

Munlik entered the ger, bowed to Erdene, and stood as though about to make a great presentation. Slowly, with all the relish of a conjurer revealing of a magic card, he removed his fur hat.

He had shaved his head.

I hadn't seen a shaved head in over fifty years. As I was taking in the significance of this sight, he threw open his winter coat to reveal his clothes: the saffron and red robes of a novice. He might have been naked, the way Erdene's hand flew to her mouth in surprise.

Munlik laughed heartily; he had his father's sense of humour. "I am not an apparition! You see before you an official novice of the monastery at Erdene Zuu."

"But Erdene Zuu is mostly ruins." I said.

"All but three temples, yes, and those badly looted. But it's enough for a start. My father has taken his ger there. He is a master again, at last. Many people are helping to rebuild it."

I shook my head in wonder. "It's incredible. I didn't know if I would ever see the day when there were sanghas chanting in Mongolian monasteries again."

"That's what my father said. Monks from all over are coming to Erdene Zuu, even old monks who can barely ride. They have dug up their buried statues and taken their thangkas out of hiding, and joined the sangha once again. My father wanted to be the first to tell you the good news."

"It's what you have all been working for, against all hope," said Erdene. "Imagine, Dash, how happy Arigh would be to know this."

"He had complete faith it would happen. But in our lifetime! As he would say, Buddha is powerful, and life is wonderful."

Munlik nodded. "And Juchin would say it was an auspicious alignment of planets." He chuckled, then became serious. He looked at me intently. "My father wants to know, will you join us?"

For fifty-three years, a part of my heart had been mourning the lost comfort of monastic life, its firm sense of direction, its shelter from the rough world. While I had been there, however imperfect I had been, I'd known what I should do, what was right and what was wrong. More sure than I had been of most things since. All but one.

I looked at Erdene. "I am not a monk," I said, as much to her as to Munlik.

"You've been as much of a monk as one could be in Mongolia, all these years," Munlik replied.

"I have tried to do what was right, after a lot of doing what was wrong. I look forward to visiting Erdene Zuu, and joining you and Chamuka in chant sometime soon. But not as a monk."

Erdene began to protest, but I held up my hand, gently, to silence her. "In my heart," I said, "I know that Erdene Zuu, however important a monastery, is not my work. I wish you all well in it. But Buddha, I believe, has something else for me to do."

Erdene and I arrived on horseback, but it was not a quiet arrival. Along with us was a dilapidated truck hauling two open-topped, wood-sided trailers on rusted axles, whose ill-fitting hitches shrieked with every bump. The truck's engine gave one final, wheezing cough before shuddering to a stop alongside us, as though exhausted from the effort of hauling its load over so many ortoo of roadless terrain. In the first trailer was our ger with all our goods, few as they were. In the second were six sheep and two spare horses. It was enough to start.

The truck belonged to Tsetseg's husband, Dejid, who was a mechanic and had started a simple transport service when his Russian-funded factory closed down and took his job with it. We were not paying customers, however. Transporting us was their gift to the new monastery.

We dismounted and Tsetseg and Dejid swung down from the truck's cab to view what lay before us. Time and the weather had conspired to reduce the monastery to the ragged outline of a mud and stone wall, punctuated by pockets of wild thyme eking out an existence in its cracks. It was spring, the season in which the land had a fleeting look of promise before it succumbed to the thirst of summer. Erdene gazed at the forlorn countryside, so different from her home, with a sturdy calm.

She put her hand to the small of her back and rubbed. At seventy she felt the hours in a saddle more than she once had, but she still preferred a horse to riding in the truck. "So this is Khovar Khan," she said. "Tell us what was here."

I showed them where everything had been; the stupa, the small temple, the gers for dharma study, cooking, supplies, and medical treatment. The site of Suren's opulent ger. The spot where I had laid my head for seven years with my master Tilik. The spot where my grand mandala had been swept into a million grains of coloured sand by the abbot's angry hand.

I described our beautiful statue of Avalokitesvara that had been hauled away. I had since learned what had become of him. In 1939 alone, 1,566 truckloads of sacred Buddhist icons and statuary had been shipped out of Mongolia to Moscow, to be melted down for the production of bullets.

We walked to the mass grave. It had sunk as the bodies within it decomposed, so that now it was indistinguishable from any other spot of ground.

"They are under here," I said, my voice cracking even after so many years.

"Will you rebury them?" Erdene asked.

I shook my head. "Their spirits have long since found new bodies. There are only bones left now. I don't want to unearth the past, I just want to rebuild what was worthy about it."

She nodded, satisfied. "Where shall we put our ger?"

"There," I said, pointing to a place at the base of the hill, "where there is a lee from the wind."

With Tsetseg and Dejid's help we unloaded the animals, ground-tethered the horses and let the sheep roam around. They moved in a tight, dazed knot, baffled by this inferior place we'd brought them to.

We erected our ger after some fortifying airag and curd, for even with the aid of a younger couple it had become a tiring job. Once we had reassembled the stove and put our few pieces of furniture in place it began to feel more like home. Along our journey we had stopped at the place near Erdene Zuu where Dorj had hidden his treasures long ago. We found them, after much trial and one broken shovel head. They were few—a prayer wheel, a golden Buddha one arm's length in height, a silver tingsha tarnished and pitted yet still pure of sound—but they constituted the start of a new temple. We placed them, with the collection of handwritten scripture books, at the northern wall of our ger to wait for their future home.

When we were set up, Dejid looked around, shifting his weight from foot to foot uneasily. "Are you certain you'll be all right here, all alone?"

"There will be others tomorrow or the next day," I assured him. "They will come from Khovd to help. I have been told so."

"Even so, we'll stay the night," said Tsetseg. "You might find tomorrow you need the truck to transport something from Khovd."

"Thank you."

Dejid looked more troubled than ever. "Won't there be ghosts?"

I nodded. "There are surely ghosts," I said, and smiled. "They will be pleased."

When we finished building the stupa and had erected a temple ger containing a rustic altar and two benches for prayers, I had to decide how to tell Tilik about our change of address. He'd been living in Moscow with his Russian wife and family for almost twenty years. We had not spoken of Buddhism or my work with the scriptures since the day he went off to Tsetserleg. Throughout that time he had continued to write fairly regularly, relaying the events of his life with a cool detachment. The science school in Irtusk, his pilot's training, his marriage to a fellow student, the job offer designing airplanes in Moscow, numerous promotions, and the births of two sons and a daughter, none of whom could speak more than a few phrases of Mongolian.

At Erdene's insistence he had brought his family twice to visit us. They stayed at our summer camp for a week in a borrowed ger, where the unchanged, ancient rhythms of our daily lives were as quaint and archaic to them as vacationing in a museum. His children were attractive, their Mongolian features dominant but in lighter skin. But they were difficult to get to know when everything we said had to be translated.

After the decades of impersonal correspondence with Tilik, I hardly knew what to tell him about returning to Khovor Khan. I wanted to explain to him the profound draw of the place for me, the sense of urgency I felt about rebuilding it now that it was finally possible. I wanted to tell him everything that had gotten me to this point, and about the joy I had felt when we'd finished the last of the scripture books. But I couldn't imagine he would either understand or care. I worried, in fact, that speaking of such things would rip the scab off a wound that had been safely closed for a long time.

After days of deliberation, I put three photos of the stupa and temple ger in an envelope with a brief note: *Your mother and I have moved to Khovor Khan to rebuild the monastery, as some others are also doing. Progress will be slow as funds and help are scarce. Buddhist patience necessary.* And I included our new address.

A month went by and no new letters came from Moscow. Perhaps he was angry I had dragged his mother away from a perfectly good place to fulfill what he thought of as my crazy monk's dreams. Perhaps he thought me so foolish he didn't want to acknowledge my actions by responding. Perhaps he was so irritated, I would only ever hear from him again through Erdene.

After one more week of fretting, I received a reply:

Dear Ahv and Ehj,
I have created a web site for Khovor Khan and posted your

photographs to it, as I noticed on the internet that many monastery projects are doing this to bring funds and helpers from all over the world. It is in Russian, Mongolian and in English. If you send more photos of your progress and tell me more about your activities there I can add them to the site. My wife will organize the internet inquiries with a man in Ulaan Baatar, who will make sure they find their way to you. It is all arranged. I hope it helps.

Your loving son,
Tilik

Erdene read the letter. "Our son, the modern man," was all she said, but I knew she understood how much it meant. There was now a crack, a chink of light in the wall that had stood between my son and me for so long.

And Tilik was right about the website. It took some time, but help began to appear. Small sums of money came from concerned Buddhists in California and England. Buddhist students looking for a useful summer experience came to build a real, cement and stucco temple hall. Two exiled Tibetan monks living in India heard about us and came to help teach dharma to our few young novices. We gratefully accepted their help, but not their fancy, commercially printed Tibetan scripture books. We have our own, in Mongolian.

Our most exciting visitor was an esteemed Rinpoche lama, famous all over the Buddhist world, who came to us as part of a tour of monasteries that were being rebuilt just like ours. He gave us some money to start a library, and offered to ordain me. I thanked him for the money, but respectfully said no to the ordination. I was never a monk and do not need to be one now. I am a husband, a father, an artist. A devout Buddhist, but not a monk. Others can run Khovor Khan and teach dharma better than I can. I want to live out the last of my years with my beloved wife, the one who hauls me from the wreckage of my own shortcomings and has guided me through all the times the light of the Path has burned too dimly for me to see.

I do have a role at the monastery, however; I teach those who come as novices and monks the sublime intricacies of traditional, Mongolian Buddhist art. A few months ago a new boy joined us. I knew from the first day that he would be an artist. In the temple hall, where he was supposed to be polishing the statues, I caught him tracing with his finger the detailed lines of the thangka that hangs there.

"Do you like the thangka?" I asked him before he even knew I had entered. He jumped back from the scroll, red-faced with embarrassment.

"It's very beautiful," he mumbled, eyes fixed on the floor.

"Would you like to be able to make one just as good?"

He glanced quickly, at me as though my words might be a trick, then looked again at the thangka. "I wouldn't be able to make something like that."

I walked over to stand beside him. "If you're lucky," I said, "Buddha guides your hand so that you can. But it takes a lot of work."

"I can work hard."

"What's your name?" I asked.

"Enq."

It means peace. "May your life reflect it," I said. "So, you want to learn?"

He looked at me in wonder. "Would that be possible?"

"The first thing to understand is this: Buddhist art is a selfless act. No artist signs a Buddhist work. The artist doesn't matter, because it's the power of Buddha that makes such beauty possible. You must remember that."

"Yes, Master."

The boy will make beautiful thangkas and mandalas one day. He's learning fast. Occasionally we discuss dharma too, informally. I try to pass on some of the things my masters Tilik and Arigh taught me. But what I want him most to understand, even if he never becomes a monk, is how important it is not to squander his precious human life.

The End

Bibliography
The Mongolian proverbs at the start of each chapter are taken from *Mongolian Folklore, A Representative Collection from the Oral Literary Tradition*. Translated and edited by John Gombojab Hangin, 1998. The Mongolian Society (Indiana University) Occasional Paper Number 21.

Other sources of history and culture include:

Two Friends: Mongolian Tales. Translated and edited by B. Khurelbat (The Mongolian Society, no date)

Stronger Than Power: A Collection of Stories , by Sandli B. Balykov. 1989 The Mongolian Society.

Modern Mongolia: A Concise History, by Tsedendambyn Batbayar. 2002 Mongolian Center for Scientific and Technological Information, ISBN 99929-5-623-2

What Witness the Bones Excavated from Khambyn Ovoo, by Hatagin Go Akim, 2004, ISBN 99929-85-10-0

Through the Ocean Waves, The Autobiography of Bazaryn Shirendev. Translated by Temujin Onon, 1997 Center for East Asian Studies, Western Washington University, ISBN 0-914584-80-4

The Economy of Mongolia From Traditional Times to the Present. By Tumuriin Namjim, edited by William Rozycki, 2000 The Mongolian Society Occasional Paper Number 22.

Tales of an Old Lama. Translated by C.R. Bawden from a Mongolian text recorded and edited by Ts. Damdinsuren. The Institute of Buddhist Studies, Tring, UK 1997.

Glossary

There are many accepted ways to spell Mongolian words using English letters; I have chosen those variations I encountered most often.

Aa – a suffix attached to names as a sign of respect

Ahv – Dad

Aimag – province

Airag – fermented mare's milk

Arigh – pure

Burhan miny – oh my god

Del – the robe traditionally worn by Mongolians both male and female, and tied at the waist with a sash. Also spelled '*deel*' in some texts.

Eejee – literally 'oh my Mum', but used in general surprise, as with *ai ho*.

Ehj – Mom

Erdene – precious

Ger – how Mongolians refer to the round felt and canvas tent often known as a yurt

Khainag – a yak-cow hybrid known for its hardiness

Muutuu – a very fine paper made by the Chinese

Ortoo – a unit of measure, equivalent to about 30km, which refers to the distance between stages on the old horseback relay system. More correctly known as 'ortoo gazar' but shortened here for expediency.

Orum – the creamy substance skimmed off the top of boiled milk

Ovoo – a pyramid-shaped pile of stones, along with offerings such as prayer scarves and coins, used as traditional offerings to the gods and still found throughout Mongolia

Sain bain uu – roughly 'how are you' but used as a general greeting

Tos – orum mixed with sugar and flour and fried. Crumbly and very tasty.

Soum – smaller districts within the provinces, also sometimes written as '*sum*'

www.ingramcontent.com/pod-product-compliance
Lightning Source LLC
Chambersburg PA
CBHW050720180626
46814CB00002B/527

* 9 7 8 0 9 8 8 0 3 7 4 0 3 *